THE BURNING

Tim Goodman

Constable · London

First published in Great Britain 2000
by Constable, an imprint of Constable & Robinson Limited
3 The Lanchesters, 162 Fulham Palace Road
London W6 9ER
Copyright © 2000 Tim Goodwin
The right of Tim Goodwin to be identified as the author
of this work has been asserted by him in accordance with
the Copyright, Designs and Patents Act 1988

ISBN 1-84119-222-8

Printed and bound in Great Britain

A CIP catalogue record for this book is available from the
British Library

THE BURNING CLOUD

1

MARIANNE

'Now my waiting is only for the long peace,' came the old man's voice.

There was a long moment's silence. Then the sharp click of a tape recorder being turned off.

Outside the window, a reluctant summer had at last cast its tepid cloak over the land. The birches, struggling to two metres high in sheltered hollows, were covered in a haze of green, as leaves hurried to break out of their long, winter prison. On the far side of the fjord, under the inaccessible cliffs of Qeqertaq Island, dark, shadowed water rippled calmly as if it had always been there. As if the solid mass of pack ice that had enchained it for six months had never existed.

It was mid-morning, and the early mist had cleared. The sun shone brightly on the snow-cloaked mountain that dominated the northern half of Qeqertaq. The old man pushed away the microphone, looked out of his window, and wondered if this year the snow would stay. Twice in the last five years scorching summers had burned off all the visible snows, even from the very highest peak, and filled the fjord with milky-white melt-water. Scorching summers! He was starting to think like a Greenlander.

Slowly he got up. He felt good today, there were no aches in his back or his legs, just a faint sleepy heaviness in his whole body that he could almost enjoy. Absently he put his hands in the pockets of his thick jacket, and pulled out a piece of paper he found there. He unfolded it curiously, then remembered it had arrived at the farm, just before he left. He looked at it, frowning.

'They are close on your track. Things are going badly for them at home, and they wish you dead. In case. You should join those whose cause is the same as yours, and who can protect you.'

Gently he rubbed a hand through his white, straggly beard. He would have to reveal this eventually, for it might mean returning would be dangerous. But for the next three months he was safe here, a thousand miles to the west. Untraceable.

He yawned, stretched, then picked up his stick, hand-carved from arctic willow, and went outside. The fjord was only a couple of hundred metres away, and he walked down towards it, following a faint footpath through the stones and thin grass. A raven flew heavily overhead, its wing tips splayed wide. The old man looked up at it, then recited softly to himself:

'The north wind blows cold,
Thick falls the snow.
Nothing is redder than the fox,
Nothing is blacker than the crow.'

Here the north wind seemed to blow nearly all year, snow fell in every month, and the foxes were grey or white. For a moment he felt a pang of longing for the collared crows, the silky chattering starlings and cinnamon sparrows of his youth.

Away from the shadow of the cliffs, the waters of the fjord were pale azurite blue, flecked with small ice floes. The high water mark was outlined by a wall of unmelted ice blocks, stained brown and red. The old man poked at one with his stick, but it did not break. For almost the first time since he had returned to his summer house, he allowed himself to glance down the line of the fjord. The small settlement of Ikerasak, a kilometre away, was just visible, brightly coloured against the grey and brown rock. He stared at it, and wondered if this year would be like the last three, or if perhaps it would not happen. It had been almost nine months since he had left. That must be a long time to her. To him it seemed like the passing of a week.

He turned back towards the fjord. Today it appeared beautiful and gentle, ready to play, the waves slapping affectionately against the rocks. But he knew that it was cold. Heartless. And as his years drew on, it was heart that he needed.

'It won't happen again,' he said to himself. 'I should not hope.'

But he dared not believe himself.

He sat down on a boulder, put his stick in front of him, and stared out into nowhere, letting his mind roam.

Time passed imperceptibly, until his peace was shattered by the sound of feet on stones, running swiftly closer. He closed his eyes for a moment, as if praying to a god he had never believed in, then turned, with a burst of excitement in his heart. A moment later his old, creased face – generally so impassive – was split apart by a smile of pure joy.

Running up the side of the fjord, the wind ruffling her thick, tousled black hair, was a girl. As she ran, she waved her hand, and shouted something, but he could not hear what it was. He waited patiently, not moving. A bubble of warm fragrant air seemed to have enfolded him.

The girl leapt extravagantly over a lichen-stained rock, landed with a splash in a puddle she had not seen on the far side, laughed, then hurried on up to him.

'Hello, grandpa,' she said, breathlessly.

He put his old hand, brown-spotted with age, on to her head, and said, as he always did, 'I'm not your grandpa.'

'Great grandpa then.'

'I'm not –'

'Great, great, great grandpa.' She grinned up at him, showing a gap where she had lost one of her front teeth during the winter. 'I'm not going to call you your name, because you always tell me I can't pronounce it properly. So you're going to have to be grandpa. It's what I've always called you, isn't it?'

He nodded gravely.

'Well then. What are you being silly about?'

'I'm sorry.' He looked down at her, drinking in her enthusiasm and her youth. 'And how old are you now, Marianne?'

'Ten, grandpa, of course,' she went on without a pause. 'I knew you were back, I saw Nils in the village, and he told me he'd brought you in. I wanted to come straight away, but Aunt Anita said I mustn't. She said you were an old man – as if I didn't know that – and you must have some time to yourself. To settle in. So she made me have my lunch first.'

'I wouldn't have minded if you had come straight away,' he said.

'I told her you'd say that,' she replied confidently. 'But she wouldn't listen. She never does. Most grown-ups don't, except you, of course. Anyway, I've found something you must come and see. It's really, really exciting. I haven't shown anyone else. Not Aunt Anita, or Adam, or anyone.'

He smiled indulgently. 'What is it?'

'No, no. Telling you would spoil it. I have to show you.' She had taken his hand and was pulling at it. 'Come on.'

'Is it far? You know I'm an old man. I can't walk far.'

'Old people can walk if they want to,' she answered. 'It's just they sometimes don't want to. Aunt Anita says her father was still going out hunting when he didn't have a hair left on his head.'

'Perhaps he lost his hair when he was still young.'

'No. I can just remember him. He was very old. Even older

9

than you.' She wrinkled her brow in thought. 'Perhaps you should wear a hat though. Your head might get chilly.'

'Are we going somewhere cold?'

'Of course not. It's summer.'

Summer, he thought briefly. This was far from the summers of his youth. From somewhere deep within him, he recalled a year the spring rains had not come, when the birds had not sung and the hot deathly night was like a blanket over his face. When the river ran low, exposing stretches of livid green stinking slime that dried and cracked, while great fish floundered and gasped out their lives in shrinking pools, and bloated herons and storks barely needed to move to find their food. Day after day the sky had stayed steely-grey, cloudless and cruel, a fitting backdrop to the vicious incandescent sun. That had been summer. Not this thin white sun, with its surrounding wisps of mare's tail cirrus, glistening on snow and ice.

'How long will it take us?' he asked.

'Not too long. Come on.'

A steady fjord wind drove up into the valley from the sea, but neither Marianne nor the old man noticed it – there was nearly always a wind, either from the sea or from the ice. They walked past the house, which Marianne regarded with solemn, wary, eyes.

'Where is the woman who lives with you?' she whispered.

'You mean Inga,' he replied, smiling. 'She is unpacking and tidying up inside. She is always tidying up. In three years she has not learned that I am a very neat and organised man. She thinks it is her who keeps me in shape. And I let her think so.'

A lugubrious-faced woman, of perhaps thirty, with ash-pale skin and fair hair scraped severely back in a pony-tail, appeared at the door.

'Where are you going?' she demanded.

'Just a walk with my friend,' said the old man, meekly.

'Do not be long, and take care not to overtire yourself.'

'Yes, Inga.'

'Why are you not wearing your hat? Put it on.'

'Yes, Inga.' Shamefacedly the old man produced a crumpled red lumberjack cap from the pocket of his heavy jacket, and put it on his bald head.

'Your dinner will be in two hours. Do not be late.'

She vanished back inside.

'She's so stressy,' said Marianne, making a face at the closed door. 'And you listened to her when she said about your hat, but not me.'

'She doesn't like coming here, but I insist. Can you guess why?'

'Because you like coming to see me?'

'That's right.'

'I knew you'd say that too,' she said dismissively. 'But it's not true. You come here for the fishing, like everyone does.'

'That was true once,' he agreed. 'But now –'

'What will your dinner be?' she interrupted.

'Milk and bread.'

She looked at him, appalled. 'Is that all?'

'Yes.'

'But that's just baby food. Aunt Anita and me and Adam eat sausages and cheese and seal meat and vegetables and all sorts of things. As well as fish, of course. Why don't you, grandpa?'

He gave a fleeting smile. 'My stomach grows angry when it is given too much to do. What are you going to show me?'

'My secret,' she said.

They walked inland, towards the inner ring of mountains, for about three-quarters of an hour. A kilometre away to their left, hidden in its saucer-shaped valley, ran the River Isortoq. A small area of grey sandy flats, held together by cushions of moss campion and crawling purple saxifrage, soon gave way to rock, and they pressed on through a rough, broken landscape of puddles, seeping water, shrinking snowfields, and ice-cracked stone, scattered with a few struggling alpine scrubs.

Marianne walked briskly, and the old man half wished she would slow down, but at the same time he found it invigorating that she did not worry about him. That she never doubted he could keep up with her. It was one of her attractions, lending him some of her youth by her very confidence in him. Eventually his breath began to come short, but he ignored it, and walked beside the girl, his eyes fixed on the ground, finding an even rhythm.

Straight in front of them was a talus slope of fallen boulders and rock debris, marking the foot of a soaring cliff. Beyond lay a jagged ridge of mountains, snow-covered, ice-carved, fencing in the inland ice, the savage, dead desert at the heart of Greenland.

'Where are we going?' he asked doubtfully.

'Not far, grandpa.'

She danced away to the left, parallel to the cliff, then turned

11

right again, where the land dropped. Following her, the old man found himself on a broad ledge. He pushed up his spectacles, and gazed at a magnificent view of Greenland at its most dramatic. At his feet, a hundred metres down, he could see the river, swinging south, then east again, as it slashed an echoing cleft through the mountains. Beyond the cleft the valley opened out; however, except for the gently sloping ledge straight in front, it was still hemmed in by great precipices. At the further end of the gorge, perhaps a kilometre away, the river ran under the shadow of the tallest of all the mountains. Thickly covered in snow and ice, it stood out from the others by its size and height, and on its shoulders the old man could see the snouts of grey glaciers, the furthest tentacles of the inland ice, which provided the water from which the River Isortoq was born.

'That's Mount Iviangeq,' said Marianne, pointing. 'It's called that because it's supposed to look like a woman's breast. It doesn't look like that to me, what do you think?'

'We are not going up there, are we?' he asked.

But she had already hurried on.

He followed, clambering painfully over the pathless jumble of rock and stone, but she was soon well ahead, accelerating as she nimbly made her way down towards the muddy river at the bottom of the mighty high-walled canyon it had carved.

The old man's legs hurt, and he knew he should sit down for a moment. A long moment. But he dare not let Marianne out of his sight. Dare not in case she got into trouble – or he did. For he was not sure he could find his way back.

A white and black snow bunting flitted away to vanish into a crack in a nearby rock wall. There was a faint ringing in the old man's ears. Gradually the sound grew, and a yellowish haze gathered round the edge of his sight. His spectacles seemed to be misting up, and there was a choking edge to the air. Then suddenly Marianne was back beside him.

'See,' she said proudly. 'What about that?'

He took a deep breath, rubbed his forehead, which was prickled by drips of cold sweat, carefully wiped his spectacles, then looked.

They were at the bottom of the valley, close to the river. On their right a razor-backed ridge swept up to link with the looming slopes of Mount Iviangeq. In front of them was a basin, thirty metres across, and near the centre of it was a small dry patch of orange-ochre mud, surrounded by grey stones, flecked with lichen. In the mud were two holes. He stared at them.

'What is it? Does some animal live here?'

'A dragon,' giggled Marianne.

As she spoke, a puff of steam emerged from the larger of the holes. Marianne laughed delightedly, as if she had arranged everything, then took his hand.

'And look over here.'

Surrounded by more red and yellow mud, with a few slate-coloured stains, lay a pool of rusty water. A small stream ran out of it, and trickled away to join the river. As the old man watched, there was a swirl in the thick opaque water of the pool, then a bubble emerged with an audible glooping sound. At the same time steam briefly filled the air. A little way beyond, more steam was escaping from a moss-covered hole in the ground, and close beside that was another, larger pool, a rich blue-grey rather than reddish, that steamed gently.

'Aren't they brilliant?' said Marianne, crouching down and staring at the bubbling little pool.

The old man breathed deeply. Now he understood the hint of sulphur in the air. 'Hot springs,' he said.

Marianne nodded. 'I've put my hand in the blue pool. It's lovely. But the red pool is too hot to stand.' She looked at him, and winked conspiratorially. 'They're my secret. I haven't told anyone, except you.'

'Thank you,' he said, aware of the honour.

They stood a little longer in silence.

'Have you ever seen anything like them before?' she asked.

'Yes,' he said.

She looked disappointed, and he hastened to explain.

'I spend the winter in a place where there are many hot springs. There is a lake, and although it is surrounded by snow, ducks stay all through the winter, because hot springs make sure it never freezes.'

'Why does no one shoot them?' asked Marianne.

He shrugged. 'People are not hungry.'

'And are the springs as big as this?'

'Bigger. There are geysers and great volcanoes.'

'What are they?'

'Geysers are fountains of boiling water that leap high up into the sky. Volcanoes are mountains that spit fire and burning rocks. There is one not far from where I live.'

Marianne looked worried. 'I do not think you should stay in such a place,' she said. 'It sounds dangerous. Is it near here?'

13

He laughed. 'Don't worry. It is in another country, and is quite safe.'

'What is the country called?'

'Iceland.'

'Is it colder than here, then?'

'No,' said the old man. 'But we will go on with our geography lesson another day. I must get home. Inga will be angry if I am late for my dinner.'

They began to walk back up the slope that led out of the canyon.

'I could bring you some of my food,' she offered. 'Secretly. So no one would know.'

'Thank you, but I have been eating bread and milk for a long time. It is enough for me now.' He glanced behind him, but although they were only fifty metres from the patch of hot springs, there was no sign of them.

'Are you sure no one knows of those springs?' he asked.

She shook her head proudly. 'No one at all. I found them last week. They weren't there last year.'

He looked at her. She instantly recognised his lack of belief, and scowled angrily.

'It's true. Except for the blue pool – which has been there as long as I can remember. But it has never steamed before. Last September I came up here, and I searched to see if there were any more blue pools, and there weren't. I would have seen the steam and things. They weren't there. That's how I know that I discovered them.' She stared at him, vehement. Almost aggressive. 'There are similar things in other parts of the country. Our schoolteacher told us that hot water comes out of the ground on Uunartoq Island. She said it was warm enough for people to sit in the pool without their clothes on.'

'Where is that?'

'Between Qaqortoq and Nanortalik. In the far south.' Marianne frowned. 'I think she said there were hot pools in other places – on Disko Island, and the east coast, but I can't remember where. I'm not very good at geography.'

The old man concentrated on walking.

Only when his house above the fjord was back in sight did he allow himself to rest. Later in the summer he would be fitter, better able to cope with walking, but after his sedentary winter it was hard. He closed his eyes and concentrated on controlling his breathing and lessening the beating of his heart.

'Are you all right, grandpa?' asked Marianne.

'Yes,' he said carefully. 'But you had better go now. In case Inga is angry.'

'With me?'

'No, with me. Don't worry, and come to see me tomorrow – if you can.'

'All right. Goodbye, grandpa.'

He felt the fleeting touch of a kiss on his forehead, like a blessing, then she was gone, running off towards the settlement down the fjord. The old man sat where he was a little longer, then opened his eyes and got slowly to his feet.

As he descended into the dry valley that led down to his house, there was a sudden crack, as if someone had trodden on a piece of dead wood. The old man stopped dead. For a moment he could not think what it was that he had heard. Then it came back to him.

At the same moment the sound was repeated. There was another crack close beside him, and rock splinters spat up at his face.

The old man, distant memories fresh in his mind, ducked behind a great boulder, and flattened himself against it. Time lengthened out. He pushed his spectacles hard against his eyes, and peered out over the bare landscape. Something moved, a hint of green where there should have been only the grey of the rocks.

Breathing heavily, he edged round the rock. As he did so, there were two more rapidly fired shots, and a bullet crashed into something, then whined away.

The old man's mind moved swiftly, easily, without panic. It was many years since he had been under fire, but there was no strangeness in the experience. It felt familiar, almost normal. He edged further round the boulder. In front of him was a stretch of broken ground, scattered with boulders, grass clumps, and rock outcrops, where a fit young man might find enough cover to escape even a man with a gun. But the old man knew his limitations.

Instead he crouched as low as he could to the ground, and pressed himself into a recess at the foot of the great rock. A second rock blocked any view of him from a distance, unless someone should come round the side of the rock and look directly into his hiding place. There the old man waited, not moving, though his limbs rapidly began to pain him. But he remembered times when the pain had been far greater.

Two minutes trickled by. Five. Ten. Still he did not move. Then he heard the sound of footsteps, and muttered voices, coming slowly closer.

The voices sent a chill of recognition down his back, and he knew that it had happened at last. After more than ten years. Yet he felt no surprise, no apprehension, barely any fear. He was an old man, he had had his run, and at last the hunters had tracked him down. He had thought it would happen before this. The only surprising thing was that they still thought he was worth the trouble. That they still thought he was dangerous.

The men stopped, barely five metres from his hiding place, but still out of sight.

'This was where I last saw him,' said a voice.

'He cannot have disappeared.'

'There is much cover out there. He could be a kilometre away by now.'

'He is seventy-two. He cannot have got far.'

'There will be trouble if we do not find him.'

'We shall find him.'

The men walked forward again. The old man was gazing at the ground, aware that nothing is easier to recognise as human than a face. The back or top of a head, especially a bald one, may be mistaken for a rock, but a face is always a face. He barely breathed.

The gravel crunched close by him, then there was a soft grunt of satisfaction.

'Get up,' said a voice.

Two men were staring down at him. They were dressed in dark green anoraks, with the hoods tied around their heads. They wore black ski masks that almost completely covered their faces, and reflective skiing goggles. In gloved hands they carried hunting rifles, with telescopic sights, and both rifles were pointed at him.

He stood up.

'What now?' said the smaller of the two men. 'Do we kill him now?'

'No. He is to come with us.'

'What if the villagers see us? Some of them are hunters and carry guns.'

'We will deal with that if it happens. First search him to make sure he has no weapon. No? All right, old man. Walk in front of us, slowly.'

'I can walk no other way.'

'If you try to draw attention to yourself in any way, we will

16

shoot you where you stand. Go down towards the side of the fjord.'

The old man began to walk downhill. As the rocks gave way to grass and plants, and they neared his house, there was a sudden call. A moment later a figure appeared from the house, and came towards them.

One of the two gunmen swore.

'Shoot, shoot!'

'No, we can't risk it. We'll have to let him go this time.'

The old man felt himself pushed fiercely in the back. He stumbled and fell to the ground. When he picked himself up, it was to find Inga running up the slope towards him. There was no sign of the gunmen.

The old man waited for her, then the two of them hugged each other.

'What was happening?' gasped Inga. 'Who were those men? They had guns. What were they doing?'

'I think they were taking me away to kill me,' said the old man softly. 'But you came just in time. Thank you.'

He held her long, bony body, and now that the danger was over the easy tears of age filled his eyes.

Two minutes later a thin, graceful Greenlander woman came running up the slope from the fjord. Marianne was beside her, holding her hand.

'What's happening?' the woman demanded. 'I was on my way to see how Adam was getting on with his trammel net up the fjord when I heard shots. I saw men who seemed to be threatening you, then they ran away.'

'They were going to kidnap him,' said Inga, breathlessly. 'They shot at him, then they tried to take him away, to kill him –'

'It is nothing to worry about, Anita,' interrupted the old man, who had completely recovered himself.

'But grandpa –' burst out the worried Marianne.

The Greenlander silenced her with a gesture. 'I think this was something to worry about,' she said firmly. 'I am going to telephone the police.'

'I would prefer you did not,' said the old man.

The woman took no notice of him, striding over into the house as if she owned it.

The old man sighed.

'It's all right,' said Marianne, comfortingly. 'Aunt Anita knows what she's doing.'

'I am not so sure,' said the old man quietly.

2

THE CHIEF

Pieter Norlund pulled up a chair opposite Larsen's desk, lit a cigarette, and grinned lopsidedly at him.

'How's things, then?'

'Fine,' said Larsen. 'And you?'

'OK. Any news of that promotion you were hoping for?'

'No.'

'It's been a while now, hasn't it? And with that smug bastard Lindegren getting the appointment in Ilulissat, I reckon you'll have to stick with handing out fishing and hunting licences, organising search and rescue parties, and clearing up drunks. Like the rest of us.'

Larsen nodded coldly, hoping Norlund would leave him, but the young man seemed intent on a conversation.

'Heard from that daughter of yours lately?'

'She rang me a few days ago, from Pond Inlet.'

'Where?'

Larsen was no longer surprised by the insularity of many Greenlanders. 'On Baffin Island.'

'Oh. And how's she liking it there?'

Larsen shrugged. 'She says people're better off.'

'Are they?' Norlund frowned. 'I remember hearing on KNR that some local councils in northern Canada have banned beer and closed down the TV film channels. That doesn't sound better off to me. What did she go there for?'

'After her father-in-law died two months ago, she wanted to leave Nuuk. I think she finds it difficult to stay in one place. And now she has a boyfriend.'

Norlund's grin grew wider. 'There's a surprise,' he said ironically, and he drew slowly on his cigarette. 'Quite a girl.'

'You're married, and about to be a father, Pieter.'

'True, true. But there's no harm in a little backsliding, is there? Everyone does it.'

Norlund gave an exaggerated wink at a long-haired, plump-faced secretary who was sitting in the far corner of the large room. The girl, named Jette, giggled delightedly, then caught Larsen's eye and hastily looked back at her work.

'When's your baby due?' asked Larsen, probing.

'Two weeks or so. A bit less maybe. Not long anyway, and that's the point, isn't it? Once women fix their minds on having babies, then baby-making goes out of the window. My father told me the best few months of his life were around the time I was born, but it wasn't until I was thirteen that he told what he meant. It seems he had several girlfriends going at the same time.' He laughed. 'After all, it was only fair for him to have some relaxation. Anyway, that's not what I wanted to talk to you about. Why not come out with Helge and me and a few others for lunch? We thought we might go to the Sky Top for a change.'

'I don't think so, thanks.'

'Worried it's too expensive? Perhaps you'd prefer the good old Kristinemut? Or how about the Thai?'

Larsen shook his head.

'I'll tell you what,' pressed Norlund. 'I've heard that, despite your age, you're still pretty strong. How about this – an arm-wrestling competition, and the loser pays for the winner's meal? That way you might get a free meal.'

Pieter Norlund was tall for an Inuit, much taller than Larsen, and well proportioned, with muscular arms, a mop of unruly black hair, and a lazily confident smile. A man in the arrogant prime of his youth. Larsen himself still worked out with weights most evenings, and was aware of the enduring strength that lurked in his broad, squat body, but he had no desire for any form of contest.

'No thanks.'

'You think you'll lose.'

'Probably.'

'Maybe you're right.' Norlund laughed again, then flexed his fingers, and knocked the ash off his cigarette with a ragged fingernail. 'Where do you go at lunchtime, these days?'

Larsen felt a hollowness in his stomach, but struggled to keep his face unreadable. 'Why should you care?' he said, with an attempt at casual dismissal.

'I'm curious. Ever since I first joined, you've just eaten a sandwich in the office. But now you're always out. What's going on?'

Larsen shrugged. 'I like going home for a bit of peace.'

'Well, you'd better be off then.'

Larsen got up, pulled on his anorak and left the police station.

The room was too hot and stuffy as usual. Gerda never opened the window, even on warm sunny June days like today. And the television was mumbling away to itself in the corner of the room. Larsen hated her habit of never turning the TV off, but there was nothing to be done about it. He would have preferred her to come to his flat, but she always refused, and would never explain why.

He sighed heavily, and lay back on the small, lumpy bed.

'I should not be doing this,' he said, mostly to himself, then corrected himself. 'We should not be doing this.'

The young woman astride him, hands on her taut, swollen belly, laughed. 'You think Pieter has no girlfriends?'

'That's not the point,' objected Larsen, looking up at her.

'Of course it's the point. My husband will not make love to me because I am pregnant. It is a problem he has. OK, fine. But why does that mean I have to give up sex? I am only twenty and I enjoy it. It's true that for the first three or four months of my pregnancy I was happy enough to avoid love-making, but not now. The closer my time comes, the more I want.'

'I noticed,' said Larsen wryly, trying not to remember that she was younger than his elder daughter.

She laughed, and stroked his cheek with her hand.

'When I went to the midwife, she told me that for first-time mothers-to-be sex was a good thing. That it would help make sure my baby does not stay too long inside me. It's the first time I've been told that it's good for my health to have as much sex as possible, and I'm not about to ignore that advice.' She moved her broad hips invitingly, and her breath came a little deeper.

Larsen reached up his hands, but avoided her stomach. He felt strongly that it was no business of his, and preferred not to touch it. A couple of weeks ago as they had lain in afterglow, the baby inside her had kicked him, and Larsen had felt uncomfortable and embarrassed. Guilty.

He briefly cupped her breasts, then ran his hands round her back, and stroked her like a cat. She arched under his touch, and smiled sleepily. He smiled back at her, then sat up, holding himself on his hands. As he did so, she ran a finger over the white scar on his left shoulder.

'How did you get this?'

'I was shot.'

'For doing something like this?' she laughed.

'No, it was during a job. At Sermilik, on the east coast.'

She considered him, her vivacious face tilted to one side.

'I think Pieter's quite wrong. I think underneath all that politeness and not talking and refusing to get drunk, you're a hard man.'

'Not me. It was a woman who shot me.'

'That doesn't surprise me either. What was she like?'

'An American. Very rich.'

'I see,' she said, with a face. 'And where is she now?'

'She is dead. I must go.'

She shook her head and pushed him firmly back down. 'No.'

'It's time I was back at work.'

'It certainly is. Come on . . .'

'Gerda . . .'

She took no notice, except to thrust against him harder. Demanding. After a moment, in spite of himself, he responded, pushing deep into her so that she gasped. But when he looked up at her a moment later, even as she settled into the driving rhythm of sex, he saw that her eyes had wandered over to the far side of the room – watching the television.

'You're late, Larsen,' said Chief Thorold.

'Sorry, sir.' Larsen glanced across the Chief's prim, well-ordered little office, to where Norlund was sitting, legs crossed.

'This has happened several times,' went on Thorold, running a fretful hand over his thinning fair hair. 'You know very well that you're only allowed an hour for lunch, and if a sergeant like you returns thirty-five minutes late, it sets a very bad example to the junior staff.'

Larsen pressed his lips together. It was humiliating to be reprimanded in front of Norlund, who was also a sergeant, but fifteen years Larsen's junior.

'A very bad example,' repeated Thorold.

'Sorry, Chief.'

'See it doesn't happen again.'

Larsen did not look at Pieter Norlund, but he sensed the younger man enjoying himself.

'Sorry,' he muttered again.

'Right. Let's get to the point. Anyone heard of Ikerasak?'

Larsen frowned. 'Isn't that somewhere near Uummannaq –?'

'Perhaps, perhaps,' broke in Thorold impatiently. 'I know there are always five or six places in Greenland that share the same name. But the Ikerasak I am concerned with is a village up the coast from Frederikshab – I mean Paamiut.'

Chief Thorold had always used the Danish names for towns.

Someone must have reminded him that it was now obligatory for public officials to call them by their Inuit names.

'But sir –' Norlund began.

Thorold raised his hand. 'Yes, Pieter, I know you were stationed in Paamiut for a year, and that there are officially only three villages in the municipality – Avigait, Narssalik and Arsuk. Well, Ikerasak was actually abandoned about twenty-five years ago, during the reorganisation, but like some other deserted villages it is still used in the summer.'

'What's happened there, sir?'

Thorold shrugged and opened his hands wide.

'I'll tell you everything I know – it isn't much, I'm afraid. Ikerasak is an isolated settlement, up one of the fjords. Very isolated. But each summer it is reoccupied by up to thirty people, who use it for fishing and hunting. Two days ago an old man was walking a little way inland of the village, when he was shot at.'

'Hunters, who couldn't see clearly,' suggested Larsen.

'Or were drunk,' put in Norlund.

'It seems not. The two men who had fired at him then tried to kidnap him. Fortunately his housekeeper and another woman arrived, and the men ran away.'

'That's it?' said Larsen.

Thorold nodded. 'Yes. Basically.'

'The man wasn't hurt?'

'No.'

'What was his name?'

'The name I have been given is Haan. Jette has undertaken a check on the census and birth records, but I cannot find anyone from that area with that name, let alone who is that age.'

'How old is that?'

'Early seventies. Of course the records from back then are fairly unreliable.'

Norlund's face was a study in disbelief. 'I am sorry, sir. I don't really understand why we are concerning ourselves with an old man who lives in the middle of nowhere, and escaped unhurt from a little trouble with some drunken hunters.'

'The Royal Greenland Police Force concerns itself with all law-breaking,' said Thorold sternly. 'There are no no-go areas.' His face relaxed a little. 'However, I agree that normally this would not be a top priority. But I have received an urgent fax message from the Danish foreign office requesting I enquire into the incident, and send them exact details of what happened, though I don't understand how they heard of it before I did. I have since contacted the Prime Minister's office here in Nuuk, but they knew nothing of the matter – and didn't seem interested. I suppose foreign affairs is still the business of Denmark, but why should events here be dealt with by the foreign office? We're not an independent nation.'

'Yet,' muttered Norlund, under his breath.

'Surely the Danes gave some explanation for their interest,' said Larsen.

'Well, not really. I faxed Copenhagen back, asking for more details, but the answer I got was not particularly satisfactory. First it repeated what they had said before – that the Danish foreign office had reason to be concerned about the matter, then it went on to say that thorough precautions must be taken by officers on the ground to ensure there was no possibility of a repeat of the incident, or of any similar incident. It also required a minimum degree of seniority in at least one of the investigating officers. My requests for further information have met with no response, so I have decided to send you two to Ikerasak. I want a thorough and speedy report, that I can pass on to the interested parties.'

When did Chief Thorold not want a thorough and speedy report, thought Larsen.

'At five this afternoon, there's a scheduled Grønlandsfly helicopter flight to Paamiut. The local police there will arrange for you to get to Ikerasak tomorrow.' He hesitated and cleared his throat. 'It seems the matter is . . . must be important. You will have to be careful and painstaking. Obviously I cannot tell you what to look for – but I have chosen the two of you with some care, and I know you will not let me down.'

He gave a brief nod, to signal the interview was at an end, then turned to some papers on his desk.

'So what the hell was that all about then?' said Norlund, once they were at the far end of the corridor that led to Thorold's office.

Larsen shrugged. 'We'll have to wait and see.'

'And what does he want both of us to go for? I mean, no offence, but the two of us could hardly be more different, could we?'

'Perhaps that's the reason,' said Larsen mildly. 'He thinks we may complement each other.'

Norlund laughed. 'I don't think I've ever noticed the Chief thinking about anything. If you ask me, the moment he started to feel he was being leaned on, he panicked. You know what he's like under pressure from above – he makes a jellyfish look tough and decisive. We're the two most senior policemen he's got to hand, so he thought he'd better send both of us, to show he was doing everything he possibly could.'

Larsen realised Norlund was almost certainly right. It was the irritating thing about the young man. He was brash, arrogant, egotistical, tactless – and usually right.

'See you at the airport,' said Norlund. 'I'm off home to throw a few things in a bag, and to take a loving farewell of my beautiful young wife. Maybe I can spin this business out for a few days, and miss the birth.'

Larsen watched him go, and thought about Gerda. In many ways she was very similar to her husband. Which probably meant their marriage would be lucky to last more than a couple of years – or was he just being cynical?

When he got back to his apartment, Larsen rang Mitti, but she was out. He left a message with some girl who lived in the same block, saying he would be away for a few days, and if she needed to contact him, she could do it through the office. He knew she wouldn't.

Ten minutes later, as he was packing, the phone rang. He snatched it up, but it was Chief Thorold, sounding oddly guarded.

'Tomas, good.'

When Thorold used Larsen's first name, it usually meant trouble.

'Yes, Chief.'

'I think that during our meeting I may not have underlined just how important this business is.'

'How important is that, sir?'

'Very. Influential people are interested in this man, Haan. I'm not sure why, but you must go to all lengths – you understand, all necessary lengths – to find out exactly what is going on.'

'Yes, sir. Of course, sir.'

'I'm relying on you, Tomas. Pieter Norlund is a very energetic and talented officer, as you know. I have great hopes for him. But sometimes he can get a little too ... enthusiastic, and step on people's toes. And occasionally he has a tendency to overplay his hand. Also, of course, we mustn't forget that he is clearly under great pressure from the imminent birth of his first child.'

Larsen thought drily that he hadn't noticed.

'I need to be absolutely certain that this enquiry will be sorted out as fast as possible,' continued Thorold, talking too fast. 'I must be able to trust you to do that.'

'Are you saying that I am the officer in charge of the case, sir?' asked Larsen ingenuously.

'No, no. Pieter Norlund and you are of equal rank, and it would be invidious to place either of you above the other. Nonetheless, you are the more experienced officer, and what responsibility there is for the smooth running of things must come down to you. You understand?'

Larsen understood. He understood that he would have no authority over his partner, but that he would bear the final responsibility for anything Pieter Norlund might do. 'Yes, Chief.'

'Good. Best of luck.'

He rang off. Larsen sat down on his bed, pulled out a tooth-pick, and carefully began to clean his teeth.

It seemed pretty clear that since the interview in the Chief's office someone important had contacted Thorold and told him again that this incident must be efficiently dealt with. No doubt Thorold was now on the phone to Norlund, saying more or less the same thing. Only probably adding that Larsen was rather slow and uninspired, and old of course to still be a sergeant. Leaving open the implication that Norlund should follow his instincts and push things on as briskly as he could.

In other words Chief Thorold was safe. Whatever happened he would have someone to blame, because he had neatly covered all options by talking to his two officers in entirely contrasting ways. Larsen felt a twinge of admiration for the way Thorold, though clearly alarmed, had handled the matter. And a realisation of how he managed to keep his job while doing so little.

The telephone rang again.

Larsen picked it up, expecting to hear Thorold's voice. It was Gerda.

'Pieter is out of town for a few days,' she said breathily. 'Come round tonight.'

'I'm sorry. I have to go away too.'

'Put it off.'

'I can't. You see, I'm going on the same job as your husband.'

'Oh shit!' she exclaimed, and hung up.

Larsen stared at the phone, wondering whether he was dis-appointed or not, then returned to his neat and ordered packing, arranging things carefully on his bed before putting them in his hold-all. He looked at his gun frowning. Policemen in Greenland almost never carried guns, but Larsen was trained and entitled to in special circumstances. He wondered briefly whether to take it with him, but the clumsy aggressive thing got on his nerves. After a moment's thought he put it away in his bottom drawer, carefully locking it shut.

3

IKERASAK

The flight to Paamiut was uneventful. Larsen began reading Hemingway's *Death in the Afternoon*, but the country and culture it described were so impossibly alien that he found himself dozing off. Norlund had changed into a brown leather jacket, sun-glasses, and camouflage trousers, making Larsen think momentarily of a sheep in wolf's clothing. After scanning a copy of last week's *Niviarsiaq* without much interest, Norlund turned his attention to flirting with a small, mischievously eyed stewardess.

Paamiut was sited near the western tip of an area of flat land, at the end of a long, ragged peninsula, deeply indented by arms of the sea. On the south side lay Kuanersoq fjord, heavily speckled with icebergs from two great tidewater glaciers fifty kilometres inland. The round, raised helicopter landing pad had once been a little way out of the town, but was now almost entirely surrounded by houses and roads, except on one side where a forest of white crucifixes marked the municipal cemetery. The town itself, with a population of around three thousand, was dominated by several grey four-storey apartment blocks.

The policemen spent the night at a minimally furnished dormitory, where their sleep was interrupted in the small hours by a fierce argument between two young men, which almost flared into blows. At breakfast the next morning Norlund was in a bad mood.

'You know the name of this place?' he growled, lighting a cigarette and looking sourly at his watery cup of coffee.

'No. I've never been to Paamiut before.'

'It's called the Millionærbarraken. The hut of the millionaire. Someone must have a twisted sense of humour.' He shook his head, and blew out smoke. 'They could at least have found us a room at Petersen's Hotel.'

'It was full.'

'So they say. And now there's no helicopter available to get us to Ikerasak.' He shook his head. 'They're supposed to be build-ing an airport for the Dash 7s here – but all that's happening is nothing at all. Typical of this country, everything takes fifty times as long to happen as anywhere else in the world. I mean, Jesus, you couldn't even buy Coca Cola until a couple of years ago.'

'I asked about transport. Apparently Ikerasak is set in very rugged terrain, and the only usable landing place is part of the foreshore. The usual helicopter pilot is away, and his replacement doesn't want to take the responsibility for landing there. So it has to be boat.'

'And boat is a lot cheaper,' said Norlund cynically. 'The Chief's just saving money, that's all.'

Larsen said nothing, but it seemed likely enough.

After finishing their coffee, they went down the main street, past a colourful, wooden church, with an elegant little bell tower, to the harbour that had given the town its name – dwellers at the river mouth. Well protected from the ocean by islets and reefs, Paamiut harbour was packed with a mass of small fishing-boats, most of whose catch went to supply the local fish processing plant. The Kalaaliaraq, the fresh food market, was already busy, with people buying and selling an assortment of fish, together with smaller quantities of seal and reindeer meat. There was even one stall offering bundles of green mountain angelica stalks, a few crowberries – clearly unripe for they were pink or purple, rather than glossy black – fresh dandelion leaves and some amethyst-capped 'Deceiver' mushrooms.

There was no sign of the local policeman, who had promised to meet them by the ferry landing, so Larsen and Norlund retraced their steps over the muddy Praestevigen creek, past the KNI bank and supermarket, to the police station. They were greeted as if there wasn't a problem, given a large mug of tepid coffee, then taken back along the road they had just walked, but this time to the south side of the harbour, where they were introduced to a thin, silent, unusually dark-skinned man. Nils, as their ferryman was called, took them to his fishing-boat and the three of them set off half an hour later.

As they left Paamiut harbour, Nils gestured at a rusting old steamer, moored to the rocks. 'The *Greenland Star*,' he said.

Larsen glanced without interest at the decaying remnant of the ship that had once been the main link between the towns of west Greenland. Already they were swinging north, cautiously skirting ice-fringed shores, and weaving in and out of a chequerboard of barren, brown and black islets. The coastline was precipitous, and unpredictable, in places extending far out into the sea, and every now and then sudden squalls of wind whipped down on them, driving the sea into a frenzy of bucketing waves, then just as suddenly lessening. Occasional giant icebergs drifted lazily by.

Over the next two hours, the snow-shrouded mountains edged further away and the intervening land became more visible. Flat, white tablelands stood out in sharp contrast to frowning black precipices, and rolling glaciated hills. The only sign of vegetation was a brownish tint on some slopes, and a few small patches of green, which beckoned enticingly like emeralds.

At last the taciturn Nils guided the boat closer inshore. There was more drift ice than there had been in the open sea, and from the front of the boat Larsen watched a party of black and white little auks waiting on a floe until the boat was almost upon them before they simultaneously dived into the water. Just to the right of them a hill, lofty and razor-edged, rose evenly to about six hundred metres. On the shore beneath it, high and dry like a stranded whale, was a huge, ancient iceberg marked with thaw marks.

'Palasipqaqqaa.' Their pilot finally spoke again. 'The priest's mountain. It is a useful marker to find the fjord entrance.'

They swung around a promontory from the mountain, then abruptly the boat lurched and lost way. Water swirled wildly around their sides, driving them towards the rocks of the nearby headland.

'What is it?' asked Larsen, alarmed.

'Currents,' said the boatman calmly. 'It's often like this when the wind meets the ebb tide.'

The engine laboured hard, and they began to make way again. Within a short distance cliffs rose up on their left also, and they followed the fjord that drove like a spear-head into the very heart of the land before them. The water was littered with shoals of small icebergs, some of them streaked with the rich turquoise colour of old glacier ice, others greyer, and dirty, marked by curving lines of small stones. A cape reared up on their left as they passed narrowing shores, heading towards a gap, only about half a kilometre wide, beyond which the fjord opened out again.

'Grindehval fjord,' remarked the boatman. 'There used to be a big whale hunt here every autumn.'

'But not now?' asked Larsen.

'We take a few in September, but the old men say many more whales used to come. Enough to supply the whole village all winter.' Nils frowned. 'Nowadays the fishermen in Paamiut make good money taking Americans out to see whales. To watch them, but not to kill them. What sense does it make? But they pay 500 kroner a head. Perhaps I will do it too this autumn, when the big whales arrive.'

He returned to his steering, as if embarrassed at his sudden burst of loquacity.

On their left were low-lying, lifeless skerries, surrounded by rocky shallows. Stony promontories jutted out into the sparkling water, and beyond lay looming cliffs. On the right the land, though still steep, was lower, and Larsen caught a glimpse of a long milky-green ribbon lake, glittering in the sun. The still-ebbing tide flowed strongly against them, through the gateway to the inner fjord, but the boat pushed its way through, leaving a broad, bubbling wake.

As they ran deeper inland, the coast grew more attractive. The lower slopes appeared to be covered with grass and bushes, and only a few rocky heights and tors broke through the green carpet. Closer in, however, Larsen could see that creeping shrubs served to disguise wide stretches of rock and stone, making the countryside appear lusher than it really was. The boat slid on, past a small inlet and a thin curving beach of grey-black sand at the cliff's foot.

As a brick-red timber-frame house appeared on the right, the boat swung in towards the shore. Ten minutes later they clambered ashore on the long pile of boulders that served Ikerasak as a jetty. The trip had taken three hours.

Nils led the way to a path that wound up the rocky side of the fjord. Beside it, plunging headlong, was a stream which Larsen realised must help keep the landing place ice-free in spring and autumn. At the top, on more level ground, the stream became broad and shallow, winding among banks of grey pebbles and dark brown mud. About it grew clumps of sedge and waving masses of arctic cottongrass, bending before the wind. The path ran on beside the stream, through a sheltered valley, thick with grass and shrubby growths of willow and dwarf birch. Scattered on either side were about fifteen timber-frame houses, with sharply sloping roofs. Many were clearly unoccupied – with broken windows, cracking walls, and in two cases collapsed roofs. However six of the houses were bright with recent paint, red, yellow and blue, and surrounded by casually scattered belongings – timber, petrol cans, fishing nets, buoys, boots, seal-skins, a clothes line, even, bizarrely, a rusting supermarket trolley. On one patch of rocky ground, two huge triangular frameworks of wooden struts had been erected for fish drying, and there were other, smaller drying frames scattered around the settlement.

Several people, adults and children, had emerged and were looking at them with open curiosity.

The woman who approached Larsen and Norlund first was unusually thin, which together with the graceful, upright way she carried herself gave an impression of height and youth. However, as she came closer, Larsen saw that her black hair, which she wore in a long plait down her back, was streaked with grey, and her face was covered in tiny lines. He guessed she must be in her early fifties.

'Good day,' she said, meeting his gaze with long, quick, sharp eyes. 'I am Anita Petterman.'

'Hi,' replied Norlund, reaching out and shaking her hand. 'I'm Sergeant Pieter Norlund, from Nuuk. This is my partner, Tomas. We're here to look into the shooting that happened on Tuesday.'

'You mean the outsider who lives up the fjord?'

'That's right. We were told his name is Haan, is that right?'

'I have never heard him called that,' she said.

'Who is he then?'

Anita shrugged. 'He comes here every year about this time, and stays until we leave. Then he goes too.'

'What sort of an outsider is he?' asked Larsen.

She stared at him. 'What do you mean?'

'I mean is he a Dane, or an American? Or from another part of Greenland – the east coast perhaps, or the north?'

'It is difficult to know. He could be from Tanu – the back of the country – but he does speak west Greenlandic, if not very well. I think he taught himself, and he has a strange accent, unlike any other I have ever heard.'

'Where does he live when he is not here?' interrupted Norlund.

Anita shrugged again. 'I do not know. He comes back to Paamiut with us in late September, but then he takes the helicopter on to Narsarsuaq.'

'Does no one live here all the year?' put in Larsen.

She gave him a scornful glance. 'We were moved from here many years ago, and the government in Nuuk tells us Ikerasak does not exist. But our families are from Ikerasak, and many of us were born here. So we still come here in early May, for the mountain trout, and the seals, and the pilot whales in autumn. There are also good catches of Greenland halibut and catfish – if you know the right places.' She looked at him hard. 'And we know the right places. But we do not tell others.'

'You needn't worry about us,' said Norlund dismissively. 'We're not here for fishing, that's for sure. Where does this outsider live?'

'Follow that track up the side of the fjord. It's about fifteen minutes walk.'

Pieter Norlund set off along the path, but Larsen stayed where he was.

'Aren't you going?' asked Anita.

'I'd rather have a drink,' said Larsen.

For a moment her initial hostility remained intact, like a solid wall, then suddenly it dissolved.

'Come and have some imiak then.'

Five minutes later the two of them were sitting in a small front room, its windows steamed up with condensation, while an old paraffin heater gave out a faint edge of warmth. They had been joined by a short, wiry, lean-faced, moustached man in his forties, whom Anita introduced as Adam, and who was pouring out large glasses of Greenland beer.

'He's a hasty man, that partner of yours,' remarked Anita. 'Goes through life in a hurry, does he?'

'A bit.'

'He won't find out much if he keeps on at that speed.' She reached forward and patted Larsen on the knee, in a motherly way. 'Young men are always impatient, so they never do anything properly. They mistake quantity for quality. Isn't that right?'

'So people have told me,' replied Larsen.

'When I lived in Aasiaat,' said Adam suddenly, nodding ponderously, 'people said young sledge dogs pull better in the morning, but for a full day's work, you need old dogs.'

They drank their beer.

'Is it good?' Anita asked.

'It's good,' Larsen reassured her, though he found it too acid for his taste.

Adam refilled their glasses, swallowed his own straight down, raised his hand, and left.

'He's off hunting,' said Anita, with more than a hint of pride in her voice. 'They say he's the best hunter in the village – but I think all they mean is that he goes hunting more than anyone else. He prefers it to fishing, he says it is an art – putting yourself in the mind of your prey, and foretelling what it will do.' She paused. 'I phoned the police about the old man.'

'What did you see?' asked Larsen.

'It was difficult to be sure. I was on a high ridge a little way down the fjord, and what I thought that I saw was two men shooting at the old man, then coming down and pointing their guns at him. Then Inga came out of the house. I did not think she was that brave, though maybe she did not realise what was happening. Anyway, the two men ran away, and when I arrived Inga said the men were trying to take the old man away, to kill him. So I rang the police.'

'How do you know it wasn't just careless hunters?'

'I know every man in this village,' said Anita. 'The men with the guns were not people I had ever seen before. And what would they have been shooting at? There are no seals up here on the hills.'

'Tell me more about this old man,' Larsen said.

'What do I know?'

'A lot, I suspect.'

'No. But I think he is a man who has experienced much, and who has learned to keep his own counsel. A man who has lived a life.'

'Why do you think that?'

'You are not really interested in my opinion.'

'I am.'

She hesitated a moment, looked at him more closely, then nodded.

'I think you are. Well, I will tell you then. For a few years, in my youth, I lived a life. Sex, drink, fights, not knowing where I would wake up in the morning, nor where I would sleep at night, or who with. Used by faceless men. Scratching for survival with my nails.' She put up one hand and clawed her fingers. 'When you have lived like that, on the cliff edge, then you recognise others who have done the same.'

'Have I done it?' asked Larsen.

Anita laughed, so that her elegantly sloping shoulders shook. 'Not you, little policeman. Oh no. Not you.'

'I have been in danger many times,' said Larsen, stung by her contempt.

She shook her head pityingly. 'So has everyone. I don't mean the car that does not stop, the plane in a storm, the slip and fall. I am talking about years lived constantly in the shadow of fear.

That is something that cannot be understood by those who have not experienced it.'

'How did it happen to you?' asked Larsen curiously.

'I was a cheap whore in Copenhagen. My pimp made sure I could not ever have children, and week after week things happened to me that should not happen. Every day I lived among those who most people never meet, who they do not even conceive of. After the last of my few friends fell deadly sick, and after a madman had done things to me with a rope and a knife, I realised I was only alive because I was lucky. I put together every krone I had – most of them stolen – and ran away from my pimp and came home. Since then I have put on weight, found Adam, helped bring up my niece Marianne – who I love as if she were my own child – and slowly taught myself to become content. But some nights I still wake up screaming.'

'I'm sorry.'

She patted him on the shoulder. 'I think you really are. I do not feel you will judge me – which is a surprising thing to think about a policeman.' She laughed, and shook her head in surprise at herself. 'I am not a secretive woman, but I do not usually tell people I have just met the story of my life. Anyway, I know almost nothing about the old man. Though perhaps you would be interested to know there are other outsiders here also.'

'Who?' enquired Larsen.

'Europeans. Two women and a man, who have come from some college to study here.'

'What are they studying?'

Anita waved a vague hand. 'Stones, plants, I do not know.'

'And how long have they been here?'

'Ten days. They are camped inland, perhaps an hour's walk – near the river. I think one of them came here before, two or three years back. We see little of them, though they have visited to buy fish and other things.'

'Perhaps I will go and see them,' Larsen said quietly.

He finished his beer in silence.

'Shall I show you the house you are to use?' Anita suggested.

It was a standard, small, detached, timber-frame house, painted bright yellow, though the paint was peeling badly. There were two upstairs bedrooms, and a kitchen, shower cubicle, and sitting-room downstairs.

'Whose is it?' asked Larsen, glancing around at a scattering of personal belongings – a few religious pictures on the walls; a pile

33

of mouldering newspapers from the year before; plates and saucepans in the kitchen; pieces of cheap, battered furniture.

'It was Hansi's,' said Anita. 'But he did not come this year.'

'Why not?'

She shrugged. 'I have not seen him for months. He may have moved. Or perhaps he is dead.'

The house felt damp and cold from its long winter vacancy, but Nils had already stacked up the supplies they had brought with them in the front room, and there was a store of driftwood outside under a tarpaulin. Larsen set up the small portable generator, tested the phone link by calling Nuuk and telling them they had arrived, then carefully unpacked their other belongings. There was three weeks' worth of dried and tinned food, and enough fuel to provide four or five hours of electricity a day for two weeks. It should be more than enough, he hoped.

The weather was clouding over as Larsen strode over a stony hillside, thinly grown with grass. Ahead lay the foothills of the mountains, and a powerful river. Close by, on a small height, stood the remains of a square stone building. A few metres away there had once been another, larger building, but the great stones were fallen and broken, and concealed by luxuriant growths of grass and shrubs. Near the ruins were two green tunnel tents, and beyond them a single, rather larger, pale yellow dome tent.

As Larsen came closer, he saw a man and a woman, measuring part of the larger ruin, and taking down notes. They looked up as he approached.

'Good day,' said Larsen politely, using Danish.

The woman stood up from where she was squatting on the ground. She was small and neat, with short fair hair, and quick, eager blue eyes.

'Good day,' she replied, pleasantly enough, but the answer was a question.

'My name is Sergeant Tomas Larsen, of the Royal Greenland Police,' he said. 'I am investigating the shooting incident near here on Tuesday.'

'I'm afraid we know nothing,' answered the woman. 'We are simply scientists, studying the area.'

'Could I ask you your name?'

'I am Sigrid Heintze.'

'And this scientific study is for what organisation?'

Sigrid hesitated.

'What does he want?' asked the man in English. He was of average height, perhaps thirty-five, with a broad, reddish face, thickly covered with freckles, ginger hair down to his ears, and a thick beard and moustache.

Larsen's English, learnt during his college days in Copenhagen, was fairly fluent, but on an impulse he decided not to reveal it.

'He's a policeman,' explained Sigrid. 'He's asking about the shooting. I told him we didn't know anything.'

'What about those –?'

'It's not important. Anyway, it's none of our business.'

'I suppose not,' the man agreed. 'And there's a lot of surveying to complete before the winter comes in and we have to leave.'

'That's if we're wrong. And we're not wrong, so there'll be even more work – which is why we can't afford any disturbance.'

'I agree the signs are fairly promising – more than I had expected. But we ought to see what Bettina thinks.'

'Bettina thinks what I think.'

Sigrid turned back to Larsen, whose round, pleasant, fattish face gave no hint that he had understood everything they'd said. 'I'm sorry we can't help you,' she said, slipping back into Danish.

'What precise work are you doing?' asked Larsen, ignoring her answer.

'We are geologists.'

'I see. Yet you seem to be working on a historical site. Do you have an official licence from the Ministry of Culture, Education and Research for such work?'

'Of course. Our trip was officially organised through Copenhagen.'

'Kalaallit Nunaat has complete home rule, and the Danish government has no authority in the internal affairs of our country. I'm afraid I must ask to see your official papers, please.'

A second woman had appeared from inside the dome tent, and joined the group. She had long loose hair dyed copper-red with henna, a smooth high-cheeked face, black-rimmed tinted glasses, long ethnic ear-rings, and skin so pale it was almost colourless, except where it was marked with large dark moles.

'What's going on?' she asked, also in English.

The other two started to explain, when there was the buzz of a telephone. The man gave an embarrassed twitch of his head, and bent down to push back the flysheet of one of the tunnel tents. He picked up the telephone, which was lying on a pile of clothes.

'Hello? Yes, that's right, it's Rob Coleman. Can you speak up, it's not a good line . . . No. No, I can't talk now. I'm sorry. The police are here . . . Some local incident, they've been asking us about our papers and such things . . . I'll phone you back later.' He switched off the phone. 'Sorry about that.'

But Larsen was far more interested in something the man had revealed when he pushed back the tent flap.

'Whose is that rifle?' he demanded.

'I suppose it belongs to all of us,' said Sigrid, after a moment's hesitation. 'Part of our supplies.'

'What is it for?'

She hesitated again. 'Hunting.'

Larsen bent down and picked the gun up by its handsome walnut wood stock. He examined it carefully.

'A Browning BAR, Mark II Safari,' he remarked. '7 millimetre mag calibre. Semi-automatic centrefire with a scope sight. A good, powerful weapon. Fairly new by the look of it. What were you planning to hunt with it?'

The man reached out for the rifle, but Larsen did not return it to him.

'What were you planning to hunt with this weapon?' he repeated.

Sigrid shrugged uncomfortably. 'We weren't sure. Reindeer perhaps. Or seal.'

'Have any of you shot seal before?'

'No.'

'Most seals sink once shot, especially in summer when they have less blubber and the water in the fjords is less salt, so there is no point in shooting them without some method of making sure of the body. More to the point, it is forbidden for tourists to hunt anywhere, without specific permission and the provision of police licenses, which are only supplied to organised groups under the control of a licensed and recognised tour operator. Do you have such a licence?'

'No. But we were worried about being so out in the wilds. What if a polar bear –'

'Polar bears are not seen here,' said Larsen dismissively. 'Do you have any other guns?'

'No.'

'Where did you get this one?'

'We brought it with us.'

36

'Airlines only permit people to travel with rifles if they complete extensive advance paperwork. I would like to see your official certificate of carriage for this gun.'

'I meant we brought it with us from Paamiut. We bought it there.'

'And what will you do with it when you leave here?'

'We were told it would be easy to sell it back again.'

'Such activities are not permitted in this country.' Larsen knew perfectly well that at least half the population of Greenland owned guns, and there was a thriving market in selling and reselling them, but it seemed a fair bet that these visitors did not realise that. 'I think you had better come down to the village, and discuss these matters with me.'

Sigrid glanced across at her two companions. 'I have to go with him,' she said in English.

'Why?'

'Don't worry. It's nothing. I'll be back soon.'

'But –'

'It's nothing. OK,' she said, turning back to Larsen. 'Let's go.'

'And I will take this also,' said Larsen, picking up the rifle.

4

THE ATTACK

When Larsen arrived back at the yellow house with Sigrid, he found Norlund already there. He had lit a fire of driftwood in the fireplace, and was using the generator to power a radiator.

'We haven't got so much fuel,' said Larsen. 'Perhaps we shouldn't waste it.'

'Making the house habitable is not wasting fuel,' retorted Norlund. 'Anyway, we won't be here long. Who's this young lady?'

'Sigrid Heintze, from Arhus in Denmark. She and two companions are doing a survey of the area – mainly geological, but also an archaeological study of what seems to be a Norse farm inland, near the river,' explained Larsen.

Norlund wasn't listening. He had taken the rifle from Larsen, and was looking it over. 'Nice weapon!' he remarked, impressed. 'Where did it come from?'

'Sigrid and her friends.'

Norlund weighed it in his hands for a moment. 'It's loaded.'

'I noticed that.'

Norlund broke it open with the ease of someone used to rifles. '175 grain bullet.' He turned back to Larsen. 'You were thinking this might have been one of the guns used in the attack? It's possible. I talked briefly to the old man, and he said the guns he was threatened with had telescopic sights, but his description is very vague.'

He closed the gun up again, took it to the door, then levelled it and peered through the scope. There was a sudden crack as he fired.

Sigrid and Larsen started violently.

'What the hell are you doing?' demanded Larsen, recovering himself.

'Checking its accuracy. I've heard the Browning BAR Mark II is one of the most accurate semi-automatics on the market. It seems like that's true.'

'What were you aiming at?'

'That.' Norlund pointed with the gun at an outcrop a couple

of hundred metres away. 'In fact I aimed for a whitish stone on the top of the rocks – which I hit. And I'm not one of the world's great shots. With a steady hand and this scope sight, I reckon it'd be hard to miss anything which wasn't either moving pretty fast, or at least four hundred metres away. So this probably wasn't one of the guns used in the attack.'

'Why?'

'Because I think I've found one of the places a rifle was fired from, and it's barely 150 metres from where the old man was standing. With this gun, I don't see how the attacker could have missed.'

All this time Sigrid was standing patiently in the middle of the room. 'May I sit down?' she asked.

'Of course,' said Larsen. 'Would you like a coffee?'

'Thank you.'

Ten minutes later all three of them were drinking strong black coffee from chipped mugs.

'It's an isolated part of the Middle Settlement,' Sigrid was saying. 'Of course we're only a few days into our work, but we reckon it probably dates from 1250 to 1300 – just about the time that the Norse settlement of Greenland was starting to get into trouble from the worsening weather. We assumed it was used exclusively for seasonal fishing, but now we've found signs of some farming as well. There are clear boundary markings of what must have been the Home Field – and Rob has suggested that they brought sheep with them each spring, sailing from the Middle Settlement, around Ivittuut.

'However, what is really interesting is that the building also seems to have been used by Inuit hunters. There's a scattering of old Inugsuk settlements in this area – especially south of here around the inland sections of Nerutussoq. The point is that the Inuit tended to avoid ice-fjords, which block up with bergs, and often have unpleasant micro-climates. Also seals prefer ice-fjords, and a settlement might drive them away. Better to live elsewhere, and hunt the ice-fjords. Anyway, this is the first case we have found of Norse ruins being directly recycled, or even perhaps shared –'

'I thought you were primarily geologists,' put in Larsen. 'This is work for archaeologists.'

Sigrid looked momentarily uncomfortable. 'The work we're doing here requires fairly extensive knowledge of recent history – and that means the Norse settlement is very relevant. We're also doing some natural history surveys.'

'Aren't geologists only interested in things millions and millions of years ago?'

'Nowadays all sciences are becoming more and more holistic. To take one example, the geology of this region is clearly reflected in its natural history – the density of moss campion can provide important information about –'

'Tell us what you know about the old man who lives up the fjord,' interrupted Norlund impatiently.

'What old man?' Sigrid looked at him with wide blue eyes.

'You have never seen him?'

'We hardly see anyone. We have been down to the village to buy fish and meat, but basically we brought everything we'll need for three months with us.'

'And you know nothing about any attack?'

'No.'

'OK,' said Norlund. 'That'll do for the moment. But we'll keep this rifle a little longer.'

'Then I'd like a receipt for it,' said Sigrid.

'As you wish.'

Norlund pulled out a small notebook, tore a page from it, wrote out a few words, and gave the piece of paper to her.

'Can I go now?' she asked, pocketing it.

'Of course.'

'After you have given us your phone number,' put in Larsen hastily.

Sigrid gave it to him, then scuttled away, relief obvious in her every movement.

'So how was the mysterious old man then?' asked Larsen.

Norlund put his feet up on a small table and lit a cigarette. 'I'm not sure. At first I thought he was being deliberately evasive, answering every question I asked with another of his own. Then I thought maybe he's just so old that his mind's going. It's difficult to tell. Anyway, although he prefers to speak Danish, he can speak west Greenlandic adequately, and he looks fairly Inuit, but he's no Greenlander. Maybe he's from Alaska, or even Siberia. He gave a pretty vague description of the attack, and if I was a more suspicious person, I might begin to wonder if it had really happened.'

'Why?'

'Well, I also questioned the old man's housekeeper, Inga. She said that she heard and saw nothing, just went out to call him in for his meal and found him outside, shivering and upset. Then some woman from the village turned up and said she'd seen an attack. It doesn't exactly sound like much to go on.'

'What about those faxes to the Chief from Denmark?'

'Yes,' said Norlund, flicking ash into the fire. 'What was that all about? It makes no sense. I reckon the Chief's made some stupid mistake somewhere.'

'Are you sure?'

'Of course I'm not sure. But we always tend to assume things are happening for good reason. This may be one of those cases where it's all bullshit. Crossed wires. You know as well as I do that Thorold's got nothing but snow water between his ears, and only keeps his job because no one can be bothered to kick him out. It's not as if he's got a chance in hell of becoming Commissioner. But by hanging on in there, he blocks everyone else off from promotion.'

Larsen looked at Norlund, in all his youthful energy, drive and certainty. Twenty-five years old, with a pathetically limited experience of life, he didn't doubt for a second that he knew exactly how the world worked. That he could handle it. So many Greenlanders were still used to subordination, to being paid less than Europeans, to keeping quiet, and saying only what they thought their bosses wanted to hear. Suddenly here was someone brash, go-ahead, almost American. A can-do person, who dared to speak back, and was openly and unashamedly ambitious.

They liked all that – the men who had promised Larsen promotion after the Sermilik seed bank affair, then gone back on their promise. Norlund's very certainty impressed and convinced his superiors. And Larsen could do nothing about it. The realisation had grown on him that he was already consigned to the trash bin – a sergeant for the rest of his working life, going through the same repetitive circuit: issuing licences; organising searches for tourists who underestimated the Greenland climate and got into trouble; sorting out pointless drink-induced murders and thefts and suicides.

'Do you want the Chief's job?' he asked.

'Sure, but I want a lot more than that. I want to run things.' Norlund blew out smoke. 'Don't you?'

Larsen shrugged. Norlund's question made him realise that, when it came down to it, he didn't want Thorold's job, didn't want to sit in an office in Nuuk. He had returned to Greenland because he loved the country, and policing had helped him indulge that love. To experience fully the land, and its people. Maybe the bosses sensed that attitude, and that was why they weren't interested in him. He was safely pigeon-holed in the right place. The country needed people like Norlund, needed Greenlanders to take over and run things, to get rid of that lingering colonial attitude that the Danes knew what was best for Greenland. But Larsen was not one of the people who would do that. He was interested in detail, not the broad picture.

'I would have liked to talk to the old man,' he said.

'Telephone him, the number's in there.' Norlund tossed Larsen his notebook, then flicked his cigarette butt into the fire. 'As for me, I'm going to bed.'

He went upstairs and closed the door to one of the rooms. Larsen leafed through the notebook. Half the pages had been torn out. The rest were empty, except for a list of scrawled telephone numbers at the back. Larsen copied the old man's phone number into his own book, then wondered briefly whether to try phoning. But it was too late. Especially for an old man.

He slumped back in his chair, closed his eyes, and returned to brooding on Norlund's casual question. It was his lack of ambition that lay at the heart of the matter, it was what had driven his Danish wife, Ann-Marie, from him.

'What do you really want?' she once asked him.

He had thought for a moment, then said, 'To be happy.'

'That's a stupid answer,' she had retorted angrily.

'Why?' he had asked, not understanding.

'Because happiness comes from other things – money, status, children, lovers, important work . . . success.'

'I'm not sure I understand what success means. For my fore-fathers it was just staying alive.'

'That was then. This is now. And I can tell you exactly what success means – getting what you want. That's why I asked you what you really wanted.'

Norlund would have known the answer, but Larsen hadn't, and still didn't. As for happiness, he had assumed that it came from within. Of course the things she had listed would be pleasant, but he lacked a devouring hunger for them, the convic-tion that he was entitled to them.

Or he had then. And perhaps that was why he had con-sciously, cold-bloodedly, chosen to come back to Greenland. But now there was an itching deep within him, that made him suspect he was beginning to regret his decision. But it was too late to do anything about it.

Larsen woke about two in the morning. He was cold, the

blanket had slipped off him. He yawned massively, then heard a door close downstairs. He slipped out of bed. Barefoot, almost soundless, he padded to the thin, badly fitting door of his room and listened. Then came a crunch of feet on stones outside, and he went over to the window.

In the pale violet-shadowed light of a lurid sunrise, he saw Norlund walking rapidly away from the house. Larsen wondered whether to follow him, but he was tired, and his usual curiosity seemed to be missing. He picked up the blanket, lay down and pulled it back over him. Almost to his own surprise, he fell asleep again immediately.

Next morning, when Larsen went downstairs, Norlund was sitting in the kitchen, drinking a cup of strong black coffee.

'How did you sleep?' asked Larsen.

'OK. What about you?'

'Not bad.' Larsen poured himself a coffee, and decided to say nothing about the previous night. He didn't want to hear Norlund boasting about his sexual conquests. 'I thought I'd go and talk to the old man, this morning. If you don't mind.'

'Why should I? In fact I'll come with you. Maybe a second visit'll get something new out of him.'

On their way up the fjord-side track, a small girl came running up behind them. She had her black hair in bunches, tied up with red ribbons, and she was carrying a small bag.

Larsen slowed, expecting her to catch them up, but she followed at a cautious distance until they came to the old man's house, when she suddenly trotted up to join them.

'Are you going to see my grandpa?' she asked.

'Is this where your grandpa lives?' said Larsen, knocking.

She nodded.

The door opened. A solidly-built Scandinavian woman, with long scraped-back fair hair, stood there. There was a taut expression on her pale, rather characterless face.

'What is it?'

'Sorry, Inga,' said Norlund easily, as if he had known her for years. 'We need to see him again.'

'He's busy,' said the woman.

'Not as busy as you, I'll bet,' replied Norlund. He grinned, pushed back a lock of hair, and put his hand on her shoulder and squeezed. 'You don't mind if we chat with him for twenty minutes or so, do you?'

Inga softened. 'All right. I'll go and tell him.'

'What about me, Inga?' broke in the little girl. 'Tell him I'm here too.'

'Run away, Marianne.'

'But I've brought something for him. A picture I did for him.' The girl raised her bag.

'Perhaps you can come back after lunch.'

'No, she can stay.' The old man stood in the doorway. 'She won't get in the way, will you, Marianne? And after these gentlemen have finished, she can show me her things.' He put his hand on Marianne's head. 'Play outside for a few minutes,' he said softly to her.

'But I don't want to. I want to . . .'

She caught his eye, and the resistance drained out of her. She turned to the door.

'I won't be long,' he called after her, then ushered the two policemen into the front room. It was pleasant and warm, with a large window that looked north-west to the fjord, and Qeqertaq Island. There were two comfortable chairs, a sofa, a low coffee table, and a desk on one side, half-covered with pieces of paper and large books. The old man settled into one of the chairs while Larsen took the other and Norlund perched himself on an arm of the sofa. 'Now, how can I help you?'

'Just a few more questions, Mr Haan, sir,' said Larsen. 'If you don't mind.'

'Of course.'

'Where do you spend the winter?'

'I would rather not reveal that fact, if you don't mind.'

Larsen was surprised.

He looked closer at the man in front of him. He was small, but round – almost fat – yet there was a force and decisiveness in his few movements that was instantly impressive. His broad face was relatively youthful for a man in his seventies, with few lines and those shallow, except for one deep-etched cleft from nose to the left tip of his short, tight mouth. He had a thin white beard and a firm chin. Above a straight, prominent nose were long, dark eyes, deeply set and quiet, under straggling eyebrows. His bald head – so clear of hair it looked shaven – was high and sloping.

'Why don't you wish to tell us?' enquired Larsen.

The man smiled, then picked up a pair of spectacles and put them on.

Larsen waited, but the man still just smiled. It seemed a

44

pleasant, meaningless smile – except Larsen realised that it did mean something. A total refusal to answer. A stone wall.

Larsen wondered whether to push against that refusal, to test how real it was. But even without probing, he sensed a steely will behind the smile. A moment later he realised that Pieter Norlund had probably noticed his uncertainty. Irritated at exposing himself, he resolved to take the attack.

'Very well, Mr Haan, I shall turn to my other questions.' Anger gave his voice the hard brittle quality of pebbles falling on slate. 'One: Is Haan your real name? Two: Where were you born? Three: Do you know why these people attacked you? Four: Do you have any idea who they are? Five: Do you expect anything similar to happen again?'

Haan appeared entirely unruffled. Briefly one of his long thin hands pulled at his chin, as if to stretch out his beard.

'The answers to one, two, three and four are all the same as I gave you to your previous questions, Mr Larsen,' he said at last, as if apologising, but with no weakness in his voice or face. 'The answer to five is that I don't know. If I was asked to elaborate, I would say that in my opinion – and I stress that is all it is – there is nothing you can or need do about it.'

Larsen nodded slowly. Norlund's suggestion that the old man's mind might be wandering was surely so much garbage. This man's thoughts were precise and clear, completely unclouded.

'You realise that hindering our investigation could put you in line for a charge of obstructing the course of justice?'

'Sergeant Larsen . . .' The old man opened his hands expressively. 'I have made no formal complaint about anything, nor did I contact the police. This is all a stupid mistake. Two men decided to play a foolish game, perhaps they were drunk, perhaps not. It does not matter. They pretended that they were in some American film, and they used me as their victim, to try to terrify me, then they ran away. That is all. It is not a police matter.'

'So you think your assailants were local men – from the village?'

'I suppose so. I could not tell.'

'There are not many men in Ikerasak. If we lined them up for you, wearing similar clothes to the people who attacked you, you might be able to identify them.'

'There is no need for you to do anything so embarrassing. For one thing my sight is not good, for another they were, as I told your partner, masked. But let me assure you, this is just a waste of your time, and of the nation's money.'

'Then why not answer our questions, Mr Haan?'

The old man leaned forward, and for a moment there was a flash of genuine intensity, passion even, in his eyes. 'Because I value my privacy, Sergeant. That is why. No other reason. But enough, I think.'

'No, sir. It is not enough. A crime has been committed. Possibly a major crime, and it is our job as policemen to deal with that.'

The man sighed, and for a moment his fleshless fingers, slightly curved from arthritis, beat a tattoo on his thin knees.

'A quick passage through the world will find many policemen whose approach to crime involves committing or compounding them. But, as you seem to be an honest man, Sergeant, perhaps you can recognise that I am not lying to you, or misleading you, though I could have done both. I am merely informing you that there is no point in continuing this conversation.' He paused, and lines of weariness appeared over his features, like a grey veil. 'Now, if you have finished questioning me, I think my friend Marianne has some things that she wishes to show me.'

Larsen did not reply. He was trying to make something of the old man, trying to place him. But somehow he did not fit. He was not a Greenlander, that was clear – but what was he? Who was he? What was he doing here? Only one thing seemed plain: that the man had intelligence, experience, and deep self-confidence, of a calibre Larsen had not met before. Used to feeling in control of situations and people, intellectually if not practically, Larsen found it hard to combat his own instinct that this man was something new. In some indefinable yet very real way, his superior.

At that moment the little girl came bursting in, pigtails flying.

'There are men outside,' she said, her long, almond eyes wide and frightened. 'Many men. They came up the fjord in two boats. They have landed and they are coming here. Men with guns.'

Larsen and Norlund sprang to their feet, and Norlund drew out a handgun.

'Stay here, Tomas,' he said swiftly. 'I'll go and see what's happening.'

The door slammed shut behind him. Larsen reached for his own gun – then remembered it was in his bottom drawer in Nuuk.

Marianne had run to the old man's arms and he was cradling

her. But as Larsen glanced across, he realised the old man was not afraid. Did not even seem to be alarmed.

'Who are these men?' he demanded harshly.

'I don't know, Sergeant.'

'But you have some idea.'

'You do not need to hear my wild theories.' He turned to the girl. 'Don't worry, little one, no one is going to hurt you.'

Larsen bit his lip, then ran to the front door. He opened it and stared outside.

Pieter Norlund, gun in hand, was crouching by a rock a few metres away. Advancing towards him was a straggling line of half a dozen men. They were dressed in grey and white arctic camouflage fatigues, and they carried rifles.

'I demand that you stop now,' Norlund rapped out, raising his voice above the faint hissing of the wind. 'I am an officer of the Royal Greenland Police, and if you do not put down your guns and stop where you are, I will be forced to open fire. Do you understand me?'

The men continued advancing swiftly, menacing and predatory in their self-assurance.

Norlund raised his handgun in both hands and pointed it at the leading man, less than a hundred metres away.

'I will open fire. This is your final warning.'

The man at whom he had pointed his gun stopped.

'Do not be a fool,' he called in Danish. 'Put away your gun and leave. This is no business of yours.'

'Last chance,' said Norlund. 'Put down your weapons.'

The man began to advance again, and Norlund fired, then flung himself to one side, almost disappearing amongst the rocks and grass tufts. The man fell to the ground. A moment later there was a volley of rifle shots.

Larsen darted back inside. Inga had emerged from the kitchen, shaking.

'What is happening? Help us, help us, they are coming back,' she babbled.

Outside Larsen could hear further shots. He pushed Inga into the front room, where the old man was still holding Marianne.

'Quick,' said Larsen. 'They're almost here. We must get away. Is there a back door?'

'Yes,' came a voice from behind him.

Larsen spun round.

A tall blond man in camouflage gear, his face broken up by

47

livid stripes of sun-block, was standing there, rifle in hand. A moment later he was joined by a second man.

'Come along, Mr Haan,' said the first newcomer coldly. 'Let's go.'

Obediently the old man took a step towards them.

There was a piercing scream.

'No, no. You can't take him,' shrieked Marianne. 'He's my grandpa, you can't.'

Desperately she clung on to the old man, her hands clenched into bloodless fists. The old man tried to free himself, but she would not let go. One of the men stepped forward and casually, emotionlessly, tore her away. Instantly she turned on him, and bit his hand savagely.

'Shit!' His detachment vanished and he lashed out. Marianne was sent flying across the room, and crashed against the book-shelf.

She screamed afresh in shock and pain, tears pouring down her cheeks. Larsen ran to her and picked her up. She felt light as a feather.

'You should not have done that,' said the old man sharply, looking his towering captor full in the face. His voice was a whip, lashing back and forth. 'The man who can ill-treat a child and feel nothing is irreparably damaged. He has cut out the most valuable part of himself, the seat of his humanity, and left nothing but rotting scar tissue. He has shrunk into a mindless tool, for others to wield as they wish.'

A flicker of emotion ran over the intruder's face, a faint flush appeared on his cheek, then he put his hand on the old man's shoulder, and began marching him towards the door.

'Come on,' he said.

'You will not get away with this,' Larsen called fiercely.

They ignored him. But as the old man reached the door, he stopped, in spite of the grip on him, and looked back.

'I am sorry, Marianne,' he said. 'But do not worry. There is nothing for you to worry about.'

'I'll find you, grandpa,' she said.

'Don't even try,' he answered. 'But perhaps I may find you again.'

He left the room, escorted by the first man. The second stayed where he was, scanning the room with ever-moving blue eyes, his gaze flickering between Inga, paralysed with terror, and Larsen, who still held Marianne.

'Who are you?' demanded Larsen. 'Don't you realise that I am a policeman?'

The man said nothing.

'Kidnapping is a serious crime,' continued Larsen. 'You will spend a long time in prison for this.'

Still the man did not speak, barely moved, except for those watchful, darting eyes. Larsen looked at him, trying to imprint everything that might help identify the man on his mind, as if he was taking a mental photograph. But there was little to focus on. The fatigues might be a uniform, but they had no distinguishing marks, no numbers or crests or maker's marks. The calf-length waterproof boots, the rifle, even the man himself, with his fair skin, close-set eyes and cropped light brown hair, were anonymous, uninformative. Mass-produced.

The man took a wary step backwards. 'I do not wish to hurt anyone,' he said. 'But if you try to follow me, I will shoot. You understand?'

He took another step backwards, and slipped easily out of the sun-filled room.

Outside Larsen could hear more shooting. As the back door shut, he handed the weeping Marianne over to Inga, then hurried to the front door, and opened it a crack. He could see nothing. He opened it a little wider. Something smashed into the door frame near his head, spraying him with slivers of wood. He slammed the door shut, and ran round into the kitchen, where he peered cautiously out of the window.

There were two small motorised boats on the fjord, with several men splashing through shallow water to them. One turned and raised his rifle. Larsen ducked, and heard the faint crack of a distant shot. When he looked again, the boats were already swinging rapidly round, and vanishing back down the fjord, towards the sea. As they did so there were half a dozen fresh shots.

Larsen went back to the sitting-room. Inga was sitting down, stroking Marianne's hair. The girl was crying quietly, limply, without stopping.

'We'll get your grandpa back,' said Larsen.

She looked up at him, but the hope in her eyes died away within a moment.

As Larsen turned to go and look for Norlund, he saw a small Sony cassette on the desk. Almost without thinking he slipped it into his anorak pocket.

Norlund's face was smeared with dirt, there were scraps of

grass and earth in his hair, and his leather jacket had a large new tear in one of the arms. He was still carrying his gun.

'You were a lot of fucking use, weren't you,' he hissed, his eyes hot with fury. 'You didn't fire once.'

'I don't have my gun with me.'

'Well, you fucking well should have. How the hell do you expect me to handle a dozen men armed with rifles by myself?'

'There were eight of them. And I never thought you could handle them.'

'I might have been able to if you'd fucking helped me. At least I made sure they knew they'd been in a fight.'

'What happened?'

'I dropped their leader, I think I got him in the shoulder. And another one of them in the leg. They sprayed the area around me, but they were shit, none of the shots came close.'

'One shot hit the door just above my head,' said Larsen.

'Which was enough to send you scuttling inside, like a whipped dog.'

'I was trying to get the old man away.'

'Very brave of you,' sneered Norlund. 'What went wrong?'

'Two of them burst in through the back door. They must have worked their way round the back of the house before the others showed themselves. One took the old man, the other held us up until they were away.'

'Brilliant! Just don't expect me to ask for you as a partner next time I'm in a tough position. Jesus Christ!' He stormed past Larsen, back into the house. 'Have you sent a message out yet?'

'No. I came out to see what was happening and –'

'And what use were you?' growled Norlund angrily. 'You could have made the call five minutes ago, which would have given us a much better chance of intercepting them before they get away.'

5

THE TAPE

'I see,' said Chief Thorold, nodding as Norlund finished his report. 'Well, I must say it sounds as if you behaved very well. Very . . . boldly. You probably should not have taken such risks – one handgun against eight rifles is scarcely sensible odds to fight under – but your bravery and formidable determination were estimable. And it shows impressive foresight that you thought to take your gun with you.'

'Thank you, sir.'

'Anyway, to press on with our business. I have some good news.'

'Good news?'

Larsen stared blankly at Thorold, then across at Norlund, wondering if he had missed something. If he was just being stupid. But Norlund's face was equally uncomprehending.

'I have just been talking with the Police Commissioner,' went on Chief Thorold, in a slightly hushed voice. 'He has informed me, unofficially of course, but . . .' He paused, then carefully began the sentence again. 'We have had an informal discussion, and I am glad to be able to state unequivocally that the whole episode can now be consigned to the past.'

Norlund sprang to his feet. 'But sir –'

Thorold held up his soft, pale hand. 'Let me continue, please. The Commissioner kindly spent some time clarifying precisely what happened. Despite the way things must have seemed to you, in point of fact no kidnap took place at all. On the contrary. The men involved were members of an élite security unit who were training secretly, under the auspices of NATO, on the edges of the inland ice.'

Larsen nodded. That at least explained why the attackers had been so disciplined and thorough.

'Anyway,' went on Thorold, 'it seems that Mr Haan – not his real name of course – was part of this training exercise. He is, in fact, an actor, and the job of one group of the men was to . . . er, seize him, while another group attempted to take control of the headquarters of the first group.' Thorold frowned a little. 'Wargaming, I believe it is called. To continue, the first attempt to capture Mr Haan was foiled, not of course by the housekeeper, who knew nothing of the matter, but by members of the defending force, who arrived in time to stop the seizure. The second attempt, in which you unwittingly became involved, was however, a complete success. Apparently the defending forces had been lured away by some trick, and the guards left behind were overwhelmed.'

'This can't be true, sir,' burst out Norlund. 'What happened was not a game. They were firing at me, and –'

'And you actually wounded two of them. Yes. The Police Commissioner had to apologise to the officer and the man involved. Of course it was not your fault, but the whole affair could have been very embarrassing. Fortunately the officer involved apparently took it very well. Neither injury was serious, and he told the Commissioner that to undertake the exercise as a live fire operation had added greatly to its reality and tension, as well as contributing to its practical use – in training terms, that is. I must say, I cannot really understand these army people . . .'

'Sir, they fired back at me,' said Norlund. 'I heard the bullets.'

'I did enquire about that, Sergeant. In fact the rifles were loaded not with bullets, but a sophisticated equivalent of paintballs – small pellets filled with a clear liquid that only shows up on infra-red viewers. If you had been hit you would have received nothing worse than a bruise, and of course anyone wearing night-vision goggles would have been able to see you glowing like a bonfire. But I gather you were not hit.'

'No, sir.'

'The Commissioner explained to me that these pellets travel much slower than bullets, and because of this they are substantially less accurate – especially at longer ranges, which probably explains their failure to hit you. Next time you face eight rifles, you should perhaps take a leaf out of Sergeant Larsen's book, and behave with more discretion.' The thin smile he gave was clearly not designed to take any sting out of the words. 'I have requested the Commissioner to ensure we are officially informed about future military exercises, and he has agreed that these events certainly revealed a failure of communication links which must be sorted out.' He stopped, and briefly regarded his immaculately clean fingernails. 'Any questions?'

Norlund scowled, but shook his head.

'Tomas?'

Larsen shrugged. 'It seems we've been made fun of.'

'No, no. Just an unfortunate misunderstanding. I believe that the officer in charge of the attack group believed you were members of the defending forces, who had disguised yourselves as civilians to confuse them. When he realised he was really wounded, not just paint-balled, the attack was already well under way. Anyway, all's well that ends well, eh?'

'Yes, sir,' said Norlund and Larsen.

'Good, good. Now, it is getting on for lunchtime, and with today being Friday, there's no real point in the two of you going back to work this afternoon, is there? In recognition of your recent difficulties, I've decided to give you both two days' unofficial leave. That means you don't need to come in again until next Wednesday.'

'Thank you very much, sir.'

'That's all right. See you next Wednesday.' He summoned up another skeletal smile. 'Unless, of course, Pieter's child has arrived by then – in which case the new father will be entitled to a few more days off.'

As Norlund and Larsen walked down the corridor, the younger man stopped to examine the torn sleeve of his jacket.

'I ought to get the bloody Danish army to pay for this,' he muttered. He pulled out a cigarette and lit it. 'I don't know about you, but I feel really pissed off about all this. I mean, what a waste of bloody time.'

'Was it?'

'Of course it was.' He blew smoke out viciously. 'I hate the armed forces – all they do is pretend to be hard men. It's the police who deal with the real thing, on the ground.'

'You mean handing out real angling licences, and telling off real drunks for being really sick in the streets,' said Larsen.

'OK, OK. But it's not only those sort of things. And even if it was, I reckon they're better than grown-ups playing bloody kids' games.'

'Yes,' agreed Larsen. He looked at Norlund sidelong. 'Except I don't think what we saw was a kids' game.'

'Not for the two I shot anyway,' said Norlund, dragging on his cigarette with an air of angry satisfaction. Then the edge in Larsen's voice, penetrated. 'What do you mean?'

'I think the Chief was spinning us a line,' said Larsen quietly.

'Why do you think that?'

'Call it instinct.'

'I'm a policeman,' said Norlund. 'I deal with facts. So what exactly are you talking about?'

'OK. Here's a fact for you. That old man, whatever his name was, had visited Ikerasak every summer for several years. That doesn't sound like an actor to me.'

Norlund considered. 'Maybe the army do the same exercise each summer.'

'Maybe. Or maybe not.'

'Oh well. It's not our business any more, is it?' He walked on. 'I'm going to make the most of things and have myself a really good weekend. If you see any soldiers, you have my permission to kick them. But right now, I'm going for a drink. Want to come?'

'No, thanks.'

'As you like.'

He stubbed out his cigarette on the floor, and walked off jauntily.

Larsen left the police station. It was one of those grey, misty days, common enough in Nuuk during the summer, when the air tasted of salt and fish. But just before he reached the soulless high-rise housing development where he lived, a fan of sunbeams broke through the greyness that cloaked Greenland's capital, and for a moment the town looked as if it had been floodlit for a gala. Then the clouds closed up again.

As soon as he had let himself into his small two-room apartment, Larsen sat down. The postcard he had received a few days ago from Mitti still lay on the side table. He picked it up and read the brief scribbled lines again.

'Hi. It's quiet here. Much quieter than Nuuk, or even Sermilik. I'm not sure if I like it. Hope you're well. Love, M.'

After a moment Larsen flicked it away. It curved across the room, and fell down the back of his bookcase. His shoulders were sore, and he massaged them as best he could for a few minutes, then shrugged several times. The stiffness faded, and he knelt down on the floor and began to do press-ups. After fifty, he got up, twisted his head from side to side a few times, and rubbed his neck. Feeling better, he went into the kitchen, made himself a coffee, then got out the cassette he had removed from Haan's house, slipped it into his own tape player, rewound it, and turned it on.

It began abruptly, the old man speaking slowly, and carefully, in his strangely accented Danish.

'Where was I born? I cannot remember. All those villages were

54

the same – a warren of narrow, straggling lanes with high windowless walls, so that people looked only inwards at their fenced-off courtyards and gardens. Tree-shaded houses thatched with stalks that could not keep out the rain, a maze of worn brick and termite-eaten wood on the hilltop. Shallow pits where women milled the grain by pounding it with stones, or winnowed it with flapping carpets of woven straw. Boys carrying goods in panniers. Communal vegetable-cutting on immemorial flat stones outside the village. Old men sucking at empty long-stemmed pipes while they sat on narrow wooden benches and watched the world. Old women squatting on their heels. Mud and dust and the warm, thick, comforting smell of animals. As comforting as the mud wall around the village.

'Beyond lay the countryside. A green terraced patchwork of fields, woods and clusters of houses, under the hot southern sun. The lines between each square, like a Go board, etched out in silver water which gleamed in the ditches and streams. Distant blue mountains cloaked in pines. A serpentine river, crawling across the quilted landscape. A world tamed and bridled by man, crushed by aeons of occupation, all unpredictability long since removed. And everywhere people. The picture is so clear in my head, that it must be real. Unless it is just the concentrated memory of a thousand similar places.

'When you have lived as long as I have, it becomes hard to separate truth from imagination, to see through the dream of your life. Your own body loses its reality. You think you are younger than you are, you see yourself younger than you are, but when you get up from the chair it hurts. When you put on your spectacles, it is still hard to read. What people say is fuzzy and distant. The senses you rely on betray you until you no longer know what you can trust. Every night you sleep a little less, every evening you go to bed a little earlier, yet it is easier to doze in a chair than in your bed. Again and again your body cries out, torn between gravity on one side and your will on the other. And your memories come at you transformed into regrets: the things you did not do, did not say, did not try. And foremost among them those days one May that could have represented a glittering flash of achievement, something no one could ever take away from me. The moments when perhaps I could have joined those who take history by the throat and briefly force her to do their bidding. But I did not have the courage, or the self-belief, or the sheer bloody-mindedness, to continue to the end of the road. Instead the memory of failure and weakness squats like a malign toad in the very centre of my life. But in more than ten years, guilt has run its course, and my own weariness drains the last dregs of its virulence.

'I have other closer concerns now. I catch death looking me in the face, and I hastily turn away, but my old neck grows stiff and it becomes ever more difficult to avoid those empty eyes, to close my ears to the elusive promise of sleep, which is harder and harder to find any other way. Meanwhile time itself shrinks, for when I close my eyes, I can still see the blue slopes of the Mountains of Heaven as clear as a photograph. But I cannot bring to mind the Hverfjall, which I see every day from my bedroom window. Enough, I am running ahead of myself.

'What happened to my childhood? I lost it on that epic odyssey – which itself is no more than a few cold flashes piercing my reluctant mind. One of my first true memories reveals me already a soldier, a determined and ruthless adult mind in a ten-year-old body. Sometimes I am almost incapacitated with fury at the unmoving, blank desert of my childhood. The rage builds up until I wish to scream and throw myself on the floor and scratch my face until pain tears the veil and reveals my past. But old men are serene. They have taken everything life can throw at them and conquered it. So I do nothing. And the anger dribbles away, like venom which leaves the place where the snake struck only to undermine the whole body.

'When I was young, I must have had a savage temper. But children were not permitted such luxuries then – unlike today. So I learned to hide the fury that stalked my heart. Not that hiding made it less – a fire that is banked up becomes hotter. I kept my face impassive, and smiled, and did what I was told. And I waited for opportunity, like a bear at a seal hole. But I missed my last strike at the seal, and now my waiting is only for the long peace.'

There was the harsh click of the microphone being turned off, followed by silence. Larsen left the tape run a little longer, then switched it off. He got to his feet and began to walk round his little apartment. It was a habit he had when thinking. His ex-wife used to tell him that he was the only man she knew who could only think on his feet.

And aloud, she might have added.

'If what is on the tape is reminiscence, not fiction, then the old man is not an Inuit,' he said quietly to himself. 'That explains his strange accent. Pieter Norlund suggested he came from Alaska or Siberia, but on the tape he speaks of trees and heat and dust.

So he must come from somewhere hot and poor. Remembering his appearance, that probably means eastern Asia. But what was he doing in Ikerasak?' He shook his head. 'I should have talked to his housekeeper.'

Then he realised that he still could. He pulled out his note-book, noted the number, and rang.

There was no answer. The phone rang on and on, without reply.

Larsen swore. It was obvious really – if the old man had gone, then there was no reason for his housekeeper to stay. He felt a temptation to forget the whole business, but what else was there for him to do this weekend? He could seek out some acquaintances and have a night out, perhaps visit the disco at the Hotel Godthab, but Larsen had not enjoyed doing that for a long time. He could hire a video, go to bingo, or visit the cinema or the solarium. He could stay in, read and watch TV. Or he could arrange a couple of days walking in the interior, around Qoorqut or Kapisillit. Somehow none of those ideas appealed to him.

He glanced down at his notebook again, and saw the number of the geologists' camp. Not giving himself time to wonder exactly what he was doing, Larsen rang the number.

He was answered by the man, speaking in English.

'Hello, this is Rob Coleman.'

'Good afternoon. This is Sergeant Tomas Larsen of the Royal Greenland Police. I apologise for calling you, but I am trying to contact the isolated house where the old man called Haan lives. There is no answer to the telephone there, and I am concerned.'

'I don't understand,' said Rob. 'I thought the old man had –'

'I would be very grateful if you could go to the house and see if it is still inhabited,' interrupted Larsen.

'But it's the best part of thirty minutes' walk each way.'

'I would be most grateful.'

Rob sighed. 'OK.'

'Thank you very much. If you could call me back when you have any news – my number is . . .'

As Larsen rang off, he realised he had just revealed to Coleman that he spoke English. Unable to settle, he walked restlessly round his apartment. He drank his tepid coffee, then made another and drank that. Four times he almost rang again, and four times he controlled himself.

It was well over an hour before Rob Coleman rang back.

'Sergeant Larsen? I'm outside the house you talked about. There's no one here, but it's a bit weird, because the lights are on in a couple of rooms, and the generator's going. I've knocked and called several times, and looked around the place, but there's no answer. Sorry.'

'You're absolutely sure there's no one around?'

'No one. I told you, I've gone right round the house, and shouted several times. Nothing. And now I have work to do, so I need to head back.'

'Thank you very much.'

'It's OK.'

The phone went dead.

6

TRACKING

Larsen buried his head in his hands and brooded. It took him ten minutes to realise that he had already made up his mind, then he glanced at his watch. Five forty-five. Chief Thorold would leave the office in fifteen minutes at the most. As it was Friday he had probably left already, but it would be as well to play safe and wait. Had it not been Friday, Larsen's plan would have had little prospect of success, but he knew there was no way the Chief would be back in the office before Monday morning. Thorold treated his weekends as sacrosanct – put aside for his pretty young wife, and for playing with his even prettier little four-year-old daughter. One of the few things guaranteed to turn the mild-mannered Thorold into something close to an angry polar bear was to contact him about work between Friday evening and Monday morning. Furthermore, with Norlund off, Helge must have been left in charge. Everything seemed to be clicking into place.

At 6.03 Larsen phoned the station.

'Hi. This is Tomas Larsen. I need a few words with the Chief.'

'Hello, Tomas, it's Helge. The Chief's gone home.'

'Damn!' said Larsen. 'Oh well, it probably doesn't matter. He should have left the paperwork on his desk.'

'What was it about?'

'My return trip to Ikerasak tomorrow morning. I've got a nasty feeling that I was supposed to reserve my ticket to Paamiut, not leave it up to the Chief . . .'

'I can't see anything about it,' said Helge after a couple of minutes.

'That's strange.' Larsen allowed himself a carefully weighted hesitation. 'I suppose you'll have to contact him at home and ask for official confirmation of my flight booking.'

'I suppose so,' said Helge, the reluctance clear in his voice. 'But –'

'The problem is that I think it's his daughter's birthday party this evening,' went on Larsen relentlessly. 'I'm afraid he won't take at all kindly to an interruption, especially when it's just a routine travel confirmation.' He added pressure with a second pause. 'Are you absolutely sure there's nothing on his desk?'

'No.'

Larsen sighed. 'He really should have remembered.'

Like everyone in the station, Larsen and Helge knew that Thorold did not enjoy being caught in the wrong by juniors.

'Perhaps it would be best if you called him,' said Helge.

'Oh no. I couldn't do that. I have to pack, and the duty officer always has the responsibility for passing things on. You know that.'

There was yet another pause. With the confidence of a good poker player bluffing hard, Larsen felt a growing certainty that he was about to scoop the pot.

'You have to get to this place tomorrow?' asked Helge, at last.

'I'm afraid so. I mean, all I need is an official police confirmation when I book the flight.' Then, as if the idea had occurred to him for the first time, 'I suppose as the duty officer you could do it.'

'You think so?' asked Helge doubtfully.

'Why not? The Chief won't even know until the accounts come in in a few weeks, and he may not notice then. If there's any problem, I'll deal with it. Anyway, the duty officer has pretty broad-ranging powers.'

'But that's in case of an emergency, isn't it?'

'Well, I am supposed to take the trip. Actually I'm pretty annoyed about it – I had plans for the weekend, if you know what I mean.' Another pause. 'I suppose if I don't get my travel confirmation, I could forget the whole trip, and go ahead with seeing my girlfriend. There'd be a lot of explaining to do on Monday morning. A lot. Especially if anything happens in Ikerasak during the weekend. But –'

'OK.' Helge's resistance crumbled. 'Go ahead and book your flight, and I'll confirm it for you.'

'If you're sure,' said Larsen.

'Yes.'

'Pity, actually. I thought I was going to get away with it.' He laughed. 'Oh well. See you, Helge.'

At one o'clock the next day, Larsen was back in Ikerasak, talking to Anita Petterman.

'No, I haven't seen the old man's housekeeper,' she said. 'Not that I usually do from one week's end to another. But I don't see how she could have left – the last boat to Paamiut was the one

60

you and your partner travelled on, and there hasn't been a helicopter here since last autumn. Maybe Marianne knows something.' Anita shook her head disconsolately. 'Not that I can get a thing out of her. Since the business with the old man, she's been a different child – as if the sorrows of the world came crashing down on her that moment.'

Marianne was lying on her bed in a small room upstairs. She was staring up at the ceiling, and her round face was a brittle mask of lassitude. She did not bother even to glance up as Anita came in.

'I've brought someone to see you, Marianne.'

'Tell them to go away.'

'It's Sergeant Larsen, he wants to talk to you.'

In a moment the little girl had changed. She shot up from her bed, and ran over to Larsen. 'Have you found him? Where is he?' Her face looked up excitedly. Imploringly.

Larsen shook his head. 'I'm sorry.'

A quiver ran through her whole body, then she crumpled back on her bed.

'Marianne, I need your help,' said Larsen.

She did not move, showed no sign she had heard him at all. Larsen hesitated, standing and looking around her room. On the wall, mounted with drawing pins, was a painstakingly coloured picture of a house, with mountains in the background. But it was creased, and partly torn.

'That's a nice picture,' said Larsen. 'Is it your house?'

'No, it's grandpa's,' came her muffled voice, shaking on the edge of tears. 'I did it for him, but then they took him away – and I'm never going to be able to give it to him.'

'Yes, you are,' said Larsen firmly. 'Because I'm going to find him. I'm a policeman. It's my job to find missing people, and I've never failed.'

At last she looked up again, with the faintest gleam of rekindled hope. 'Never?'

'Never,' he lied. 'But you have to help me. So I want you to come up to his house with me, and tell me everything you know. All right?'

Quarter of an hour later, cloud hung low overhead as the two of them walked by the edge of a low cliff. Below lay a stony beach vanishing before a dark, rising tide. A gusty wind snatched at Marianne's hair and blew it around her face.

'So,' said Larsen, 'no one had ever come looking for him before?'

'That's right. He says Ikerasak is his own secret place, and he won't let anyone see it.'

'Listen, Marianne, did you ever ask him where he spends the rest of the year?'

'Yes. He said it was in another country. A country with boiling fountains and burning mountains. Is there such a place? Or was he making fun of me?'

'There is such a place. It is called Iceland.'

'That's right. That's what he said. Iceland. Has he gone back there?'

'I don't know. Did he mention the name of any place in Iceland?'

'No, I don't think so. Though he said that he lives by a lake that doesn't freeze. But Inga comes from there too, so you can ask her where it is. Look, there's the house.'

'I thought the generator was still going.'

'Maybe it's out of fuel. But Inga wouldn't leave it on when she didn't need it. She goes on and on at me when I just forget to turn a light off.'

At that moment it began to rain heavily, pattering on the rocks. Marianne ran for the house, and Larsen followed her. The door was open, and they burst in, dripping. Then a thought came to Larsen. He went back outside and looked at the door frame. The hole was very clear, as was the gleam of a bullet embedded in it. So Thorold was wrong – the men who had seized the old man had been armed with bullets, not paint-balls. But why? And why had they been such bad shots?

'Come here,' came Marianne's voice behind him. 'Come here quick!'

He hurried after her.

Someone had turned the house upside down. Every surface had been stripped bare, every shelf cleared, every cupboard and drawer opened and its contents flung to the ground. The kitchen was a chaos of pans, utensils, and broken plates and mugs. Every container of food or drink had been emptied, and the floor was thick with rice, coffee, flour, sugar and salt. The fridge had been tipped over on its side, and a puddle of rancid milk filled the air with its smell. Larsen went upstairs, to find the cupboards had been emptied and the beds stripped – their sheets and duvets flung on the ground. He returned downstairs, to find Marianne was still standing in the kitchen, looking around disapprovingly.

'Aunt Anita tells me off if I drop just a little bit of food,' she said. Then she frowned. 'Do you think Inga did this?'

'No,' said Larsen. 'I think a thief did it. A wicked man, who we'll catch and put in prison.'

Marianne considered this. 'Do you think it was those soldiers, who stole away grandpa?'

'Perhaps. But first I would like to know where Inga is.' He looked around him again, then his face changed. 'We came in by the front door, didn't we? But the back door is open.'

'Shall I close it?' Marianne took a step forward.

'Stop!' rapped out Larsen abruptly.

She obeyed, her face twisted in shock, as if he had slapped her.

'Don't move,' said Larsen sharply. 'Stay where you are.'

He began to walk forward slowly, his heavy boots crunching over broken glass and china. Marianne watched him wide-eyed.

'Look!' he said. 'Some one trod in the coffee, and they've left footmarks out of the door. All right, you can move now, but don't tread on those footprints, and follow me carefully.' He paused. 'I'm sorry I shouted at you, but . . .'

'I know,' said Marianne. 'You only did it because you want to find grandpa.'

'That's right. OK, let's go, and careful where you step.'

They followed the brown stains out of the back door, then round the side of the house, where they pointed down towards the shore. But once they were out of the shelter of the house walls, the traces vanished.

'I need a hunter to follow the tracks,' muttered Larsen.

'I'll get Adam,' said Marianne. 'He told me he could follow a reindeer from here to the Iceblink. He's the best tracker. I'll get him.'

When Adam arrived, half an hour later, Larsen explained what he wanted. Adam listened carefully, gave Larsen a characteristic sidelong glance, then gently stroked his greying moustache with a thick, yellow-stained finger.

'How much?'

'It depends how long –' began Larsen.

'300 kroner if I find the tracks, nothing if I don't.'

'OK.'

With barely a glance at the ground, it seemed, Adam led them down to the fjordside, then followed the edge of it about half a kilometre, heading north towards the mouth of the River Isortoq. A curving ridge of old moraine swung out towards a grassy hummock which projected into the widening fjord, opposite the northern tip of Qeqertaq Island. They followed it, passing a brackish lagoon, enclosed by the ridge, and made their way on to black seaweed-slimed rocks which showed the hummock was cut off at high tide. On their right, the low-lying, swampy delta of the Isortoq, with many separate streams flowing out into the fjord, created an intricate jigsaw of land and water.

'Here,' said Adam, pointing at the far end of the thin-grassed hill, where there was a rocky promontory, with the water rolling up against it.

'How can you be so sure?' demanded Larsen, suspiciously.

'See, there's the mark of a heel, here someone stumbled, and that rock over there has scraping against it from the side of a boat.'

'Why should anyone come up the fjord, away from the sea, to get in a boat?'

'Perhaps so no one saw them,' suggested Adam, and he gave a quick, cunning glance at Larsen. 'It's a good place to bring in a boat, if the wind is not blowing from the ice, because deep water comes right up to the shore.'

'But they would be seen going back past Ikerasak.'

'They do not need to travel past the village. On the far side of Qeqertaq is a channel to the sea. It is not much used, for the currents there are often strong, as are the winds, and in places it is so narrow a single large berg can block it. But the channel is there. People who know this country, or have a good map, do not need to be seen. If they do not wish it.'

Larsen's hopes fell. 'You think Inga was taken away from here?'

Adam considered, his long slanting eyes darting around the ground where they stood. Suddenly he turned to Marianne.

'Go down by the waterside, and see if you can find anything.'

'OK.' The little girl scrambled down among the rocks. 'Around here?' she called.

'Yes. Now walk back towards the ridge. That's right. Keep an eye for any signs that people have been there. The sergeant and I will look up here.'

'What is it?' asked Larsen, dropping his voice.

Adam pointed to a patch of gravel and loose stones that was churned up and scattered. Nearby some grass had been flattened and torn.

'Someone was dragged along here,' he said. 'And they were struggling. But I don't think they were taken to the boat – see how the scrapes on the rock are leading that way. We had better search very carefully.'

It was Larsen who found the narrow little inlet, like a knife cut in the northern rock face. In the black oily-looking water a body was washing slowly to and fro.

Larsen scrambled down to the water's edge. The body was battered and torn, and parts of the face had been eaten into by birds or fish. But despite the empty eye-sockets and the grey waterlogged skin, there was no doubt that it was a woman's body. Inga's body.

7

RISA

It was sleeting as the red and white Grønlandsfly Bell 212 helicopter dropped slowly, delicately, on to the rippled grey sand of the foreshore, close to the high tide mark. The moment the helicopter settled, bouncing on its skis, the door opened, and two people got out, ducking unnecessarily low. The taller one led the way up on to the rocky shore. Both wore thick waterproof jackets, the hoods up, and carried bags in their gloved hands. Larsen went forward to greet them, and there was a roar of noise and a blast of air as the helicopter took off again, rapidly vanishing out over the sea.

'Good day, doctor,' said Larsen, speaking in Danish, as nearly all of Greenland's doctors were still of Danish origin. He offered his hand.

The leading newcomer, who was slightly taller than Larsen, laughed, and replied in the same language.

'I'm afraid Dr Lynge is a busy man. Especially when faced with the prospect of having to set off into the wilds at three o'clock on Saturday afternoon. What you get is me – Nurse Risa Poulson. This is my son, Edvarth.'

Larsen felt as if he had put down his foot on a step that was not there. He had not expected a woman, let alone a woman who had brought her child.

'Good afternoon,' he said, to cover his confusion.

'I wouldn't say so. Let's find some shelter.'

'It's quite a long walk.'

'How long?'

'Twenty minutes – maybe a bit longer.'

'Great!' she sighed. 'Here, you can carry this bag for me. Come on, Edvarth, let's go. If I don't get a cup of coffee soon, I'll collapse with acute caffeine withdrawal.'

They set off up the stony way to Ikerasak. Larsen had still not seen the nurse's face, which was well shadowed by her anorak hood.

'Why did the helicopter leave so fast?' he asked, walking alongside her.

'The weather's expected to worsen. So he threw us out, and got himself out.'

They walked on. The sleet, now mixed with snow, was blowing directly in their faces, driven by a vicious wind that swept straight off the ice cap. At last they reached the top of the ridge, and the village became dimly visible below them, through a curtain of snow.

'Is that it?' asked the nurse. 'No wonder they emptied the place.'

'The fishing's said to be very good.'

'That'll give Edvarth something to do.'

The boy, hunched and miserable, looked at his mother, and Larsen caught a glimpse of a fine-featured, pale-skinned teenager. Then the snow blew harder, lashing into their faces, and they bowed their heads and pressed on.

'I suppose I'd better give you some information about the body, where we found it and –' said Larsen, half-way down the final, steep descent to Ikerasak.

'No, thank you,' the nurse interrupted sharply. 'I prefer to consider the matter without prejudgements. I'll ask you any questions I need answers to.'

Larsen had reoccupied the house where Norlund and he had stayed during their last visit to Ikerasak. After arriving, he made coffee while Edvarth and Risa went upstairs, stripped off their wet clothes, and unpacked their bags.

When Risa reappeared twenty minutes later, Larsen was surprised by her physical presence. She was not only tall, but broad also, bigger than many men, and her body gave an instant impression of physical strength. Her black hair, untouched by grey, was tied up in a neat bun, high on her head, so that it was impossible to tell how long it was. Her face was almost square, with fine long eyes and high cheekbones, and her large mouth had a faint twist to it. She was wearing a thick multi-coloured sweater, and woollen trousers tucked into mud-stained boots, and Larsen guessed she was in her late thirties.

She also gave him a vague, haunting sense of familiarity, but he could not think where from. He watched her pour herself a cup of coffee, and swallow it straight down, even though it was still scorchingly hot. She poured another, then sat down in the chair opposite him, and confidently, unselfconsciously, stretched out her legs.

'It's good to be dry,' she said.

'Does your son want some coffee?' asked Larsen.

'Edvarth will come down if he wants anything.' She looked up and intercepted Larsen's questioning look. 'What is it?'

'I just wondered . . .' Larsen stopped.

'You wondered why I brought him – is that it?' She didn't even wait for his answer. 'I'd say that was my business, wouldn't you?'

'Of course. I'm sorry.' He paused. 'How long do you expect to be here?'

She laughed harshly. 'In other words why bother to bring my son out here for just one night? You won't leave the subject alone, will you? Have you got children?'

'Yes. Two daughters.'

'And do they ever worry you?'

'Well . . .'

'You leave that to your wife, I suppose. Well, Edvarth has been running with the wrong sort of young men lately, and I don't have a partner to watch him while I'm away. Nor a friend that I'd trust. It's true I expect to be out of here tomorrow morning, but even a single Saturday night is plenty of time for a fourteen-year-old to get himself in serious trouble. Let alone the chance that I might be stuck out here for several days.'

'I'm sorry,' said Larsen.

'It's not your problem. And you don't need to worry, he won't be a problem. At the moment he's sitting on the bed listening to music on his personal stereo, and feeling sorry for himself.' She yawned, then sat up and gave Larsen a critical frown. 'You don't really look like a policeman.'

'What do I look like?'

'You don't behave like a policeman either. I thought you'd answer, "Well, I am," and then start talking about the body.'

'You haven't answered my question.'

'Probably because I don't know the answer. I suppose I could imagine you as a hunter from some wild place in the north or east. You've got that sort of squat, powerful build. And you look very patient – someone who could sit by a hole in the ice for five hours till the seal finally popped up, and then move very fast.'

She reached out and without warning picked up his right hand. She looked at it attentively for a moment, then delicately brushed one of his fingertips.

'Could you feel that?'

'No.'

'I didn't think so. You've had frostbite.'

'I've only got nine toes too.'

'At least you waste less time cutting your toenails. So you

have been a hunter? No, on second thoughts I don't think so. Your fluent Danish means you've probably spent time in Denmark, and that doesn't fit with being a hunter. Perhaps you've been on some scientific expedition to the north – but then why would you be a policeman? Sorry, I'm talking too much. Greenlander men often find me difficult to deal with, because I'm like a European, I never stop talking. But I'm right about you having lived in Denmark, aren't I?'

'Yes. Several years. I suspect maybe you have too.'

'Maybe,' said Risa. 'Immaqa. Maybe. The word that sums up Greenland. Maybe. Perhaps. Could be. On the other hand. Let's play safe and not commit ourselves. Will the plane come tomorrow? Immaqa. Do you love me? Immaqa.' She smiled without real humour. 'Of course I've lived in Denmark. Greenland women are supposed to laugh a lot and not talk, aren't they? Even when they're pissed.'

Larsen said nothing.

'I was two years into my medical training in Copenhagen, then Edvarth happened. So out went any chance of my being a doctor.'

'You're married then?'

'You think so?' She swallowed her second coffee as fast as the first.

'Have I met you before?' Larsen suddenly blurted out.

She looked at him, then shrugged. 'Perhaps. I worked in Nuuk for several years, and every now and then there were dealings with the police.' She scratched her chin with another oddly masculine gesture. 'I'm a bit unusual and people tend to remember me. I don't remember you.'

'Why did you move from Nuuk?'

'You may not look or behave like a policeman, but I can see why you are.'

'Why?' asked Larsen, genuinely interested.

'Because you like asking questions and finding things out.'

Larsen opened his mouth to speak, but she anticipated him.

'OK, I wanted a change, and a new staff controller was appointed at the hospital, who I didn't like, and who didn't like me. Paamiut's been a good move. The new video conferencing facilities, linked up to Nuuk and Copenhagen, mean local hospitals are much more interesting places to work than they used to be. Now we don't have to send patients away if it's anything worse than food poisoning or frostbite. And while I think of it, is it all right if we stay here tonight?'

'Of course. I mean, it's not my house, I've just borrowed it, but as long as you don't mind sharing a room with your son . . .'

As if on cue, the boy appeared at the top of the stairs.

'Want a coffee?' asked his mother.

He shook his head. 'I thought I'd go out for a bit,' he muttered.

'Sergeant Larsen says there's good fishing here.'

'Haven't got any fishing stuff.'

'Try some of the people here,' suggested Larsen.

'I don't know them,' answered the boy, not looking at him.

'That doesn't matter, I'm sure one of them would lend you a rod. And it's a good time to look for mountain trout in the fjords at the moment, they –'

'I know,' said Edvarth, and slipped out of the door.

'Social, he isn't,' remarked Risa. 'But a good boy at heart. At least I think so.' She stood up. 'Right, this seems a good moment to get down to work. Let's see the stiff.'

Outside the sleet had stopped, and the sun was trying to break through the low clouds. Inga's body was round the back of the house, placed in a depression in the ground so the permafrost would keep it refrigerated, wrapped in blankets, and covered with a waterproof tarpaulin and large flat stones to keep off the foxes.

While Risa rolled up her sleeves, patted her hair, to make sure it was well out of the way, and opened up her bag, Larsen moved the stones. He felt as if he was stealing a corpse from a graveyard.

'Shall I bring it inside for you?' he asked, lifting the tarpaulin to reveal the swathed shape that had been Inga.

Risa, who was pulling on a pair of disposable latex gloves, looked around, then shrugged. 'I should think we'd all prefer not to use the kitchen table for a post-mortem,' she remarked. 'I'll do the initial examination out here, it's as good as anywhere and there aren't too many flies around. After that we'll see.'

Larsen, always squeamish, looked away as Risa unravelled the blankets and exposed the body. To his relief she asked him to take notes, so he was able to sit down on a nearby rock, and concentrate on writing.

'OK,' she said briskly. 'The body is that of a Caucasian woman, probably from one of the Nordic countries, and in her late twenties or early thirties I'd say. The body appears to have been in the water for around two or three days, and there are clear signs that animals, presumably fish and/or birds, have damaged the corpse in that time, though not seriously. Due presumably to the cold, there are almost no signs of decomposition.'

There was a pause, then Risa let out a sort of grunt.

70

Larsen glanced up, then hastily looked away with a feeling of nausea. The nurse had Inga's head in her hands, and was painstakingly investigating her mouth, her nose, and her empty eyesockets.

'It is impossible to be certain if drowning was the cause of death without undertaking an autopsy,' she went on. 'However, the victim was clearly struck an extremely hard blow on her right temple shortly before her death – the severe bruising demonstrates it could not have happened after she died. The blow, which must certainly have incapacitated her, could have been the direct cause of death, or death may have occurred as a result of exposure in seawater with a temperature barely above freezing, or by drowning. Whichever way, it seems probable that the victim never recovered consciousness from the blow.

'The possibility that the blow on the temple was accidental cannot be ruled out at this time, nor that it was sustained after the victim had fallen in the water – possibly as a result of being thrown against a rock. However, it is hard to ignore the force and precise placing of the blow, just below the squamous suture, and the consequent fracturing of the squamous part of the temporal bone, possibly driving bone fragments into the petrous temporal.'

'What does all that mean?' asked Larsen, struggling to keep up with her quickfire comments.

She went on as if he had not spoken. 'Combined with the lack of any similar damage to other parts of the skull or upper body – which I would have expected in the case of the body having been thrown violently against the rocks by waves – my conclusion would be that the blow was in probability a deliberate act, undertaken by someone with a working knowledge of skull structure, and intended to kill or disable the victim.'

'So it was murder,' said Larsen.

This time she looked at him. 'I'd say so. But that's my opinion. Not a fact.'

Half an hour later Inga's body was again wrapped up under the tarpaulin and the rocks, and Risa and Larsen were having another coffee.

'I hate doing post-mortems,' remarked Risa.

'I didn't notice.'

'You mean you thought I was enjoying it?'

'Of course not, but . . .'

'But I didn't start moaning or feeling faint. When you have to scrape the remains of some young man off the wall of his bedroom, after he's blasted his head away with a rifle, you don't like doing it, do you? But you do it as efficiently and unemotionally as you can, because you're a professional. Well, I'm a professional too, and I'm not going to let the pathetic indignity of a naked corpse get to me. Though I'd prefer something stronger to drink than coffee. Have you got anything?'

'No. In fact I've hardly got anything. I didn't expect to be here for more than two days.'

'You mean you hoped you wouldn't be here for more than two days. Anyway, it's just as well. If he catches me having a few drinks, Edvarth's going to feel pretty badly done by, after the go I had at him last week. Any idea why someone should hit that woman on the head and dump her in the fjord?'

'She was the housekeeper of an old man who was staying a little way up the fjord. Last week the old man was shot at and almost kidnapped, then three days later a group of heavily armed men, who looked like soldiers, took him away. Now his housekeeper appears to have been murdered.' He shrugged. 'I can't make anything out of it.'

'I didn't think detectives were supposed to say things like that,' said Risa. 'Who was the old man?'

'According to my boss, he and the soldiers who snatched him were part of a NATO exercise. But that doesn't fit with some things I've found out. He's been coming here for some years, and according to people here, nothing like this has ever happened before. Also I think he's from eastern Asia, and it seems he spends most of the year in Iceland. What would an old Asian man be doing spending three months a year in Ikerasak, and nine months a year in Iceland?'

'Hiding,' said Risa.

'From what?'

'How would I know? OK, so he spends most of the time in Iceland – do you know whereabouts?'

'No.'

'Not round Reykjavik, I'll bet.'

'Why not?'

'Because I've been to Iceland, and Reykjavik may not be the hip European hub that Icelanders like to pretend, but it gets passing traffic. It wouldn't be easy to disappear there. But most other parts of the country would be pretty safe, I'd guess.'

'So why does he come here each summer?'

'Iceland opens up for tourists a bit in the summer, so maybe he's making sure no one finds him. Or perhaps he's a masochistic freak and really likes it here.'

Larsen rubbed his chin thoughtfully. His thick stubble, one of the few physical features he had inherited from his Danish father, seemed to be growing even faster than usual.

'You could be right,' he said at length.

'Of course. Any other little problems that you need sorted out? No, don't answer that. You'll say your life, and I don't do lives. Not even my own. Especially not my own.'

Larsen laughed. 'There is one thing I'd like to ask – what do you suggest I do next?'

'If that's an invitation, I've heard better.'

Larsen started. 'No, no,' he said instantly. 'Nothing like that. I'm sorry . . .'

'Forget it, I was just joking. Do you mean about our wretched friend outside – who could easily be an Icelander, judging by her physical appearance?'

'I think her murder must be linked to the old man's kidnapping.'

'Sounds fair. If you ask me, you'd better backtrack on the old man – which means going to Iceland, if you've got any address to try. But you're going to tell me you haven't. Right?'

'Hverfjall. Does that name mean anything to you?'

She shook her head. 'Is it somewhere in Iceland?'

'I think so.'

'OK. We can phone a friend of mine who lives in Reykjavik and ask her. Or we can if you've got a phone. My mobile gave up the ghost a few days ago.'

Half an hour later, as Larsen was making liver pâté sandwiches in the cramped little kitchen, Risa came in and gave him his phone back.

'You took a long time,' he said.

'Of course. I haven't spoken to Thora for two or three months, I couldn't just ask her something then ring off. Anyway, it's Saturday, so calls are cheap.'

Larsen grunted, and finished spreading the liver pâté. 'You're going to give me bad news about Hverfjall, aren't you?'

'I suspect you pride yourself on being a good judge of women, Sergeant Larsen. Which is often a foolish thing to believe. The news is actually good – when I mentioned the Hverfjall, she knew it straight away. It's a huge black volcanic crater near Lake Myvatn. Rather famous – she said asking an Icelander about the Hverfjall is like asking a Greenlander about the Ilulissat ice fjord, or an Englishman about Dartmoor – whatever that is. Does it help you at all?'

'Are there a lot of houses near it?'

'I was way ahead of you there, Sergeant. I asked about that too – so you see, at least three of the minutes I spent on your phone were productive. Thora said there's a place called Reykjahlid, with a few houses, a camping site and a couple of hotels, and a handful of isolated farms on the edge of a lake. That's it.'

Larsen nodded. 'A lake was mentioned. So there's a good chance this is the right place. I think, if you don't mind, that I'll join you on your flight back tomorrow.'

'Maybe,' she said. 'Immaqa.'

Next morning sea mist hung low and thick over Ikerasak like a net, trapping everything in its fine moist mesh. There was a cold fret in the air, but not a breath of wind. Coming downstairs, Larsen peered out of the window, and cursed.

'Unless this clears, there's no chance of leaving here today,' he muttered.

'No,' agreed Risa. She was fully dressed and sitting curled up on the battered sofa, struggling with a crossword in the previous week's *Sermitsiaq* newspaper, her hand round a mug of coffee. 'This was forecast, you know.'

'What?'

'Why do you think Dr Lynge was so determined not to come here? Why do you think Edvarth and I arrived with a bag full of spare clothes and food, and dressed up as if it was April rather than June?'

'How long will it go on for?'

'Last I heard they expected unbroken mist or light rain, with some sleet or snow, for the whole Paamiut area until Tuesday or Wednesday.'

'Jesus Christ!'

Larsen sat down and thought. He had never intended to ask for help, but he dare not risk the whole case falling apart because he was trapped in Ikerasak. So he would have to share, and there was only one person he could do that with. Much as he loathed the idea.

He pulled out his phone.

'Hi,' came the confident voice at the far end.

'Pieter, it's Tomas.'

'How're you doing? Want to take me on at that arm-wrestling competition then? I've been hearing that you're still a tough

74

proposition.' He laughed. 'What can I do for you at this disgustingly early hour?'

'I'm in Ikerasak.'

The tone of Norlund's voice changed sharply. 'What are you doing there?'

'The old man's housekeeper has been murdered. But listen, I've got a line on where to find the old man himself, or at least news of him. The problem is the weather's closed in and I can't get out. Do you reckon you could look into it?'

Larsen could almost hear Norlund's brain ticking over, and the rapid realisation that whoever found the old man would probably get all the prestige. Followed by dawning caution. A battle in his head.

'The Chief told us to leave the matter –'

'I understand if you don't want to risk it, but as you were in on the start of the case –'

'OK, OK. Go on.'

'It's in Iceland.'

'Shit! That's not so easy.'

Larsen realised Norlund must be thinking of Gerda and the baby that was due any day. Silently he swore at himself.

'I'm sorry,' he said. 'Of course you can't think of going anywhere with your wife about to have a baby. How is she?'

'More like a basketball holder every day. But that's got nothing to do with it. She doesn't need me, in fact she says I'm just in the way. I can probably fix a flight to Iceland – I've a friend who works for Grønlandsfly. Where exactly are we talking about?'

'It's by Lake Myvatn, in the north of the country, but –'

'There are a few direct flights from Reykjavik, but he'll probably need an internal flight to Akureyri or Husavik, then a bus,' remarked Risa, who had put aside the crossword and was openly listening.

'Did you hear that?'

'Yes. Who's the woman?'

'A nurse, don't worry about it.'

'Struck lucky, have you, Tomas?' There was a chuckle. 'That gives hope to us all.'

Larsen ignored the aside. 'Once at Lake Myvatn, you'll need to look about. The house is within sight of a great black volcanic crater called the Hverfjall.'

'You're not making it easy, are you, Tomas? Are you sure all this stuff is the real thing?'

'Of course I'm not. Look, perhaps it'd be best if you forgot all this; when I get out of here, I'll handle it myself.'

'But the sooner we do it, the better chance there is of finding the old man,' said Norlund shrewdly, picking up on Larsen's thought. 'Right? So get on with it.'

Larsen found himself almost smiling. Norlund had behaved exactly as he had suspected: unable to resist a hook with a double bait – a journey offering the chance of dramatic success, combined with an opportunity to behave with the bold insubordination of someone in an American film.

'The old man can see the Hverfjall from his bedroom window. Apparently there aren't many houses this could apply to.'

'How did you find this out, Tomas?'

'Just asking around.'

'And you say his housekeeper has been murdered?'

'It looks like it. I'll deal with that side of things. With you taking on the Iceland end, we ought to come up with something.'

'What about the Chief?'

'He won't be in the office until tomorrow morning, and we're not expected in till Wednesday. That's a good stretch of time.'

'Yes.' There was a pause at the far end of the telephone. 'I didn't realise you were like this, Tomas.'

For a moment Larsen felt a glow inside him. 'Like what?'

'You know, going out on a limb and taking risks, stuff like this.'

'Everything depends on circumstances,' said Larsen. 'Incidentally, when we were staying in Ikerasak, you went out in the middle of the night. What were you doing?'

'Christ! You don't miss anything, do you? I just couldn't get to sleep, that's all. There were half a dozen mosquitoes whining round my head that wouldn't leave me alone, so I went for a short walk.'

'Right,' said Larsen, and rang off.

'You don't like him, do you?' said Risa, her eyes back on the crossword, though she had not solved any new clues.

'What makes you think that?'

She didn't reply.

Larsen hesitated, but there was an air of waiting around Risa that encouraged him to go on.

'I suppose I'm jealous of him. He's younger and tougher and sharper than me, he's the same rank as me, and still on his way up. I stopped rising a long while back.'

'And you don't like him,' she repeated.

8

MYVATN

Pieter Norlund had managed to get a flight to Keflavik in Iceland, and stayed Sunday night in a guest house. Next morning he caught a plane for the forty-five minute flight to Akureyri. After landing, he showed his police ID card, and enquired about the possibility of hiring a plane to take him back to Greenland. It seemed it would be less difficult than he had feared.

Encouraged, he went into the town, booked himself on the Myvatn bus, then visited the police station, a fine building overlooking a pleasant, busy square. Norlund found himself envying the high-tech appearance, and the pleasant surroundings. But in Iceland everyone seemed to be tall, blond, and Nordic, and the bleak blue eyes of the efficient policemen stared right through him as they inspected his sallow skin, long eyes, and thick black hair.

When he explained who he was, and asked if they knew anything about an Asian man living by Lake Myvatn, disbelief crept into their cold faces. And of course they had every reason to look at him like that – why travel a thousand miles to ask the question, when he could have phoned? Humiliated and angry, Norlund left the station as fast as he could.

On the bus, Norlund brooded. He had a growing suspicion that he was behaving like a complete fool. As the bus crawled along the mountainous, unsurfaced road, he realised he had spent large sums of police money without a hint of official authorisation. Staring out over the barren lava fields, he wondered why he had agreed to do what Tomas Larsen asked him to, and found he could scarcely remember the reasons that a day before had seemed so urgent.

It was mid-afternoon when the bus reached Reykjahlid. Norlund knew he should start his enquiries immediately, but he felt strangely reluctant. Instead he strolled up towards some corded basalt rocks that lay over the area, remnants of a past volcanic eruption. It had been drizzling, and the wet basalt covered the land with a slick, black overlay. Beyond lay Lake Myvatn, and the snow-streaked mountains to the south, dominated by a vast black crater, which the bus driver had told Norlund was the Hverfjall.

After a few minutes he returned the way he had come. Reykjahlid was a small settlement – two hotels, an Esso petrol station, a café, grey houses, a couple of shops, and some battered grass with sheep on it. Norlund made his way to the supermarket and asked about the old Chinese man.

The man at the service counter shrugged. There was no one like that here. He would know. Not many people lived in the village, most just arrived in the summer, for the tourist season, and many houses were rented out. Perhaps this man was renting a house. June was a good time to rent out houses, before there were too many flies.

His assistant, a lively girl, was more forthcoming. Two or three days before, she had been cycling down the east side of Myvatn when she saw an old man, perhaps Chinese, she wasn't sure, walking up a track heading away from the lake with two other men. She had been surprised, because few old people came out here, and because he had obviously not been an Icelander.

Norlund asked if she could tell him anything else, but though she thought she might have seen the man once or twice before, she wasn't sure. And he had certainly never been in the shop.

As Norlund set off along the road she mentioned, a stiffening wind swung round to the west, and sent the clouds scurrying away before it. Within minutes the sky had changed to a glorious washed-blue, richer and with deeper colour, it seemed, than the same sky would have had in Nuuk. The mountains that ringed the lake were bathed in sunshine, and shone with an ochre radiance. All except for the Hverfjall. That sombre, black crater, towering above its neighbours, swallowed up the light and gave none back.

After leaving Reykjahlid, the road split. The left fork turned east, climbing past a large industrial plant on the side of the hill. Norlund, following the directions given by the girl, took the right fork, which curved down the far side of the lake. A little way along he found himself looking into a bay that was almost cut off from the rest of the lake. The water in it was steaming, but a pair of wigeon, the drake handsome with chestnut head and black and white body, the duck discreetly ruddy brown, swam on it unconcernedly.

Beyond a small forest, the land opened out. On one side lay a rough country of boulders and eroded rock faces, broken up by wiry bushes and deep ravines, which stretched away towards the great black crater. The other side was a sharp contrast, grass, sheep grazing, and fences, sloping down towards the lake shore. Norlund walked on and came to a stony by-way, pitted with deep holes, that led away to the left, towards the hills.

Noticing new wheel tracks on the ground, he followed the by-road up a slope. Beyond the next ridge, completely hidden from the road, he found himself looking down on a small, stone-built farmhouse, with a few hens scratching optimistically in the gravel outside. Norlund hesitated, unsure whether to walk boldly up to the door, or to try to get closer without being seen.

The decision was made for him.

'Don't move,' came a voice in his ear, speaking English. At the same time Norlund felt the muzzle of a handgun pressed against the nape of his neck.

A large hand ran swiftly, professionally, up and down his body, checking for concealed weapons, and removing Norlund's wallet and mobile phone. The man took a couple of steps backwards, and made a call.

'There's some guy here, creeping around, who I've just picked up . . . He's certainly no Icelander, that's for sure . . . No, I don't think anyone else saw . . . OK.'

The gun was jabbed in the small of Norlund's back.

'Head for the house,' said the man harshly. 'And don't even think about making a break, or you're history.'

Trying to convince himself this was a mistake, Norlund obediently walked down to the house, where he was taken round to the back entrance, and pushed along a narrow hall, and into a room. Although the farmhouse was built of stone, everything inside was of stripped, polished pine. The man with the gun, large, with short fair hair, told Norlund to sit down on the broad, wooden sofa and to put his hands palm down on his knees. He sat down opposite, gun in his hand, and watched him in cold silence.

When Norlund started to explain who he was, the man gestured intimidatingly with his gun, and Norlund closed his mouth. At last another man came in. He was lean, quick-spoken, grey-bearded, with dark eyebrows over his blue eyes, rapid nervous movements, and a face etched with many lines. The man with the gun stayed where he was.

The second man began to question Norlund. The first language he used was Icelandic, and although Norlund was able to follow some of what was being said to him, he shook his head. The man

79

then tried English, only to switch to unaccented Danish, rattling questions at Norlund faster than he could possibly answer. What was his name? What was he doing here? Where had he come from? Why? Why was he lying? Norlund answered cautiously, giving out as little information as he could, while taking care everything he said was the exact and literal truth.

The questioner clearly did not believe him and suddenly, in mid-sentence as it seemed, he switched from Danish to another language. One that Norlund did not understand at all, and that sounded strange in his ears. He looked blank, and shook his head. The man immediately tried a fifth language, similar to the previous one, which Norlund understood no better. He tried to explain that the only languages he knew were Greenlandic, Danish, and some scraps of English, but they told him to be silent. When he persevered, the man with the gun slapped him back-handed in the face. Hard.

The interrogation went on for a long time, darting from one language to another, with Norlund continually shaking his head, except when the questions were in Danish. Then, abruptly, the questioner muttered something, and went out. He came back a few moments later, holding a medical syringe.

Norlund could feel sweat prickling on his forehead, and for the first time there came the touch of nauseating fear.

'What's that for?' he demanded.

'Roll up your sleeve,' said the man, testing the syringe as he spoke.

'But what is it for?' he repeated.

'To stop you lying to us.'

'I am not lying to you.'

The questioner gave a thin smile, and took a step towards Norlund, syringe at the ready.

At the same moment Norlund flung himself forward, towards the man with the gun, who was taken completely unawares, and knocked sideways. Norlund seized the hand that held the gun, clutching the man's wrist and forcing the gun back so that it pointed at the roof. There was a deafening sound and a blast of heat in his face as the gun fired, but Norlund continued to drive the man's hand relentlessly back with his powerful forearms. There was a shriek of pain, and the gun fell to the floor, as the man collapsed backwards, writhing. Norlund dived for the gun, scrabbling on the carpet, but before he could reach it agony sliced through him, so that he jack-knifed and the breath exploded from his lungs. For a second he thought the second man had stabbed him in the back, then he realised he had been kicked savagely in the kidneys.

A moment later the gun was snatched up. With a desperate effort to ignore the crippling pain, like fire in his guts, Norlund staggered upright and put all his remaining strength into a great hay-making punch. He struck only air. A second later something slammed sickeningly into his head. He doubled up and tried to scream, but could not. His legs turned to water, and he collapsed to the ground, almost incapable of thought, desperate only to get air in his lungs and to escape that insupportable pain.

He was barely aware that his left arm had been pinned to the ground. He did not even feel the slight prick of pain as the hypodermic was slipped through his skin.

When he woke, Pieter Norlund's head felt as if it was being crushed. A red-hot beating pain lashed the inside of his temple. Another pain ran from his shoulders, channelling along his spine, and penetrating like barbed steel into the back of his skull. His aching eyes were swollen and tender, and would not focus properly. There was a fetid taste in his mouth, and his tongue felt huge and clumsy.

When he closed his eyes, it made the pain worse, so he opened them again. He was lying on his back on a hard bed. The ceiling appeared to be vibrating, continually moving down towards him, then rising away again. He stayed where he was, trying to control the nausea that filled him whenever he moved, and becoming gradually aware of an appalling sensation of pressure in his groin. It was at least two minutes before he realised that he had to urinate. Immediately.

With a stupendous effort, Norlund staggered to his feet, clutching hold of the wooden bed-head. Gasping, he looked around, but the room was bare of anything except the bed and a chair. Norlund reeled over to the far corner of the room, leant his head against the wall, which seemed to revolve around him, unzipped his jeans, and pissed against the wall. The feeling of relief was overwhelming, briefly swamping all his aches and pains.

He retreated from the steaming puddle, and sat down on the bed. He was freezing cold, and had begun to shiver. The bed had only a bare mattress on it, but his leather jacket was lying on the chair. He put it on and zipped it up, but still he shivered. And he had found a new pain, a throbbing rawness in his left upper arm.

Desperate to keep warm, he stood up and began to walk to and fro, between the door and the bed. Whatever had happened to him, whatever was about to happen to him, he must gather his wits.

Ten minutes later his legs were shaking uncontrollably and he had to sit down on the bed again. His mouth felt as dusty and dead as a dry river valley, but there was nothing to drink in the room.

To take his mind off his overwhelming thirst, he tried to piece together what had happened since he had been seized. Somehow the memories did not come together, did not gel. There were only shattered fragments, drifting in and out of focus – a man with a gun; another man questioning him; lights; sickness; darkness; hunger; blows; and questions. Hundreds of questions. Questions he could not answer. Questions in languages he did not understand. Questions about people he had never heard of. Questions that made no sense at all.

Gradually one part of the interrogation came back to him. They had asked him his name, who his parents were, who his family were. And of course he had answered truthfully. They had asked him about the place he was born, so he had told them about Sisimiut: its straggling, hilly main street, the oldest church in the country, the whalebone arch and the dogs, life at the long, low Knud Rasmussen High School with its Danish flag outside, the open-air swimming pool, the shipbuilding yard and the cod fisheries. But why should these unseen men care about his childhood?

With an effort Norlund broke his mind free of what had happened to him, and began to take more of an interest in his surroundings. Gradually the veil that had enveloped his senses was lifting and he began to see clearly, and to smell the sharp stench of his own urine.

The room had a window, but it was blocked off by a layer of wire mosquito mesh, which Norlund wrenched down. Beyond lay steel shutters. He pushed them a few times, experimentally, but they were well-pinned into the wall, and locked fast. Norlund peered through the thin gap in the centre of the shutters, and realised there was a second pair of shutters beyond them. There was no possible chance of escape that way.

He went over to the door. It was wooden, thick and solid, with massive hinges. Cautiously he tried the handle, but it too was locked. If he tried hammering, it would just disturb his captors. He looked around the bare room, but there was nowhere to hide, and the door opened outwards into the corridor. There was no switch, so the light must be operated from outside.

He retreated to his bed. His clothes he now realised, stank, and there were stains on them, blood perhaps. His pockets were empty, his ID had gone, together with his money, his knife, his handkerchief, everything. Norlund lay down on the bed and stared at the gloomy, stained roof, and at a few midges flying round and round. One of them circled the light, then flew straight into the bulb.

Its body fluttered to the ground.

Norlund realised that the single bulb was the only source of light. If he took it out, the room would be overwhelmed in darkness, and he might have a chance of ambushing whoever came into the room. On the other hand removing the light bulb would warn them that he was awake, and that he was planning something.

The beginnings of a plan came to him.

After putting his hand inside the sleeve of his jacket to protect it, he pulled out the scorchingly hot bulb, then waited for it to cool, before slipping it inside one of his jacket pockets.

It probably wouldn't work, but Pieter Norlund was not a man to lie on a bed and wait for things to happen. He had to do something. Anything. So he sat on the edge of the bed, his jacket huddled close around him, and began to shout.

'Help me, for Christ's sake! Help me. It's dark, I can't stand it. Help me.' Then he screamed. 'Let me out,' he bellowed. 'I must get out. It's dark. I'm going crazy. Help me.'

9

EDVARTH AND MARIANNE

Edvarth stared gloomily at his feet and scowled. Not only had he been dragged out to this boring backwater, half a day's boat trip from anywhere, but now they were stuck here until the weather improved. Maybe for days. To make things worse, the fish weren't biting. And the mosquitoes were.

Edvarth loved fishing, and in the months since his mother and he had moved to Paamiut, he had discovered several good places within two or three hours' walk of the town. But Ikerasak was new, and he had no sort of feel for the area. However he had gathered up the courage to ask for advice from Yelmar, a tiny, shrivelled, bow-legged man of around forty, who lived alone in one of the houses.

Visiting Yelmar had been an eye-opening experience for Edvarth, like stepping into the world of fifty years before. Outside, fish dried on a rickety pyramidal construction built of driftwood, and there were two fine spotted sealskins stretched on frames. Inside was an old-fashioned sleeping platform, a beaten earth floor, and an open fire partly fuelled with blubber from which black oily smoke gushed; a pail served for a toilet, and beer bottles, rifles, fishing gear, filth and flies were everywhere. The stench in the house made Edvarth's eyes water, but Yelmar was a pleasant, good-natured man, with an easy smile, and as well as lending the boy a three metre coast rod, he also suggested a couple of possible places to try.

To the rod Edvarth had added a line, long-throw spoonbait and an artificial lure, all borrowed from two brothers, Jokum and Kunarat who appeared to live with the same woman in a small house with only one – large – bed.

It amounted to pretty good equipment, yet here he was, at seven in the evening on a rising tide, fishing a perfect-looking sound, with nothing, not even a hint of nibble, in two hours. And he had been looking forward to fresh grilled mountain trout for supper.

Suddenly sick of the whole thing, he dismantled the rod, put the gear into his rucksack, and set off further up the coast. He soon reached the mouth of the River Isortoq, and rather than try to ford it, he turned and followed its southern shore. He needed to move, to use up some of his energy. To take his mind off his anger at his mother.

As he penetrated inland, the ground became more rugged, and the river cut deeper and deeper into the rising hills. On the far side a tributary stream joined the main river, its steep, south-facing valley green and lush. The amount of snow on the slopes above grew, and the walls of the valley rose higher. A cream and grey wheatear flew away swiftly to land on a pointed rock at a safe distance, flirting its tail and brilliant white rump. Behind him, fog still lay heavily over Grindehval fjord, though the highest razor-edged tip of Qeqertaq Island was visible, apparently floating on the mist. Ahead a damp, snow-freckled cliff rose up, where the river swung in a sharp left-hand elbow, round a steep hillside.

Edvarth froze.

Two hundred metres away, scuttling along the bottom of the valley by the far bank of the river, was a figure in winter camouflage gear. As Edvarth stared, the figure glanced back, then ducked down low and darted off up the side of the hill, vanishing among the rolling rock edges.

It seemed strange that the man – if it was a man – should run away. Oddly frightening. After a moment or two Edvarth turned and set off back the way he had come. But walking away did not lessen his disquiet. In fact the further he walked from the cliff, the more he felt a shapeless fear snapping at his heels. Three-quarters of the way down the valley, with the fjord opening out like a gateway, he heard a fall of stones behind him. Edvarth spun round, his nerve-endings prickling with anticipation, but although his eyes scanned the slopes and rocky heights around him, he saw nothing. He hurried on, only to glimpse movement out of the corner of his eye. Again he stopped and swung round.

Surely that was something, someone, high on the crags on the north side of the river, moving parallel to him, slipping in and out of the rocks, vanishing into the shadows below an overhang.

Edvarth's breath was coming fast, and he could feel his heart accelerating.

'I'm imagining this,' he said to himself. 'I've thought myself into this.'

Yet he did not believe it. A moment later he seemed to see that fast-moving shadow shape again, getting closer, poised on the brink of the cliff.

Panic caught the boy in its bony grip, and he began to run. Clutching his rod as tightly as if it represented safety, he sprinted wildly south, towards the village. As he did so, he plunged abruptly back into the fog bank that hung low over the fjord, cutting visibility to less than a hundred metres. The mist redoubled his anxiety, for it needed little imagination to conjure up menacing shapes in the ever-shifting featurelessness.

Constantly looking behind him, Edvarth did not stop until he was past the promontory where Inga's body had been found, and he glimpsed the now-deserted house, where the old man had lived, appearing out of the greyness.

Descending into a marshy valley, he suddenly saw a small figure perched on a huge glaciated boulder by the side of the fjord. It was the little girl, Marianne. She was hugging her knees and staring across the water towards Qeqertaq Island, and its rampart of sheer cliffs.

Although she was only a few metres from him, she seemed entirely unaware of his presence.

'You're getting cut off by the tide,' called Edvarth, after giving himself a few moments to recover his breath.

'So?' she replied, without looking round.

'You should get back to the shore while you still can.'

Marianne uncurled herself, and slipped easily off the boulder. Her feet, in wellington boots, splashed into the shallow water, and she waded back to the shore.

'There,' she said. 'Happy now? Why were you running like that?'

He shrugged. 'I was late.'

'What for?'

'Nothing much. It was a good thing you got back from there while you still could.'

'Why?' Marianne looked up at him defiantly. 'Once I sat there the whole time the tide went up and down. You were running away from something, weren't you? Because you were scared.'

Edvarth gave an unconvincing laugh. 'Course not.'

Marianne sat down on the ground. 'Do you want to know a secret?'

'OK.'

'Sit down then, and I'll tell you.'

Edvarth hesitated. He had little experience in dealing with younger children, and no particular interest in them, but Marianne offered an alternative to staring up at the mist-choked sky, running from phantoms, and failing to catch any fish.

'You must promise not to tell anyone else,' she said.

'Sure,' he said, a little patronisingly.

She bent towards him and stared at him intensely, as if to

judge his trustworthiness. At last she lowered her voice. 'There are people hiding out in the mountains,' she whispered.

Edvarth's heart began to thud again. He felt suddenly cold. 'What do you mean?'

She glanced round. 'They may be watching us now, hiding in the mist. But if we keep our voices down they can't get close enough to hear. We'll see them if they try to creep up on us.'

'This is just a game, isn't it?'

Marianne looked up at him, and her eyes were dark and shadowed.

'No,' she said, shaking her head so that her glossy black hair in its bunches swung about her broad cheeks. 'No, it's not a game. Inga was murdered. Someone hit her on the head, and threw her into the fjord, and she died. I didn't like her much, she was always complaining when I took my grandfather out for walks, but this isn't a game. They are hiding out there. The killers of Inga.'

He realised that she was frightened. As frightened as he was. But struggling not to show it.

'I saw them too,' he said, without meaning to.

'I guessed you had. Where?'

'I was walking up the river valley, near where it swings south, when I saw a man. He ran away, but I think he came back and followed me afterwards. Or else there was another man following me, in the hills on the far side of the river.'

'What did he look like?'

'I don't know. I couldn't see. Who are they?'

'The killers of Inga,' she repeated, scarcely raising her voice above a breath. 'They look like us, but they are hard to understand.'

'How do you know?'

'Two days after my grandfather was taken away, I was walking near the head of the fjord. One of them was behind a rock, he hadn't heard me coming. When he saw me, he sprang up, looked around, then came over and spoke to me.'

'What did he say?'

'In Danish – not Greenlandic – he said: "Do you know where the old man is, the one who lives with the fair woman?" '

'What did you say?'

'I stared at him, and he said it again. I was scared, so scared I didn't seem able to speak. Suddenly he turned and ran away. I think he'd seen Nils's fishing-boat, out on the fjord. But I've never told anyone about this. I hoped it didn't matter.'

'Until you heard about Inga,' said Edvarth.

She nodded. 'I spoke to one of the murderers of Inga,' she said, and suddenly she gave a great convulsive shudder. 'Are they going to murder us next?'

'Why should they?'

'I don't know. A few days ago Inga told me she had done something that she shouldn't have. Is that why they killed her?'

Edvarth saw that the little girl was still shaking, and he bent down and put his arm round her.

'Don't worry,' he said. 'It's grown-up stuff. Nothing to do with us.'

'Then why are they watching us? What do they want with my grandfather? Did they take him away? Did they kill him? Why are they still here?' There was a growing vein of hysteria in her tone.

'I don't know. Perhaps we've just got things wrong. Or missed something important, that explains it all. Sometimes I lie on the ground and watch birds or insects, and you can't tell why they do what they do – but there's always a good reason.'

'You mean we could watch them just like they watch us?'

He hadn't meant that at all.

'We don't know where they are,' he objected weakly.

'I think they're up the Iterdla valley.'

'Where's that?'

'It's the river that runs into the Isortoq from the north.' She had stopped shivering, and her face was suddenly alight with excitement. In a few moments the savage touch of frightening reality had faded back into a game. 'Let's find them. Tonight.'

'Tonight?'

'We'll creep out after we've been put to bed, and look for them. Don't forget to bring some food, and we'd better leave a note saying where we've gone. Just in case. OK? I'll meet you here, at midnight.'

And suddenly she was gone, loping easily back towards the invisible village, as if the way was not a hard track, rising and falling over a series of steep ridges, creeping around stony barrens, and past pools where mosquitoes lurked in predatory clouds.

When Edvarth, footsore and tired, got back to the house, his mother was in the kitchen, preparing some dried vegetables.

'All right, where's the fish?' she said, without looking up. 'Let's get them cooking.'

'I didn't catch anything.'

She looked up in amazement. 'But you're brilliant at fishing, and everyone says the fishing here is really good. I was expecting you back with twice as much as we could possibly eat.'

He shook his head. 'I didn't get a bite.'

'So what am I going to tell Sergeant Larsen when he comes in?'

'You've always told me men shouldn't rely on women to get them their food.'

Risa laughed. 'That's true,' she admitted. 'But I get you your food.'

'I'm your son. He's no one. Just a cop.'

'Just a cop,' she repeated, then took a breath. 'Oh well. It's going to be a dull supper – some rye bread past its best, and a few dried vegetables. I suppose I could open a tin of luncheon meat. Wait, I've a better idea – you can make up for your failure by buying a couple of fish off someone.'

'Why do you want to impress the policeman?'

'Maybe because he's polite enough to let us stay here, without making any difficulties. Here's some money, go and see what you can get.'

Edvarth went over to Yelmar's house, knocked and then opened the door. The little man appeared, accompanied by a cloud of oily smoke.

'I wondered if I could buy some fish,' said Edvarth.

'You mean the rod was no good? Could you find no line? I told you to ask Kunarat . . .'

'I did. I went fishing, but I caught nothing.'

'Ah. Then you tried in a bad place.' Yelmar nodded his wizened face with an air of deep wisdom. 'And now you wish to buy fish. Very well, I will sell to you. But you would do better to catch your own.'

As Yelmar was unhooking two rose fish from a string that hung in one corner of the room, Edvarth suddenly said, 'Are there any other people round here? I mean except for those living in the village.'

Yelmar looked up, slitting his eyes, like a dog in the sunshine. 'Sometimes people come here,' he said vaguely. 'People climb the mountains, or go to look at the ice, or they even go fishing.'

'Are there any people like that around now?'

'Why?'

'I thought I saw someone, in the river valley.'

'No wonder you caught nothing. There is no reason to fish the rivers for another three weeks. What money have you got? Give me 20 kroner, that will do.'

Edvarth took the fish, holding them by the line through their gills.

'What about the person I saw?' he said.

'It was probably just Karadi or Jokum or Enok. Or one of the other men.'

'What would they be doing in the hills?'

'Hunting grouse perhaps. Looking for foxes, or reindeer.'

'I thought they were fishermen.'

'You ask a lot of questions,' said Yelmar. 'But all fishermen go hunting at times. Just as Adam, who is a hunter, goes fishing.'

'So you think I saw someone from the village. I could try to find out who it was, couldn't I? By asking.'

Yelmar opened his hands. 'I do not say there are no outsiders in the hills. Some years ago a fireball appeared in the sky over Paamiut, a great rock in the heavens they said, that lit up the winter night like a mighty flaming harpoon, then broke itself to pieces in the mountains near the Iceblink. The next summer many people came to search for it, though I do not think they found it. Perhaps this is like that.'

'So there are outsiders here then?'

'People have said so,' Yelmar mumbled. 'I do not go up the Iterdla. There is nothing there except a few skinny ducks, so what is the point? Take your fish home before it rains.'

It was spitting before Edvarth got back. Larsen had also returned, but he said nothing, and they ate in silence. Twice Edvarth intercepted glances between his mother and Larsen, glances he did not understand, but that somehow unsettled him. He stared out of the rain-speckled window, and wondered if Marianne had been serious about going out that night.

Edvarth generally slept with all the deep concentration of a teenager, but he was woken by stealthy movement. He opened his eyes, and in the grey twilight saw his mother slip out of her bed, and pull her sweater round her. He almost spoke, but something told him to stay silent. As he watched through half-shut eyes, she glanced in his direction, then crept out of the room, and across the landing at the top of the rickety stairs. She knocked quietly at Larsen's door.

'What is it?'

'I can't sleep,' said Risa. 'Do you mind if I come in and talk?'

A momentary pause.

'Sure.'

The door opened, releasing a brief gleam of light. Risa slipped in, and closed the door behind her.

There was a murmur of conversation.

After a couple of minutes Edvarth sat up. There was an acid

taste in his throat, and a burning anger in his heart. For a moment he wondered whether to throw open the door that was shut. That shut him out. Instead he looked at his watch. It was midnight, and only then did he remember the little girl who might be waiting alone for him. At the same time the thought of walking through the wilderness offered a way of escape.

He got up as silently as he could and dressed. As he padded softly downstairs, he heard his mother laugh. A soft, deep, beckoning laugh. His face twisted into a fierce snarl.

Outside the rain had stopped, though in the cool pearly half-light he could see the cloud ceiling still hanging low over the fjord. Marianne was waiting a few metres from the front door.

'I thought we were going to meet up by the fjord,' he said quietly.

'You were late. I was coming to get you.' Her young, round face was nervous, anxious to be persuaded. 'Perhaps this is a silly idea. We don't even really know where to look.'

'Yelmar mentioned the same place that you said – up the Iterdla. How far away is that?'

'Perhaps an hour and a half.' She paused. 'Are you really going to look for the watchers?'

Edvarth remembered that murmur of conversation in Larsen's room, and his mother's soft, teasing laugh. His stomach churned and he nodded grimly. 'You go back to bed. I'll tell you about it tomorrow.'

His determination had infected her, and she shook her head stubbornly.

'I'm coming with you. If I don't come, you won't be able to find your way. You don't know where to ford the Isortoq, or which side of the Iterdla to follow. Or anything.'

'You're too young to be out this late.'

'I'm ten. I'm not afraid. And I'm coming.'

As they set off, a hooded figure appeared walking into the village. Edvarth tensed and almost dived for shelter behind the nearest house, but Marianne merely nodded.

'Hi, Karadi. Good hunting?'

'No,' grunted the man, who seemed entirely unsurprised to see the little girl out after midnight. 'The foxes and hares have left us these past days.'

'Maybe it'll be better soon.'

'Maybe I'll return to Paamiut soon.'

The children walked in silence, through the half-light. A

91

breeze whispered over the stones, and they could hear waves slapping gently against the shore.

By the house where the old man had lived, Marianne looked east, towards the ring of mountains that shielded them from the great inland ice sheet. One mountain stood out from the others, marked out by its unique shape, and the way its dark lower slopes were entirely bare of snow.

'That's Mount Iviangeq,' she said, and her voice shook a little. 'I took my grandfather there.'

The ground rose rapidly, as they cut inland from the side of the fjord and crossed the high ground of the Isortoq watershed. It was hard walking, over stony slopes, interspersed with streams, small lakes and pools, and hump-backed ridges. After half an hour, the ground suddenly feel steeply away into the valley, a hundred metres below them. Marianne led the way along a track, which rapidly disappeared in the rocks, leaving them to scramble down to the river as best they could. The Isortoq was an intimidating torrent of sandy-grey glacier meltwater, roaring and tumbling, foam-flecked, towards the fjord.

'How're we going to cross that?' demanded Edvarth, eyeing it doubtfully.

'The water's high,' agreed Marianne, frowning. 'It looks as if the thaw's happening really fast, even though it hasn't been particularly warm lately. If it rises much more, it'll cover the crossing.'

'What crossing?'

She pointed upstream, to where a ridge of harder rock, flanked by boulders, rose out of the centre of a wide fast-flowing stretch of shallows.

'Most of the summer you can cross the river there without going more than ankle deep at the most. But today . . .'

When they tried to cross, Edvarth found himself calf-deep, and fighting the fierce, slashingly cold, current to keep his footing, while Marianne clung grimly to his waist. They were both wet to well above their knees when they finally made it over. Marianne stopped and emptied the water out of her wellington boots, while Edvarth wished he had put on something more substantial than jeans.

As they left the wide, exposed reaches around the Isortoq, and began to climb the south-facing rift that housed the Iterdla, it felt distinctly warmer. The sun was rising, a rosy disc through the mist, as they plunged in amongst tall thickets of willow and birch. Around them they glimpsed birds singing, black-headed Lapland buntings and rose-chested redpolls.

Suddenly there was a loud rustle in the greenery to their right. Edvarth spun round.

'What's that?' gasped Marianne, wide-eyed.

'Just a fox,' said Edvarth reassuringly.

He moved towards the sound, pushing aside branches, then stopped and pointed.

In a muddy patch, where a small stream trickled down the hillside, there were the outlines of large footprints, and a faint path vanished into the undergrowth. They looked at each other, then cautiously, with frequent pauses, began to follow the path which climbed up the side of the valley. Every now and then it was marked by more footprints, or broken branches.

At last Edvarth, who was in the lead, stopped.

'Look!' he hissed.

'What is it?' Marianne was right behind him, and without thinking she took his hand.

Someone had hacked through a tight ring of gnarled arctic birches, and it was possible to see what looked like a rough overgrown bank. They pushed through the branches, and found to their surprise the remains of a house, situated on a flat ridge of rock. The walls were a mixture of lichen-stained stone and turf, mostly around half a metre high. They looked very old, and were scattered with leaves and twigs from the trees. But there were also signs of far more recent habitation. A square of grass had been levelled out inside the walls, and there was a small fireplace in which lay blackened stones and a few charred sticks. Marianne found a steel tent peg and an empty camping gas canister half-concealed by the lush grass. There were also more footprints.

'Is this what we were looking for?' asked Marianne.

'Perhaps. Except that it doesn't look as if anyone's been here for two or three days – see how wet and soggy the fireplace is. And the man I saw was only yesterday.'

'They must have moved,' said Marianne solemnly.

'Could you find this place again?'

She nodded.

'Good,' said Edvarth, after a few moments' thought. 'Then we'd better head back to the village and tell someone what we've found.'

'Isn't it our secret?'

Edvarth put a hand on Marianne's shoulder. 'Someone has been killed,' he said softly.

Marianne nodded. 'Let's go,' she said. 'Now.'

10

LOST CHILDREN

Risa drifted up from a delicious post-coital doze, and yawned sensuously. She reached out a hand, and found Larsen's chest close beside her. She ran her fingers through his hair, then kissed him. He opened one eye, that looked as if it had never been asleep, and smiled at her.

She rolled closer, feeling his powerful body against her own, and smiled back.

'One of the great advantages of being a nurse,' she mused, 'is that I never travel without a supply of condoms.'

'That's not a very romantic thing to say,' objected Larsen.

She laughed. 'But true. I'll bet you haven't any.'

'No.'

'Well then.' She pushed back the thick mass of her black hair, then bit him on the shoulder. 'And the good news is that I've got plenty more.'

He raised himself on his elbow, and looked at her, then gently stroked her rather large, loose breasts which had been uncovered by the blanket. A faint questioning frown had spread over his broad face. He opened his mouth to speak, and she instinctively put a finger over his lips.

'I was lonely,' she said softly, answering what she had not let him ask. 'That's all you need to know.'

'No, it isn't.'

'I suppose not. How truthful do you want me to be?'

'That's a silly question.'

'It is, isn't it? After all, you're a policeman – and a nosy one at that.' She stopped, and wrinkled her brow in thought. 'You've been married, haven't you?'

'Yes. Once.'

'Did she divorce you because you were always cross-examining her?'

He laughed. 'It was nothing like that.'

'Why did she then?'

'I thought I was the nosy one. And how do you know I didn't divorce her?'

94

'Because you didn't. Did you?'

'No.'

'So, what was it then? In exchange, I'll tell you what you want to know.'

'What's that?'

'Why I came in here and had sex with you,' she said simply. 'Do we have a deal?'

'I suppose so.'

'Go on then. Why did your wife divorce you?'

'She was a Dane and she hated living in Greenland. Also she wanted me to . . . to be a success, I suppose.'

'And you didn't give a centimetre on either front, did you?'

He had never thought of his divorce in those terms before. 'You either live in one place or another – how can you compromise?'

'Maybe by compromising in other parts of your life.' She looked at him calculatingly. 'But you're stubborn aren't you? Just like me. Anyway, my turn now and because I'm feeling generous you can have not two, but three reasons. One is that I've never really enjoyed sex when drunk, but the opportunity usually only arises when I am drunk, so I end up not doing it, or not enjoying it. That didn't apply tonight.'

He bent over and smelt her warm, salty scent, then kissed her again, longer and harder. She responded, pressing her body against him, then suddenly pulled back.

'Don't you want to know the second reason?'

'OK.'

'Because I like you and I trust you. Probably a mistake. My track record on men is not great, in fact it stinks. I'm going for the golden boot award, for a lifetime's achievement in picking losers. But at the moment you'll do.'

'Thank you. And the third reason?'

'I've changed my mind. I'm not going to tell you that. Or not yet anyway.'

She looked at him frankly for a moment, then pushed away his hand, which had crept under the blankets.

'Not now. If I don't get back to my bed, Edvarth'll notice – and I'll have to either apologise, or justify myself, and I don't want to do either. The young are very puritanical about their mothers.'

She got out of bed, and put her hands behind her head to coil up her shoulder-length hair, unashamedly naked. As he watched her, she bent down to kiss him quickly, then slipped on her jumper, and went out, carefully closing the door behind her.

Larsen, with a rich sweet sense of fulfillment, lay back and closed his eyes. He heard Risa going back into her room, then coming out again and going downstairs. He hoped she might be about to make him a mug of coffee. Instead he heard the front door open, and a moment later steps came running back up the stairs.

'He's gone,' Risa burst out, flinging his door open.

He started up. 'Who?'

'Edvarth, of course, for Christ's sake. He's gone. His bed's empty, there's no sign of him. Shit! I knew I shouldn't have –'

'He's probably just gone out for some early fishing,' interrupted Larsen, reaching for a sweatshirt.

'He left the fishing gear behind. And don't tell me he's gone for a walk – my son doesn't go for walks. He's gone, I tell you.'

'What's the time?'

'What does that matter?'

Larsen looked at her wide, worried eyes, her face across which ageing lines had suddenly spread. He reached for his watch, saw that it was quarter to six, and started to get out of bed.

Two minutes later they were both dressed, looking around the sitting-room and kitchen for any hint as to where Edvarth might have gone.

'I'm sure you're worrying unnecessarily,' he said, in his most reassuring tone. 'He's probably just . . .'

At that moment, the front door opened abruptly. Anita came in.

In contrast to Risa's barely concealed fear, bordering on panic, the thin, graceful Anita seemed composed, but there was a cigarette in her hand, and she drew on it heavily.

'I wondered if either of you have any idea where Marianne has got to,' she said, exhaling the smoke. 'She seems to have disappeared.'

'Edvarth has gone too,' replied Risa.

'Marianne left this,' said Anita.

She handed Larsen a piece of paper. In a large, painstaking script was written: 'We have gone to find the watchers. Don't worry. M.'

Risa was reading it over his shoulder.

'It says we. They must've gone together,' she said instantly. 'But where? And who the hell are the watchers?'

'Adam told me a few days ago that there were people in the area he did not know, and that he thought they didn't want to be seen,' said Anita. 'Others have said the same. I suppose Marianne, or your son, has seen them, or heard of them, so they've gone searching.'

Risa's eyes were wide. 'A woman has just been murdered,' she said. 'And now my son, with a little girl in tow, is wandering around looking for the murderers. Jesus Christ in hell! He must be out of his skull.'

Larsen made a determined effort to break free of the spell that the two women seemed to be spinning around him.

'Let's organise ourselves, and see if we can find out what has happened –'

'We know what's happened,' interrupted Risa.

'No, we don't. And there's no point in rushing out into the countryside looking blindly. First we must check if anyone has seen either of the children this morning, or if anyone knows where they've gone.'

'But –' began Risa.

Anita put her hand on her shoulder. 'He's right,' she said gently.

Twenty minutes later Larsen was talking to the two women again, together with Adam, who had joined them.

'From what Karadi and Yelmar said, it sounds as if they've gone to the Iterdla valley, so that's where Adam and I'll go to look for them. You two stay here –'

'I'm not staying here,' snapped Risa hotly. 'I'm not one of your accommodating little Inuit women. My grandmother rowed umiaks, and knocked down men who annoyed her. Edvarth's my son, and I'm helping to look for him.'

'As you wish,' shrugged Larsen. 'But what if they come back while we're still away? Someone should be waiting for them.'

'That sounds like a job for this accommodating little Inuit woman,' said Anita.

Risa began to apologise, but the older woman waved it away.

'We'll take my telephone with us,' went on Larsen. 'So you can contact us if there's any news. Here's the number. We'll ring you if we find anything. Right, let's go.'

'Not until you two have better boots than those,' commented Adam.

'There's no time to waste,' burst out Risa desperately.

Adam shook his head with stolid stubbornness. 'Bad boots cost much more time than finding the right ones.'

Ten minutes later Risa and Larsen, in borrowed knee-high sealskin boots, were following Adam north out of the village.

Anita watched them go. After a few minutes tears began to run down her creased cheeks.

The sun was casting long shadows as Risa, Adam and Larsen came to the River Isortoq. It was in spate, pouring down into the fjord, muddy ochre with glacial silt, but also white-foamed and fierce, like a creature that had this moment been unleashed. Fragments of ice bobbed and spun in its heaving waters.

Larsen and Risa stopped, nonplussed.

Adam merely tucked his loose trousers into his boots, then waded along the clearly marked division between the yellow turbulent river water and the dark quiet water of the fjord, cautiously testing each footstep before he made it.

'I thought river outflows were dangerous,' said Larsen.

Adam took no notice, and after a moment Risa and Larsen followed him. Gradually they made their way further and further out into the fjord, before Adam turned and began to make his way back towards the far side of the river.

Above them there was a harsh cry, and Larsen saw the flittering white wings of an arctic tern flying elegantly up the fjord, hunting for small fish in the shallows. A few moments later he and Risa emerged from the water on the far side of the river, to see Adam already casting around for tracks.

'Good boots,' remarked Larsen, whose feet were still completely dry.

'Any sign of the children?' asked Risa.

Adam shook his head. 'No. But there's another crossing upstream. Perhaps they used that.'

They passed briskly over sandy flats on the north side of the Isortoq delta, then a stretch of open rocky ground, before descending into the deep valley of the Iterdla.

'We'd better check both sides,' said Adam.

Without waiting for a reply, he made his way over the fast-flowing river, leaping easily from rock to rock, then began to walk up the eastern bank of the river. Larsen and Risa walked parallel to him, separated by fifteen metres of crashing, bubbling, stone-fanged water.

As the walls of the valley began to draw in, the scattered clumps of grass and alpine plants also began to come together. The thickets of willow and birch became taller, thicker, larger, until Adam had vanished from sight in the scrub as – for much of the time – had the river itself.

Hot and sticky, Larsen and Risa sat down against a great

boulder. A cloud of mosquitoes gathered, and Risa flapped her hand at them distractedly.

'We should have brought head-nets,' said Larsen.

'Let's get on,' she replied, getting back to her feet.

'We don't want to tire ourselves out,' he said. 'Remember the rule for hiking in Greenland – take a break every hour.' He produced a bar of chocolate, and broke it in half.

Risa ate her half rapidly, impatiently, still standing, then turned on Larsen.

'Phone up and see if there's any news,' she demanded.

'What's the number?'

'I don't know. I thought you did. Shit, shit, shit!'

'It doesn't matter. If they had anything to tell us, they would have contacted us.'

'I suppose so. OK, let's get on.'

The ground was rising sharply, and the tangle of birch and willow made a wiry maze that was hard to penetrate. At last, sweating and short of breath, they emerged on a steep slope, where a waterfall thundered down, covering them in fine spray. There was no sign of Adam. Risa started to scramble rapidly up the steep slope near the waterfall. Larsen sighed and followed. At the top he found her sitting on the ground, unconsciously arranging her hair, and looking around.

'I can't believe a ten-year-old child would have covered this much tough going,' she said.

'Maybe they went a lot slower than us,' suggested Larsen, sitting beside her. 'We've done this in an hour, they might have taken two or three times as long. And Marianne knows this countryside – there could be easier routes.'

He produced a pair of binoculars from his pack, and began to scan the surrounding countryside. Now that they were in the foothills, there was less vegetation, and the countryside was dominated by scree slopes, rugged ridges, pools of open water, and rolling, stone-strewn rock on which the deep striations of ancient glaciers were clearly visible. Snowfields speckled the area as it rose towards the inner mountains, and the deathly white ice cap beyond.

Larsen put down the binoculars, and glanced at Risa. Her face was grey.

'This is pointless isn't it?' she said. 'We'll never find them like this. We don't even know if they really did come this way.'

'Don't worry,' said Larsen, then realised what a stupid thing it was to say.

Risa turned on him savagely. 'Stop trying to comfort me, for Christ's sake.'

She snatched up the binoculars, and turned and climbed fluently, athletically, up a rocky tor immediately behind them. Reaching a ledge near the frost-shattered top, she again began to scan the countryside. Suddenly, as she looked north, up the course of the river, she seemed to tense. For a long time she barely moved. Abruptly she climbed swiftly back down, handed Larsen the binoculars, then pulled out a bottle of water she was carrying at her belt, and took a long swallow.

'What did you see?' he asked.

'I think it was a tent,' she said. 'But it was through a gap between two cliffs, which made it difficult to be sure.'

'Let's go and look.'

'The children didn't have a tent.'

'Perhaps the people camping know something.'

'What about Adam?' She seemed strangely reluctant.

'He knows his way around well enough.'

It took them another half an hour of stiff walking to reach the cliffs. The Iterdla had shrunk to a busy stream, bustling through a cold, damp canyon, where water dripped off steep black walls, and the ground was littered with fallen and broken rocks. Eventually Larsen and Risa found themselves in a high valley, with ribbon lakes down the centre of it. Half a kilometre away, beside the nearest lake, was a dark blue semi-geodesic tent, with a large porch.

Larsen stopped. He suddenly felt vulnerable. He had no weapon, no support except Risa, and no one knew where they were, except perhaps Adam. He pulled out his telephone and tried to contact first Norlund, then the geologists' camp, but the high cliffs blocked all radio waves, and he received nothing but crackles and white noise static.

Risa was already striding purposefully forward.

The tent was empty. Inside were two sleeping bags resting on sleeping pads, a variety of heavy clothing, cooking gear, bottles of methylated spirits, and some food. Risa began investigating a pile of spare tent pegs, boots, first aid gear, thermos flasks, twine, and insect repellent. However, Larsen's attention was drawn to two pairs of ski masks and goggles hanging from a hook on one of the poles.

As he stared at them, remembering the attempted kidnapping, Risa tossed a small guidebook over to him. It was written in a language and a script he could not understand, but the letters were surely Chinese, or some related language.

While he flicked through the book, Risa left the tent, a look of resignation on her face, then immediately darted back inside.

'They're coming,' she hissed. 'Two men – they've both got rifles.'

'Did they see you?'

'I don't think so. They're quite a way up the valley still, and I ducked down straight away. What do we do?'

For a moment Larsen's mind whirled. This was a chance to sort the whole business out, but the men had guns, and he had no business risking Risa's life as well as his own.

'You head back,' he said urgently. 'Get help. I'll stay here and –'

She was shaking her head. 'No way.'

'But –'

'Don't be a fool,' she hissed urgently. 'You're unarmed, and you'll never catch them both unawares. Once we're out of this valley, you can call in help from Paamiut, and we'll be able to trap them easily.'

'But –' he began again. Even though he knew she was right.

'Come on!' She dragged him out of the door of the tent.

They headed back the way they had come, keeping low and trying to use every available scrap of cover. As they climbed towards the narrow canyon, the ground became more and more bare, and Larsen was wearing a bright red sweater – which he had picked to be especially visible, in case the children might see it.

They were two hundred metres short of the gorge, when they heard shouts behind them.

'Run!' said Larsen.

Risa sprinted forward, running fast and direct. Larsen deliberately moved more slowly, darting unpredictably from side to side. Within a minute Risa was out of sight, hidden by the boulders under the overhanging cliffs. Larsen accelerated and joined her.

'Why didn't they shoot?' asked Risa.

'Perhaps they're out of ammunition,' he replied. 'Or they think it'll be easier to follow us. Or they're frightened we've got friends nearby and this is a trap. Or they're innocent hunters with no reason to shoot. Save your breath. We've a long way to go.'

Half-way through the gorge, as Risa pressed on ahead, Larsen stripped off his red sweater, and threw it up towards a ledge. It fell neatly three-quarters behind a rock: with some luck the sight of it would hold their pursuers up for a few minutes. He hurried on, emerging from the ravine on Risa's heels.

'Where now?' she gasped.

'Back the way we came. But don't run, not yet. We must save our energy.'

Fifteen minutes later Risa glanced back over her shoulder again.

'They're there!'

Larsen looked back.

Two figures were perhaps a kilometre behind them.

'Go!' he said.

The two of them set off down the valley, towards the woodland, with its promise of shelter. Larsen ran steadily, keeping to the rear, and trying to cover Risa's back from any shots. After all, he thought to himself, as the breath rushed in and out of his lungs, she has a boy to look after – my children don't need me. Risa ran much better than he had expected. She was tough and strong, with long well-muscled legs, and she kept going without seeming to feel the pace, even beginning to lengthen her lead. When she vanished over the slope by the waterfall, she was thirty metres clear of him. Larsen stopped by the first birches, and looked back, but the lie of the land prevented him seeing far, and there was no sign of the men with rifles.

In the wood, they heard or saw nothing of their pursuers, and when they reached the grey sands near the mouth of the Isortoq, they saw Adam. With him were Marianne and Edvarth.

Risa let out a cry of joy, ran over to them, and hugged Edvarth.

Larsen followed more slowly. He was exhausted, his legs and back ached, his throat was sore, and there was a pounding pain in his head. Nevertheless, the discomforts faded as he saw that the children seemed all right.

'What happened?' he asked.

'They got lost,' said Adam. 'And this little wicked one,' he ruffled Marianne's spiky hair, 'she fell over and hurt her knee. So the boy had to carry her back, which took him some time – as you can imagine.'

'He had to keep stopping for rests,' said Marianne. 'And he kept bumping me. It wasn't comfortable. See, my knee has swollen up like a balloon.' She pulled up her trousers, then looked disappointed. 'There's the graze, where it bled, but the swelling's going down already. You saw, didn't you Adam? Like a red balloon.'

'Your Aunt Anita, will give you more than a swollen knee for behaving like this,' said Adam.

Marianne looked entirely unimpressed.

But Larsen glanced over his shoulder, towards the wooded valley behind them.

'We should get back to the village as soon as we can,' he said.

'It's all right,' said Adam, and pointed. A small open fishing-boat was coming over from the far side of the fjord. 'Kunarat is on his way. After I found these two and helped them down here, I walked up the shore. There's usually someone fishing nearby in June, and when I saw Kunarat, I signalled to him to come and get us.'

'What with?' asked Larsen.

'This is my mobile phone.' Adam produced a small case, and opened it to show a slightly concave mirror. 'I carry it every-where – either for signalling or for making a fire.'

'Or for looking at your ugly face,' laughed Marianne.

Adam waggled a knobbly finger at her with an air of mock anger. But Larsen looked back over his shoulder again, then sighed. It had occurred to him that it was Monday morning, and time to telephone Chief Thorold.

11

ESCAPE

At last there was a rattle of keys, and a moment later the door opened, revealing two men silhouetted against the light in the corridor outside. A powerful torch flashed into Norlund's face, dazzling him so he could see nothing except a savage whiteness that seemed to drill inside his head.

'Help me,' he gasped. 'I can't stand it in here. I'm going mad.'

'Shut up,' growled one of the figures.

The other took a step into the room and tried the light switch. Nothing happened.

'Shit! The bulb's gone.'

'Let me out of here,' begged Norlund hysterically. 'Please, for God's sake, let me out of here. I'm starving. I'm dying of thirst. I can't bear the darkness. Let me out. I'll do anything, anything.'

He fell to the ground below the bed, grovelling. The torch beam followed him.

'For Christ's sake,' said one of the men, his voice heavy with disgust. 'And it stinks in here.'

'It's been a long time,' said the other. 'OK then, you, shut up making that foul noise, or I'll kick you to sleep.'

Norlund whimpered. He knew he must not be impatient, because he would only get one chance – which he dare not waste. He needed to find out how many people there were in the house, whether the old man was there, and whether there was any realistic chance of escape. And he was well aware that at this moment his captors would be at their most watchful. In a while their caution might lessen.

'Come out of there, but remember – we both have guns trained on you, and if you make the slightest movement that we don't like, we'll shoot you dead. Understand?'

'Yes, sir. Of course, sir. Please don't hurt me, sir.'

Ten minutes later Norlund was sitting in the plain, well-equipped kitchen, eating. He ate desperately, stuffing the greasy sausage and tomatoes into his mouth like an ape. Grunting. Drinking two large mugs of milk straight down and begging for more. His guards watched him with their guns in their hands, and disgust on their faces.

A fresh morning sun shone through the window and warmed Norlund's blood. Without seeming to, Norlund was taking stock of his surroundings, noting that the window was double-glazed and locked shut, although the shutters were drawn back. The food made him feel better. Stronger. But his guards had not relaxed their vigilance.

As an experiment, but also because he needed to, he begged to go to the lavatory. They made him sit on the toilet with the door open and both of them outside the door, watching his every movement. Back in the kitchen, one of the guards made a large thermos flask of coffee. The other stood at Norlund's back.

'Should we make anything for the others?'

'No point. We don't know what time they'll be back.'

'What about him?'

'He doesn't drink coffee. Make him some tea. Weak.'

At that moment the door opened. Norlund glanced up, and a shaft of excitement lanced through him.

The man who came in, walking slowly and carefully, and sat down at the far end of the pine kitchen table, was the old man he was looking for. His eyes behind their thick spectacles drifted across to Norlund, then avoided the Greenlander's gaze, moving on to the window.

'It seems a fine day.'

'It is, sir. And enough of a wind to keep the flies under control.' To Norlund's surprise, the guard spoke to the old man politely, with respect. 'We've made a cup of tea for you.'

'Very weak, I hope. When I was a child, we drank only hot water, and I find I am going back to that again. It is enough to just wave a teabag in the steam.'

As the old man sipped his tea, Norlund watched him carefully, and found him somehow formidable. He no longer suspected for a moment – as he had that first meeting – that the old man's mind might be wandering.

There was a quality of stillness about him, as if he never made unnecessary, unconscious movement. As if every time he even blinked or breathed, he had carefully weighed up the action, and it was planned and executed with a minimum of wasted effort.

He was very short, and round, but noticing his thick thighs, Norlund thought he might have been powerfully built in his youth. Except for a thin white fringe over his ears and round the

105

back of his head, there was not a hair on his gleaming skull, which came to a sharp point at the top. His white beard and thin moustache were carefully clipped, and he had a broad nose and a small mouth. His long eyes, half hidden behind thick, black-rimmed spectacles, seemed continually to look beyond what was in front of him to somewhere far away.

The old man's face was a labyrinth of tiny wrinkles and creases, and there were laughter lines round his mouth – or they seemed to be laughter lines. His arms were long, and his hands large, with massive almost swollen fingers. He wore loose baggy trousers, and a heavy woollen jersey, but his feet – flat and faintly discoloured – were bare.

He sipped his tea delicately, then suddenly turned to Norlund.

'It is pleasant to meet new people,' he said. 'Sometimes I go months without seeing a fresh face. There are people who do not like me to make new friends.'

'He's not a friend,' said the paler of the two guards.

'I can make up my own mind about that,' answered the old man, with the barest hint of a smile. 'But certainly this young man, whoever he is, looks the worse for wear.'

Norlund's spirits rose, as he realised that the old man was deliberately concealing their previous meeting.

'He won't be here long,' said the guard.

'Why not?'

'Ask the boss about that when he comes back.'

'I will. I will also ask him about myself. I gather we are moving soon.'

The guard looked at Norlund and said nothing.

The old man turned to Norlund, and spoke in west Greenlandic. 'You are one of the policemen who were in Ikerasak, aren't you?' he said calmly, as if he were talking of the weather. 'What are you doing here?'

The guards seemed taken aback, and turned to each other, frowning. It was obvious they could not understand, but were not sure what they should do.

'I came here looking for you, but they do not believe me.'

'No, they wouldn't.' A sudden urgency came into the old man's voice. 'Can you tell me, how is Marianne?'

For a moment the name meant nothing to Norlund. Then he remembered the little village girl, who had been with the old man on the day of the kidnap.

'She misses you,' he said, instinctively.

106

'I must ask you to stop talking a language that we cannot understand,' broke in the blond guard.

'I thought hearing his own tongue would put him at his ease,' shrugged the old man. 'But if you don't want me to, captain, then I won't.'

'Einar, take the intruder back to his room,' said the captain, before turning back to the old man. 'Meanwhile I wish to know what the two of you were talking about.'

'I merely asked him where in Greenland he came from.'

'How did you know he comes from Greenland?'

'I can recognise an Inuit face when I see one.'

The younger guard escorted Norlund out of the kitchen and along the corridor to the door into the dark room.

'Please don't send me back in there,' begged Norlund. 'Not alone. Not without a light.'

The guard opened the door, his gun ready, and gestured inside.

'Please, please, I can't stand the darkness.'

'Get in!'

Norlund, visibly shaking, staggered into the room, then as darkness enfolded him he whipped the light bulb out of his pocket and flung it to the ground. It exploded in a savage burst of noise, and Norlund screamed as loud as he could.

The guard muttered a curse and started forward into the gloom. Before his eyes had a chance to adapt themselves, Norlund clubbed his hands together and launched a massive blow, carrying every ounce of his strength.

It struck home on the side of the guard's jaw, and the man stumbled forward. At the same moment he fired his gun. There was a deafening blast, and the bullet crashed into the wall, then ricocheted away, whining. Norlund kicked out, and caught the guard's wrist, sending the gun spinning away over the floor. The guard lunged out, but Norlund kicked him again, catching him full in the face, then darted across the room to snatch up the gun.

As he grabbed it, he heard the other guard running along the passage. He levelled the gun as the captain appeared.

'Don't move,' he rapped out.

The guard hesitated, and Norlund fired. The bullet smashed into the wooden wall, close to the guard's head.

'Put your gun on the floor by your feet,' shouted Norlund. The captain obeyed. 'Now kick it away down the passage. OK. Come in here, slowly. Over there, by your friend. Don't try anything, or I'll shoot again. And shoot to kill this time.'

'You won't get away with this –'

'Shut your mouth!'

Norlund moved round the far side of the room, to the door. The key was still in it. He closed and locked the door on the guards, then picked up the second gun and slipped it into his jacket pocket.

'If either of you make any attempt to escape,' he barked through the door, 'I will kill you both.'

There was no sound from inside.

Norlund, breathing heavily, ran back to the kitchen. The old man was still sitting there. He looked up as Norlund came in.

'Now we find out who was right,' he said quietly.

'What are you talking about?'

'I was just telling my friend, Captain Eklund, that you are a Greenland policeman, who tried to protect me in Ikerasak. He said I was quite wrong, and that you are an assassin, sent to kill me. Now I will find out if I was right, as it seems that I am completely at your mercy. If you wish to kill me, you had better do so quickly.'

'I'm not here to kill you,' retorted Norlund irritably. 'I've come to take you back to Greenland.'

The old man nodded. 'I am glad I was right,' he said. 'But I'm afraid –'

'No,' said Norlund. 'You're afraid nothing. You come with me now. I have a plane on standby at Akureyri airport, so if there's anything you need to take with you, get it now. We leave in five minutes.'

'What if I don't want to come with you?' asked the old man.

Norlund stared at him in confusion. The idea had not even occurred to him.

'Don't you?' he asked, rather weakly.

The man did not answer for at least a minute. His face was twisted in what looked like pain, and his old boneless fingers clenched into a fist. At last he let out a long breath. But it was as if he had been defeated, and his face was covered by a shadow of bitterness.

'I will come,' he said.

'Then get some shoes on – and a warm coat,' said Norlund, retaking control. 'Grab some food too. I'll look for the things they took from me. Is there a car here?'

'Yes. But what about Captain Eklund and Einar?'

'One of them said other people are on their way here – which is one reason I'm in a hurry.' A sudden thought came to him. 'I don't even know what day it is.'

'Tuesday morning.'

Ten minutes later, Norlund had hot-wired the four-wheel drive Daihatsu, and he and the old man were driving at a blistering, bouncing pace, along the rough track towards Lake Myvatn.

Four and a half hours later the four-seater plane Norlund had hired was flying low over the Denmark Strait, towards the coast of east Greenland. The late spring pack still lay thick over the sea, a massive, infinitely complex, broken pavement: pancakes of fresh pure white; blue-tinted second year ice; mountainous icebergs; fragile glassy new ice; and everywhere the thin black scars that revealed leads of open water.

'I think it's time you told me your real name,' said Norlund, turning towards his companion.

The old man shrugged. 'I think of myself as Wan Li.'

'What sort of an answer is that? I asked you your name.'

'I gave it to you. I have used several names during my life, but that's the one I was given as a child.'

'You're from China, aren't you?'

'Yes.'

'Then what the hell are you doing here?'

The old man sighed wearily. 'I am a political refugee – seven years ago I was granted asylum and the right to live in Iceland, but each year I spend the summer in Ikerasak. And now I wish to go back there. Is that enough?'

'No. Who were those people who seized you?'

There was a clear hesitation, before the old man answered.

'As far as I know, and I may be wrong, they were people who wished to stop me from doing something I should do, but that I am not going to do. But they do not believe me. Though I have been told there are people who wish to see me dead.'

Norlund felt as if the old man was spinning thin, almost imperceptible webs in his mind. 'I don't understand.'

'Neither do I. Sergeant Norlund, I am grateful to you for all that you have done, but it has been a long day, and I am very tired. You must please let me rest.'

He lay back in his seat, put his hands in his lap, and closed his long, heavy-lidded eyes. Within a few minutes his shallow, even breaths spoke of sleep.

An hour and a half later the plane landed at Kulusuk, on Greenland's barren east coast, under the shadow of a steep mountainside. Norlund and the old man got out, and walked to the airport building.

'I have never been here before,' said the old man, looking around him with interest. 'It's harsher than Ikerasak, and there's still so much snow around. What do we do now?'

'You go inside and warm up,' said Norlund. 'I have to phone my Chief.'

The old man vanished inside. He was walking very slowly, but held himself proudly upright.

Norlund got out his mobile, which he had found together with his other possessions in a neatly labelled box on a desk in the main room of the Lake Myvatn house. Two minutes later he was speaking to Chief Thorold.

The Chief's initial reaction, when Norlund told him where he was, was ice-cold, but he showed no surprise.

'Your co-conspirator, Tomas Larsen, had already told me to expect a call from you, Pieter. Before we go further, I would like to make a few things crystal clear. You had absolutely no excuse for behaving in this reckless fashion. You received no authorisation to spend large sums of taxpayers' money, as you have been doing, and your behaviour has nothing – absolutely nothing – to commend it. Frankly you will be extremely lucky if you are not heavily fined and expelled from the service for rank insubordination. I blame myself for allowing you far too much leeway in the past.'

'But Chief, I've got the old man back. I rescued him from armed men who were holding him.'

'Norlund, let me repeat this to you just once more. Listen very carefully. The whole incident was simply part of a secret NATO exercise –'

'No, it wasn't, Chief. It was a kidnap. These guys seized him and took him away against his will. I've sorted it out, and now he's back in Greenland, where he wants to be. And if you contact the Icelandic police, there's still a chance that we can have the men involved arrested. I left them locked in a house on Lake Myvatn.'

'But –'

'Chief, someone somewhere was lying to you. Everything points to a major crime having been committed. Just give me a couple of minutes to take you through it – OK? One – the old man didn't want to stay in Iceland, he wanted to come back with me. That means he was taken against his will. Two – no one in Ikerasak knew anything about this so-called exercise, even though he goes there every summer. Three – if everything was so innocent, how come I was imprisoned, interrogated, and beaten up? And there's what looks like a hypo mark in my shoulder. Four, and this is the clincher – what about the murder of the old man's housekeeper, which Tomas must have told you about? There's no way the story about a NATO exercise can cover all those facts. You must see that.'

There was a long pause at the end of the telephone.

'OK,' conceded Thorold finally. 'I can see the points you're making, and I'm not saying there aren't some good ones among them. There's certainly more to this than meets the eye.'

'You said it.'

'So you're at Kulusuk now?'

'Yes. And I don't like it, Chief. Once those men get free, it won't be hard for them to track us, and if I can hire a plane, so can they. They could arrive any time.'

'What are you suggesting?'

'I think we need the old man in Nuuk as fast as possible. Once there he'll be safe, and we can question him in detail – and try to sort the whole business out.'

'Perhaps.' There was another pause.

A flurry of sleet whispered down the mountainside. The runway, marked off by thin orange posts connected by wire, was brown and nondescript. A few yellow luggage trolleys and some mobile steps marked Flugeflag Islands lay around as if no one was interested in them. Norlund listened to the faint crackling of his mobile, and found himself glancing nervously up at the sky above.

'If this man is really being searched for, then I'm not happy about him being brought to Nuuk,' said Thorold at last. 'It would be very easy to find him here. I think you should take him somewhere unexpected. Somewhere only you and I know about. Then you can get to know him, and question him, while I make fresh enquiries – and try to discover just what is going on. Perhaps you should return to Paamiut and link up with Sergeant Larsen again.' Thorold gave a cough, and there was an edge in his voice. 'He too has been totally ignoring my orders.'

'Surely Ikerasak would be one of the first places they would look for us.'

111

'I am not, of course, suggesting Ikerasak, but I think you and Larsen should continue your work together. Meanwhile I will consider the matter. Contact me from Paamiut. Any questions? No? Right, goodbye then.'

Norlund switched off his mobile and brooded. The Chief had sounded on the edge of panic. Probably he was afraid that his bosses knew things he didn't, so he wasn't sure whether to tell them everything or nothing. It sounded as if he had decided on the second alternative – by hiding the old man in Paamiut, Thorold could keep the problem at arm's length, and be able to deny any knowledge, until the situation grew clearer. But Norlund wasn't happy about it.

The old man appeared at his elbow.

'More travelling,' said Norlund. 'We're going to Paamiut.'

The old man nodded. 'And then on to Ikerasak.'

'No. That would be too dangerous. They know about Ikerasak, and will probably look for you there again.'

The old man shook his head. 'They will never think of us returning to the same place, because they know of no reason why we should.' Into the strange, swooping old voice had crept a clear ring of certainty – of the utter confidence of command. 'Unexpected repetition is a trick I have used before.'

'What do you mean?'

'You are not interested in the long past of an old man.'

'At the moment we have nothing but time.'

'As you wish.' The old man's eyes were far away. 'The Americans attacked a hill in our line near Kaesong –'

'Are you talking about the Vietnam war?' interrupted Norlund.

The old man laughed, and patted Norlund on the shoulder. 'We are talking about Korea, even longer ago. I hid the main mass of my men not on the summit, or even close to it, but near the bottom. After the few troops I left guarding the hill were put to flight, the Americans saw the land opening out in front of them and advanced down the hill – into my trap. I retook the hill at little cost to myself, and much cost to the Americans. Two months later they attacked the same hill, and I did exactly the same thing. This time they were a little more circumspect, and did not push on headlong, but I made sure my troops did not show themselves. Eventually the Americans lost patience, as they do, and they advanced, and the same thing happened again.'

112

'Would you have tried it a third time?' enquired Norlund curiously.

The old man shook his head. 'No. For they would probably have assumed I had no other plan, and so been prepared. Anyway, there is another reason why we must return to Ikerasak.'

'What is that?'

'Because otherwise, I will not come with you.'

'You have no choice.'

'On the contrary, I have many choices. I could ask the pilot who brought us here to take me back. Or I could go up to those Greenlanders over there and ask them to let me to stay with them for a day or two. They would not say no to a venerable old man like myself, who speaks their language. Or I could take the helicopter to one of the local settlements, Tasiilaq or –'

'OK, OK,' said Norlund hurriedly. 'If possible I'll take you to Ikerasak.'

'Thank you very much,' said the old man, bowing his head politely. And without even the faintest appearance of irony.

'But there is a problem,' said Norlund, more to himself than to the old man. 'I will have to work out a plan in case we are followed.'

Next day Norlund walked into the Nuuk police station. Beside him was a small figure, well wrapped up, with a thick anorak, hood up, and dark sun-glasses. Chief Thorold was talking to Helge as the two men came in, and when he saw them, his face hardened.

'What is the meaning of this?' he demanded in a low, dangerous tone. 'I ordered you to take –'

'This is Rikki, Chief,' said Norlund.

The old man removed his thick anorak, took off his sunglasses, pulled down his hood and ran a hand through his dishevelled black hair, then yawned massively, revealing a mouth with more gaps than teeth.

'Can I go now?'

'Sure,' said Norlund. 'Jette, please show Rikki out the back way.'

'Into my office, Norlund,' snapped Thorold, his thin face drawn and angry.

Despite his apparent confidence, Norlund's heart was beating hard. After joining the police, he had rapidly won the goodwill of Chief Thorold, and everything had gone smoothly, until that bizarre trip down to Ikerasak. Suddenly the world had seemed

113

to lose all contact with its usual order and routine, pushing him into piling risk on risk. Now he had somehow been lured into the biggest gamble of his life, for if he had misjudged the situation, his whole career was on the line. He gathered his courage and followed Thorold into the office.

'Explain!' demanded the Chief, the moment the door was shut.

'I was worried we would be followed, Chief. You yourself agreed it was a danger, so I decided to let them follow me. But I couldn't risk taking the old Chinese man, Wan Li, with me. So I paid 300 kroner to an old Greenlander, who was booked on the flight anyway, to pretend he was Wan Li.'

'Where the hell is the real man?' Norlund had never heard Thorold swear.

'He'll be on tomorrow morning's flight to Narsarsuaq, from where he's booked on to Paamiut.'

'Are you seriously telling me that you left the man who caused all this trouble alone and unprotected in Kulusuk?' snapped Thorold, glaring at Norlund from his chair. 'Have you gone insane?'

'The Kulusuk Grønlandsfly rep, a very reliable woman, is looking after him tonight, and will put him on his flight tomorrow. One of the stewardesses will then ensure that he catches the connecting flight. As he has no money and no credit card, there is nothing he can do, except what he is supposed to do. He knows I'll meet him in Paamiut, and take him on to a safe hiding place – an alpine hut by the old settlement of Igdlorssuit, on one of the branches of Kuanersoq fjord.'

Thorold looked at him dubiously. 'You're not lying to me about this as well, are you?'

'No, sir.'

'Hm. And do you think that you were followed?'

'Yes, Chief. I do. A plane arrived in Kulusuk from Iceland early this morning, and two men, Danes or Icelanders, booked themselves on to the same plane as me, though I managed to lose them at Nuuk airport by catching a taxi.'

Thorold grunted again, and drummed his fingers on the table. 'I shudder to think what our spending figures are going to look like for this quarter, after the flight bills you and Larsen have run up.' He relapsed into silence.

And suddenly Norlund guessed what was about to happen. Larsen would be told to bring Wan Li back to Nuuk, there would be an internal enquiry, and the whole thing would turn out to be a tangle of mistakes and misunderstandings. Perhaps even Inga's murder was nothing to do with the old man – maybe the nurse had been wrong, and it wasn't a murder at all. The whole incident would vanish like snow cover before the föhn wind. And all that would be left was a memory of him and Larsen behaving like complete fools – and being fined a huge sum of money to pay for all the flights they had taken.

Only then did he remind himself what had happened at the house beside Lake Myvatn, and in that moment Norlund was again sure something sinister was going on. But how could he prove it?

'. . . rejoin Larsen at Frederikshab – I mean Paamiut,' Thorold was saying. 'Assuming Wan Li arrives, the two of you are to stay with him in the hut you mentioned awaiting further instructions from me. No more unauthorised flights. No more rushing around the place like crazy American tourists. Do you understand?'

'What about the murder?' asked Norlund, then cursed himself for making more problems. This was a time to play safe, and watch and listen.

'Your job is to concentrate on this man, Wan Li. I will deal with the murder – if it was a murder.'

'Yes, sir.'

'The slightest hint of further insubordination, and you will be instantly suspended. Do you understand?' said Thorold sternly.

'Yes, sir.'

'That's better.' What passed as a smile settled over his thin, pale lips. 'I still believe you have it in you to be an excellent policeman, Pieter. But it is of the first importance that you learn to be less headstrong. Frankly I blame Tomas Larsen for not settling you down more – that was why I wanted him on the case, but it seems all he has done is make things worse.' Again that cartoon of a smile. 'Now, you had better contact Larsen and make sure he understands the situation. Then you'll want to get back home to your wife. Tomorrow morning you will be on the flight to Paamiut.'

The moment Norlund had left, Thorold picked up the phone and began to dial, then seemed to think better of it, and put it down again.

He sat where he was without moving, but an observer would have seen that suddenly his face seemed to age.

He picked up the telephone again.

115

12

KIMBERLEY

Rob Coleman was sitting outside, smoking a pipe. He did not really like smoking, but when combined with wearing a thick layer of insect repellent, it usually ensured he was not too bothered by the ravenous mosquitoes that plagued Greenland's inner fjords in summer. However, today he was frowning, and scratching his reddish hair irritably. Although there were distinctly fewer insects around than usual, those present were apparently obsessed with his scalp.

The scientific expedition he was a member of was primarily interested in the geology of the Ikerasak area, and especially any signs of nascent, or resurgent, volcanism. However, they were also investigating other aspects of the Grindehval fjord complex: studying the Norse/Inuit farmhouse had gained them funding from the University of Iceland, while a census on plants and insects had ensured research money from Aberdeen University. Rob's own speciality was the study of how natural history reflected underlying geology, and he was responsible for compiling a variety of data on the area, including a detailed breakdown of all butterfly sightings: butterflies were an important early indicator of any possible climatic change.

The day before, Rob had visited a plateau under the shadow of Mount Iviangeq, where there was an extensive basin dominated by raised acid bogs, standing pools, and shrubby vegetation. When the area had been surveyed some years before, it had been identified as one of the prime localities for butterflies in south-west Greenland. Furthermore, several pairs of Greenland white-fronted geese had been found nesting, which was as far south as the species reached. However Rob's visit had revealed no butterflies, despite good weather conditions, and no geese either. Even the snow buntings, wheatears and redpolls which populated most of the ice-free zone of Greenland were only present in very small numbers. Rob also noticed that some of the larger plants and trees seemed to be damaged, or even dying, as if the winter had been exceptionally hard, or there had been a sudden freeze-up again within the past few weeks. But neither was the case, and he could make no sense of it.

Bettina came walking up the hill to their camp. Her primary responsibility was the archaeological aspects of the trip, but she was also in charge of finding fresh food. Just now she had a fishing rod over her shoulder, and a discontented expression disfigured her smooth, oval face.

'Sigrid around?' she asked.

'No. She went down to the village. Nils was due in this morning, and she wanted to see if he'd got those supplies from Paamiut we asked for. You didn't have any luck then?'

'Nothing,' she said bitterly. 'All the trout have just vanished. It's crazy. They should be shoaling in the estuaries, getting ready to head up the rivers for spawning, but there's nothing. As if they had never existed. Last week, when I was out the far side of Palasipqaqqaa, they were all there as usual, beating each other up for the privilege of getting hooked, but Grindehval fjord's like a graveyard. Talking of which – along the high water mark there seem to be an unusually high number of dead creatures – crabs, small fish, starfish, and three birds.'

'Maybe it has something to do with global warming . . .'

'Talk sense, Rob.' Bettina took off her tinted spectacles, breathed on them, then cleaned them on her jumper, with nervous, staccato movements. 'I know the effects of global warming are highly complex, and we're a long way from understanding them, but why should they include driving the saltwater trout out of this particular fjord, but not the next one along?'

'It may be a localised phenomenon. The melting of glaciers might have exposed deposits of some heavy mineral which is polluting one of the meltwater streams, which in turn flows into the fjord.'

'What about your butterflies and geese? The geese nest on higher lakes that wouldn't be affected by polluted run-off, and I can't see your theory does anything to explain the lack of butterflies.'

'Butterfly numbers are cyclical – you know that. We must have just arrived at the down point of the cycle.'

'More like the no-butterflies-at-all point. And it's not only butterflies. Have you noticed how there are fewer mosquitoes than usual?'

'Different weather patterns. A lot of cold, low cloud. Or perhaps more wind.'

'No. I was looking at the statistics. They're comparable to the last survey expedition, no significant variation at all.'

'Arctic wildlife is unpredictable, they have to be to survive in such a marginal environment.'

'That's debatable too, at least here in the low Arctic. More and more I think Sigrid's theory may have something to it.'

'We've seen no concrete signs yet.'

'What about the ignimbrites? I found some more.' She produced a couple of pebbles of foamy white rock.

Rob took the stones and studied them briefly. 'They look the same as the others, and those're well over a thousand years old. There's no sign of a vent, you know that. Sigrid thinks there isn't one at all, my feeling is that if it exists, it'll be very small, and under the ice.'

'Then why haven't we found any samples of Palagonite Tuff? If the vent was under the ice one would expect there to be . . .'

Rob had stopped listening. He was looking past Bettina, an expression of surprise on his face. Bettina turned also, then put her spectacles back on.

Coming up the hillside was a clean-cut, square-jawed woman of perhaps thirty. She had shortish, curly, brown hair, heavy eyebrows, a nose-stud, and a look of unflinching determination on her angular face. She was dressed in what Bettina recognised as an expensive Patagonia Infurno jacket, she wore high quality Meindl walking boots, and on her back was a large, fully waterproof North Face rucksack, sealed shut. As she came closer, it became clear that as well as being well-built, she was also very tall, at least two centimetres taller than Rob, who found it off-putting but also dimly attractive.

She stopped beside them.

'Hi,' she said, in an accent straight from the Appalachians. 'Do you guys speak any English?'

'A bit,' said Rob. 'I am English.'

'OK. Right. Good. My name's Kimberley Persac, that's generally shortened to Kim. I'm an American, as you probably guessed – from Lexington, Kentucky to be precise. Kentucky Kim.' She grinned.

'You're hiking?'

'Sure.'

She took off her rucksack, plonked it casually on the ground, then sat down on it, and stretched out her long legs.

'Nice, here,' she said, after a moment. 'What are you guys about?'

'We're conducting a scientific study,' explained Rob.

There was another long pause. The newcomer was seemingly unmoved by any trace of embarrassment. 'Anyone else round here?' she asked, gesturing further inland.

'No, no one,' said Rob.

'I thought I heard there was some old guy, living by himself.'

'Where did you hear that?' asked Bettina, speaking English with care.

'Some guys down in the village. I didn't get everything they said, their English wasn't up to anything at all, but that was what it seemed to be.'

'You don't speak Danish or Greenlandic?'

Kimberley laughed. It was an attractive, easy laugh, infectious, and accompanied by a pleasant smile. 'No, I don't speak Danish or Greenlandish, or any -ish except English. Terrible, isn't it? I'm ashamed of myself, but that's the way it came out.'

Bettina looked at the newcomer with a strange, tight, almost predatory expression on her pale face, then gave a characteristic flick of her long, henna-ed hair. But Kimberley was focusing her attention on Rob.

'Maybe I just misunderstood everything,' she said, with a self-deprecating smile. 'I usually do. But I sure got the sense there's a house along here someplace.'

'There is,' said Rob. 'But you're well off line for it. It's close to the water's edge – a good twenty minutes' walk away. You can see it from up there.'

Kimberley climbed the outcrop he pointed out, and produced a pair of armoured Leica binoculars. She focused them down towards the glittering waters of the distant fjord.

'Yeah, I got it. Who lives there?'

'No one now,' said Rob. 'It used to be some old guy called Haan, I think. Then weird things started happening.'

'Tell me.'

Rob opened his mouth, but Bettina interrupted him before he could start.

'It is a lot of nonsense,' she said firmly. 'People here have very little to talk about, except fish and seals and weather, so they create all sorts of crazy stories. Nothing to take any notice of.'

'I love stories,' said Kimberley. 'All kinds of stories.'

'I would prefer you told us your story,' said Bettina. 'We've never had walkers round here before. It is a pretty valley, but very isolated, with the difficult approach by sea, and the Iceblink to the north –'

119

'The what?'

'A place where the inland ice comes right down to the sea. Presumably you specially chose to come here – why was that?'

'Just chance,' shrugged Kimberley. 'I was in Paamiut, looking for somewhere to go, somewhere good and special, you know, where the rubber really hits the road good. Though I suppose that's a dumb phrase in Greenland, with there being no roads worth talking about. Anyway there was this guy in the port, and he was coming out here, so I thought, why not? And it was brilliant, massive icebergs, and eagles overhead on the boat trip. Brilliant!'

'You look well equipped,' said Bettina, glancing at the rucksack.

'You said it. That's equipment coming up close to $3000 in all. I mean, no way was I going to get myself in trouble – everything had to be the best.'

'Even that isn't always enough,' said Bettina. 'Greenland is real wilderness, and things can always happen. Especially when you travel alone.'

'Sure, sure. But travelling alone is what I do. I'm used to it, in fact I prefer it.'

'You know the Arctic well, then?'

'Not the Arctic. But I've been some wild places, and some of them pretty cold: Colombia, China, Kashmir, Kazakhstan, Tibet, and I've looked after myself OK so far.'

There was a call from down the valley. Sigrid, small and blonde, was coming up the hill. Behind her walked the solid figure of Tomas Larsen.

'Brilliant news!' said Sigrid excitedly, as she joined the group outside the tent. 'My records show the water temperature in the fjord has increased by 0.3° since we came, and that's even making an allowance for the weather. I told you, there's something happening here . . .'

'This is Kimberley Persac,' said Rob. 'She's an American hiker.'

Sigrid stopped, glanced at the American woman who towered over her, and momentarily bit her lip. Then she brought up a bristling smile.

'Yes, I heard – she came in with Nils this morning. Down in the village he was telling anyone who'd listen how much money he was making as a passenger ferry. Sorry, maybe I shouldn't have said that. Anyway, that's not the point. Sergeant Larsen has got some news for us.'

Kimberley was listening to the exchanges in Danish, a puzzled expression on her face.

'What's she saying?' she asked Rob.

'She's one of our team. She was just telling me some stuff about our work,' explained Rob in English.

'Is the guy she's with part of your team too?'

'No. He's a policeman.'

'Oh right,' said Kimberley. But the casual phrase had no connection with her response to the information. Her wide, slightly bulbous eyes were nailed to the approaching Larsen, and her long, lean body seemed suddenly tense.

'What's a policeman doing out here?' she asked, after a moment.

No one answered. But as Larsen arrived, she turned to him. 'Hi. Do you speak English?'

Larsen nodded. 'A little.'

Sigrid, Rob and Bettina exchanged glances.

'So what are you doing round here? I mean a policeman, in this tiny little place. It seems weird.'

Larsen replied quietly, in his careful English, 'I thought I should stop by and give you all a warning.'

'What about?' asked Rob.

'There are two men camping further inland,' said Larsen. 'Up the valley of the Iterdla. I want to talk to them, but they do not seem anxious to talk to me.'

'I don't understand,' put in Kimberley. 'I mean if you want to talk to someone, you just do it.'

'Not out here. I intend to . . . round them up. And it's possible there may be trouble. I wanted to make sure you knew what was going on.'

'When is this happening?' asked Bettina warily.

'Now.' Larsen gestured out to where a small motor boat was creeping up the fjord. 'I'm about to join the others.'

'I'll come with you,' said Kimberley instantly.

'I don't think that would be wise –' began Larsen.

'Crap!' she retorted. 'You've got guys from the village helping you, haven't you?'

'Yes, but they're volunteers who know this area –'

'I'm a volunteer too.'

Larsen shrugged, and glanced at the other three. Rob Coleman was looking at Kimberley. His hand was rubbing through his

121

thickening beard. Somehow Rob irritated Larsen, but he pushed the geologist out of his mind, and strode off towards the water-side, Kimberley at his side.

Rob, Sigrid and Bettina watched the tall American and the broad short policeman walking briskly away.

'What was all that about?' demanded Rob, at length. 'Why did you keep interrupting me?'

Bettina shook her head. 'There's something weird about that woman,' she said. 'I mean what the hell is she doing here?'

'She explained that . . .'

'Not to my satisfaction she didn't.'

'Go on,' said Sigrid intently.

'OK. Nils barely speaks Danish, let alone English, so how did she have the faintest idea of where he was going?'

'She probably got someone in Paamiut to explain,' said Rob.

'Possible, I suppose. But what's special about Ikerasak – why should anyone think of coming here?'

'Good point,' said Sigrid, nodding. 'The place is hard to get to, and there's no hiking map of the area, no mention of it in any of the guidebooks I've seen.'

'And all that stuff about someone in the village telling her an old man lived by himself up here,' went on Bettina. 'As far as I know no one in the village speaks more than a few words of English, so who told her, and why, and how did she understand?'

'What're you saying here?' enquired Rob.

'I don't know. Just that it looks like she's telling lies. I've no idea why, but –'

'I have,' interrupted Sigrid. 'We all agreed that we had to keep our research secret. If anyone finds out, there's a real danger our work will be pre-empted.'

'Come on. You're fantasising,' protested Rob.

'Am I?' said Sigrid intently. 'This is the big one, Rob. The really big one. If we're right, this is our chance for international publicity, big research funding, a prestige university chair. The whole deal. A lot of people want that.'

'If we're right.'

'Yes. And things are looking better all the time.'

'How do you work that out?'

'The figure on the water temperature must be another indicator. Surely you can see that. I'm not going to risk anyone else getting on to it.' Sigrid clenched her fist. 'I've worked on this for five years, and it is all ours,' she hissed.

13

CAPTIVE

Larsen lay flat on his stomach. In front of him was a low thicket of alpine rhododendron, spotted with pink flowers and intergrown with taller birch scrub. Beyond he could see the dark tent. There was no sign of life, but Adam had assured him that the men were inside.

As the minutes slipped by, Larsen continued to scan the area, until he saw the flashing reflection of a mirror away to the right. Then a white shirt was waved further up the valley. Everyone was in place.

Larsen took a deep breath, got to his feet, and walked down towards the tent. It took more nerve than he had expected to stand up, knowing he was an open target for men with rifles. Men who had almost certainly committed at least one murder already.

There was no shot. No sound. Nothing. He walked on.

When he was just ten metres from the tent, there was a sudden scuffle of movement inside, and a man sprang out, rifle in hand, and gestured to Larsen to leave. Larsen shook his head. At the same moment five other figures rose up in a semicircle around the tent. Adam, Jokum, Karadi, and Yelmar all held their own hunting rifles. The man started violently, then hissed something in an urgent voice, and the second man appeared beside him, also clutching a gun.

'Put your guns down,' Larsen said quietly in English.

The men stared at him as if they did not understand. The rest of Larsen's team were coming rapidly closer, with Kimberley leading the way. Larsen repeated his words.

Slowly the man in front put his rifle down on the ground. His companion followed suit more reluctantly. As Adam arrived from the right, he picked up the two rifles, and regarded them with interest. He was joined by the other villagers. Kimberley moved round to stand immediately behind Larsen.

'Will you please come with us,' said Larsen.

With no warning the man at the back flung himself sideways and darted through the gap left by Kimberley. Springing over some rocks, he sprinted off up the hill. Yelmar raised his rifle, but Larsen put out his hand to stop him shooting.

'Take this one back,' he said to the others. 'I'll follow the runaway.'

'I'm coming with you,' said Kimberley.

Larsen gave no sign he had heard, and set off up the hillside, after the fleeing figure. However Kimberley paused to snatch one of the rifles from Adam, before hurrying after him.

The ridge was hard and bare, a rising stretch of loose grey shale, with hollows, frost-shattered outcrops, and small streams. The sun was breaking through the clouds that had cloaked Ikerasak for the last three days, and suddenly it felt hot. Larsen, sweating, pushed himself on as best he could, but he had never been a great runner. The man in front was young, fit and strong, and soon extended his lead.

As his quarry vanished from sight, Larsen slowed, and Kimberley, running lithely, joined him. She looked ahead up the empty ridge.

'Shall I go on after him?' she said. She was hardly even short of breath.

Larsen shook his head wearily. 'Too risky,' he said. 'And we've got one of them.'

As they rejoined the others, Adam loped past, rifle in hands.

'I'll catch him for you,' he said, with a brief nod.

'I don't want him hurt,' called Larsen.

'I'm doing him a favour,' said Adam drily.

He set off up the hill at the steady hunting trot of the arctic wolf, who never grows weary or discouraged.

Three hours later, the man they had caught was sitting in a battered chair in Larsen's house. At the man's back stood Karadi, Yelmar and Jokum. Unable to understand English, they were smoking and talking to each other in low voices. They seemed less interested in the man they had captured than in the tall American woman, at whom they threw frequent curious glances. Kimberley was watching the prisoner closely, her bright eyes alight with interest.

Their captive was no more than twenty-five, and good-looking. His straight black hair was thick and glossy, his narrow face quick and alive, and he had a strong, jutting chin. Larsen was sitting on the table, trying to interrogate him, and using his best English, but the young man did not appear to understand a word.

'Are you Chinese?' he demanded for the third time, speaking very slowly, and trying to hold back a rising anger. 'Chinese?'

The young man shrugged.

At that moment Adam appeared, with the second man. Adam had an air of modest triumph about him, and a large smile on his faintly foxy face.

The man Adam brought in was about the same age as his partner, though there was an indefinable air that revealed him as the leader of the pair. He had very short cropped hair, and liquid, rapid-moving eyes. There was a clear-cut, hard-edged pride evident in his posture, and in his stubborn mouth, but over his fine-featured face hung an expression of ingrained exhaustion.

'It wasn't hard to find him,' remarked Adam. 'I think he wanted to be caught.'

Larsen turned to the newcomer, who had slumped sullenly on to another chair. 'What is your name?' he demanded.

The man sighed. 'Ze Shu-fan.'

'What nationality are you?'

'Chinese, of course.'

'Of course. And what are you doing here, in Greenland?'

The answer was defiant, spat out as if launching a blow at Larsen: 'Fighting for the freedom of my country.'

Larsen stared at the man, and recognised the iron gleam of the fanatic. But he could make no sense of the answer.

'What do you know about the death of Inga Brønnestedt?'

'I have never heard the name before. Who was he?'

'A woman. She was found a few kilometres away, last week. She had been hit viciously on the head, probably with a gun butt, and her body was thrown in the fjord.'

'I know nothing about her.'

'Ask him about the old man who lived up the fjord,' said Kimberley.

Larsen and Shu-fan both turned and looked at her. Larsen opened his mouth to silence her, then realised she knew things he did not.

'You ask him,' he said quietly.

Kimberley came round to face Shu-fan. At her back, the watching villagers grew quiet.

'You were looking for the same man as me, weren't you?' she said.

'I do not know who you were looking for,' Shu-fan said stolidly.

The other Chinese man was also intent on Shu-fan.

'A man half the world heard of for a few weeks, in 1989,' said Kimberley. 'A man who is said to be dead.'

Larsen turned to Adam. 'Watch these men. Make sure they do not escape.'

Adam nodded.

'You promised we would be paid for this,' reminded Yelmar. 'Helping the police. It is important work, isn't it?'

'It is important work,' confirmed Larsen, then gestured to Kimberley to come outside

The sun was still shining through a mesh of thin mackerel cloud, and cool breezes slid off the glittering waters of the fjord. Inland, the mountains were invisible, masked by persistent low cloud.

'What is it?' asked Kimberley.

Larsen put his hands in his pockets. He had had the feeling throughout this case, from the first day, that he was being kept in the dark, and he was sick of it.

'Who are you?'

'Like I told you, a hiker . . .'

'How do you know about the old man who used to live here?' interrupted Larsen sharply. 'And what do you know about him?'

'Not much. Just what someone in Paamiut told me . . .'

'Crap! No one in Paamiut knew anything about him. Anyway, you speak no Danish, let alone Greenlandic, and it's clear you knew what you were looking for here long before you arrived.'

He looked up at her with angry eyes. 'I am not a fool, American woman. Because I am short and overweight and middle-aged, because I cannot run and my skin is not white, because I earn little money and I live in this cold backwater of the world, does not mean you can lie to me safely.'

'I never thought –'

'No. That is right. But it is time for you to start. I want to see what is inside your expensive rucksack.'

She gaped at him. 'No way. I'm not showing you my stuff.'

'Then I shall take it from you, and look myself.' He stared at her, his head slightly to one side. 'Because you are American, you think you can do what you like, but I'm afraid that is not true. Now get your rucksack, bring it out here, and open it up.'

Reluctantly, flushing red with anger, she went back into the room, eyes lowered to avoid meeting anyone's gaze, and picked up her rucksack, then returned to where Larsen was waiting for her. Under his eyes, she unsealed the rucksack, unzipped it, and slowly began to pull things out and put them on a large flat rock.

A few minutes later Larsen was vigilantly checking through her belongings.

'Very expensive camera, satellite phone, Magellan GPS, tape recorder, top quality laptop with Internet connections.' He glanced at the passport in his hand, then paused to give her time to speak. She said nothing, so he went on. 'Pack your things away, Miss Persac, and while you do that, you can explain to me what an American journalist is doing in Ikerasak. And if I don't like your answers, I shall make sure you are stuck here the rest of the summer.'

'You can't do that.'

Larsen smiled grimly. 'You think not? Just how would you get out of here if I confiscated your passport, phone, money, computer? This is real wilderness – not like your deserts and mountains dotted with petrol stations, motels, and pizza parlours. There are only two ways in and out of Ikerasak – one is helicopter, and that will not come here unless there is a Class 1 emergency. You are not an emergency. So that leaves Nils's boat. If I tell Nils he is not to take you out, he will not. He knows that without police permission, he is not allowed to operate as a ferry, so I can cut off ninety per cent of his income like that.' He snapped his fingers. 'He will not risk that for anything you might promise him.'

The two of them stared at each other. The slim, high-cheekboned American, with all the confidence that came from working in a glamorous job in the most important country in the world, combined with a provokingly attractive appearance. And the squat, greying Inuit man.

But Kimberley had not been a journalist for ten years without developing the ability to read people.

'OK,' she said, surrendering gracefully. 'What do you want to know then?'

'What are you doing here?'

'You mean you can't guess?'

'I want to hear from you, please.'

'OK. As you know perfectly well, the guy up the fjord was a big-time celebrity some years back. Sure he only emerged from the cover of the Chinese Communist Party for a few days, but that doesn't lessen the impact he made. One minute he was another of those blank apparatchiks who sit in the second row at party conferences – as Second Secretary of the Beijing party I think he rated around twenty-eighth in the national hierarchy. Then he made that speech at the bottom of Chang'an Avenue, in front of thousands of protesting students and the world's media, saying it was time for the rulers of China to hand over more power to the people. That the Communist Party had become divorced from real life and that it was run by corrupt old men who didn't trust the Chinese people. In that moment he became one of the symbols of a liberation movement.

'A senior member of the administration had deserted his own government. More, he went on and told the listeners how he had fought for the revolution, how he had fought in Korea and defeated the Americans, and how as a one-time general he was sure the People's Liberation Army would never attack its own people. And they believed him. Thousands of people in Beijing, tens of thousands, maybe more, were suddenly sure the army would come over to their side. And Mei Tei was cheered wildly, fanatically, as he shook hands with student leaders by the Gate of Heavenly Peace. We all thought freedom was finally about to happen. Five days later the tanks rolled into Tiananmen Square, thousands died, and China was hurled back into the iron grip of dictatorship.'

She stopped repacking her rucksack. And Larsen, watching her face, saw the emotion flickering over it like lightning out of a grey sky.

'You were there?' he asked.

She shook her head. 'I was at college. I was watching it on the TV, with some friends. But I've never forgotten it. And maybe it's one of the reasons I ended up becoming a journalist – so I could share my feelings with others.'

She returned to repacking her rucksack. 'Anyway – you have to understand he's a man who meant something to me – still does. A man who put himself on the line for his people. In the West hero is a cheap, devalued word, it means a rock star or a film actor or a football player, at best a soldier or policeman doing the job he chose to do. Not someone turning their back on all their previous life. Someone coldbloodedly choosing to face death for other people, because that's what their conscience tells them they should do. Like Mei Tei did.'

'How did he end up here?' asked Larsen.

She wasn't listening. The story continued to pour from her. 'Some time ago I heard from a contact of mine who works for the CIA what had happened to Mei Tei. He'd escaped after two or three years in prison in north-western China, fled into one of the ex-Soviet republics, and then applied for political asylum some-where in Scandinavia. It's taken me a year to find him. Not working all the time, of course, I had a living to make, but when I could. And at last I found him, or thought I had. Just at the very moment when he might be important once more.'

She pushed the last few things into her rucksack, and zipped it up, then lost herself in her thoughts.

'What do you mean?' prompted Larsen.

'You must realise the Chinese government is in trouble – the economic collapse in Japan and south-east Asia hurt it more than most people thought, then there was trouble repressing that

128

religious cult, the Falun Gong. Floods and famines over the past two or three years have also made people angry, and now discontent is spreading even into the countryside. Of course there's tight news control, but we know about protests in several Chinese cities, and at Wuhan there even seems to have been a temporary occupation of the Communist Party offices. Rumour says some sections of the army are growing restless too, as the government runs out of money. But there are no real leaders of the resistance. That's where Mei Tei could step in.'

Larsen thought back to the old man in his house overlooking Grindehval fjord. 'He is old.'

'So was Nelson Mandela. And he forged a new South Africa.'

'Mandela was the leader of his liberation movement. Your Mei Tei is just a bureaucrat who once stepped out of line. And surely if he had wanted to become a leader of resistance, then he would not have hidden himself away here.'

She shrugged. 'Perhaps he thought there was no hope. But now there might be, and he would be incredibly valuable. As a former administrator, and an ex-general, he'd reassure people. Chinese politics changes so slowly that many of the ruling élite must have known him, and men who wouldn't allow a student leader anywhere near the reins of power might accept Mei Tei. And so might the protesters. That's why he's so important – the man who could change China.'

Larsen's mind was struggling to come to terms with everything she had told him, with the sudden enormous expansion of the case he was dealing with. It seemed bizarre that the fate of great nations should touch this wild and lost part of Greenland, and even more ridiculous that the old man who enjoyed going for walks with Marianne might be thought of as the leader of 1300 million people.

If she was telling him the truth.

'OK,' he said at length. 'I'm going to continue with the questioning. If there's anything you want to say, signal to me, and we'll talk about it out here first.' He stopped, then put his hand on her bony arm.

'What is it?'

'You haven't told me why you think this man, Shu-fan, is here.'

She looked at him, then opened her hands. Long, tapering hands, white, untouched by the slightest hint of physical work.

'I reckon it's obvious,' she said unflinchingly. 'The Chinese government's probably confident of handling separate protests by the students and the city workers, and regional trouble in

Tibet and Xinjiang too. Even unrest in the bureaucracy and the army. But if someone could unite the different strands of discontent, then it's a whole new ball game. I think they found out where Mei Tei was, like I did, and they've sent people to kill him. I think that guy in there is an assassin.'

Shu-fan and his partner were sitting in the same places, with Adam, Karadi, Jokum and Yelmar still behind them.

Larsen took his position at the desk.

'Did you come here to find Mei Tei?' he asked sharply.

'Of course,' replied Shu-fan.

'Why?'

'To get him to speak out in our favour. Perhaps to persuade him to come back to China – when the time is right.'

Larsen masked his surprise. 'You chose a strange way of asking him for support.'

'What do you mean?'

Everyone seemed to think he was an idiot who knew nothing. Larsen's fist tightened over his pencil, then gradually loosened again.

'Very well,' he said calmly. 'I will go through your recent actions. Wearing ski masks, and carrying rifles, you and your partner attacked Mei Tei ten days ago. After the arrival of his housekeeper ruined your plan, you arranged for an assault on the house and the kidnapping of Mei Tei, and then murdered the housekeeper.'

Shu-fan shook his head. 'I do not know what you are talking about. Where is Mei Tei?'

'Why did you kill Inga Brønnestedt?'

'We have killed or hurt no one.'

'What about the attack on Mei Tei ten days ago?'

Shu-fan reached up and rubbed his chin, on which thin black stubble was just visible. 'That was not serious.'

'Explain,' said Larsen sharply, leaning forward.

'Several weeks ago, when he was still in Iceland, I tried to contact him through that woman who works for him . . .'

'Inga Brønnestedt, yes. How did you know her?'

'We found out who she was, then simply approached her and asked her to give Mei Tei a letter, which outlined the situation in China, and begged him to join us.'

Larsen wondered whether to switch his line of attack, then decided to leave the murder until later. He glanced at Kimberley Persac. Her face was as intent as a cat at a mouse hole.

'Why did you not go and see Mei Tei and talk to him your-selves?'

Shu-fan's eyes fell away. 'We thought it best that he did not see us.'

'Why?'

'I am telling you. After he received the letter, we waited, but he made no attempt to contact us. Our resistance group had suspected he might be reluctant to help – after all, he has done nothing since the Tiananmen Square massacre – so we decided to use our back-up plan. First we sent an anonymous warning that he was in danger, then we followed him here, to Greenland, contacted the woman again, and paid her to tell us when he was out, so that we could fake an ambush. We dressed ourselves up as frighteningly as possible, and attacked him on his way home. Of course we were not going to do anything to him, it was to make him think – to realise – that staying in Greenland was no longer safe, and that he must confront the real world again.'

Why don't people think that Greenland is the real world? wondered Larsen. It is to me.

'What do you mean?' he said.

'The idea was to force him to leave his hiding place. Then we would offer to protect him, and in exchange he would help us. We felt driving him out of isolation would psychologically encourage him to take a firm stand. To offer himself as a symbol of resistance to the men who govern China. Anyway, we had arranged for the housekeeper to chase us away, but of course he would expect us to return soon.'

Larsen changed his point of pressure. 'You are talking about the woman who is now dead.'

'I know nothing about that. I only spoke to her a few times.'

'Why was she helping you?'

'I told you, we paid her. But we also had to convince her that we were not Mei Tei's enemies. She was fond of him, and would not do anything against him.'

'So who killed her?'

Shu-fan said nothing.

'Perhaps it was just coincidence,' put in Kimberley, then caught Larsen's eye, and went a little red.

Larsen folded his arms, and frowned in concentration, remov-ing himself from the small crowded room, from everything except what lay in his mind. Carefully, painstakingly, he probed his thoughts.

Parts of what Shu-fan said dove-tailed neatly with what he

had observed. Most importantly, it explained why the two men who assailed Mei Tei had not simply shot him down, and why they taken to their heels at the sight of Inga, rather than killing her too. But why had she been murdered a few days later?

'What else can you tell me?' he demanded, bringing himself back to the present.

'Nothing.'

'And you have committed no crime except threatening behaviour?'

'We had every right to do what we did,' Shu-fan said, his face lit by pride and total belief. 'We are not only trying to save the soul of our nation, but also the lives of thousands of people. Perhaps more. No one knows how many died after Tiananmen Square, and the crisis now growing upon China is worse. If the old guard triumphs, the repression will be correspondingly worse. I believe Mei Tei can help to prevent that. What it comes down to is that anything we do that may save lives and free our nation is right. More, it is necessary. A historical necessity. We have to do it.'

Larsen sucked in his cheeks. For a moment his mind went back a dozen years to the pictures that had gone through the world like knife thrusts: the nameless young man using his defenceless body to bring a whole column of tanks to a halt; the weeping, wild-haired girl pleading with stone-faced soldiers; the lone man carrying the bloodstained clothes of his friend; the V for Victory signs waved by despairing students running to join a fight they could not win. All united by a determination to die for what they believed in. And in that moment he saw the same expression on the face of Ze Shu-fan.

'We have to,' repeated the young man fiercely, then turned and spoke to his partner. The two of them exchanged volleys of quick, sharp sentences.

Larsen broke their conversation with a voice like iron. 'And that was why you murdered Inga Brønnestedt.'

'No.'

'You have just said that the historical necessity of freeing your nation permits you to do anything. So killing is justifiable.'

Shu-fan set his jaw. 'If I felt I had to kill someone, I would.'

'Even someone completely innocent?'

'If it was necessary, yes. The good of the individual must bow to the good of the many.' Larsen was struck by the appearance of Marxist slogans in the mouth of someone who obviously considered himself a fierce anti-Communist. 'But the death of this woman was not necessary, and we did not kill her.'

'I would say you had the clearest possible motive for murder.' Larsen's voice was clear, precise, utterly lacking any hint of emotion.

'I don't understand.'

'You believe this old man may be the best chance your country has of freeing itself. You admit your plan is to pressure him into joining you. The focus of that pressure is to expose his weakness, to convince him that assassins are on his trail, and to reduce him to friendlessness. That is why you killed Inga Brønnestedt.'

'I would not do that.'

'You just told me that you would,' said Larsen gently.

Shu-fan opened his mouth, then slumped forward and hid his face in his hands as he saw the gaping trap he had fallen into.

Larsen signed to Adam to come over to him, then spoke quietly in Greenlandic. 'Is there anywhere in the village where we can lock these two up?'

'Yelmar has a shed round the back of our house. We could put a plank across the door to stop it opening.'

'I use that shed,' objected Yelmar, joining the conversation. 'Though I suppose –'

'How much?' said Larsen.

'A hundred kroner.'

'OK.'

'A day,' added Yelmar hastily.

'Maybe. We'll see. Anyway, take the man who hasn't been talking and put him in there, with some food and water if he wants it.'

Yelmar nodded, and he and Jokum ushered the younger Chinese man out. Shu-fan looked up and watched his partner taken away.

Larsen leant forward. 'If you want me to believe you, then you must help me. I need the answers to many more questions.'

'I will answer anything that does not put my friends or co-workers at risk.'

'How were you supplied?'

'We brought enough with us for several weeks, and our guns meant we could hunt if necessary.'

'How did you get here?'

'A seal hunter from Qeqertarsuatsiaat brought us – we thought it would be less noticeable to approach from the north, rather than Paamiut. We disembarked on the far side of Qeqertaq Island, and made our way round here. I am an experienced mountaineer, I have ...'

The words died in his throat, and he let out a strangled half-scream.

14

TREMORS

Larsen's brain reeled. The world seemed to be dissolving into liquid chaos. His paralysed body, even as it sat securely in a chair, felt as if it was falling to the ground. Yet there was no ground, nothing solid to provide security. Around him came distant shouts of shock and blind terror, but they were far away, at the end of a long, writhing tunnel. Nothing to do with him. Even though the terror they expressed was also present in him, a swirling cloud of fear he could not fight. He felt an overwhelming desire to hurl himself flat on the floor, close his eyes, and lie there until the anarchy that had seized everything in its nauseating clutch faded.

There was a violent clashing sound, the crash and thud of falling objects, and a feeling of rapid shocks, like angry blows delivered from two different directions. Gradually normality re-established itself and, to his astonishment, Larsen found himself sitting exactly where he had been. Nothing seemed to have changed, except that the coffee cups were on the ground and puddles of coffee were soaking into the wooden floor. Adam and Karadi were struggling unsteadily to their feet, their faces rigid with the aftermath of shock.

The overwhelming silence was broken by a shrill laugh. It was Shu-fan.

'Haven't you guys ever felt an earth tremor before?' he said. 'When I was stationed in Xinjiang, we used to have them every few months.'

'I felt one in Colombia one time,' said Kim. But her attempt to sound calm was betrayed by her quivering voice. 'It wasn't like that.'

Simultaneously Adam and Karadi burst into an explosion of questions. Larsen, still shaky, but confident in his ability to hide his fear, did the best he could to calm them.

'It was just a shaking of the earth,' he explained.

'I have never heard tell of such a thing in Kalaallit Nunaat,' said Adam.

At that moment the earth shook again, but not nearly

as strongly as the first time, and without the same hideous, irresistible sense that reality was being ripped apart.

'Aftershock,' said Shu-fan, as that strange, powerful shuddering died away. 'There'll probably be more spread over a few days, but much less violent.'

The door swung open again and Risa stood there, Edvarth trailing in her wake. Behind them were several other people.

It occurred to Larsen that the house where he was staying had become a de facto town hall.

'What the fuck was that?' demanded Risa, wide-eyed, breathless.

'Apparently it was an earth tremor,' explained Larsen.

'I've never known anything like it before.' Risa looked around. 'When I was at school, we were taught that Greenland is made up of the oldest rocks on the planet. I'd have thought that made us safe from this kind of thing – or was our teacher just talking trash?'

Larsen looked helpless. 'I don't know.'

'It gave me the crawls,' went on Risa, almost accusingly. 'I couldn't walk properly – it was as if my legs had turned to jelly.'

At that moment Anita burst in. She had a gaping cut in her head, which was sending a trail of blood down her left cheek, but she seemed unaware of it.

'Is Adam here?' she gasped.

He sprang forward. 'What is it? Marianne . . .?'

'No, no. I just wanted to make sure you were all right.'

'You're hurt,' he said.

'Only a scratch. Marianne slept through the whole thing, I can't think how.'

Risa came over to her. 'What happened to you?'

'I fell over. It was nothing . . .'

'Let me see.' Risa examined the cut in a businesslike way. 'It's not nothing, and it needs treatment. I suppose I'd better check the rest of the village as well.'

A couple of minutes later Larsen heard Risa, with the brisk, no-nonsense manner of the medical professional, telling people outside that there was nothing to worry about. The inhabitants of Ikerasak, unconvinced, drifted nervously away, discussing the event animatedly.

Larsen was finally left with Shu-fan and the American. He glanced at them, and felt at a loss, with no idea of what to do.

The sudden realisation that this case had the potential to directly affect the lives of untold millions had bewildered him. Mentally he had suffered an earthquake as violent, and as unexpected, as the tremor that had shaken the ground a few minutes before. But the psychological impact was harder to recover from.

Before he could rally his shattered forces, Kim was leaning down looking at him, with a pleading look on her face.

'Let me interview him,' she begged. 'Please, Sergeant.'

'But –'

'No, don't but me. Look, this trip is all me. I've paid for every last cent of it, and believe me it cost a fucking fortune. Greenland has got to be one of the most expensive places to go in the world, no question – as hard to reach as the Third World, but you pay First World prices. At the moment I stand to make roughly minus $10,000. But a heavy duty interview with our friend here is going to go someplace towards levelling things up.'

'You mean you would sell the interview?'

'Of course. I mean, Jesus, this is what I do! Everyone knows that China's bubbling like a hotpot coming to the boil. This guy's got an angle that not many people know. Now, if I –'

'This is a murder enquiry,' broke in Larsen firmly.

'Come on.'

'No.'

'Sergeant!' she appealed, her hands wide open. 'You have to help me on this one. I can make it good for you too. You know, kind of mix you into the story – people'll be real interested. Look, I'm not some unknown – I've had stuff published in *Time*, the *Washington Post*, the London *Guardian*, I've done TV stuff for CNN, you name it. When I file this story, people're going to want it. Believe me. And you can be a part of it.'

Larsen gave her a cynical smile.

'I mean it,' she insisted. 'It could be real good for you. Maybe a promotion, something like that. And anyway, it's important. It matters. It's big.'

Realising she was not persuading him, she switched approach.

'OK then, listen. I'm willing to offer you something I've never given anyone else any time. You can go through the story before I send it off, check what you want in it, and take out things you don't like. How about that? You can be a bloody censor. OK?'

'Don't tell me you've never had your work censored before,' said Larsen.

'Sure I have. But I told you how much all this means to me.

And what I haven't ever done is actually to offer censor powers to anyone. I'm giving them to you. OK? Please, Sergeant.'

Yet again Larsen saw pictures of Tiananmen Square flash subliminally across his mind. The thought of all the faceless nameless people who had died weighed down his conscience, and brought a fresh wave of fear upon him.

'I will tell you what I will permit,' he said at last. 'As long as you make no reference to the murder, direct or indirect, you may interview Shu-fan.'

'Great!' She bent forward and to his astonishment kissed him on the cheek. 'Thanks a million times.'

'OK. But there's something you have to do in exchange. I'm putting Shu-fan in your charge – it's your responsibility to make sure he doesn't escape.'

'How can I do that?' she said, startled.

Larsen shrugged. 'You could pay Nils, or Karadi, or one of the others to watch him. Or maybe you'd better put him with his partner in Yelmar's shed.'

'You're telling me to lay more of my money on the line?'

Larsen nodded. 'I'm relying on you,' he said seriously. 'If this man gets away, you're not the one who'll get into serious trouble. I will.'

She considered. 'You've got a deal.' She turned to Shu-fan and, to Larsen's astonishment, spoke to him in Chinese. He answered in the same language, and they spoke together for a couple of minutes, then walked out together.

'It's OK,' said Kim, over her shoulder. 'He's promised he won't try to get away. He'll talk to his comrade too, so we won't need the shed after all.'

'What makes you think you can trust him?'

'He wants the publicity. Just like most of us.'

She left.

Larsen had a conviction that he had made a bad mistake. If Shu-fan was lying, then he would take the first opportunity to escape. Or what if Kim was not the person she seemed to be? Perhaps he had fallen for some elaborate trick. On the other hand, it was clear Shu-fan did not realise that Mei Tei had returned to Greenland. And Larsen knew he would shortly have to go to see Norlund and the old man.

Two hours later, Larsen was called by Norlund, who sounded tense and distracted.

'Meet me at the landing place at ten tonight.'

'I thought I was coming to Paamiut.'

'Change of plan.'

'How about the old man? Is he –?'

'I'll tell you tonight.' Norlund rang off.

That evening Larsen went down by the fjord-side. The deep velvet shadows of the inner mountains, which themselves showed deep blue in front of a paler sky, lay heavily over the oily water, and where the sun was sinking, to the far north-west, there was a crimson glow in the sky, which caught the water of the open sea, and lent it flashes of transient reflected colour. The black sand of the foreshore glimmered. A faint noise crept into the silent landscape, and with it came a narrow beam of brilliant light, springing rapidly closer across the sea. The helicopter arrived in a thunder of noise and wind and glare. The Huey blades were still rotating as the door opened and Norlund came down.

'Where's the old man?' shouted Larsen, above the roar of the engine.

'He hasn't arrived yet,' replied Norlund. 'His flight was delayed.'

'Jesus, Pieter! You didn't leave him alone, did you?'

'It was necessary. I will explain.' Norlund glanced at the pilot, who was sitting by the controls, chewing gum. 'Let's go over there.' He pointed along the track back to Ikerasak.

'OK,' shrugged Larsen. He yawned. He felt tired and uncomfortable, and there was a stiffness about Norlund that he found irritating.

'What's been happening to you?' said Norlund, as they began walking back along the track.

Five minutes later Larsen finished describing the capture of the two Chinese men. Norlund seemed barely interested. Instead he glanced back over his shoulder, towards the helicopter, its lights just visible in the gathering gloom.

'I sent Wan Li to Paamiut by the southern route,' he said distantly. 'The plan is for him and me to hide out in an alpine hut near Paamiut, until the heat dies down.' He frowned. 'Is he the same man as this Mei Tei you are talking about?'

'I think he must be. But where have you been?'

'I acted as the bait for anyone trying to follow us, and came back via Nuuk.'

'Did you see the Chief?'

'Yes.' A momentary pause. 'I also saw my wife.'

'Has she had the baby yet?' asked Larsen, with a sudden sick feeling at the pit of his stomach.

'Very soon. She told me she had been taking precautions to ensure that there was no problem with the birth.'

'Good.'

'Good. Yes. Do you know the best way for a woman to make sure her labour starts in good time? Apparently it is to have sex. Did you know that?' He didn't wait for an answer. 'So yesterday, when I got home, she suggested I should oblige. I reminded her that I found pregnant women unattractive. So Gerda told me that fortunately other men didn't.'

Larsen stared at the ground. There was a stone by his foot, stained with grey and orange lichen.

'In fact,' Norlund ground on relentlessly, 'she told me you've been doing everything you could to help make sure that she gave birth to the baby in good time. That's right, isn't it?'

Larsen said nothing.

'Isn't it?' snarled Norlund, pushing his face at Larsen's.

'You've had your fun with other women,' retaliated Larsen.

'That is not your business. My wife is my business, and you've been screwing her behind my back. I don't even know if my baby is my own.'

'Don't worry –'

'Don't worry! Don't worry! What sort of crap is this you're selling me?' And suddenly Norlund exploded. 'You little piece of shit!' he snarled.

His fist scythed towards Larsen's head.

Larsen recoiled instinctively, and the blow caught him on the breastbone. It sent him staggering backwards, and he almost lost his balance as he stumbled over loose stones.

Norlund lunged after him, his lips bared back from his teeth like an angry dog. Larsen twisted away, and Norlund's clutching hands missed his throat.

'For Christ's sake, Pieter . . .' he gasped.

Norlund swung his fist at Larsen's stomach. Desperately Larsen blocked the blow, but Norlund countered by hurling a cluster of punches at him, his fists arcing in on Larsen's face with blistering speed. As Larsen tried to intercept the punches, Norlund changed his tactics, and began to hit Larsen in the body, rapid, straight-armed jabs, then he returned to Larsen's face again. Larsen fought back. He caught the taller man hard on the cheek, and knocked his head back, but it made no difference to that crazed assault.

Norlund unleashed another massive right hook, and as Larsen swayed back, Norlund grunted, and threw himself bodily forward. Larsen responded with a short clubbing blow, which caught Norlund on the side of the neck, rocking him. Larsen threw a second punch, then tried to break away, but another huge swinging blow caught him full in the stomach. It ripped through Larsen's muscles like a spear thrust, and a surging column of pain seemed to cut him in two. He doubled up, just as a flailing uppercut exploded against the side of his jaw. Unable to breathe, Larsen crumpled, gasping frantically for air to fill his empty lungs. A moment later a fresh blow sent him tottering to the ground.

'Pieter,' he gasped. 'Don't.'

There was no response, except the lashing out of a boot, that caught Larsen solidly in the ribs.

Norlund kicked again, but Larsen had recovered enough to grab Norlund's foot, and twist it round. Norlund let out a yelp, and crashed to the ground in his turn. Larsen crawled over to him and pinned the younger man to the ground, his knees trapping Norlund's arms, his heavy body pressing him against the stony ground. There was a trail of blood trickling from Larsen's mouth and a fast-growing swelling on his left cheek.

'Pieter,' he said. 'You must stop this. You must . . .'

Norlund's eyes were glazed and insane. He twisted and hooked out his leg, so that it caught Larsen round the throat, and wrenched him backwards. As he was brought slamming backwards, striking his head against a rock with a thud, Norlund jack-knifed upwards, then flung himself forward, so that now it was him who was on top.

Larsen lashed out wildly, but Norlund took the blows on his forearms, imprisoned Larsen's hands with his own, then bent forward and sent his forehead crashing sickeningly into Larsen's face.

'Pieter, stop! Stop!' screamed Larsen, as blood filled his mouth, and ran down his chin.

The only response was another stunning blow from that stone-hard forehead. With a huge effort Larsen hurled his body up. Caught unawares, Norlund lost his grip, and Larsen squirmed half-free, but Norlund snatched up a rock, and hammered at him. The blow caught Larsen on the shoulder and fresh pain lanced through his body. He tried to block the attack, but Norlund knocked aside Larsen's arms, and the rock battered into him again and again.

In desperation Larsen used every scrap of strength he had left to rip himself free. He staggered to his feet and tried to run, but stumbled and fell forward on his face. Norlund straddled him, and began striking him blindly with the rock. Larsen, helpless on his face, his arms trapped, slumped into a red haze of pain and nausea, that faded into black unconsciousness.

Suddenly, overhead, came the harsh call of a passing gull, hurrying back to its roost.

It acted as an alarm call. Norlund froze, then took a deep breath, and stared around him, as disorientated as if woken from deep sleep. He flung the bloodied stone away, scrambled off Larsen's back, and looked down at where his partner lay in a small hollow, daubed with blood, unmoving.

'Fuck!' he muttered, then turned and ran off through the gloom. Back to the waiting helicopter.

The helicopter pilot looked up. 'You took a while,' he remarked.

'We had a lot to discuss.'

The pilot laughed. 'Discuss?' he repeated. 'That's not what it looks like.'

Half an hour later they landed at Paamiut. Norlund went straight to the small building which served as the heliport.

'How long ago did the delayed flight from Narsarsuaq come in?' he demanded.

'About an hour and a half.'

'Did an old man get off.'

'Immaqa. Maybe.'

Norlund produced his police ID. 'I need to trace a passenger on that flight.'

A few questions were asked, a steward was found, and Norlund heard that a man who was clearly Wan Li had been on the flight. But he had left the heliport after they landed. Alone.

Norlund swore. Then a thought came to him that perhaps Wan Li, aware he might be being followed, and able to speak Greenlandic, had already got a boat to the alpine hut. It was approaching midnight, and Norlund was exhausted, and aching from his fight. He made his way to the Hotel Paamiut, took a room for the night, and fell asleep within moments.

Early next morning he returned to the harbour. The boatman who had been hired to take them up the fjord was there, but he had spent the evening in a bar, and knew nothing of Wan Li. However further enquiries around the harbour revealed that a man who sounded like Wan Li had been looking for a boat the previous night.

'He spoke to Gustavi,' said one of the fishermen, nodding. 'I heard them arguing. The old man said he had no money, but that he would pay at the destination. Gustavi refused to take him, but someone else did. I'm not sure who.'

'The old fool,' muttered Norlund. 'I told him to stay here until I came. He must have thought I was already at the hut.' He glanced around. 'Where's Gustavi?'

'Oh, he will not be up for some hours yet. Until midday at least.'

Norlund sighed irritably. 'I do not have time to wait. I want you to take me up Eqaluit, to Igdlorssuit.'

Kuanersoq fjord was speckled with rocky islets, milky green ice floes over which the waves washed, and small bergs, the size of a cottage, so the first half of the journey was not easy. At last they reached the head of the Eqaluit inlet, disturbing a huge vulturine sea eagle from its feasting on the remains of a dead seal. The hut, which served as a base for hunters, fishermen and an occasional hiker, was just visible a little way up the western shore, facing a small river valley. As Norlund jumped ashore, he saw clear marks of another boat having been recently drawn up on the thin strip of sand. There were also footprints leading along the faint track that zigzagged up the steep slope to the hut.

'Have you got a phone?' Norlund asked the boatman.

The man pointed to the mobile hooked up on the side of the boat.

'OK.' Norlund pulled out his notebook, and copied down the number. 'Stay here a few minutes. If I don't return you can go, and I'll give you a call if I need you again. OK?' He handed the boatman a couple of notes.

The boatman nodded.

As Norlund hurried up the track, rolling clouds brought a wave of drizzle with them.

It was a fairly steep climb, and Norlund thought the old man must have found it hard going. As he approached the hut, he stopped, suddenly worried that there had been a mistake. That the old man would not be there. Then, to his relief, he heard a sound of movement inside. Norlund composed his face to cold severity, for he was angry that the old man had ignored orders and come up here by himself. He strode up to the hut, and threw open the door.

15

THE END OF THE CASE

The morning was very windy. A fierce south-westerly lashed the ground, scattering the last rags of low cloud and mist, and the sun shone with a brittle brilliance. There had been another slight tremor during the night, and few people in Ikerasak had slept, but Risa felt a partial sense of relief, for she and Edvarth were leaving. And if there was one reason that Risa felt reluctant to go, it was not a reason she allowed herself to admit. As a practical woman she knew she must continue to live her life in the way it had gone for some years. What would happen when Edvarth left home, she did not know. Perhaps he would not leave – many young Inuit men did not. But except for a little tourism and a few shops and bars, the only real employers in Paamiut were the fish processing plant and the maritime training school. Somehow she could not see him working in either place.

Nils had promised to take them on his boat after lunch, so Risa was packing their few belongings. She was surprised there had been no sign of Larsen since the previous evening, but assumed he had come in late and gone out early. Nevertheless, she felt angry, for he knew she was due to leave the moment the weather improved. The packing took almost no time, so Risa began to clean the house. Sensing his mother's mood from the noisy way she was tidying up, Edvarth slipped away to see Marianne. He had grown fond of the quick, determined, serious little girl, and he wanted to say goodbye.

Marianne was not looking happy when he came into the house where she lived with Anita and Adam. She was on her own, wrapped up in a blanket, with the leg she had hurt stretched out in front of her on a stool.

'Hi,' said Edvarth. 'How are you?'

'Bored,' she said, her small, round face crinkling into a sterner frown, as if his arrival had made her even more bored. 'Aunt Anita won't let me out until tomorrow, but there's nothing wrong with my knee any more. I think she's doing it to punish me.'

'You could read.'

'I've read all my books a hundred times. I want to go out and look at my secret place, the place no one knows about except me and my grandpa. I was going to show you, but now you'll have to wait until tomorrow.'

Edvarth gave the embarrassed smile of a fourteen-year-old boy confronted by a strong-willed, young girl. 'That was what I was going to tell you. We're leaving Ikerasak today.'

'What?' Marianne sprang up, sending the stool tumbling to the ground. 'You can't leave today.'

'I'm sorry. My mother has to go back to her job.'

'Why can't she do it here? I'm sick. I'm hurt. She ought to look after me.' Marianne collapsed melodramatically back on to the chair. 'I can't walk.'

'It's only a sore knee,' said Edvarth.

'Men!' said Marianne bitterly. 'First my grandpa. Then you. No one ever stays with me.'

'It's not my fault . . .'

She wasn't interested in excuses. 'When are you going?'

'Soon.'

'Look, I'll tell you where my secret place is . . .'

'Marianne, I don't have time.'

The girl scowled. 'Go, then,' she said, and turned away from him. But Edvarth could hear that she was crying.

'I'm sorry,' he said again. She did not move, did not seem to have even heard him. After a moment he fled.

When he got back to the house, the fishing rod he had borrowed was outside the front door. Recognising the hint, Edvarth picked it up and took it back. Yelmar was sitting on a bench outside his house, gutting fish. He looked up as Edvarth came towards him.

'Thanks for lending me this,' said the boy.

Yelmar took it and laid it down on the ground. 'Is Nils taking you back today, then?'

Edvarth nodded.

Yelmar returned to gutting his fish, with swift confident strokes. 'He may be late.'

'What do you mean?'

'He went out yesterday, and he's not back yet. If he found a good fishing ground, he may be away for another day or so.'

'Oh. Thanks.'

For some reason, Edvarth found he was pleased at the news.

Risa had given up the cleaning and gone to look for Larsen. There was no sign of him in the village, but she remembered he

144

had said something about revisiting the geologists' camp. There was plenty of time before they were due to leave, so Risa set off at a brisk pace.

At the camp, Sigrid Heintze was sitting on a rock, out of the wind, typing into a laptop. As Risa approached, she looked up.

Her round fair face was alight with excitement and elation. 'It's happened,' she said, the words tumbling out of her. 'What I predicted. It's happened. I can scarcely believe it. They can't have missed those tremors – and they'll be arriving soon, hiring helicopters, coming as fast as they can. But we were here first. We've done it, and we've got the data.'

'Are you talking about the earth tremors?' asked Risa.

'Incredible wasn't it?' said Sigrid feverishly. 'People have been saying that the fish round here vanished a week or two ago. And we noticed there were almost no butterflies or birds either. It's as if somehow they knew this was going to happen. I've heard that in China they've managed to predict earthquakes by studying the behaviour patterns of pigs and chickens and farmyard animals.'

'I thought we didn't get earthquakes in Greenland.'

'No, that's not true.' Sigrid slipped easily into an academic lecturing style of speaking. 'There just aren't very many – and those are generally mild, maybe a maximum strength on the Richter scale of 4.1. There are actually two different sources of potential earth tremors here in south-west Greenland. One is proximity to the mid-Atlantic ridge, which is a major area of instability – look at Iceland, thirty odd volcanoes and hot springs all over the place, together with occasional earthquakes. The other is the fact that the Greenland ice sheet is receding, and the melting of ice caps has been demonstrated to cause earthquakes as the weight of ice is removed from the crust and the land readjusts. Global warming could mean earthquakes growing much commoner here.'

'Great!' said Risa. 'I was looking for Tomas Larsen.'

Sigrid wasn't listening. 'But it's never happened before, not like this, not in the whole history of geology. It wouldn't have happened this time if it hadn't been for a run of luck, but so what?' She clenched her fist triumphantly. 'I can just smell the lecture tours, the special papers, the universities begging me to join them. This is the big one, the lottery win. The moment that first tremor hit us, I knew I'd just fixed my life.'

'So you haven't seen Tomas Larsen then?' asked Risa, who could not have been less interested in Sigrid's life.

'What? Oh no. Sorry.'

Sigrid returned to typing hectically on her laptop.

Risa returned to the village. As she got back to the house, she heard a phone ringing. It was in Larsen's room, and she picked it up, surprised he'd left it behind.

'Hello?' she answered cautiously.

'Risa, is that you? This is Dr Lynge.'

Her heart fell. 'How did you get this number?'

'You gave it to me, don't you remember? Because your mobile doesn't work. Apparently there's been an outbreak of measles in Narssalik. Three children and two adults have caught it, and it sounds serious in a couple of cases. I'm tied up here, but I thought you could get out there today.'

'Not today, doctor. The boat can't leave until one, so I won't get to Paamiut before at least four.'

'Forget the boat. I've just spoken to the harbourmaster, and he says that as long as this wind persists any approach to Paamiut from the north would be very difficult, perhaps even dangerous. But don't worry, I've fixed a helicopter for you. It'll be with you in an hour or so, and will take you straight to Narssalik.'

As she came back downstairs, Risa was met by Edvarth.

'We can't get back to Paamiut today,' he said. 'Nils has gone off with his boat and –'

'It makes no difference,' said Risa, thin-lipped and curt. 'A helicopter's on its way for us.'

She ignored his crestfallen face.

Quarter of an hour later the two of them left the house, carrying their belongings. Anita was outside.

'Going?' she asked.

'Yes. Back to work.' Risa hesitated. 'I meant to say thanks to Sergeant Larsen, but he seems to have vanished. You haven't seen him, have you?'

Anita gave her a calculating look. 'Yesterday evening Adam saw the policeman on his way down to the landing place. Later he heard a helicopter land, stay for a short while, then leave again. Probably he was on that.'

'It would have been nice if he'd told us he was going,' said Risa. She was suddenly angry again at the wordless desertion. Even more than before. Perhaps because she was angry with herself for caring.

On their way along the track south, Risa shifted her heavy bag from one hand to the other, and wondered why, if he had left Ikerasak, all Larsen's belongings were still in the house.

'We must hurry,' she snapped, as Edvarth slowed and glanced over his shoulder, back towards the village.

'Why? The helicopter will wait for us, won't it?'

'The landing area is only clear of water for a few hours around low tide, and the pilot won't stay long.'

They continued round the side of the rugged hill, descending into a valley. Suddenly Edvarth stopped, and put his bag down on the stones.

'We must get on,' snapped his mother.

Edvarth shook his head, and put his finger to his lips.

'What is it?' asked Risa, in a quieter voice.

'I heard something.' Edvarth frowned and listened. 'There.'

Risa heard it this time. A faint scraping sound. 'It's just falling stones.'

As she spoke, there came the distant sound of rotor blades, and the helicopter appeared over the ice-flecked sea, flying in towards them. But Edvarth was climbing the hillside. Half-way up he vanished out of Risa's sight.

'Edvarth,' she shouted urgently, as the sound of the helicopter grew louder. 'There's no time to waste.'

But Edvarth was calling for her. She recognised the panic in his tone, put down her own bag and scrambled up after him.

'What is it?'

'The policeman. I think he's dead.'

Three weeks had passed when Larsen again entered the central police station in Nuuk.

Jette, small, dark and friendly, glanced up as he came in.

'Haven't seen you for a while,' she said. 'Been in a fight or two, have you?'

Larsen caught a glimpse of himself in a small mirror that hung on the wall. His broken nose still looked raw, the skin on his face retained the yellow smears of bruising, and there were slowly-healing scars on his forehead, and his cheek. But he was at last feeling himself again, and incredibly nothing had been broken except his nose. Even the aches were less every morning.

'I lost,' he replied.

'How did I know that?'

'Anything happen while I've been away?'

'You'll get most of what's been going on from the Chief. He's had his usual ups and downs, but the last few days he's been a real pussy cat – purring away over his new car, a great big four-wheel drive Volkswagen, which he can use to drive all the way from one side of Nuuk to the other, and back again. I did ask myself what's the point?'

'To show he's the Chief,' said Larsen.

Thorold was absently smoothing down his thinning pale hair with his hand when Larsen came in. His expression contained a rich medley of emotions, but his voice was friendly.

'Well, Tomas, after very serious consideration, I've decided to pass over all the dubious goings-on you and your partner got up to. I'm sure you won't behave in such a foolhardy manner again, especially after your incredibly fortunate escape. As you no doubt know, the doctor considered that a second night outside in the state you were in would have probably been fatal.'

'Yes, sir.'

'Anyway, I put the blame for most of this at Pieter Norlund's door. I must say I am very disappointed in Norlund. It never occurred to me that he was such an unreliable and violent officer.'

'I think the fault was more mine than his, sir,' Larsen said stolidly. 'It was I who . . .'

Thorold smiled and held up his hand. 'Very good of you to offer to take the blame, Tomas. But it's not necessary, I assure you. Pieter Norlund has been discharged from the Royal Greenland Police Force.'

'What for, sir?'

'Violent assault upon another officer for one thing, and desertion of his duty for another.'

'Desertion?' repeated Larsen, staring.

Thorold coughed slightly, and a stern expression spread over his pale face. 'After he arrived in Paamiut, we lost all contact with him. Until I received this.'

It was a short, typed note. 'Chief, I'm sick of being a policeman. I've had enough of this country too. Like being a cop, it's only for suckers.' At the bottom was a crudely scrawled signature.

'Where was it sent from?' asked Larsen.

'Narsarsuaq airport.'

'There's no question that Norlund sent it?'

'None at all. That's his signature, and he booked an SAS flight from Narsarsuaq to Copenhagen the same day this was sent. The booking clerk, the ticket officer, and one of the stewardesses all remember him. He was travelling alone, and he got out at Copenhagen. We have no other news of him.'

148

'Has his wife heard anything?'

'No. Not a word. She gave birth to a baby girl two and a half weeks ago, and is now back home. We have shown her the letter, but she seemed unmoved. I do not think there was a deep relationship there.'

'No,' said Larsen, thinking of Gerda. 'No, I don't think there was.'

'He has clearly lost himself in Denmark, like so many others. As the only thing he could be charged with is spending police money without authorisation, and as it would cost more to track him down than he spent, I have decided to forget the whole business. And of course,' Thorold gave a somehow unconvincing smile, 'it does improve your chances of promotion, Tomas. One rival out of the way, eh?'

Larsen summoned a ragged smile of his own. 'What about the Mei Tei business, sir?'

'Ah, yes.' A shadow passed over Thorold's countenance. 'Well, it was all a bit of a mess. Though I must say, you demonstrated great doggedness, and one or two flashes of inspiration, in uncovering part of what had happened.'

'Thank you, sir. I learnt a lot from –'

'Quite so, quite so. I should make the point that there were some wild inaccuracies in your depiction of events. However the two men you captured were indeed working for a resistance group dedicated to overthrowing the Chinese government and, as you found out, they were trying to frighten the old man who calls himself Mei Tei into joining them. They have been put on a flight to America, after official notification that they are no longer welcome to return to Denmark or Greenland.'

'What will happen to them?'

Thorold shrugged. 'Not our problem. Maybe the Americans will give them asylum.'

And if not, they would be sent back to China, where they would quietly disappear, thought Larsen. Then he picked up on the Chief's careful choice of words.

'What do you mean the man who calls himself Mei Tei?' he asked.

'The man is an impostor.'

'An impostor!'

'I'm afraid so. He seems to have fooled many people, including Shu-fan and his party, and at least two Western governments, so you should not feel bad that you were also taken in. But I am informed there is no longer any doubt about the matter. The real Mei Tei is dead.'

'I do not understand. Who were those armed men who kidnapped him?'

'You should have listened to what I told you at the time, Tomas,' said Thorold, looking pleased with himself. 'They were members of the Danish Special Forces. Although there was suspicion of the identity of the Chinese man, final proof was lacking, so it was decided he must be removed from Ikerasak, partly in case he was in danger, mainly for questioning. I must say, I cannot see why they thought it necessary to send so many armed men in. Anyway they took him back to his main asylum, in Iceland.'

'Near Lake Myvatn, yes.'

Thorold nodded, though his thin-lipped mouth was now tight shut. Like a trap.

'Was it you, or Norlund, who discovered that?' he asked, after a moment.

'Me, sir.'

'There was some surprise that the hideaway had been discovered. I suppose the old man let it slip.'

Larsen said nothing.

'Anyway, it would have been better if you had not informed Norlund. As you know he set off to Iceland by himself, found the man, and brought him back to Greenland. But you will be glad to hear that Danish Special Forces tracked them, and the impostor was rearrested and taken away – presumably to Denmark. We won't be troubled with him again, that's for sure. So there you have the whole story. Everything has ended happily – as you can see.'

Larsen nodded. 'Happily,' he repeated. 'The Danish have covered up their blunders. The Chinese resistance have been made fools of, and the Chinese government does not have to face a dangerous enemy.'

'It is never wise to meddle with international politics, Tomas,' said Thorold warningly. 'Greenland, I mean Kalaallit Nunaat, is a small country, and should not get involved in such things.'

'Yes, sir. There is one thing left though.'

'What is that?'

'The murder of the housekeeper, Inga Brønnestedt, sir.'

'Ah, yes.' Thorold breathed in then out through his teeth. 'Sadly nothing can be proved. At least not with enough evidence to bring the matter to court. I'm afraid it is one of those unsatisfactory situations where we must let the case drop. The bane of policing, I call them. But they do occur, and we all have to put up with them, eh?' His smile did not spread to his eyes.

'What do you think happened, sir?'

Thorold shrugged. 'I think it is suggestive that the woman had just ended a sexual liaison with one of the Ikerasak men, and begun a new one with another.'

'That goes on all the time, without murder resulting,' said Larsen, aware as he spoke that harping on about a subject that the Chief clearly wanted to see closed could damage his chances of promotion. On the other hand, he doubted that he had any real chances of promotion.

'True,' said Thorold. He hesitated, then went on. 'There is another possibility, but you must understand that no discussion of this case is to go beyond this room.'

'Yes, sir.'

'Inga Brønnestedt had been in touch with the two Chinese men, and had sold information to them. After the arrival of the Danish forces, and the removal of the old man, she did not tell Shu-fan and his companion what had happened. I suppose she thought she could make more money out of them by pretending the pseudo-Mei Tei was still living there. That is why the two men were still camping in the mountains after their quarry was gone.'

Larsen nodded.

'Anyway,' continued Thorold, 'it seems very possible that Shu-fan and his partner found out they were being fooled, and killed her – either in revenge, or in fear she might expose them. However we have no evidence, and the men denied it, so we couldn't charge them.'

'I suppose the Danish government didn't think it was worth prosecuting them either,' said Larsen.

Thorold looked at him. 'I think the Danish government is well aware that this episode does not show them in a good light. Anyway, that is how things stand, and that is as far as they will go. A little unsatisfactory in some areas, I agree, but it is time to settle back to the usual round of work. Talking of which, there is a case of larceny in Blok P that I would like you to look into this morning . . .'

That evening, after work, Larsen went round to Norlund's flat, and rang the front door. There was no answer. An elderly woman appeared at the next door.

'They've left,' she said. 'The girl had a baby, and the father

151

took off. Like men do.' Then she peered at Larsen with shrewd eyes. 'You used to come round here sometimes, didn't you?'

'I'm looking for Gerda.'

'She's gone back to her mother. Like girls do.'

'Where's that?'

'One of the older houses looking down on the sea. Jonathan Petersensvej, number 30 I think. I suppose her husband found out it was your kid. I hope you'll look after the little thing.'

'It's not mine,' said Larsen.

Her lip curled in disbelief.

Gerda and her family lived in a detached house, rather than one of the grey, sprawling apartment blocks which held most of Nuuk's soaring population. It was crowded and hot, and Gerda was cooking in the cramped little kitchen. She looked little different from the last time he had seen her – her belly still rounded though less than before, her breasts full, her face round and determined. She looked at him without surprise.

'Pieter's left me.'

'I know.'

'My fault, really. I told him about you.'

'Why?'

She shrugged. 'I don't know. He was getting on my nerves with his refusal to sleep with me. Mind you, now I'd be only too pleased. Would you like to see Nuka?'

The baby was fast asleep in a basket, sprawled under a knitted blanket, with her tiny hands just visible. Her long eyes under long eyelashes were closed, her big lips partly open. Her head was scattered with long thin black hair, making a faint halo around her face.

'She doesn't sleep much,' remarked Gerda, gazing down at her dispassionately. 'But she eats well. It's good I've plenty to give her.'

Larsen bent down to look at the baby more closely, and remembered Vigdis when she had been a baby. But she had not looked at all like Nuka. And it was eight years since he had seen his younger daughter. Half her life. She was almost an adult now. Gently he touched one of Nuka's tiny hands, but she did not move.

'Any news of Pieter?' asked Gerda.

'He's gone to Denmark – did they tell you?'

'They did, but I'd already guessed. I think he was an ambitious man, though God knows what he'll do there.' She seemed to be

152

talking about someone she had barely known. 'Do you want a coffee?'

'No thanks.'

'OK.' Gerda looked at him. 'You're worrying about me, aren't you? That's kind, but you don't need to. I'm with my family – there's nothing for you here.'

'I suppose not. I'm sorry Pieter ran out on you.'

She shrugged. 'There are other men out there. When I'm ready.'

As he left, Larsen again glanced down at the baby. Suddenly Nuka opened her eyes wide and stared up at him. The eyes were beautiful, almond-shaped and a colour that was indescribable, a rich amalgam of blue, purple and brown. Larsen stared down at them entranced, then smiled at the little girl, waving his fingers at her.

He walked out into a grey, cool evening, with a wind rising from the sea. Heavy clouds were slowly rolling in over the Davis Strait.

16

DECISION

Larsen was lying on his bed, reading a science fiction novel. Outside it was one of those rare perfect late summer days when the August sun shone down on Nuuk as if it meant it. Larsen's window was wide open, and he half wanted to seize this chance and go for a long walk – but somehow he could not gather up the energy.

Suddenly irritated, he flung the book aside, and got to his feet. A copy of the *Herald Tribune* lay on the floor – he had spent far too much on it two days before because of the headline plastered across its front page: 'China on the Brink'.

The story had not been worth the hype of the headline. Apparently there had been strikes and rioting in three or four cities, two members of the government had been expelled from office, and certain areas of the country had been made no-go areas for Western journalists because of 'banditry' – but that had happened before. One top American Sinologist had announced China was facing a massive internal crisis which could threaten the Communist Party dictatorship. Another equally eminent expert declared this was just the usual reaction to a couple of poor harvests – and the sacrifice of a few officials and some government food aid would soon sort matters out.

On an inside page there was also a short feature on the so-called lost leader of China's resistance – Mei Tei, whose death had just been announced. He was a Sichuan farmer's son, who had been taken on the legendary Long March by his parents when only a child. He joined the Red Army as a teenager, and had fought the Japanese, the Chinese Nationalists, and the Americans during the Korean war. Despite the savage twists and turns of Chinese politics, he had steadily climbed the political ladder, and in the 1980s was linked with the liberal wing of the party, and its leader, Zhao Zhiyang. Then had come 26 May 1989 when, at the age of sixty-one, he had been the only member of the ruling hierarchy to speak out publicly in favour of the students who occupied Tiananmen Square. For a short while it seemed the uprising might have found a leader, but even before the army's attack, Mei Tei was arrested. He had been imprisoned for two or three years, escaped to Kazakhstan, and was granted political asylum in an unknown place in the West. There he stayed quietly, until 1997 when he returned to China, and wrote a long, formal apology for his past actions. He had been given work as a minor official in Xinjiang, and had died in Urumqi of cancer some weeks earlier.

Larsen thought back to the quiet-spoken old man, with the thoughtful face. He could imagine that man had, for a fleeting moment, felt the wings of history touch him with an outstretched feather. Yet he was a fake.

Larsen threw the newspaper in the bin, made himself a coffee, and sat down in front of some televised English football. Suddenly the telephone rang.

'Is that Tomas Larsen?' asked a woman's voice, cautiously.

'Who is this?'

'It's Risa.'

He felt a tightening sensation in his throat. 'How are you?'

'This is not a social call, Tomas. I'm in Ikerasak, and the old Chinese man is here.'

'What?' Larsen almost dropped his telephone.

'I was called out here because a couple of people had gone down with a gastrointestinal infection – I think they'd been eating a seal that had died some time before. Anyway, I brought Edvarth with me, and he went to see Marianne. She told him the old man arrived back the same day we took you off to hospital, and he's been here ever since. Living with Marianne, Anita and Adam.'

'This has to be a mistake.'

'No. I've just met the man. Anita told me he was a distant relation of theirs from Canada, who's lost his family, but I'm sure it's him.'

'How can you be sure? You never saw him.'

'Tomas, will you stop being such a bloody questioning policeman. I'm telling you, the man staying with Anita and Adam is not some old hunter from Igloolik. He carries himself like someone who means something, who's wielded power. You don't see that in many of our people. And why should Marianne say it was him if it wasn't? You know how she loved that old man.'

'True. But –'

'Shut up saying but. It's him. Nils must have brought him here – he was supposed to be ferrying me and Edvarth that day, but he mysteriously vanished.'

'But I was told –'

Risa exploded. 'I don't care what the fuck you were told, Tomas. He's here. There are no minders, no housekeepers, no security guards, no soldiers, nothing. Just the usual summer population of Ikerasak – and this old Chinese general.'

Larsen recovered his balance. 'He's not an old Chinese general. He's an impostor. The real Mei Tei went back to China three years ago, and died a few weeks ago.'

There was a long silence at the end of the telephone.

'Died?'

'Yes. Cancer. It was in the newspapers.'

'Then it must be true!'

'My Chief told me the same thing.'

'You told me he likes to believe exactly what he's told by his superiors.'

'Yes, but –'

'Look, Tomas. I don't know what the hell this is all about, but strip it down any way you like, and you've still got a murdered woman, and an old Chinese man who was kidnapped.'

'It's sorted out.'

'Is it? I'm glad you're so confident. It's always nice to know that you don't have to do anything, isn't it?'

'Risa,' he protested. 'That's not fair.'

'What's fair? I think there's a lot of shit about this business – and not just in the fact that you haven't tried to contact me once since I left you in the hospital. Anyway, if you change your mind, or if you think maybe you need to know a bit more, then ring me.' She gave him her mobile number, then added abruptly, 'And if you don't call me, you can fuck off for good.'

The phone went dead.

Larsen sat there in confusion, struggling with contradictions, suddenly attacked by emotions he thought were under control.

His eyes fell on the cassette recorder, and he remembered the tape of reminiscences. After searching it out, he listened to it again, and found his doubts growing. The passing reference to 1989 sounded convincing, and why would an impostor record his memories anyway? Perhaps there were other clues in the tape – for example where were the Mountains of Heaven that the old man referred to?

Larsen searched his atlas without success, then rang a friend who worked in the library on Skibshavnsvej.

'I'm trying to trace the Mountains of Heaven.'

'Not on our maps, I'm afraid, Tomas. Try the Church of Our Saviour.'

'I'm serious. I think they may be in China, or somewhere nearby, probably under a different name.'

'I'll do what I can.'

A while later the librarian rang back.

'The Mountains of Heaven, otherwise known as the Tien Shan, are in Kazakhstan, on the Chinese border. Why on earth are you looking for them?'

'Crossword clue,' said Larsen.

'You do tough crosswords.'

'True. Thanks.'

Larsen's face hardened. The real Mei Tei had taken refuge in Kazakhstan, and the tape referred to a range of mountains in the same country. It looked more and more as if Risa was right, and the case was surrounded by a thick cloud of lies.

If the real Mei Tei was dead, as everyone said, then that was that. But the Chinese government had good reason to persuade people that he was dead – so anyone who claimed to be Mei Tei could be dismissed as an impostor, and the resistance would lose its leader. And the Danish government might collude in the deception to avoid angering China – one of the prime demands in exchange for political asylum was usually that the subject cease all political activity.

But if Mei Tei was not dead, then people must surely be looking for him: Danish Special Forces; members of the Chinese resistance; journalists like Kim Persac; perhaps others. And what of the murdered Inga? He found it hard to think of Shu-fan as a murderer. The man had been an idealist, but for all his bluster, he had not come over as a fanatic who would cold-bloodedly kill for his ideals.

Larsen resolved to return to Ikerasak, but this time he would have to do it more carefully, and take care to cover his tracks. Then, in a flashing moment of inspiration, he saw a possible way.

He rang Risa back.

'Hello?' came her sharp, businesslike tones.

'It's Tomas.'

'Well?'

'You're right. It needs looking into.'

'So what're you going to do?'

'It won't be easy, the Chief says the case is closed. But I'll try to be on tomorrow's flight into Paamiut. If you don't hear from me, make sure Nils is in the harbour, ready to bring me to Ikerasak. OK?'

'OK. But look, aren't you going to make people suspicious by coming back here?'

'I don't think so,' said Larsen. 'I've an idea.'

There was a pause at the far end of the line.

'You sound as if you're laughing, Tomas,' said Risa, her tone mingled accusation and suspicion. 'I don't understand.'

'You will.' He rang off.

First thing next morning, Larsen went in to see Chief Thorold.

The Chief was filling in a complex report form, and his face was a mask of pedantic concentration.

'What is it?' he asked, without looking up.

'There's a missing person alert in Paamiut, sir,' said Larsen. 'I'd like permission to go and investigate it.'

'Out of the question,' said Thorold, still not looking at him. 'The police on the spot can handle it perfectly well.'

'Well, you see, there's something else, sir,' said Larsen awkwardly.

This time Thorold did look up. 'Yes?'

'As you know, I'm due five days' leave over the next two months, and I'd like to take them from today.'

'That's unacceptably short notice,' snapped the Chief.

'I know, sir. I'm very sorry. You see . . .' Larsen looked away, then at the ground, then back at the Chief, who was watching him with an odd expression on his face. 'You see, there was a woman I met in Paamiut, a nurse . . .'

Thorold laughed. 'I see. You want to spend the week with her, and you want the police to fly you there and back.'

'It's more than that, sir.'

'Well?'

'I want to marry her, sir.'

Thorold stared at him in astonishment. 'I didn't think you were the marrying kind, Sergeant. Well, I know you tried it once – but that was a long time ago, wasn't it?'

'I want to try again, sir.'

'Brave man. About this trip to Paamiut though, I'm sorry. We can't possibly afford to put it on police expenses.' He folded his arms judicially. 'But as this is a special case, I'll tell you what I'll do. A couple of weeks ago there was a fight on the flight from Nuuk to Narsarsuaq, so I'll send you on that – as a security precaution, you understand. That way Grønlandsfly can pay.

And from there you'll probably be able to fix yourself a lift on the connecting flight to Paamiut. OK?'

'Thank you, sir. Thank you very, very much.'

Thorold beamed with the self-satisfied contentment of someone who is able to do a favour without it costing them anything. 'Of course you realise that this is not to be taken as any sort of precedent, Tomas?'

'Yes, sir. Of course.'

'Best of luck.'

'Thank you, sir.'

There was no sign of Nils at Paamiut harbour, and Larsen muttered curses as he walked slowly up and down, looking at the fishing-boats. After a few minutes he recognised Nils's battered vessel, the *Sea Wolf* – but it was empty. Larsen considered for a moment, then walked along the quay to a largish shack at the far end. It was like a hundred similar places that Larsen had visited, full of people, hot and sweaty, the music drowning a chatter of words.

Nils was by the bar, sitting on a stool. He emptied a can of beer down his broad throat, then turned back to a group of men around him, continuing to talk in an animated manner, and waving his hands so that he almost knocked over someone else's beer.

Larsen pushed his way over towards him.

'I mean who is he?' Nils was saying. 'What's he doing in Ikerasak? I've been warned not to tell anyone about him, but why not? If people are looking for him, what do they want him for? What's it all about? A mystery, that's what it is.'

'Where's he from?' asked a large, blond man.

'Who knows? He's not from round here, or from Tanu. Not from Denmark either. So what the fuck is he doing in this arse-end of nowhere?' He began on another beer, before continuing. 'I mean, it's nothing to me. Ferrying him in and out is all money.'

Larsen tapped Nils on the shoulder. He started, then grinned broadly.

'Have a drink.' He waved towards Larsen. 'This man, I forget his name, is a policeman. In the bad old days he could have checked our ration cards, and arrested us for drinking when we weren't allowed to.' Nils laughed loudly. 'But now he can go screw himself!'

'Police!' said the fair man, with a sarcastic whistle. 'We'd better watch our steps here, boys. If we get troublesome he might arrest us and ... er. What exactly might he do to us?'

'Put us in prison?' suggested another Greenlander, joining in the fun. 'Oh dear, the nearest prison is hundreds of miles away.'

Nils almost choked on his beer.

'Cut out the comedy,' said Larsen wearily. 'You're supposed to be taking me to Ikerasak.'

'So I am,' said Nils, slipping off his stool and standing unconvincingly at attention. 'You and some more stores. They're in the boat ...' He almost lost his balance, and gave a giggle. 'Not that I should say that out loud, or these fuckers will be slipping away and stealing them.'

'Let's go,' said Larsen impatiently.

'Haven't finished my drink.' A light flashed across Nils's saturnine countenance. 'Hey! Maybe you could tell my friends here what that old man is doing hiding away.'

'I don't know what you're talking about. Let's go.'

'You see,' appealed Nils. 'No one'll talk about it. That Anita, she got sore when I tried to find out what was going on. I mean, isn't a man entitled to ask a few questions now and then?' He finished his can of beer, then turned his attention back to Larsen. 'For that matter, why're you going back?'

'There was a murder there,' Larsen reminded him.

'Inga.' A strange expression flashed across his face, and vanished. 'I think maybe she just caught her head on a rock, then fell into the water. Enough people do that. Especially when they're drunk.'

'Like you,' said Larsen wearily.

Nils glowered.

'I'd get drunk if Yelmar had just started screwing me – like her.' He frowned, sensing his words had come out wrong, then pulled out a cigarette and lit it with some difficulty. 'But I'm not drunk. Look. I can even stand up.'

The people around clapped as he demonstrated.

'Awesome,' said Larsen. 'Now come on.'

The trip to Ikerasak seemed to take longer than usual, but Nils guided the boat with his usual confidence. It was hard to believe that the efficient, silent man at the wheel was the same as the garrulous show-off in the waterside bar.

There was no sign of life at the landing place.

'Where is everyone?' asked Larsen.

'Some have gone back to Paamiut,' replied Nils, manoeuvring the boat in towards the stony beach at the foot of the steep slope.

'The fishing has been bad this summer, and the shaking earth has frightened people.'

'Who's still here?'

'Anita and Adam and Marianne, because Adam spends most of his time hunting. Then there is Yelmar, who is a good enough fisherman to catch fish when no one else can, and who says he has spent every summer in Ikerasak since he was a little boy and he is not going to stop now. Aqqaluk and Mada have stayed also with Enok, and Jokum, Kunarat and Johanna – but they've been ill, and will probably leave as soon as they can. The geologists are still here too. They are very pleased about something.'

At that moment there was a distant roar. Larsen looked about warily, then saw a plane, a sliver of silver high in the white sky, leaving a jet-trail behind it.

'Planes have passed over us several times,' said Nils. 'It has hardly ever happened before.'

'Perhaps they've changed one of the flight routes. Is Risa here?'

'The nurse? She arrived yesterday morning to treat Kunarat and Johanna. I do not know if she is still there.'

'When did everyone leave?'

'Most left a week ago, after the latest earthquake.'

'And no one else has been around?'

Nils sucked in his cheeks thoughtfully. 'There've been a few people around Ikerasak these last weeks. Tourists even.'

He backed the boat up, until it nudged against the flat stones that made up the beach, then gestured to Larsen, who took the rope, splashed into the shallow water, and looped it through one of the mooring rings. Nils followed him ashore, tied off the back half of his boat to a second ring, then began to unload the supplies. Larsen helped him, putting the boxes on the shore, above the high water mark.

'Do you often get tourists here?' asked Larsen, as they trudged back and forth.

'No. Never before. But it is the way things are going – people from outside who come to look at eagles, whales, icebergs, whatever. It would be cheaper for them to stay at home and look at things on television.'

'Were any of these tourists around when Inga was murdered?'

Nils looked at him in surprise. 'Why should a tourist murder Inga?'

'Maybe they are not tourists.'

Nils brooded on this for a while, then shook his head. 'I don't

161

know what you are talking about,' he said, setting off up the slope into Ikerasak, carrying several crates.

Larsen picked up a couple of boxes and prepared to follow him, when there was a rattle of stones, and Marianne appeared, springing sure-footed down the path.

'I thought it was you,' she said. 'Risa said you were coming. Shall I help you carry things?'

'Thank you.'

She snatched up some tins and followed Larsen up the hillside.

'Are you going to talk to grandpa?' she asked breathlessly.

'That's right.'

'It's good that he's back, isn't it? And staying with Aunt Anita and me too. But he seems different.'

'How different?'

She frowned. 'Sort of nervous. I think perhaps he is worried. Sometimes he goes for walks, and when I try to go with him, he sends me away. He has never done that before. Perhaps it is because of poor Inga. I mean, I never liked her, but I suppose he did – and of course Nils did.'

Larsen stopped. 'Why did Nils like her?'

Marianne looked at him wide-eyed. 'They were friends,' she said.

'Close friends?'

'Of course. When he came to see her, they would go into Inga's room and not come out for a long time. Grandpa and I were always pleased when that happened, because we could do what we liked, without Inga interfering. Sometimes they had terrible rows and shouted at each other. One time she threw the cooking pots at him, which was fun. I watched from outside. But another time they fought each other, like dogs, snarling and hitting each other, until Inga hid in the bathroom and locked the door. That was horrible.'

'Nils told me that Inga was . . .' Larsen paused. 'A friend of Yelmar's.'

Marianne shrugged. 'After the fight, Nils did not come back, but I don't know about Yelmar. I never saw him at grandpa's.'

It occurred to Larsen that he had been so certain Inga's murder was linked to Mei Tei, that he had made no attempt to look into the background of Inga herself.

'Come on,' said Marianne impatiently, and she set off up the path again.

162

17

MEI TEI

The old man was sitting in an upright wooden chair, looking at Larsen through his thick spectacles. Marianne was sitting at his feet, and the old man's wrinkled hand gently brushed her thick black hair.

'Good afternoon, Sergeant,' he said courteously.

'There are questions I need to ask you,' said Larsen.

'Need? Is that the word?' He glanced up. 'Anita, please make tea for our guest.'

Anita was already coming in with a pot of tea. Larsen sat down opposite the old man, and set out his tape recorder on the table.

'I would prefer to interview you alone,' he said.

'They stay if they wish,' the old man answered. His voice had an underlying determination that sounded immovable.

'As you like.'

The old man slowly produced a cigarette, lit it and began to smoke.

'I shouldn't do this, should I?' he said. 'But I think it is too late to worry now.'

Larsen turned his tape recorder on.

'Tomas Larsen. Interviewing, August 3rd. Could you tell me your name?'

'Wan Li.'

'So you are not Mei Tei?'

'Mei Tei was a leader of the Hsiung-nu nomads, who inflicted a humiliating defeat on the Han emperors over two thousand years ago.' He sighed. 'China's history is like anklets of stone, that keep the nation always bound down.'

'Are you telling me that there is no Mei Tei now?'

'In a way that is precisely what I am telling you.'

'In a way? What do you mean?'

'Mei Tei is a name I adopted. In my youth I wanted to model myself on the great Russian revolutionaries – and as they took pseudonyms like Lenin, Stalin, and Trotsky, so I called myself Mei Tei, after the man who rocked an empire.'

'So you are Mei Tei then?'

'I was once. Now I prefer my real name, Wan Li. With old age I have rediscovered myself.'

Larsen hesitated. A strange clarity was stealing over him. He felt apart, distanced from the gloomy room. Everything seemed to be coming into sharp, tight focus. The old Chinese man was looking at him. Waiting.

'The Chinese Communist general, Mei Tei, is said to have died of cancer a few weeks ago while working as a minor official. Do you claim that is a lie?'

'Do you believe it?' countered the old man.

'Why should people say a man is dead when he is not?'

'Perhaps because they think and hope that this man, who is me, soon will be dead. But explaining what is in the Chinese media has always been an unwinnable game.'

Larsen considered that for a moment. 'Can you provide evidence the Chinese claim is a lie?'

'Evidence as to who I am,' mused the Chinese man. He gave an ironic laugh, then lay back and closed his eyes for a long moment. 'I suppose I am that evidence.'

'What are you talking about?' interrupted Marianne. 'I don't understand.'

'The Sergeant wishes to know if I am who I say I am.'

'Of course you are. That's a stupid idea.'

Larsen reached out and clicked off the tape recorder. 'You can talk to me off the record, if you prefer.'

'To satisfy your curiosity, you mean.'

'No,' said Larsen, sensing hostility creeping into the air. 'I am trying to find out what happened to the woman who was your housekeeper.'

'I do not know what happened to Inga. Why should you think my name, and who I am, is relevant to her death?'

'Inga Brønnestedt was murdered,' said Larsen. 'Someone smashed her head in, and threw her into the fjord. I want to know why and who did it.'

The old man bent forward in his chair. His face was set and vehement.

'Millions of men and women are killed without good reason every year. Everyone in the West knows about the First World War and the ten million who died, but who knows how many died in the Chinese wars between 1911 and 1949? Twenty million perhaps? Maybe more. But they were just Chinese, so it is not important. Yet if a couple of Americans die in Kosovo or East Timor, then we will all be told, and international government

164

policies will change. In China half a million can die without leaving a shadow on the face of the world.'

'That is not my problem,' said Larsen, fighting against the entanglements of a long lost past.

'Which is what everyone says.'

'Whether one person dies, or a million, they are all individuals. As such, they deserve respect and that means their killers should be brought to justice.'

'Ah. Justice. More slippery than any eel.'

'My job is to find and arrest Inga's killer.'

'You shouldn't be talking about these things,' objected Marianne suddenly. 'I don't like it.'

The old man patted her on her head again. 'Go and look for Edvarth,' he said.

'I want to stay here. With you. In case you go again.'

'I am not going.'

Reluctantly she stood up, then darted forward and kissed his lined old cheek, before turning and running upstairs.

The old man looked after her. 'I have upset her,' he mused. 'That kiss was a reproach that I deserved.'

He turned his attention back to Larsen. 'Let us get this over as quickly as possible. I do not know anything about the death of Inga. I did not really know her, even though she had been with me for several years. She was equable, pleasant, busy, with almost nothing to say, except when she told me off for doing things that I should not.'

'I have been told that she recently ended a love affair with Nils, and began a new one with Yelmar. Is that true?'

'I never troubled myself about Inga's private life.'

'So you weren't interested in her?'

'I am sorry for her, I hope that you find who killed her, but I cannot help you.'

'I am not convinced.' Larsen crossed his legs. 'I think the time has come for you to explain how and why you came here.'

There was a long silence. Wan Li took a deep breath, and absently pushed his spectacles up his nose.

'I heard the tape you made,' said Larsen.

'Inga thought I should record my memories, so one foggy morning I started. Just to please her. But then the sea mist cleared and the sun came out.'

'Why did you tape them in Danish?'

The old man laughed. 'You are trying to catch me out,' he said, and to Larsen's surprise he seemed suddenly more friendly, more approachable. 'You think that if I was the real Mei Tei I would have made my records in Mandarin. But I have barely spoken Chinese for eight years. The West is much easier to comprehend if you think in Western languages, English and Danish. Anyway, I was making the tape for Inga, not for myself.' He paused. 'I cannot remember doing very much. I have always preferred to immerse myself in the day itself, not its predecessors.'

'I would like you to go on with the story,' said Larsen quietly.

The old man considered, then shrugged. 'Where do you want me to start?'

Larsen said nothing. As he watched the old man fixedly, he saw pain scuttle like a mouse on to the lined face. At last he raised his hands, then let them fall limply on to his lap.

'I suppose you wish the story of the deconstruction of Mei Tei. It began after the speech in Tiananmen Square, when I was arrested for daring to say in public what everyone knew was true. I was taken to Harbin, in Manchuria, and put in prison.' He gave a bitter laugh. 'Like a fool, I had believed Mao Ze Dong when he said "crude coercive methods should not be used, only painstaking methods of reason." But old ways are still popular. I was confined alone in a cell that did not give me room to lie down or stand up. The only light was a small ray that crept through the ventilation grille during the daytime, and I had to perform my bodily functions on the ground. Occasionally the guards threw in buckets of cold water mixed with disinfectant, which washed my filth down a drain, and also served as a bath. It was high summer, and stiflingly hot – the air was stagnant, and the walls sweated. But when winter came, there was ice on the floor.

'At intervals I had to stagger down the corridor to the interrogation room. There I was questioned about my allies in the army, in the bureaucracy, in the party. Who had I spoken to? What about? When? What plans had I hatched against the state? They always asked the questions very politely, sometimes they called me "sir". But if they did not like my answers, then the guards beat me.

'Occasionally, perhaps through boredom – they seemed to find the whole process boring – they used different methods. I was hung from the roof by my wrists and punched; stones were heaped on my back until my lungs felt about to collapse; electric cow-prods were used on my naked body, especially my genitals. A favourite was to tie me to a chair, push it over so that I lay on my back, and then put a sodden towel over my face, so I could not breathe properly. After I passed out, they would wake me with kicks, or the burning ends of cigarettes.

'I am no hero. I have lived a long time, and real heroes rarely do. The only reason I did not tell them about my accomplices was because I had none. What I did, I did on my own. But it is hard to be sure when pain clouds your mind and you scream and shout to lessen the pain.

'After some months I must have convinced them, for they put me in a more comfortable cell, stopped beating me, and started my re-education. Pleasant young men discussed political theory with me, and helped me write a detailed confession of my wrongdoing – a piece of elaborate fiction that has since been published under my name. But one of the guards – one of the worst of them in fact – was bribed to help me escape. Although I suspected it was a trap, I allowed the guard to smuggle me out of the prison one night. I was driven hundreds of miles by a man whose face I never saw, then another man took me through a high snow-choked pass in the Tien Shan, into Kazakhstan. The man returned to China, and I was left alone, to walk down the mountainside, and so into Almaty, where seventy years before a far greater man than I, Leon Trotsky, was also exiled.

'Some time later I applied for asylum in Denmark, and they made me promise not to indulge in any political activity. I agreed, happily. They also insisted that I live in secrecy, and eventually I was sent to Iceland. One summer I persuaded my minders to allow me to visit Greenland, and I fell in love with your country: the purifying snow, the good-natured people, the stripped-down essentials of living compared with the brutal geopolitics of China, or the grim reserve of Iceland. Since then I have come here each summer. I think these visits to Ikerasak are almost the only thing that has helped me to withstand my past. And the great betrayal I committed.'

Wan Li's face was a mask of anger, of self-disgust.

'What great betrayal?' asked Larsen.

'Those who arranged my escape had assumed I would publicise what was happening in China, that I would assemble an official opposition, that I would become a sort of icon of their cause. But I did nothing. For one thing I detest any form of hero-worship. For another, I felt I had nothing left within me to draw on.' He stopped. His eyes had sunk deep within him.

Larsen waited.

'But at the heart lay a simple fact,' Wan Li went on at last. 'I did not have the courage, even though I now see that surrendering to fear is only a temporary escape. The expectations of those I betrayed never left me. And now they have returned.'

167

'You mean the attempt to make you join the Opposition, by pretending there was a plot to kill you?'

The old man nodded. His face changed, as if he had shrugged aside the emotions that a moment before had wholly dominated him. Once again he had become calm, discursive, though Larsen sensed that the change was not a calculated one. Wan Li was so drained, he could no longer keep up the same pitch of emotional intensity.

'It is hard to know how real a threat Shu-fan and his people represent to the Chinese government. They are young, and that is important. Change is the business of the young. But he will have to be far cleverer than he was with me if he is to achieve anything. The fake kidnap was a stupid idea, which only served to alarm the Danish security forces.'

His rasping breath sighed in and out.

'I would be no use to them anyway,' he added.

'They don't think that.' Larsen probed deeper. 'Why not do what they want? Then you wouldn't have to feel guilty that they helped you and received nothing.'

'That is not the chief source of my guilt,' retorted Wan Li, with a momentary burst of barely concealed anger. He clenched his fist. 'It is the whole condition of the Chinese people – and how I did nothing to improve it. Nothing.' Gradually the fist uncurled, and fell back on his lap, and again he took refuge in analysis. 'When I was young and became a Communist, I thought I would make a difference. But Communism preaches that individuals do not matter, only historical forces. Perhaps I am now a true Communist, because I no longer have the slightest belief that I can change anything. I am old and tired. Very tired. And the moment I must leave Ikerasak looms in front of me like a black cliff.'

He closed his eyes.

After two or three minutes, Larsen went out. Anita was in the kitchen, frying small cubes of fresh seal meat with potatoes and onion.

'Did you get much from him?' she asked, looking over her shoulder.

'Yes. He explained a lot.'

She nodded. 'Over the past weeks I have had some long talks with him also. He's not the quiet, unreadable man he pretends to be, but nor is he a happy man, except sometimes when Marianne is with him.'

'It must be difficult for you having him stay here,' said Larsen. 'Why? He eats little, drinks less, and tells wonderful stories when he is in the mood – of war and treachery and love and destruction. Stories of a sort that we rarely hear in Greenland. Also he loves Marianne, and she loves him.'

'It is another mouth to feed. And of course there are the earthquakes . . .'

She laughed. 'You are being nice to me because you want something.'

Larsen nodded. 'Tell me about Nils and Inga.'

She stirred the food thoughtfully. 'They were lovers – if that is what you mean. Sometimes. Off and on. Nils has a woman in Paamiut who he lives with, and who he has had children with. But he also comes out here every summer, and sees Inga – until now. Since she was killed, he has been drinking heavily.'

'I noticed.' Larsen scratched his chin. 'Did they argue a lot?'

Anita looked at him pityingly. 'Have you ever been married?'

'Yes.'

'Did you ever argue?' She didn't even wait for him to answer. 'On the day I stop arguing with Adam, I will know that either we are tired of each other, or one of us is dead.'

'What about Yelmar?'

'He is like Najanguak, the gull, who stays close, hoping to dart in and steal from others.'

Larsen left the house. Sitting on a rock outside was Risa.

'Well?' she said. 'Is the old man who he says he is?'

'Anita thinks so.' He looked at her, and brought up a smile. 'How are you?'

'OK.'

'And Edvarth?'

'Good. Time away from school has been good for him. And he likes Marianne, he treats her like a little sister.'

There was a pause.

'What are you going to do?' asked Risa, at length.

'I don't know.'

Larsen looked at Risa, and his confusion deepened. Used to seeing his life in front of him in precision-drafted straight lines, he felt himself struggling with uncertainty over the real reason he had come to Ikerasak. And that in turn threw a thick, disorientating mist over how he should proceed.

Seeing Risa's eyes on him, he tried to avoid the emotional maze he felt closing about him. 'If he really is Mei Tei, then he is an important man. I am not used to dealing with important men.'

'You deal with them like anyone else,' said Risa. 'Cut him up, and he's the same mixture of blood and meat and muscle and bone as the rest of us.'

'You're thinking like a nurse.'

'You'd better start thinking like a policeman. And to a policeman, I'd have thought that everyone was equal.'

'No. I look at that old man, and he makes me feel like a child. Stupid. Incapable. Knowing nothing of the real world.'

'Edvarth doesn't feel like that. Neither does Marianne. Why should you?' Suddenly Risa took a step forward, put her hands on his shoulders, and shook him. 'He's just another old man, Tomas.'

'No, he's not. He's a man who has left his fingerprints on the world. And yet he is still tormented by his failure. How can I take my own problems seriously, when I see his?'

'Yours are as real as his.'

'I don't believe that. I . . .' He hesitated. 'I'd better contact my Chief and ask for advice.'

'I thought you hadn't told him anything about this.'

'I think it's time I did.'

'Are you sure that's wise?' asked Risa cautiously. 'The moment you reveal where the old man is, he'll probably be taken away like he was last time. But this time for good.'

'What else can I do?'

Risa looked at him, an almost cynical expression on her round, sharp features. 'I can think of several possibilities. But they all require you to start with one vital thing that you haven't done yet.'

'For Christ's sake,' growled Larsen, feeling like a great lumbering polar bear, fresh from hibernation, at the mercy of an aggressive, fast-moving dog. 'Leave me alone.'

'You asked for my advice. Now I'm giving it to you.' Larsen opened his mouth to reply, but she held up her hand. 'One more thing, then I've done. What you have to do, Tomas Larsen, is very simple. Make up your mind.'

'About what?' he retorted irritably.

'About whether you really want to find out who murdered Inga. About what you think should happen to the old man. About who is making the decisions.' She pushed her face towards his, and for a moment he felt her breath warm on his face. 'About what the hell you want to do with your life.'

His heart beat hard in his chest as their eyes locked.

'We just had a one night stand, didn't we?' she said softly, then turned before he could answer, and walked away.

170

18

A WALK IN THE MOUNTAINS

Twenty minutes later, Larsen was still sitting alone, struggling with his racing thoughts. A thin wind hissed through the grass. The door opened behind him, and he saw the old man emerge, with Marianne holding his hand.

'My friend here has something that she wishes to show me,' said Wan Li.

'It's a fire,' said Marianne. 'It keeps burning. On and on and on.'

'Maybe someone keeps feeding it.'

She shook her head. 'It's not like that. I'll show you, then you'll understand.'

'Where is it?'

'Up in the mountains.'

'That is much too far for me just now, Marianne –'

'Wait,' interrupted Larsen. 'There's something I must ask you.'

'Oh no,' Marianne scowled. 'Not more questions.'

'Well?' said Wan Li.

'I am thinking of contacting my Chief, to tell him where you are.'

'As you wish.'

'But what do you think?'

'Many things,' said Wan Li.

In the last half-hour he had become a different man. He had put his mask of benign impassivity back on, and there was no longer any hint of anguish or exhaustion.

'I mean about this. About telling people where you are.'

'It is not a question of people knowing where I am. It is a question of what I do when people know.'

Larsen thought for a moment. 'You mean all that matters is whether you choose to help the Opposition or not.'

'Are you sure that is what I meant?' enquired the old man, and Larsen seemed to glimpse a glitter dancing in his long brown eyes.

'Come on, grandpa,' insisted Marianne.

'Not yet, my dear. For one thing you are not dressed warmly enough – your aunt told me that you must always wear a thick sweater, a waterproof jacket, and walking boots. For another, I have changed my mind. If you are going to drag me across the barrens, I must have some food and a rest first. After that I will go where you wish.'

Larsen returned to his house, and phoned Chief Thorold.

'What is it?' A faint sound that might have been a laugh. 'How is your wooing going?'

Larsen answered quickly, not giving himself time to think. 'When I reached Paamiut, I discovered the person I was coming to see had gone on to Ikerasak. I followed her – and found that the old Chinese man, Wan Li, has returned there.'

The answer was like a whip crack. 'What?'

'Yes, sir. He wasn't taken away by the Danish Special Forces, he's been here ever since Norlund brought him back from Iceland.'

'You're sure?'

'I've just been talking to him, sir.'

'But the man is a fake.'

'I'm not sure that's true, sir. I think people have been lying.'

'I see.' There was a long pause, pregnant with uncertainty. 'I need to think about this. Perhaps you'd better come straight back to Nuuk, and –'

'What if someone else knows where he is, sir?' objected Larsen.

'Yes.' Another pause. 'Yes, that's true. All right then, Tomas, perhaps it would be best if you stayed where you are and kept an eye on him. You could also finish your investigation into the death of that woman at the same time. Keep me posted on your progress. Good luck.'

He rang off abruptly.

Larsen looked at his mobile with a wry expression, then went back to his house, made himself coffee, and got some rye bread and cheese. It was sunny, and he ate his lonely meal outside, then closed his eyes, soaking up the heat on his face. He suddenly felt a fierce desire for more heat, more sun, for a land where the dominant colour was green, and where you didn't have to scratch a living by killing those few creatures able to survive on the unforgiving frozen soil or in the ice-choked sea. But his feelings faded – like the sun, which drifted behind clouds.

He stretched, and looked out over the countryside. Wan Li and

172

Marianne were climbing the nearest hill. The little girl seemed to be talking non-stop, gesturing vivaciously, as they toiled higher, then disappeared out of sight.

He yawned, closed his eyes again, slipped into a doze, and woke suddenly as his head fell. A thought sprang into his mind, and he pulled out his phone.

'Hi?' said an American voice.

'Kim – it's Tomas Larsen.'

'Who? Oh, you're the policeman I met in Ikerasak. Nice to hear from you, Tomas. Can I help you?'

'I was thinking I might be able to help you.'

'In what way?' Her voice was wary.

'You're still in Greenland?'

'Sure. I have to file a few stories before I go, or it's a bankruptcy hearing for me.' She sighed. 'I was so sure I could sell that interview with Shu-fan, but nobody'd touch it. They said that with things in China being how they are, they didn't want hearsay, needed more facts, that kind of stuff. Editors are so chicken-shit these days. So now I'm in – God, I don't know, I can't get my head round these names. Sounds like a duck. Qaqortoq, that's it. Doing a piece on how tourism does or doesn't fuck up life in Greenland.'

'Does it?'

'It's so fucked anyway, what's the difference?'

Larsen felt a sting of anger. 'Is that what you're writing?'

'Hey, that was just a joke. I love this place and I'm doing a beautiful lyrical piece on the great blue icebergs, and the tundra turning red in the autumn, and the whole last frontier, Greenland's icy mountains bit, complete with suitable pix. It's only for the SAS in-flight magazine, but it's bucks. So what's this about?'

'The old Chinese man is back.'

Her whole voice changed in an instant. It became quick, demanding, excited. 'Back where?'

'In Ikerasak.'

'How do you know?'

'I'm here with him.'

'Don't let him go anyplace. I'm on my way.'

The phone went dead.

Larsen put away his phone. It sounded as if SAS's magazine might have to wait for its article on Greenland. He wondered briefly if he had done the right thing, then a cold breath of wind made him glance up towards the distant encircling mountains of ice. As he did so, he thought he glimpsed a thin column of smoke, but the wind strengthened and he could not see it any more.

The journalist hadn't even asked him why he was telling her. Not that Larsen himself was sure. Except for an instinctive sense that a media presence might provide a protection – though against what he did not know – and the fact that he liked the talkative American woman.

Abruptly he felt a convulsive shiver in the earth, and heard a rumble like distant thunder. Anita appeared close by, throwing out her washing-up water on to the stones. He went over to her.

'Have you had many of those shakings?' he asked.

She nodded. 'I'm getting used to them. They used to wake me up in the night, but not now. Why?'

'I just wondered. Are they getting weaker?'

'Not that I've noticed – though none have been as bad as the first one.'

'That's strange – I thought aftershocks were supposed to fade.' He frowned. 'What exactly did Marianne say she had found?'

'A fire that never goes out.' Anita smiled. 'She has a great imagination.'

'Maybe not.'

'What do you mean?'

'Maybe nothing.'

Larsen set off up the hill, striding through the thin grass that grew on the lower slopes, then on higher, where the stones were interrupted only by small streams and cushions of alpine plants, bright with flowers – purple saxifrage, moss campion, roseroot, scurvy grass. Behind him, Anita stood and watched, a concerned expression on her fine face.

Some way on Larsen saw tents in a depression. Hastily he changed direction and hurried down the hill. The geologists' camp had been moved about two kilometres closer to the eastern mountains, and all three of them were there, talking earnestly among themselves.

'This is what you're here for, isn't it?' interrupted Larsen breathlessly, gesturing towards the mountains.

'Of course,' said Sigrid, looking up at him. 'When we came on our last field trip, three years ago, we found hints of pre-volcanic activity. Since then we've been monitoring the area as closely as we could, and last year I predicted a seventy per cent chance of a volcanic birth in this area within five years. It's never been done before – no one has ever predicted the birth of a volcano.'

'But why all this secrecy?'

'Don't you understand? This is our volcano. We predicted it, no one else. If we'd discussed our theories with others, it would have become public knowledge and our work would have been subsumed in other people's. We didn't want anyone else to know for as long as possible so that we could accumulate data and prepare for the event. Of course, people will soon be arriving –'

'You said that before, after the first tremor,' broke in Larsen. 'But no one has come yet. Have they?'

'They will. It's just they haven't realised its significance yet.'

Larsen looked at her, and recognised the same single-minded focus that he had seen in Shu-fan.

'Why did you move your camp?' he asked.

'We need to be close enough to get as many detailed measurements as possible. You have to realise just how big an event this is, geologically speaking. New volcanoes are rare, and that's what we've got here.'

'We've picked the site carefully,' said Bettina. 'A full-scale eruption would mean the possibility of flooding as a portion of the ice cap melts and breaks through the remaining ice. But the waters would come down the Isortoq valley, which is away over that ridge. We'd have ample warning of any lava flows, and of course we've got radar scanners for estimating the speed. Most important, there's no possibility of a pyroclastic avalanche as this is a new volcano, and the flows are linked to the collapse of old lava domes.'

'We're not absolutely sure about that,' put in Rob. 'There was that deposit of welded tuff we found, which is usually considered to be the result of pyroclastic flows, and don't forget that calcalkaline feldspar –'

'In a glacial erratic which could have been brought from anywhere within hundreds of kilometres. This is a new volcano,' insisted Sigrid flatly. 'There's no question.'

'What if it isn't? What if the main body of the volcano is under the ice, and –'

'You've no evidence for that, Rob.'

'I've just given you my evidence. And we haven't yet undertaken a thorough survey of Mount Iviangeq –'

Larsen realised that they were going on with an old argument.

175

'What is a pyroclastic avalanche?' he interrupted.

'An explosive outpouring of superheated ash, pumice, steam and other gases,' explained Bettina. 'They used to be called *nuées ardentes* – burning clouds. The most famous wiped out Pompeii, and another killed the entire population of Saint Pierre in Martinique – thirty thousand people – except for one survivor who was in the death cell deep underground. Recently there's been Mount St Helens in the US, Pinatubo in the Philippines, Merapi in eastern Java, and La Soufrière on Montserrat.'

Larsen stared at her, as if at a snake. 'Are you telling me that Ikerasak is in danger?'

Bettina shrugged. 'Pyroclastic flows are very dangerous, yes. Fifty people died in a pyroclastic flow at Mount Unzen in Japan in 1991, and Mount Lamington in New Guinea killed several thousand in 1951.'

'But there's no risk of that here,' said Sigrid. 'You see –'

'Is the village in any danger?' repeated Larsen, spitting out each word.

'It's impossible to be completely certain,' admitted Bettina. 'There's always a chance of gaseous emissions. That's why we have firefighters' masks.' She gestured at three masks connected to oxygen tanks that were stacked up in the porch of one tent. 'In a worst case scenario, they'd give us time to get up on to high ground, out of the gas cloud.'

'So there's real danger then?'

Bettina's long henna-dyed hair was showing its straw-coloured roots. She pushed it away from her face, where the breeze was blowing it.

'There could be,' she admitted. 'It's unlikely that any effect would reach the village, but it's very hard to be sure. You can smell a trace of sulphur in the air now, when the wind's from the east, so there might be a major release of sulphur dioxide.'

'Likely, I'd say,' put in Sigrid. 'At some point in the cycle of eruption. But – as with all volcanic phenomena – the solution is usually just to climb. The higher you are, the safer you are likely to be. As long as you're not climbing straight for the vent.'

'Why the fucking hell haven't you warned anyone before?'

'It was just a theory,' said Bettina.

'It isn't now.'

'What're you doing?' asked Sigrid, as Larsen pulled out his phone.

'It sounds to me as if Ikerasak should be evacuated.'

'You're panicking unnecessarily,' said Sigrid. 'The village is a good five or six kilometres from the vent. It's in no danger.'

'I'm not willing to risk that,' replied Larsen. 'Hello? Hello . . .'

Five minutes later he put his phone away.

'I can't get through to anyone, there's just hisses and crackles.'

'It's the same with ours,' said Rob. 'We haven't been able to contact anyone for two days.'

Larsen glared at him, then with an effort calmed himself down and concentrated on the reason he was there. 'Have you seen an old man and a child pass by in the last half-hour?'

'No, why?' asked Sigrid.

He ignored her. 'Where would you see a fire that doesn't go out?' he demanded harshly.

'There may be some burning gas escapes in the gorge below Mount Iviangeq,' said Bettina. 'But you can't get there along the south bank of the Isortoq any more. There was a rock-fall about a week ago, so now you have to cross the river.'

Larsen turned and hurried off in the direction Bettina pointed, then heard someone calling him. He stopped as he saw Rob following him, waving.

'What is it?' Larsen asked impatiently.

'There's something I think I should tell you.'

'Be quick, then.'

Rob glanced back over his shoulder, then regained his breath. 'It's complicated, but we've been very short of money for this work. I suppose I shouldn't say this, especially when everything's turned out so well. But Sigrid's been obsessed with the project for years, and she's done everything she possibly can to raise the necessary cash.'

'Yes?'

'I think one way she did it was by providing people with information.'

'What people? What information?'

'I'm not sure.' He glanced back again. 'I've just heard fractions of conversations, that sort of thing. But it seemed to be about that old man – she was talking about him to someone.'

'Are you sure?'

'I think so.'

Larsen slapped the heel of his hand into his other palm, then knitted his fingers. His mouth was a narrow slit. 'When was this?'

'Several times since we got here.'

'You should have told me before.'

'I know. I'm sorry, but I didn't want to spoil things.'

'I haven't time for this now. But we'll go into it in more detail later. OK?'

Rob looked worried. 'I don't want to get Sigrid in trouble. I mean, this project is all down to her. She set it up, sorted it out, financed it, everything. She's the driving force. But when I heard about that woman having been murdered, I started to think . . .'

'I'll be back,' said Larsen, and hurried away.

'Wait, there's something else,' called Rob.

It was too late. Larsen was already vanishing up the hillside. Rob watched him go.

'What was that about?' demanded Sigrid, as Rob returned to the camp.

'I thought I saw someone in the hills this morning, I was telling him about it.'

'You shouldn't talk to the police,' said Sigrid. 'It just causes trouble.'

'I suppose you're right, but . . .' Rob raised his hands weakly, then sat down. 'I was going to warn him about the possibility of lahars as well.'

'There isn't going to be a lahar,' said Sigrid firmly.

After a few minutes Larsen spotted his quarry. Marianne and Wan Li were perhaps a kilometre ahead of him. They had crossed the river on the stepping stones, and were walking steadily up its far side, towards the gorge from where the river emerged, freed from its glacial chains. And from where smoke was oozing. Larsen followed them as fast as he could.

As he descended towards the river crossing, he saw that the river had changed. Rather than the sluggish, silt-laden yellow creature he remembered, it had become a grey-brown torrent that almost covered the great age-old stepping stones. Larsen stopped above the stones and frowned. The Isortoq looked like a stream in the first flush of the spring thaw, but this was the beginning of August and there was no reason for it to be so full or so violent. It also occurred to Larsen that there were almost no fragments of ice in the fast-flowing water.

Cautiously he clambered down to the side of the water, and on to the first of the stepping stones, then put his hand into the turbid water.

It was like no meltwater stream he had ever touched, for the water was not bone-crackingly cold, but warm. Pleasant. Larsen stared down at the swirling water in astonishment, then crossed the stones. As he started to climb the northern bank, he was spattered with spray and there was a thunderous roar. A metre-high wave of water, hurling rocks before it, came foaming down the valley.

Larsen scrambled hastily up the hillside, to continue his pursuit. When he caught Marianne and Wan Li at the mouth of the gorge, they seemed unsurprised to see him.

Almost directly above them was a hanging glacier of extreme steepness, from which a small stream came bursting down, over the black-sided rocks. All around the unmoving, yellow-stained air was thick and hard to breathe, with a stench of sulphur.

'It wasn't like this last time,' said Marianne. She wrinkled her nose, coughed, then pointed. 'Look, the river's all blocked up.'

A little way in, where the gorge was at its narrowest, a massive rockfall had filled it to a height of thirty or forty metres. The river poured through gaps in a hundred brown and grey waterfalls that hurtled down the rockface and joined together in a surging mass of water.

'I do not think we should be here,' said Wan Li sombrely.

Larsen walked forward a little, past a frost-shattered column that jutted out from the eastern cliff, blocking their view further up the valley. He had to put his hand over his mouth and nose, as he stared through acrid, coiling smoke.

The widening U-shaped valley, which stretched beyond the gorge into the hazy distance, was half full of steaming, brown water, held back by the rockfall. Closer, only five hundred metres away, an island stood out of the water. It was perhaps twelve metres above the water, cone-shaped, and in its heart was the dancing red of a flame. Larsen scrunched his smarting eyes up and stared, but it was impossible to see clearly through the heaving boiling smoke that filled the steep-sided valley.

Suddenly the rocks beneath him quivered, as if some vast sledgehammer had struck them, and he felt a moment of nausea. There was a staccato crackle, like the sound of gunfire, and Larsen instinctively flung himself on his face, then realised that what he had heard was a volley of stones lashing into the cliff-face. He stood up again, then coughed some more. His nostrils were stinging, and black cinders filled the air, fluttering down all around him.

Within the echoing vault of the cliffs, strange sounds were hurtling back and forth, explosions, cracks, hisses and roars intermingled with the thunder of the steaming water escaping down the valley. The rocks quivered again, but less violently.

Boulders crashed down from higher up the cliffs, and there was a fresh volley of stones, lashing into the water like the shrapnel of artillery fire. From high above, as if in answer, came a noise like thunder and a huge mass of ice broke free from the snout of one of the hanging glaciers on the far side of the valley. Accompanied by great solid-looking clouds of powdered ice, the glacier fragment crashed down headlong into the water, sending brown waves hurtling round the steaming lake.

Larsen retreated swiftly from his precarious perch. Behind him Wan Li had his old arm round Marianne's thin shoulders. Her face was white and she was shivering.

'Let's get away from here,' she said. 'It's scary.'

'I agree,' said Wan Li.

'So do I,' said Larsen.

Thirty minutes later the three of them reached the stepping stones over the river. But they were no longer there. The roaring river had swallowed them up.

'We're cut off,' said Larsen unnecessarily.

A moment later, as if in response to his words, the ground shook again.

19

EVACUATION

The helicopter landed on the slick, wet foreshore with a heavy beating of its rotors. Two people scrambled out, and hurried up beyond the high tide line. Gradually the blades slowed, and the sound lessened. The pilot leaned out of the door.

'Three and a half hours, max,' he shouted. 'After that the tide'll be back.'

'OK.'

The two hurried off up the track to Ikerasak.

Risa was talking to Edvarth, outside the house where they were staying.

'But mum, you told me you were going to take a few days off . . .' he protested.

'Well, I'm not,' she retorted. 'We leave as soon as Nils can take us back to Paamiut. I've work to do, and a living to earn. You know that.'

'I don't want to go back yet, mum.'

'When we first came here, you moaned and complained the whole time. Now it's the opposite. It's time you sorted yourself out and learned to make your mind up, Edvarth.'

A look of outraged innocence took over the boy's face. 'What about you then? You keep changing —'

'Don't be insolent,' she broke in, her voice like knife-edged crystal. 'I am the head of this family, and we do what I say. Understand?'

'No need to get stressy,' muttered Edvarth, slouching away.

Risa glowered after him, then savagely kicked a stone.

There was a sound of people behind her, and she looked round.

A man was coming up the path from the mouth of the fjord. He was a Dane, thin, serious-looking, with a beard and moustache, his long hair in a pony-tail, a single pearl-drop earring hanging from his left ear. Beside him was the American journalist, Kim, her expensive North Face rucksack on her back.

Risa nodded at them coldly.

'Good afternoon,' said the Dane in a soft-spoken voice. 'Can

181

you help me? I wish to gather the village together, and talk to them.'

'Why?'

'I'll explain, but it's important that there are as many people as possible present.'

'How did you get here?' asked Risa, her mind going off on a tangent.

'By chopper. But we don't have long. There may not be a chance of another visit for some time – the weather outlook is overcast, with rain.'

'Surprise me.' Risa looked across at Kim. 'You travel in style,' she remarked in English.

The American looked faintly embarrassed. 'I was coming here anyway,' she replied. 'But at Paamiut, I found out that Mikkael was on his way here too. Listen, where's that old Chinese guy? I need to see him right away.'

Risa shrugged, and pointed to Anita and Adam's house. 'He's been staying there.'

'Thanks.'

Kim adjusted her rucksack, and hurried off, her face set.

Twenty minutes later ten people were gathered around the serious Danish man.

'Right,' said the Dane. 'Is everyone here?'

'Nils is out fishing in his boat,' called someone.

'OK. Well, my name is Mikkael Holm. I work for the Greenland Geological Survey, and as you must've all noticed, there have been some unusual things going on round here lately – especially the earth tremors.'

'Are they what has driven away the fish and animals and birds?' demanded Aqqaluk, a sinewy, hatchet-faced man wearing sun-glasses. 'I have never known so bad a hunting and fishing season.'

'Perhaps,' said Mikkael. 'Though there are other possible causes too – sulphur pollution, smoke, the apparent rise in ambient temperature, other chemicals . . .'

'What are you talking about?' demanded Anita.

The man looked a little flustered. 'Sorry. I'm trying to explain. This area is the focus of completely new and unexpected seismological disturbance, incorporating vulcanicity that may possibly demonstrate vulcanian features . . .'

There was a rumble of discontent among the listeners. Risa stood up and put out her hands. As silence came down, they could all hear a distant continuous sound, like the roar of breaking waves, but the fjord below them was still.

'Mikkael,' said Risa, clearly and slowly. 'Will you explain in simple words what you are doing here and why you want to talk to us, for no one understands what you are talking about.'

The man nodded, and his pony-tail flopped limply up and down.

'Let me start again,' he said. 'Something totally new is happening here.'

'You're telling us what we know,' called out Aqqaluk.

'He's not telling me anything at all,' commented Yelmar. 'I can't understand this Danish nonsense.'

Risa, who was still standing, frowned. 'Keep silent and listen,' she said sharply, in Greenlandic. 'I will explain at the end.'

Mikkael glanced nervously at Risa.

'Go on,' she said.

'After the small earth tremors you have been experiencing first registered on our instruments, we began to analyse satellite pictures and also sent out a couple of planes for fly-pasts. Basically, what we think is happening is that a new volcano is being born. This is a very rare occurrence indeed. With the partial exception of the Loki fissure in 1996, the last we know of, in this hemisphere, was the island of Surtsey off the coast of Iceland in 1963. It is even more extraordinary, in that there are no volcanoes in Greenland at all. Shortly we expect to have at least two, possibly more, teams of expert vulcanologists arriving to monitor what is taking place, but of course this area is very isolated, with awkward access, and the precise location of the infant volcano, tucked away in a deep valley on the very edge of the inland ice, makes it extremely hard to see. Because of this there has been some delay in organising an expedition – and we have had to make do with seismological soundings, and satellite photographs.'

Risa could hear a mutter among the listeners, but no one raised their voice. After a moment, Mikkael continued.

'The cause of this phenomenon is a source of much argument. Three-quarters of Greenland is ancient Canadian shield rock, a minimum of one and a half billion years old, so no one expected any volcanoes or earthquakes here. However the south-western portion of the country is somewhat different – there is newer rock there, much of it igneous, and the famous hot springs in Uunartoq fjord provide direct evidence of low-level volcanic activity. Nevertheless, it must be admitted that the presumption

Greenland was not a volcanically active area is the main reason why original warnings of activity in this area were ignored. Global warming has caused glaciers to retreat in several parts of the country, and it was assumed that the tremors which accompanied the birth of the volcano were merely crustal readjustments caused by the removal of the ice cover, and not linked to any volcanic activity . . .'

Risa raised her hand, and Mikkael stopped speaking.

'I realise that as an expert it is hard for you to put this in easy words, even when you are trying,' she said. 'So can I ask something?'

He gave a vague, weak smile. 'Of course.'

'You are saying there were signs of what is happening, but some people got it wrong, and only now are they sure. Is that right?'

'Well . . . crudely, yes. Though there is substantial research to be done before we can be certain of the development of events. Anyway, as I said –'

'Don't repeat it,' interrupted Risa. 'That's all we need to know.' She turned to the others, and switched to Greenlandic. 'There is a volcano, a burning mountain, growing not far from here. They have only just realised this, and they wish to say sorry for not telling us sooner.'

'So what?' said Yelmar.

'They want to know why this matters,' translated Risa.

'Yes, of course. That's why I'm here.' Mikkael hesitated again, and brushed a nervous hand through his beard. 'Well, to put it simply, we think that it is advisable for you all to leave.'

There was a whisper as those who could understand Danish explained what Mikkael had said to the others. Gradually a complete silence fell.

'Why?' said Risa, at last.

'Well, we don't know how big or fast this volcano is going to grow. But in previous cases, such as Paricutin in Mexico, new volcanoes have expanded extremely rapidly. Within a week of its first appearance Paricutin was over 150 metres high, and it went on growing steadily for two years.'

'But I know where this new mountain is – my daughter found it,' objected Anita. 'It's over an hour's walk from the village. How can that be dangerous? And why should its growth over two years worry us? We will leave here in a few weeks and go back to Paamiut. Next spring, we can see.'

There was a mutter of agreement.

Mikkael's lined, sincere face took on a slightly panicky expression.

'Volcanoes are very unpredictable,' he said. 'And our advice is that you are in dangerous proximity to this one. A full-scale eruption here, so close to the inland ice, is likely to prompt serious flooding. The combination of volcanic activity with large areas of ice can also cause lahars –'

'What?' demanded Risa, impatiently.

'Lahars are dangerous and unpredictable mud-flows that can travel many kilometres at great speed. They are very destructive indeed. There is also the chance that this is not a new volcano, but a reborn one. If so, there is a possibility of explosive activity.'

As Risa tried to explain what he had said, there was a hubbub of discussion. Everyone started to offer advice and opinions, and Mikkael's attempts to continue what he was saying were choked off.

It took five minutes for Risa to regain control.

'So you think we should leave?' she said.

'Yes,' said Mikkael, nodding earnestly. 'Of course you cannot be made to depart, but if you stay here, then you are taking a risk.'

'And when should we go?'

'As soon as possible.'

'What does that mean?' demanded Anita. 'Today? Tomorrow? Next week? In three weeks' time?'

'Ideally within the next twenty-four hours,' said Mikkael. 'The volcano is growing more active, and there are indicators of a possible major eruption – the latest satellite pictures appeared to show a measurable swelling of the land around the vent, though it was hard to analyse because of the ice and water that covers much of the area. Analysis of the emissions also appears to show rising quantities of sulphur dioxide.'

'How are we expected to go?' called out Adam. 'The only boat big enough to move many people is Nils's, and he is not even here.'

'Nor can he move all of us in a single day,' put in Yelmar. 'And if I know Nils, he will make sure it costs us plenty of money.'

'And what if he doesn't want to leave?' said Anita.

'The government has agreed to lay on a helicopter to help the evacuation,' said Mikkael. 'It will cost you nothing, but –'

'It is over two kilometres to the only place that the chopper can land,' objected Aqqaluk. 'How are we to . . .?' The rest of his objection was lost in the rising tide of complaints.

'There's a helicopter waiting now,' shouted Mikkael, above the hubbub. 'It will take as many people as it can carry, with their belongings, but it has to fly in . . .' He looked at his wrist-watch. 'In just under two hours. If anyone wishes to be on it, then you had better hurry . . .'

At that moment there was a roar above the village, and everyone glanced up. Circling overhead was one of the red and white twenty-four seater S-61N helicopters that were usually only used for transport between the main towns of the country.

'Look,' said Adam. 'They've sent a big chopper. They must take this very seriously.'

As the helicopter began to drop towards the distant foreshore, there was a sudden rush. Everyone hurried back to their houses, to get as much as they could, before leaving. In a moment the crowd had changed from resentful and suspicious to panicky. The revelation that the government thought the situation worrying enough to disrupt the transport schedules and send a helicopter from Narsarsuaq, over two hundred kilometres south of them, had convinced everyone in a moment. There was no longer any question whether they were going to leave. Within minutes people were pouring out of their houses, bowed under sacks, boxes and bags, heading down the track towards the mouth of the fjord.

'Well,' said Risa, turning towards Mikkael, a faint smile on her face. 'You didn't need to bother, did you? All it needed was the sight of the S-61. I suppose I'd better collect my erring son, wherever he is, and our things –'

Anita interrupted her. 'Marianne's up there,' she said, gesturing up the valley, towards the distant faint column of smoke. Her thin face was lined with care and worry, and Risa felt a shiver of fear down her spine.

'Edvarth didn't go with her, did he?' she asked.

Anita shook her head. 'She went with the old man. That American woman's gone after them.'

At that moment Edvarth appeared up the slope from the fjord. 'What's going on?'

'We're leaving,' said Risa sharply. 'The helicopter is to take all of us out of here.'

An hour and a half later, as the tide sidled up the open beach of glacial sand, the S-61 flew, loaded with people and possessions to maximum all-up weight. The much smaller Bell remained, with Edvarth, Risa, Mikkael, the pilot and Anita inside. Adam had set off to find Marianne, and they were waiting for him to return.

But the pilot was getting worried as the sea crept closer and closer.

'I can't stay here much longer,' he said, for the fifth time.

'You must wait,' said Anita, on the edge of tears. 'You must.'

'The water's still twenty or thirty metres away,' objected Risa.

The pilot shook his head. 'The sand gets wet as the tide rises, and we might get bogged down before the water reaches us. I can't wait more than another couple of minutes.'

'What about Adam and Marianne?' protested Anita, putting her shaking hands on the back of the seat in front of her.

The pilot shrugged.

'It'll be all right,' said Mikkael soothingly. 'There's no reason to expect an immediate eruption. We are just making sure no unnecessary risks are taken.'

'I thought you said you didn't know – one way or the other.'

'There's still Nils and his boat,' added Risa from the front seat. 'He can take everyone who's left.'

'OK, let's go,' said Mikkael.

The doors were slammed shut, and the rotors accelerated. Anita was trying to stem tears, but Risa was frowning.

'Everyone,' she repeated her own words. 'Of course! We haven't told everyone. There're those bloody geologists. And Tomas.'

Sick emptiness struck at her, like a physical blow. Her head spun in panic. As the pilot went through his take-off routine, Risa grabbed his shoulder.

'Wait!' she shouted. 'We must warn the others. Have you got a phone?'

'It's no good,' bellowed Mikkael. 'The volcano is disrupting all reception. That's why we couldn't warn you all earlier.'

Risa turned to look at him, then knew what she must do. She flung open the door, and sprang out on to the sand.

'Mum!' screamed Edvarth. 'What the hell are you doing?'

'Don't worry,' she shouted back, ducking down as the wind of the helicopter blew her heavy anorak around her. 'I've got to go back. Stay with Anita, I'll be in contact.'

Edvarth lunged after his mother, but Mikkael caught him.

'We'll come back tomorrow,' he bellowed, and slammed the door shut.

The helicopter swung up into the air, then circled twice. The pilot pointed down at a boat, looking like a toy, that was making its way south from the inner reaches of the fjord.

'That must be the missing guy,' he shouted. 'He's heading back towards the village, so there shouldn't be a problem.'

On the beach, Risa was still staring up at the vanishing helicopter, as it set off south-east over the icy sea and the black cliffs of the priest's mountain, towards Paamiut.

'Why the fuck did I do that?' she muttered to herself. 'Still, at least Edvarth's out of the trouble.'

She took a deep breath, and set off back up the track.

The village was empty. She went into every house to double-check, then made herself two large sandwiches with some of the food she had left behind. While she ate, she took out a notebook and wrote a list of names. Tomas Larsen. Adam. Marianne. The old Chinese man. Nils. The three geologists. And herself. There were still nine people left around Ikerasak. No, ten. That stupid American woman, Kim, as well. And she found her eyes once more creeping up towards the mountains, and the thin plume of smoke. Above it clouds had gathered, like skuas over a seal carcass, and Risa saw a flicker of lightning. Then a second.

At the same time there was a rumble deep in the earth, then a distant roar – like white noise – and a strange fuzziness swept over the landscape so that for a moment she thought she saw a moving wave sweep through the solid ground towards her. Then a series of brutal earth tremors almost knocked her to the ground.

'Jesus Christ!' she muttered, clinging on to the shuddering wall. 'What the hell am I doing here? The only person who is my business is Edvarth, and he's away. So why did I come back? I must have been out of my stupid skull. And what the hell do I do now?'

The world reeled again, and she fell to her knees. The foul smell of sulphur was harsh in the air, and she began to cough. Suddenly from above, she heard sharp noises on the roof of the house. She ran to the window and looked out. Tiny pebbles and cinders and fragments of what looked like red clay were flying through the air, falling on the village like rain, beating down on the houses. A window near her cracked, then so did a second. One of the shapeless pieces of clay fell to the earth close by and Risa saw flames momentarily leap from it, while the grass it fell on blackened. Only then did she realise that it was lava. Burning lava, thrown six kilometres from the volcano. And she felt fresh fear lance through her.

Risa cowered in the house for two hours, until the bombardment lessened. The rattle of stones, the heat of flying lava, and the blackness of ash and cinders, ceased to descend on deserted Ikerasak, and she took up her courage, put up the thick hood on her oilskin coat in case more fiery bombs fell from the sky, and went out.

She had barely gone five hundred metres, when, above the fading rumbling of the volcano, she heard a boat's engine. She looked down the steep slope, and saw the battered shape of the *Sea Wolf* chugging down the fjord, towards Ikerasak. Risa ran back as fast as she could, and scrambled down the path to the fjord-side, waving and shouting. Nils had already seen her and swung the boat in.

'What's going on?' he called.

'Nearly everyone's gone,' she said. 'There's a mountain breathing fire and rock out there.'

Nils's stolid, round face showed nothing, but he tied up his boat, and joined her on the shore. 'I've never heard of such a thing.'

'Apparently some people thought such a thing might happen, that's why those geologists came out here. Have you seen them?'

Nils shook his head. 'I was fishing.'

Risa sensed something odd in his behaviour, in his manner. 'Edvarth said there were almost no fish round the head of the fjord at all.'

'Maybe he's right.'

'Did you catch anything?'

'No.'

'So what were you doing?' demanded Risa, more and more sure that he was hiding something.

He gave the smile of a schoolboy, found out by his teacher. 'Some people paid me to take them up the fjord, round the far side of Qeqertaq Island.'

'Why? What did they want?'

Nils shrugged. 'I did not ask.'

'Who were they?'

'I do not know.'

Risa angrily reached out, took his shoulders and shook the fisherman hard. 'Tell me,' she spat out, between clenched teeth.

'There is nothing to tell. They were hunters. They had guns and binoculars, and camping equipment. They wished to hunt for reindeer in the hills. That is all.'

189

'Were they Greenlanders?'

'Maybe,' said Nils vaguely.

'How many of them?'

'Two.'

'When are you to pick them up?'

'They didn't say.'

Risa stared at him. 'They must have said. They can't walk back to Paamiut from here.'

Nils said nothing.

'You're lying,' she snarled at him.

Nils shook his head.

For a moment Risa was tempted to shake him again, then she remembered Nils's boat might represent the only way of leaving Ikerasak for her and everyone else left behind. Especially if the predicted bad weather prevented the helicopter from returning.

She took a deep breath to calm herself. 'We have to find the others, and get them out of here in your boat.'

Nils glanced at the sky. Massive purple-black clouds boiled menacingly over the inner ice. The bottom of the cloud bank was dyed red as clotting blood, and seemed to flash on and off with a weird inner light.

'There's a lot of water coming down the river,' he said.

'What do you mean?'

Nils looked up again. As he did so the earth trembled once more. The unceasing distant noise changed suddenly, into what sounded like repeated volleys of rifle fire.

'Strange things are happening to the tides and currents – it is as if I am feeling my way through waters I have never crossed before. Everything is new. Nor is it only that. There are many dead fish in the fjord, some of them deep sea fish, even sharks, and dead birds too.'

'Which means we must hurry.'

'Yes,' he agreed. 'I do not want to stay here.'

'Neither do I. So we'll just get all the missing people together, then we can go.'

Nils looked at her. 'Where will you find them?' he asked pointedly.

'Up the valley,' she said vaguely.

'I do not want to stay,' he repeated after a moment. 'I will take you, but the sooner we are away, the better.'

'You must wait a little. There are several people out there – Adam and Marianne, the geologists, the old man . . .'

Nils's face was set and stubborn.

'All right,' said Risa. 'How much?'

'What do you mean?'

'You know what I mean. How much do you want in exchange for staying until I come back with the others?'

Nils thought for a moment. '5000 kroner.'

Risa stared at him.

'5000 kroner,' he repeated, more confidently.

'But –'

'Decide quickly,' he interrupted. 'Either you and I leave now. Or you go to find the others, and I will wait, and you will pay me an extra 5000 kroner.'

'You are exploiting us,' she said furiously. 'Making us pay too much.'

'Listen to me,' he retorted. 'I only know a little part of what has been happening here this summer, but it has cost me much. More than you and your friends can ever repay. I am not just talking about the fish I have not caught, the birds I have not trapped, the peaceful surroundings that have been taken from me. I am not just talking about my boat and my life that you are asking me to endanger.'

The placid, easy-going Nils was transformed, his face contorted with the power of his inner feelings, words springing from his lips like water from a cracking dam.

'I am talking about my woman, who was murdered. Inga was beaten about the head and thrown into this very fjord, and no one has found out who did it, or why. No one has said to me that they are sorry, that they will try to do something for me. She is gone, and nothing can repay me for that. So I must do things for myself. Understand? 5000 kroner for waiting – then the usual fare to Paamiut for all of you. If you do not agree – I leave now.'

Risa opened her mouth to continue the argument, then shrugged. 'OK.'

'I saw someone going up towards the river crossing,' said Nils.

'You're sure?'

'Yes.'

She nodded and set off up the hill.

Nils moored his boat, lit a cigarette and watched as she climbed the steep track, and vanished out of sight. In the distance smoke was thickening over the hills. The ground trembled again, and waves slapped up against his boat. Nils tossed his

191

cigarette butt overboard. He lifted his battered blue baseball cap, and scratched his head.

On the one hand there was the prospect of 5000 kroner. On the other, there was that mountain. He had seen the big chopper from Narsarsuaq overhead, and he knew that sending it must have cost the government far more than 5000 kroner. And the Kalaallit Nunaat government did not spend serious money without very good reason.

He lit another cigarette.

In the distance there was a fresh explosion. He looked towards the mountain, and saw, arching through the sky, a smoke-trailed volley of rocks and stones. They fell short of the fjord, but he found himself wishing that he had asked for more than 5000 kroner.

He sat in silence for half an hour, then got out of the boat, and climbed the path to Ikerasak.

The village was empty, but there were burnt scars where pieces of flaming lava had landed. Nils looked around, shading his eyes, then collected his belongings and returned to his boat. He cast off, and soon Ikerasak was fading in to the distance behind him. The rumbling of the mountain grew faint.

20

ERUPTION

As Larsen, Marianne and Wan Li stood above the thundering river, they heard someone shouting. Marianne let out a cry and waved her hand. A few moments later Adam joined them. His placid face and his powerful appearance raised everyone's spirits.

'I have been looking for you,' he said. 'We must go.'

'How?' asked Larsen, gesturing at the river. 'It's impossible to get across.'

Adam nodded. 'We must go further down.'

'Will that be safe?'

'The river's warm,' broke in Marianne excitedly. 'It's steaming.'

'We cannot stay here,' said Adam.

As if in confirmation of his words, there was a roar from the volcano at their back, far louder and fiercer than any they had yet heard. A breath of hot, pungent, sulphurous air, laced with black smoke, passed by them, and the ground shook again. Stones and earth rattled down the slope into the river below them.

Larsen remembered what Bettina had said about poisonous gas.

'We ought to get up on to high ground,' he said, pointing at the great rock ridge that towered above them.

Adam looked at him as if he was mad.

'There's no way of getting the child and the old man up there,' he said. 'If we go back down the valley, we can wade across the Isortoq at its mouth, and be back in Ikerasak within an hour and a half. That's how I got here.'

As the four of them made their way along the north side of the steaming, tumbling river, Larsen kept remembering the precarious boulder dam holding back the great lake of yellow water. He constantly looked around for possible routes of escape, but the broad river valley was typical of Greenland, its high steep walls hacked out by past glaciers.

After twenty minutes or so, Wan Li let out a sigh. 'I would like to stop for a few minutes,' he said.

'We need to keep going,' said Larsen, glancing anxiously behind him, to where smoke and steam hung over the distant Isortoq gorge.

'When I was a small boy, I took part in the Long March,' said Wan Li, with sudden sharpness in his voice. 'At first I was carried on my mother's back, but she died. And I had to walk. Six thousand miles across the mountains, swamps, deserts and poison grass plains of China, all the time under attack. Even so, Mao allowed us rests. He knew that if we rested for a little, we would rise refreshed and strengthened. Those who continued without stopping were the ones whose bodies we passed on the road.'

He sat down on a rock, and Marianne joined him. He stroked her thick black hair absently. 'This is your Long March, my little one.'

'Is it far now, grandpa?'

'That is what I used to say,' he replied, and his face was sad, lost in the distant sorrows of his youth. 'Every day I said it as we started, and every day I said it as we stopped. And always my mother said the same thing. "It is closer than it was." After she died, I no longer had anyone to ask, but it did not matter, for by then I knew the answer.' He sighed. 'Life is the longest march. Though for some it seems nothing but a quick stroll downhill, with a precipice at the end of it.'

Larsen leant against a bluff. Adam stayed standing, looking down the valley.

'Anyone want some biscuits?' said Marianne suddenly.

She produced from her pocket a packet of cracked digestive biscuits and offered them round. Everyone took two, and Larsen realised just how hungry and thirsty he was. But no one else said anything, and Larsen, his limbs aching, closed his eyes and tried not to listen to the growling of the infant volcano, like a far-distant artillery barrage. Tried not to feel the quiverings in the ground beneath his feet.

'Look,' said Adam suddenly. He pointed down the valley, to where the river swung briefly north under a looming cliff.

Larsen stared in the direction the hunter was pointing. The low sun, away to their right, sent deceptive shadows across the bare landscape, and he found it hard to make sense of the frost-shattered ridges and loose scree slopes that lined the bottom of the cliff, or of the black tumbling precipice, free of any hint of vegetation or colour.

'What?'

'People. Straight down from the summit shaped like a man wearing a hood. Just above the valley floor there's a low cliff, then an area of loose paler rock. To the left of that is a small stream, coming down the hillside in a cleft, but it is almost dry, and by the side of it, maybe a hundred metres up, there are two people.'

Larsen tried to follow Adam's instructions, but he could not even see the stream, let alone people beside it.

'What are they doing?'

'I would guess they were lying in ambush. This valley is sometimes used by reindeer, and they have chosen a perfect place to pick the animals off as they either enter or leave, for there is no other way in or out, except over the mountain sides.'

'Are they people from the village?'

'Unlikely,' said Adam. 'Everyone knows there have been very few deer this summer.'

'So who could they be?'

Adam shrugged. 'Occasionally hunters come out here from Paamiut. As well as the deer, there are usually foxes, hares, and ptarmigan, though again, this year has been poor. But I would say they are placed for large game.'

Larsen sucked in his cheeks. 'You're sure they are hunters?'

'What else would they be doing up there, watching the mouth of the valley?'

'That is what I was wondering,' said Larsen, under his breath.

He had a horrible sensation of being caught between two inexorably closing steel doors. Briefly he remembered the seed bank in Sermilik, where a year ago he had been trapped, seemingly without any chance of escape.

'We will find out soon enough,' said Adam. 'They are on the same side of the river as us, and we will pass within twenty or thirty metres of them.'

'Is there no way we can keep further away?' asked Larsen, licking his lips.

'Why?'

'Because I do not like these men lying in ambush. They must have seen us, mustn't they?'

Adam nodded. 'They probably have binoculars, and we are making no attempt to hide.'

'Then why are they not waving to us, or coming down to meet us? Can you still see them?'

'No. But they must be in the same place. Any attempt to climb either up or down would expose them instantly. From that point of view, it was not so good a spot to hide themselves. They may be well sited and well hidden where they are, but they cannot change position without warning their prey. They are probably inexperienced in hunting reindeer.'

The cold hand on Larsen's stomach tightened its grip another notch. And suddenly he was certain. 'They're not hunting reindeer. They're hunting us.'

'Why should they be?' demanded Adam.

'Why should Inga have been murdered?' Larsen swung on Wan Li. 'It's you they want, isn't it?'

The old man looked at him carefully. 'You think Shu-fan and his friend are back?'

'No,' said Larsen. 'I think it's worse than that. Shu-fan would not hide. His attempt to scare you into leaving failed, so why do the same thing again? He would simply try to persuade or force you to come with him.'

'You are not a fool, Tomas Larsen,' said Wan Li slowly, nodding.

'You mean the same thing had occurred to you?'

'Yes. It may be that these men are Inuit hunters, but . . .' He paused, and absently stroked Marianne's head again. 'I would like a cigarette.'

Without a word, Adam produced some cigarettes. The old man lit one with the ease of long experience, then looked at Larsen again, through the thin veil of smoke. 'What do you think this is about?'

'Why the hell are you asking me?' retorted Larsen. 'You know better than I do.'

Wan Li said nothing. Larsen looked at him, then turned to Adam. 'Any movement by those men?'

'No.'

'And they can't get closer to us without you seeing them?'

'That's right.'

'Watch them. Tell us if you see anything.' Larsen turned back to Wan Li. 'Very well, I will tell you what I think. There was another recently occupied campsite up the Iterdla, besides that of Shu-fan.'

'You mean among the trees, in the remains of the old house?' said Marianne. 'The place me and Edvarth found.'

'That's right.' Larsen's attention remained tightly focused on Wan Li. 'My guess is that now we know why the Chinese have announced you are dead. Because they expect you to be very soon. I think the Chinese government has tracked you down, and they have decided that killing you would remove any danger of you coming out of exile.'

'Permanently,' agreed Wan Li. He flicked ash to the ground. And to Larsen, he seemed oddly younger. As if the cigarette had removed fifteen years from his age. 'But why should they bother?'

'You were the only member of the government to speak out publicly in favour of the students at Tiananmen Square, and you were also a general.'

'In the People's Liberation Army.' An ironic smile took over Wan Li's face. 'What does that mean today?'

'It means,' said Larsen, 'that the government, like Shu-fan, thinks you may still be capable of uniting the open resistance in the towns, universities and regions, with simmering discontent in the ranks of the army and the bureaucracy. And they fear that combination would be enough to destroy them.'

'They fear correctly,' said Wan Li grimly. 'Millions recognised that 1989 was time for change, a great leap forward. But the corrupt, arthritic old men who had sat at the top for a generation knew they would be the first casualties of any change. So they reacted with instinctive savagery – like a man beating a barking dog to death, though the dog only wanted its food. Now most of them have gone, replaced by courtiers who made their way up by kowtowing and flattering and grovelling at the feet of the old men. Licking up their shit.'

Larsen and Marianne stared at him in surprise, but Wan Li took no notice.

'I think you are right, Tomas Larsen,' he went on. 'The men who wait at the mouth of the valley are men sent to murder me.'

Silence fell over them like a great cloak.

'What are we going to do?' said Marianne at last, her face snow-white and lined, like an old woman's.

Wan Li looked down at his feet. 'I am tired,' he said. 'Tired of watching shadows. Tired of living with fear as my wife. Tired of hiding. Tired of being Mei Tei. I could tell them that I will do nothing, that their fear is a phantom, without power or reality, but they will not believe me. They have never been willing to believe me.' He ground the cigarette butt on the stones. 'There comes a moment when the deer's resolve breaks, and he lies down and gives himself to the wolves. A rifle bullet would be a welcome release. There is nothing to fear in a moment's pain, then sleep. I shall leave the three of you here, and walk on by myself.'

'Don't go, grandpa.' Marianne reached out her thin arms and put them round the old man, as if she could hold him there. 'I won't let you. You mustn't leave me. You mustn't.'

'It is best that you let me go,' said Wan Li, getting to his feet, then bending down and kissing her frightened face.

'No, it isn't,' said Larsen sharply.

Wan Li stopped. 'What do you mean?'

'It will not be best for Marianne if you give yourself up,' said Larsen in a voice that permitted no contradiction. 'Inga knew something of these men, so she was murdered. The same will happen to us after you have gone. They will kill us too, and it will be easy enough – we are unarmed, and trapped.'

Wan Li's face was a creased study in thought.

'You may be right,' he said at last. 'But . . .'

'But how do we get out of here alive? Ask the expert. Adam, have they moved yet?'

'No.'

'Can we get away from here, without them realising?'

'Why are you asking me? I have never been hunted.'

'Let me put it another way. If there was a herd of reindeer at the entrance of the valley, how would you get within easy shooting range?'

The hunter scanned the area around them with the predator's eye for minutiae. 'If the wind was from us to them, I would go into that recess in the cliff, out of their sight, then climb the cliff. The first three hundred metres are hidden from the mouth of the valley. After that they probably would not notice me because I would be high above them. At the top, I would go along the ridge, then down the further side, so that I was downwind of them. But that would take us further from Ikerasak, and from the place to cross the river.'

'It also takes us further from the ambush. Let's do it.'

'The other two will not be able to,' protested Adam.

'They will have to,' said Larsen. He felt a sudden wash of relief at the news that there was a way out of the valley, however hard.

'Come, little one,' said Wan Li, putting out his hand to Marianne. 'On with our Long March.'

'So you're not leaving, grandpa?'

'No. I'm coming with you. Now, save your breath. You will need it.'

Once they were hidden in the bay in the mountains, Adam looked upwards. It was not a sheer cliff above them, but it was steep and difficult. His eyes ran up and down, calculating possible routes.

'What if our friends down the valley wish to know what we are doing here?' Wan Li quietly asked Larsen.

The policeman raised his hands helplessly. 'We must hope that they just think we're having a rest.'

Above them the sun was vanishing behind a thin haze.

'OK,' said Adam suddenly. He grabbed Marianne, and hoisted her on to his broad shoulders.

'It's time to climb,' said Larsen to Wan Li.

'I'm not sure that I can,' said the old man, sighing again. 'Perhaps if I stayed here . . .'

'Stop pretending to be a hero. Let's go.'

Adam led the way up the rocky slope, with Marianne gripping tightly. Larsen followed with Wan Li, as they toiled up the slope, zigzagging across the rugged face, slowly climbing higher and higher. In some places Larsen had to stand below Wan Li and give him a foothold, pushing him upwards as much as he could. At other places, Larsen went on ahead, then pulled the old man upwards. He was far lighter than Larsen had expected, and the policeman suspected he might have had more difficulty with the solid shape of Marianne perched on his shoulders, than he did helping Wan Li.

Fortunately much of the early climbing was not too difficult, though the old man was soon panting, and wincing. As they went up, and it grew steeper, Larsen had to spend more and more time climbing above Wan Li, then dragging him over the most difficult bits.

Without noticing, they emerged from the shadow of the cliff and clambered on and on. Suddenly the earth shuddered afresh, and fragments of smoking rock and tiny red shards of lava mingled with stones and pebbles that came scuttling down on them from the cliffs above. In the distance they heard the volcano rumble again.

Wan Li pulled himself on to a broad ledge, then fell forward on his face.

'I can go no further,' he gasped. 'I am sorry.'

'I need a rest too,' admitted Adam.

He deposited Marianne beside the old man, then sat down, leaning back against the rock face, breathing heavily. Larsen joined them, looking out over the land beneath.

They had come a long way. Much further than Larsen had thought. The river had shrunk to a yellow-grey ribbon in its shadowed valley, and they stood just below the shoulders of the surrounding mountains, which protected the lowlands around Ikerasak from the great mass of the inland ice – the frozen heart of Kalaallit Nunaat. Before them tumbling hills ran away north-west, towards a distant yet searingly bright line of white that marked the very edge of sight, the gleaming twenty-kilometre-wide wall of ice that was the Iceblink, where the ice cap came down to the sea. Far closer at hand was the dark cleft of Grindehval fjord, but Ikerasak itself, and the sea, were hidden by the angle of the mountainside. So, on the inland side, was the volcano, but they could still hear it, snarling to itself, like a huge dozing creature.

'I feel better up here,' said Larsen, slowly recovering his breath.

'Why?' asked Adam.

'It's safer. Are those men still there?'

Adam poised himself on the brink, and peered down, shading his long sharp eyes.

'I cannot tell. There is no sign of them on the open rock faces around the place where they hid. Is that why you feel safer?'

'Partly. But there are other things – water, avalanches, gas clouds. I don't know. Anything.'

'We'll have to climb back down,' remarked Adam. 'Some time.'

'Not into that valley,' said Larsen.

'And not yet, I beg you,' said Wan Li, who was lying down, his eyes closed.

'I thought the climbing was exciting,' said Marianne. But her drawn face and huge dark eyes betrayed the fear she was bravely fighting to hide.

The noise from the invisible mountain was fading slowly. Marianne had put her head in Wan Li's lap and closed her eyes; she did not move, and her breathing was soft and regular. The old man's eyes were also shut, and his creased, dried-up face was relaxed, as he leant back against a rock-wall.

Time edged past. Larsen thought that they ought to be moving

– the volcano seemed to be calming down, and they could not stay hidden in the hills for ever. On the other hand any attempt to get back to Ikerasak risked revealing themselves to the men out there.

Unable to make up his mind, he sat and waited for a decision to come to him. But rather than think around it, he simply felt the aches and pains in his body, and tried to let his mind roam free. It seemed reluctant to travel. All he saw before the backs of his eyelids were cliff faces; steaming water; the burning pyramid emerging from the yellow lake; and most vivid of all, that precarious dam, and the untold mass of water, poised to sweep suddenly, irresistibly, down the Isortoq valley.

He was startled out of himself by a sudden sharp and present noise. The other three had also started violently awake, even though the sound was the most mundane in the world – the ring of a telephone.

For a moment they all looked around wildly, then Larsen realised it was the telephone clipped to his belt, which he had entirely forgotten. He pulled it out and answered it. The line was very bad, but he could just hear what was being said.

'Tomas?'

'Yes. Who is it?'

'Jette, from the office. Thank God I'm through to you, I've been trying for hours. Where are you?'

'Nowhere interesting. Half-way up a mountain, with an old man, a child and a hunter. There's a flooding river immediately below us, and a newly erupting volcano close by, threatening to spew out poisonous gas. Also armed assassins are watching the only exit from the valley, so there appears to be no way of getting out of here. How can I help you?'

There was a pause, then a brittle laugh. 'You're exaggerating, aren't you?'

'Believe me, Jette my dear, I'm understating the case, and if you have any imaginative suggestions as to what we should do – risk the murderers, the poisonous gas, the river, or the mountains – then I'd be grateful.'

There was another nervous laugh from the far end, hastily cut off. 'I have some bad news, Tomas.'

'Bad news!' echoed Larsen. He looked around him and shook his head. 'Given where I am at the moment, I suspect there's almost nothing you can tell me that won't cheer me up.'

'No, Tomas. This is real bad news.'

Instantly his mind flew to Mitti. 'What is it?'

'Pieter Norlund.'

'What about him?' Larsen asked, letting out his breath in relief.

'His body may have been found up the fjord from Paamiut.'

'Go on.'

'There was no identification on the body, which had been buried in a shallow grave under stones. A trapper found it – though foxes had found it first –'

'Look, Jette,' interrupted Larsen, 'I thought we knew for certain that Norlund had thrown in his job and gone off to Denmark. There was that resignation letter from him, and he was positively identified as having taken a flight from Narsarsuaq to Copenhagen. Why should anyone suspect he's a nameless body in a grave near Paamiut?'

'Well, it's not quite so clear in fact.'

'What does the Chief say?'

'He's certain that it's not Pieter's body, but –'

'Could you put me through to him?'

'Well, you see – I'm not at the office.'

Suddenly, through the hisses and crackles, Larsen heard the emotion in her voice. And realised what it meant.

'You weren't told to contact me, were you, Jette? You're doing this on your own. Because you . . . liked Norlund.'

'No.' Was that a hint of tears in her voice? He couldn't tell, the line was on the edge of breaking up. 'I didn't like him. The man was a shit. But we shared a lot.'

I shared things with him too, thought Larsen briefly. 'What makes you think this body is Norlund's?' he asked.

'According to the policeman on the spot, a boatman has stated that he took a policeman up the fjord, it's called Eqaluit, to near where the body was found, and left him there. It wasn't any of the local police – and we know Norlund was in Paamiut that day. As for the ID on the flight, it was very vague – just a man who looked like a Greenlander, with Norlund's ticket, and papers. But if Norlund had been murdered, then the killer could have taken the ticket and the papers, couldn't they?'

'If you keep thinking like that, you'll be after my job soon,' said Larsen. 'So what do you want then?'

'I was told you were in Paamiut. I thought you might be able to go and see the body. I know it's a nasty job, and the whole thing may be a mistake, but someone ought to make sure, shouldn't they? And you're the nearest person who knew Norlund.'

'Except that I'm stuck on a mountain.'

'I didn't know that.' Her voice died away.

'You're right,' said Larsen, after a moment. 'Someone should check. But I'll have to have transport out of here.'

'Where are you then?'

'Back in Ikerasak.'

'Ikerasak! But I saw about that place on the TV news. There's a volcano erupting there, and they're evacuating everyone by helicopter.'

'The sooner they evacuate me, the better.'

'So all that stuff you just told me was –'

'True. Yes. Now listen, don't ring me again, Jette. If the phone goes off when I'm stretched out half-way over an overhang, I might just give up and let myself fall. I'll ring you when I can, OK? But I'd be seriously grateful if you could contact the Chief and tell him I'm stuck on a mountain, possibly with gunmen after me. He might be able to think of some way of getting me out of here. OK? And I'll take you out for a meal when I get back to Nuuk.'

'It's a deal. Good luck.'

'I need it. Thanks, Jette.'

The others were all looking at him as he put away the phone.

'Something someone wants me to do in Paamiut,' said Larsen. 'If I can get there.'

'The chances are not good,' said Adam calmly.

'What do you mean?'

This time they could all see what Adam was pointing at. About a kilometre away towards the end of the ridge, and a little below them, two men were climbing.

'Our friends are after us,' said Adam. 'You were right – they're not hunting reindeer.'

At that moment the mountain roared again, louder than ever, screaming out its challenge to the whole earth, a thunderous ear-smashing burst of noise beyond the borders of pain, so that all four of them clutched their heads, closed their eyes and perhaps screamed themselves – though it was impossible to tell in that raw hurricane of sound. An impenetrable wall of noise that swallowed them up and went on and on, timelessly, unceasing, unbearable, until Larsen's head seemed on the very brink of physically splitting apart. Only then did it begin to fade away.

The four of them sat on the ledge, in stunned silence, trying to recover from the assault on their senses, scarcely aware of the rain of ash that falling on them. Suddenly Marianne gave a fresh scream and pointed.

Round the corner of the ledge, from the direction of the ice cap, they saw something sweep down the hillside. It was a huge dense cloud, several hundred metres high, and as wide as the valley. Yet it did not look like a cloud, there was nothing thin or insubstantial about it – rather it seemed like a living creature. A huge, tortuously writhing snake, half-concealed in a swirling, boiling vortex; a serpentine maelstrom of black and grey and brown and white, crested with tongues of fire, that tumbled irresistibly down the bare slopes, travelling as fast as a speeding car, and carrying before it inexorable, inescapable malevolence.

Deep in the earth, gases had been driven up from the fiery heart of the volcano, and held trapped under stupendous pressure. Now they had finally burst free and exploded out into the atmosphere. The result was the deadly burning cloud that they now saw rolling below them, a lethal combination of super-heated steam, volcanic ash, fragmented lava, and gas, laced with incandescent dust and red- and white-hot fragments of rock, flanked and fronted with great boulders, flung from the earth by the explosion, which hurtled forward like the battering rams of an unstoppable army.

A massive wave of suffocatingly hot, fetid air struck them a mighty blow, emptying their lungs, and tearing at them with invisible talons, struggling to send them fluttering from their eyrie, to fall and be obliterated in the featureless anarchy that now swirled ever closer below them.

As they watched in terror, the inky bank of cloud washed up against the mountain they had climbed, completely concealing everything beneath in a seething black conflagration. Lightning flashed and forked through the darkness. It seemed that unformed matter from the primeval chaos at the very start of the universe had found a gap into the solid world, and was pouring in inexhaustibly, carrying with it the certainty of instant annihilation.

The air was full of a thousand different sounds: crashing, hissing, cracking, rolling, thundering, as if a vast storm had swept over the very last and ultimate battlefield – Ragnarok, Armageddon – and united with it. There was a foul stench of burning, a nauseating taste in their mouths, and venom seared their lungs.

Instinctively all four of them pulled back from the edge as far as they could, struggling to avoid the blasting heat and the lethal gases that swathed and surrounded the cloud. Crouching down, making themselves as small as they could, they pressed their faces hard against the damp rock to protect themselves from the apparent certainty that their smouldering skin would be scorched from their blistered and baked flesh. In that moment, death seemed certain, for there was nothing to breathe but burning dust. The air, that a moment before had given them life, had been replaced by superheated poison, and liquid fire.

A timeless infinite stretch of agony later, it was gone. The heat began to fade, and their desperate, swollen lungs found something to breathe. The stench remained, as did more heat than they had ever felt in that country of ice, but the most savage onslaught had passed. Yet none of the four moved. They stayed where they were, thankful only that there was once more air to breathe, and that the temperature was slowly dropping. Grateful that somehow, miraculously, they had been permitted to survive the passage of the cloud of death.

21

FIRE AND WATER

As Risa reached the top of a bare slope, on her way to the geologists' camp, she stared in disbelief. At the bottom of the next valley, where previously there had been a small stream, she now saw a broad, brown river, with wispy spears of arctic cotton grass emerging from the fast-flowing water.

There was also someone on the far bank.

Risa hurried down a steep crag, then picked her way cautiously across a multi-coloured swamp of red, yellow and green lichen and silver-grey reindeer moss. Water oozed thickly from under her boots, which sank several centimetres into the spongy surface with every step. Approaching the river, she saw, with sudden disappointment, that it was the American, Kim, who stood on a stony bank, pushing a bulging yellow waterproof bag into her rucksack.

'Hi,' Risa called, and squelched down to the waterside. 'What're you doing?'

'Getting ready to go inland,' said the American. She looked across at Risa with suspicious eyes. 'Why?'

'I just wondered.' The nurse gestured at the river. 'Last time I came here, you could jump over the stream.'

'The volcano must be melting the ice.'

'Yes. Did you wade across?'

'I tried,' said Kim. 'But I wouldn't recommend it.'

Risa studied the river. It was pouring fiercely down the valley, nowhere less than ten metres wide. The ridges of hard rock that had previously made it a simple business to cross had vanished without trace.

'How deep is it?' she asked.

Kim ran a hand through her wet, spiky hair. 'Shoulder-height some of the way. At least head-height in the middle, I didn't try putting my feet down. In fact I came pretty close to being swept away. Believe me, that water's got real muscle.'

'You mean you swam?' said Risa.

Kim nodded and turned back to strapping shut her black and chestnut-brown rucksack.

'But why did you cross anyway?' pressed Risa.

Kim looked up impatiently. 'I'm a journalist, OK? I want to interview that old Chinese guy, Mei Tei, or whatever his name is, and I'm not going to let a flooded river stop me. How about you? Why haven't you got out of here like everyone else?'

'There're people who still haven't been warned about the volcano.'

'Why not phone them?'

'Some of them may not have phones. Anyway, have you tried using yours?'

Kim pulled out her mobile and tried first one number, then another, then a third. While she did so, Risa glanced at the edge of the river, then took a few steps back.

'It's still rising,' she muttered.

'The phone isn't working,' said Kim at last.

'Neither is anyone else's. So what do we do now?'

'I don't know what you do. I know what I'm going to do.'

'I must cross,' insisted Risa.

Kim looked at her. 'I don't think so,' she said flatly. 'I'll warn these people for you. Who are they?'

'I have to find Sergeant Larsen,' said Risa. 'I think he's with the geologists.' Competitiveness flared within her. 'Anyway, how come you're telling me I've no chance of crossing this river safely, when you just did?'

'I had equipment to help me, stuff I was advised to bring to Greenland if I was going to do any serious hiking. I was warned that rivers here can be real big problems.' Kim put her phone away, picked up her rucksack and slung it easily over her shoulders, then turned back to Risa. 'Look, if you have to come, why not walk parallel to me, and maybe there'll be somewhere narrow enough to get a rope across.'

'Have you got a rope?'

'Sure.'

The two women began walking up opposite sides of the river. Kim walked fast, and Risa had to hurry to keep up with her – the more so as the south bank remained boggy, and difficult walking.

Twenty minutes later, as the land began to rise again, they came to a place where the water had sliced through a band of harder rock. The width of the river shrank to a fraction of what it had been, as it transformed into a fast-flowing cataract. The redoubled force of the current seemed to change the very colour of the water, from muddy yellow to streaked brown. On either side, ragged, sharp-edged buttresses of wet black rock rose up perhaps ten metres high.

'We'll try here,' shouted Kim, above the roar of the water.

Risa looked around her doubtfully, but Kim was already pulling a coil of rope out of her rucksack. She carefully tied one end around a rock pillar, checking the knot several times, then attached a stone to the other end, glanced across estimating the distance, and threw it. The first throw ended in the river, and Kim pulled it out swiftly, hand over hand, then threw the dripping wet stone with its attached rope again. This time it landed within a metre of Risa, who picked it up and tied the end off on a rock on her side.

'Is it good and tight?' shouted Kim.

Risa tested it, as she had seen Kim do. 'It's OK.'

'Good.' Kim was carefully tightening the rope on her side, until it straddled the river, as taut as she could make it.

'Right,' she called at length.

Risa looked at the slender rope, stretching out six or seven metres above the great smooth sweeping torrent, with its irresistible currents, and vicious whirlpools. She felt herself break out into a sweat.

'Are you sure this is OK?' she shouted. 'It means losing your rope.'

'I can use it to get back,' Kim replied. 'It'll be a lot easier than another swim, especially if the water keeps rising. Anyway, don't trouble yourself about me. Come on over.'

Risa felt her legs shaking. 'I don't think I can do it.'

'Sure you can. It's no problem. Look.'

Kim took a grip on the rope, gave it several fierce tugs to test it yet again, then swung her right leg over it, and hanging underneath the rope, using her leg as a grip, and pulling herself along hand over hand, she crossed the river in a few moments, and stood by Risa.

'See.'

'Did they teach you that in journalist school?'

'Summer camp in the Allegheny mountains. Now, you follow me.'

Swiftly, easily, Kim crossed back over the river.

Risa did not allow herself to think, but pulled herself on to the rope, hooked one leg and one arm over, and tried to drag herself as she had seen Kim do. The rope lurched sickeningly from side to side, and the water roared in her ears, as she clawed herself forward, a few centimetres at a time. There was spray around her, in her face, and the rope was cold and slippery, cutting at her desperately gripping hands. Somewhere, lost in the clamour, she heard Kim shouting, but she dared neither open her eyes, nor listen. Caught in a nightmare of terror, each uneven lurch from side to side threatening to send her plummeting to her death, she dragged herself on, snail-like, trying to ignore the pain in the crook of her arm and behind her knee. It seemed never-ending. Nausea surged through her. The rough wet rope rasped at her face, her hands felt as if they were burning up, and every locked muscle in her body screamed for release.

'You're there,' she heard Kim shout, seemingly in her very ear.

Convulsively she opened her eyes, saw Kim reaching out her hand, reached out her own, and lost her grip. She slipped sickeningly, and found herself swinging from the rope by one hand. Teeth clenched, she held on with all her power and desperately flailed out with her other hand, grasping for the rope. Her arm was paralysed, her fingers slithering away.

There was no choice, she did not have the strength to hold herself any more. For an incongruous second she found herself thinking that if she had taken more care over her weight, maybe she could have held herself longer. Then blackness rose up in her brain, and she let go and dropped – a few centimetres, on to firm rock.

'Fucking hell!' she exclaimed.

Kim laughed. 'You'll find it no trouble next time.'

'You what?'

'Let's go.'

'Where're we going?'

'Up there.' Kim pointed to a steep-sided, conical kame, perhaps a hundred metres high, that reared up out of the stony open ground. 'We should be able to see more clearly from the top of that.'

Three-quarters of their way up the hill, the ground shuddered savagely, so that the two women staggered and fell against each other. A moment or two later, a great rolling clangorous burst of noise struck them like a physical blow. The noise went on and on, paralleled by the shuddering of the tortured earth. As it finally faded, a foul chemical smell ripped at the back of their throats, and stung their eyes, like acid, accompanied by wave after wave of scorchingly hot air.

The air was suddenly dark with ash, falling gently, silently, all around them. Like black snow.

'I think the volcano just blew,' said Kim.

'What does that mean?'

'Christ knows!'

'I suppose that's true,' said Risa. 'Let's stop here. We could rest and . . . have you anything to eat or drink?'

'Sure.' Kim wasn't listening. She scrambled round the side of the hillock, and finding a vantage point, pulled out a pair of small rubber-armoured Leica binoculars and focused them up the valley. 'Fuck!' she exclaimed.

'What is it?'

'There's some sort of weird black cloud coming out of the mountains. It's got these bizarre folds hanging on the side, like huge brown and purple curtains. No, they're vanishing. Jesus Christ! There's lightning coming out of the cloud, going up into the sky. And the thing itself is massive, it looks like water almost, boiling water, but black as ink. It's gushing out round the river, and spreading all over the lower ground. It's going fast. So fucking fast!'

'Is it coming towards us?' asked Risa, scrambling round to join her.

'It's going everywhere. Yes, it's coming straight towards us, but . . . Holy shit! We've got to get away from here. Now!' There was raw panic in the American's voice.

Risa looked back, over the ground they had just crossed.

It was bare, empty of any shelter, vanishing under the steady rain of ash.

'There's nowhere to go,' she said breathlessly.

'I don't care. I'm out of here.'

Kim sprang to her feet, to run, but Risa grabbed her, and pointed towards the cloud. 'It seems to be slowing down.'

Kim put the binoculars back to her eyes. 'You're right. It's stopping. In fact it looks as if it's, I don't know, solidifying almost. As if it wasn't a cloud at all, more an avalanche, and it's got as far as it can.'

A fresh wave of burning air struck them so fiercely that they could feel the skin on their faces stiffen and crack. Hastily they retreated to the protected lee of the hillside.

'I'm not going out in that,' said Risa, shivering.

Kim glanced at her, then reached out and the two hugged each other in silence.

'I'll make us some food,' Kim said at last.

An hour later, they climbed to the top of the hill.

'See anyone?' asked Risa.

Kim scanned the area with her binoculars. 'No. And the ground seems sort of black and brown. Hang on, I'm not sure, but I think I can see some tents in a dip. Maybe a kilometre away.'

'Let's try,' said Risa.

As they approached the hollow, the women became aware that the land they were approaching was radiating heat. There was a clear line of blackened and cracked stones, that must have been brought hurtling over the land by the great flowing cloud, to fall at its furthest extremity. Entering the area that had fallen under the wave, they found the ground was completely hidden under a thick skin of ash and cinders. The few plants they could see were scorched and smoking, killed in a moment. A metallic-smelling haze sprawled over the country, and low yellowish-black clouds concealed the sun and the sky. The soles of their boots grew hot, and the heat began to penetrate through to their feet. Risa bent down and touched the charred and splintered stones beneath her, then drew back her hand hastily.

'It's too hot to touch,' she said.

'It'd probably be a whole lot hotter, if it wasn't for the perma-frost just below the surface,' said Kim. Her face was grim.

The geologists' campsite looked as if a huge wildfire had swept through it. Two of the tents were no more than blackened aluminium tent poles with rags of fabric hanging from them. The plastic ropes had fused to the heavy duty tent pegs. Belongings were scattered randomly in the omnipresent ash. Metal objects – the cooking stove, tools, spoons and knives and pots – were discoloured, but largely undamaged, as were a variety of instru-ments: a theodolite, tripod, and radar scanner. A tiltmeter had been broken by the intense heat, a computer monitor had clearly exploded, and the keyboard was burnt brown and partly melted. Almost everything else had been utterly destroyed. A column of interleaved blackened strips might have been a pile of clothes. Books had been reduced to ash, waterproof bags and sacks had become pools of unidentifiable smoking plastic.

On the far side of the camp, the destruction was even worse. The large tent had been almost completely vaporised, the poles were bent and twisted, and flung far from their places, and the ground showed streaks and signs of fire-blasting. Jagged shards of metal gleamed all around, like shrapnel after a bomb has fallen.

'What happened here?' asked Risa in a hushed voice.

'I should think it was where they stored the fuel bottles for cooking,' said Kim. 'They must have exploded in the heat – gone off like grenades.'

Fear had seized Risa's throat like a strangling hand.

'We wouldn't have stood a chance if the cloud had reached us,' she muttered softly, realising that if Marianne and Larsen and the others had been caught in the open, then they must be dead.

'No,' agreed Kim, looking around the landscape that, in a few seconds, had been transformed from grey to black. 'But these guys clearly weren't here when it struck. I wonder where they are.'

'They probably saw what was coming, and managed to run away.'

'I don't think anyone could have run from that cloud,' breathed Kim. 'It came fast. Very, very fast.'

As she spoke, Risa had a nightmare vision of what might so easily have happened: first sight of the black cloud of destruction rolling towards them; the instant terror; the desperate doomed run; and then the moment they were caught – searing pain, and almost immediate death, as the deadly cloud swallowed them up into the darkness of infinity and extinction.

She glanced up the valley, towards the source of that wholesale devastation.

'Will it happen again?' she said. 'Another cloud?'

'Christ knows,' replied Kim, and her voice was shaking. 'Do you think maybe we should get the hell out of here?'

'Nils is waiting at the village with his boat. I promised him 5000 kroner if he would stay.'

'Great!' said Kim, without listening. Then the words went home. '5000 kroner – that's pretty serious money.'

'He wouldn't stay for less. But you must have lots of money – I mean that rucksack, the binoculars, the flights, and everything.'

'I spent every cent I had,' said Kim. 'In fact I spent a lot of money I haven't got – my credit cards are flat against their ceilings. You see, this is a massive gamble – like my last throw. If I can fix a really good, exclusive, interview with Mei Tei, and syndicate it world-wide, that's my name made, and I'll be in among the big players. If not . . .'

'Yes?'

'If not, then I thought maybe I'd give up the whole journalism thing, and get married and have kids.'

'It's that easy?' asked Risa, thinking. She looked up, and stared out at the the towering snow-capped mountains further inland.

'There's a guy back in Cincinnati, where I live, who wants to marry me – but what's the point if I'm globetrotting for stories? Anyway, what now?'

'No one was here when the cloud struck, so there has to be a good chance we can find someone alive.' Risa resisted the festering fear within her.

It was Kim who found the cavity in the rock, three hundred metres from the camp, facing away from the mountains. It was a narrow crack, perhaps a metre wide, and twice that high, going deep into the rock face, with a partial roof overhead, making it almost a cave.

Kim peered inside, and then let out a breathless gulping sound, staggered a few metres back, and was violently, unstoppably sick.

Risa came over and looked along the crevice, which was still burning hot to touch.

The three geologists, Sigrid, Rob and Bettina, were crammed into the crack, where they must have fled for shelter when they saw the cloud coming. Their bodies were interlaced and twisted, so that it was impossible to see where one of them ended and another started. They were scarcely recognisable as human, limbs shrivelled, clothes and skin blackened and welded together by the irresistible heat. Except for their faces, which were scarcely touched. All three wore breathing apparatus, and although the tubes and straps and filters were scorched and discoloured, the face-plates had survived intact and the expressions of agony were caught perfectly, the last despairing scream of pain trapped forever in the ghastly three-dimensional photograph that was reality.

Ten minutes later the two women had still not said a word, only moved away from the recess of horror. At last, spontaneously, they held each other. The tall American bent her head and rested it on Risa's broad shoulder.

'It must have only been a moment,' Risa said softly.

'If only one couldn't have seen their faces,' muttered Kim. Her whole body was shivering. 'They're like the bodies at Pompeii, all twisted and writhing, but those just look like brilliant statues, statues that touch you with their pain, but still only statues. Not real. Not part of life. Here, you see the faces, you recognise the people, and ...'

She began crying. Risa continued to hug her and let her weep.

Then gradually she became aware of a new sound, and looked around.

The deepest part of the bowl was close by, beyond the tents, which were on a hummock, and Risa noticed a pool of filthy water, covered in a thick black scum of ash and floating fragments of pumice.

She frowned. She could not remember having seen the pool before, nor could she understand why the burning cloud had not boiled it away. Then she saw the pool was growing.

'What is it?' asked Kim, aware of the tension that had come into Risa's sturdy body.

Risa pointed.

In two or three places on the lower, south side of the depression, which they had entered by, water was running down. Even as they watched the streams grew bigger and stronger, and fresh ones appeared. The pool at the bottom of the depression was growing faster, lapping up towards the remains of the tents.

Kim fumbled at her belt, and produced her mobile, but yet again she was unable to make any contact, and in frustration she hurled the phone to the ground. It bounced on a rock, and tumbled down in a chute of pebbles, to vanish into the water.

'Let's get out of here,' said Risa.

The two of them ran towards the far side, where the rocky sides were higher. Behind them the streams were growing and increasing in number, pouring into the depression ever faster.

'What the fuck is going on now?' panted Kim, as she scrambled up the rocky bank as fast as she could, the rucksack shaking on her back. 'How can it be fire one moment, water another?'

Risa, surefooted and strong, and with nothing on her back to impede her, was already reaching the top. She put down a hand and helped her companion up the last section. Below them ash-skinned water, thick with mud, had covered the floor of the depression, the campsite was starting to vanish, and the water was already climbing the rock wall they had just ascended.

As they reached the top, they looked north, towards the valley of the Isortoq, and gasped.

The river itself was vast, bloated, and growing with such speed that it was no longer possible to see where it had once run. Where half an hour before had lain a blackened and burnt desert, there was now a lake, growing and spreading as they watched. The land, briefly heated to incandescence by the pyroclastic surge from the volcano, was now being cooled equally suddenly by ice meltwater, and a thickening fog of steam, blackened with ash and dust, had descended further inland. In every direction, except to their right where the ground rose steeply towards the foot of the mountains, was a huge mass of sandy yellow water, stained and streaked black and grey, spreading across the tumbled lowlands leading down to the fjord. Hillocks were becoming islands, which shrank and vanished underwater in their turn; larger hills were transformed into archipelagos; gullies and small valleys became roaring cascades for a few minutes, then as the water continued to rise, their flow lessened and they disappeared without trace. Streams became rivers, rivers became vast lakes. The rugged and varied countryside was vanishing under featureless water.

'The eruption must have melted part of the ice cap,' said Risa. 'We'll have to head for high ground.'

'It's rising so fast,' said Kim.

'The ground underneath is frozen, so it can't soak down. And the high ridges near the fjord probably mean it's difficult for the water to run off into the sea. I guess it might rise a lot more.'

The depression at their feet was almost full, and water was approaching the ridge they stood on from other directions, creeping swiftly over the burnt ground, pushing a line of blackened flotsam before it.

Risa looked around them, taking in the lie of the land as best she could, then pointed along the ridge. 'Let's go.'

As they pushed inland, the water rose on each side, leaving them nowhere to go except forward. A large rocky outcrop slowed them badly, and the solid ground behind vanished underwater with terrifying speed. Still the flood grew and spread in every direction, swallowing up the land, and in the distance they could hear the thundering roar of untold millions of tons of water pouring down the gorge from the melting ice cap. The ridge was narrowing now, barely twenty metres across, as the water closed in. In one place they had to jump a water-filled crevasse, in another they splashed through ankle-high water, to higher ground. Still the flood rose.

It had started to rain, black-flecked rain falling from the dust-engorged clouds that hung low above, like filthy curtains. Kim was growing tired, and Risa could hear her panting.

'I have to stop,' the American gasped at last. She sat down on the ground, her shoulders bowed, then unbuckled her rucksack and put it down beside her. 'I can't carry this any further.'

'What's in it?' asked Risa.

'Food, waterproofs, clothes, sleeping bag, cooking stuff, mattress, tent, everything I brought. But –'

'We may need those sort of things,' said Risa resolutely. She picked up the rucksack and pulled it on herself. 'Let's keep moving.'

The land was starting to rise towards the mountains, but after quarter of an hour, the ridge came to an unexpected end in a sudden cliff. The foothills lay just ahead, with the promise of safety, but between the ridge and the foothills lay a hundred metre gap. Surging, scum-foamed currents, scattered with slabs of ice, poured through it, whipped up into waves, crashing against rocks that had not felt their angry touch in centuries.

Kim stared at the pouring flood in despair. 'We can't cross that.'

Risa looked back along the ridge they had been following. It was vanishing as she watched, turning into disconnected islets, which themselves were disappearing under the still-rising water. 'We don't have any choice.'

'But how . . .?'

'How did you manage to swim across the river?'

'I inflated my mattress and used it as a raft. And I've got a waterproof drysuit. But that river was only a tenth the width of this, and I barely got across. I kept thinking I was about to get swept away or dragged under.'

'I told you – we don't have a choice. If we stay here for long we're going to be caught by the water anyway.'

'But –'

'But nothing, there's no point,' said Risa sharply. 'You must swim over.'

'How about you then? Aren't you going to swim as well?'

'No.'

'Why not?'

'Because I can't swim. There's not much call for it in Greenland.'

'You mean you're going to stay here?'

'I'm going to be on this floating mattress of yours.'

'But it won't take that much weight.'

'Thank you.'

'I meant with the rucksack as well.'

'We'll have to hope you're wrong. Come on, there's no time to waste.'

Five minutes later Kim had put on a black drysuit over her

T-shirt and underwear. Next she pulled a rubber mattress out of her rucksack, and inflated it with a foot pump. Risa had gone through the rucksack, and kept only those things she thought might be useful: cooking equipment, waterproofs, two changes of clothes, dried food, binoculars, a compass, and the mattress pump in case they had to cross more water. She kept the tent separate in its own bag, in case it was too heavy, then tied the rucksack shut as tightly as she could, and stuffed it into a waterproof sack, which she also sealed shut.

Behind them, on the point, was a pile of belongings they were deserting: the rest of Kim's clothes, more food, maps, notebooks, books, even her $4000 laptop, Nikon camera, and tape recorder.

'How am I to interview Mei Tei now?' Kim had objected.

'Write it down.'

They turned away. Risa glanced back over her shoulder, in case they had forgotten anything useful. She noticed a large, high-quality knife in a sheath, and remembered her grandfather had always said that in the wilds the most important thing to have was waterproof clothes, and next came a knife. There was no time to undo the rucksack again, and she had no belt, so she hastily strapped the sheath to the inside of her leg, then joined Kim at the water's edge.

The American's face was white as a sheet, and she was shaking her head.

'This isn't going to work. The currents will just sweep us away. Or the mattress won't hold you. Or you'll be knocked off by waves. Or –'

'Let's do it.' Risa's voice had the snap of command.

Obediently Kim pushed the mattress out on to the swirling water, then took a couple of steps out into the flood herself, so that she could hold it, bobbing like a boat. Risa passed across the rucksack and tent in their bags, and Kim put them on top of the mattress.

Risa hesitated a moment, bit her lip, then took a step into the water.

'It's not as cold as I expected,' she remarked bravely.

Even before she had finished speaking, she realised she was wrong. It was bitterly cold, clutching her foot in a bone-freezing embrace that took her breath away.

'Jesus!' she exclaimed, in spite of herself. 'Can you really swim in that?'

'For a while.'

The mattress bobbed unsteadily, and with infinite caution Risa lay down on it, trying to spread her weight as evenly as possible. The rucksack was under her chest, the tent by her side, and her hands were stretched out to hold the two edges of the mattress, while her legs were splayed out either side.

'OK,' said Kim. 'Don't move your body, or the whole thing'll tip over. But paddle with your hands if you can. I'm going to need all the help I can get, if we're to get across.'

'Let's do it,' said Risa again.

With a sickening lurch, the mattress floated heavily out into the swirling water. Kim virtually threw herself after it. With one hand she gripped on to the mattress, while with the other she tried to swim. A current was soon pulling them away from the shrinking ridge, out into open water.

Kim began to kick as hard as she could, paddling with her free hand, while small vicious ripples slapped into her face. Risa too put out her hands and paddled them in the freezing, ice-flecked, water. Gradually they began to make headway towards the mountains. Then the main current of water caught the mattress, and it briefly swung round as waves slid over the side, and water, chill as liquid ice, seeped under Risa's body. The flow grew steadily stronger, and a fresh eddy caught them, and spun them round helplessly again, faster than before, and more water slopped up on to the surface of the mattress, so that Risa lay in a freezing pool. But the current had carried them in the right direction, towards the far side. As it lessened, and the mattress ceased revolving, Kim kicked again, as hard as she could, pushing the unwieldy raft towards the far shore.

Agonisingly slowly, the rocky shore opposite crawled closer, until it seemed within reach, just twenty metres away. Fifteen. Kim was tiring fast, her breath was coming in great sobbing gasps, her kicks carried less and less power, and they were getting no closer. Then Risa realised there was a brisk current running parallel to the shore, and it was carrying them along, preventing them from reaching land. Glancing ahead, she saw that the edge of the mountains would soon start retreating from them, and they were about to be swept into the centre of a new lake, at least two kilometres wide, that had opened out between the head of the fjord and the great semicircular crescent of the mountains.

But closer was a rocky headland, a last outflung fraction of the uplands before they fell away, and the current was carrying them directly towards it. Risa watched that ragged strip of land grow closer. Soon it was only ten metres from them. Less. Then the current swung away from it, and out towards the middle of that deadly lake.

'Let go, Kim. Let go, and swim,' shouted Risa, as loud as she could.

The exhausted Kim obeyed instinctively, and sank, then resurfaced, brought up by the buoyancy of her suit. A few splashing strokes, and she floundered ashore on the spit of land, water dripping off her. But a sudden surge in the current had almost swung the mattress right round again, and carried it onwards at accelerating speed. Risa hesitated a moment, then lunged forward, seal-like, into the bitterly cold water.

She would have screamed in shock, but she immediately vanished underwater. Desperate, panic-stricken, she kicked, and found herself bursting back to the surface. In her arms was the thing that had saved her life. Barely aware of the fact, Risa had plunged off the mattress still holding the plastic bag that contained the rucksack. The air trapped in it had dragged her back up, and now gave her just enough help so she was able to kick wildly a couple of metres closer to the shore, where Kim had waded out up to her chest, and grabbed her.

The two of them struggled ashore, and collapsed. But within minutes, the still-rising water was running up to their feet. They picked up the rucksack, and climbed thirty or forty metres above the water level, to a small, protected corrie, where they collapsed again. The sodden Risa was shivering convulsively, and she had to strip off her clothes, and put on some of Kim's that she had kept in the rucksack, and which had miraculously stayed more or less dry. They were totally the wrong size for her, too long and much too narrow, but they were all they had. Meanwhile Kim had stripped off her suit and put on the other change of clothes. It was still raining, and both women put on waterproofs. Risa sat down wearily, but Kim looked out over the lake beneath them. The mattress was a dot on the water, far away.

'That was a Therm A,' she muttered. 'Cost a fortune.'

'Just as well,' remarked Risa. 'A cheaper one probably would have sunk with me on it.'

'I suppose so.' Kim picked up the foot-pump for inflating the mattress and flung it into the water. 'The tent's gone too, so we'd better not be stuck out here too long. Talking of which, where exactly are we?'

'I don't know.'

'Open up the rucksack, and we can check on the GPS.'

'What's that?'

'Global Positioning System. It's a way of using satellites to find out where you are and where you need to go. It's in that pocket there, a handset that looks a bit like a mobile phone.'

'I'm sorry.' Risa shrugged helplessly. 'I didn't know what it was, so I left it behind, on the ridge.'

'Brilliant! There goes another 400 bucks. Oh well, don't worry about it. At least we're alive.' Kim sighed. 'Though I could do with a cigarette.'

'Do you smoke?' asked Risa.

'No.'

After a little they lit the stove and cooked themselves a pack of dried noodles. Warm food sent life flooding through them, and they gradually felt better.

'You need swimming lessons, Risa,' remarked Kim. 'It would make things a lot easier next time we're swimming for our lives in a flood.'

'I'll remember that,' said Risa. 'And you need to put on some weight, so that I can wear your clothes.'

They laughed.

'I'll go see where we have to go next,' said Kim.

As she got up, there was a rattle of stones down the slope above them. Kim looked up hopefully. Then her hopes crashed in ruin and fear.

Two men in hooded anoraks, rifles in their hands, were advancing on them. One of them raised his rifle and pointed it at Kim.

'Jesus Christ in hell!' muttered Kim. 'I know those guys.'

22

ON THE ICE

Marianne, Wan Li, Adam and Larsen stood on a flat patch of marshy ground, intersected by small streams, many of which were still frozen. Around the plateau mountains rose up into mist, which took away edges and contrast, and drained what little colour there was from the lifeless landscape. Waves of fog, dyed darker and thicker by a rich addition of volcanic smoke, rolled sullenly overhead, depositing a steady grey drizzle. The poor light of late evening was misleading and flat, concealing more than it revealed.

'How far ahead of them would you say we were?' asked Larsen.

Adam shrugged. 'It cannot be far. They had a chance to catch us, except that they turned aside, downhill. I do not know why. Perhaps they thought they could cut us off. Even despite that, if it had not been for the mist, I think they would have found us again, but we have a chance. A small chance.'

Larsen glanced at the little girl and the old man, who were holding each other. Fortunately they were warmly dressed, with anoraks, thick oiled sweaters and waterproof boots, but he could see they were both shivering.

'They won't be able to keep going much longer,' he said softly.

Adam was not listening. He was lost in thought. Aware that the hunter, with his detailed knowledge of the area, was the only person who could keep them alive, Larsen fell silent.

'We saw that the eruption has caused huge flooding,' said Adam at last. 'I think it will get worse before it gets better, which means there is no point in trying to get down off the mountains until we are clear of this region.'

Larsen opened his mouth to object, then stopped. Adam went on, without seeming to have noticed.

'We are close by the Akugdleq glacier, a sort of arm jutting out from the inland ice. If we can cross that, it should be fairly easy to get down to the lower hills south-east of Ikerasak, which should be free from any danger of flooding, and from there it's not far to the helicopter landing place.'

'How long is this going to take?'

'Eight or nine hours – if we're lucky.'

'And if we're not?'

'Then we won't make it at all. Last summer I took some climbers to the glacier. There may still be hints of a track, but crossing a glacier without equipment will be very dangerous.'

'I prefer the ice to assassins. Let's go before we all freeze where we stand.'

'Some say ghosts roam the ice cap.'

'I don't envy them.'

An hour later, at the foot of a slanting, grey ice wall, carved by thin rills of water, Adam found the old footholds. He climbed first, with Marianne on his shoulders, followed by Wan Li, and finally Larsen. Gradually the ragged, streaked ice surface levelled out, and the footholds vanished, but the going became no easier, for as they made their way up the mist grew thicker, a freezing mist that left dirty ice crystals on their hair, and around their mouths and noses.

'It will be easy for them to follow us if they discover those footholds,' remarked Adam, during one of their rests.

Larsen shrugged. 'We have made our choices.'

On the surface of the ice lay snow which had frozen, so there was a hard crust, but frequently they broke through and sank up to their knees or deeper, and progress was agonisingly slow. Marianne had to walk on her own through the snow, which she did with stolid resignation. Adam went first, probing cautiously with each foot before leading them on, and the others all trod in his footsteps. In places turquoise meltwater streams ran over the ice, reducing the surrounding area to a morass of wet slush. Elsewhere parallel lines of hummocks, each lump of ice the height of a man, made the going hard. The mist writhed and thinned as a cold wind blew from the east, and the drizzle lessened. Eventually the crimson disc of the new rising sun crept through, its long rays reflecting off the snow and ice, and dazzling their bloodshot eyes.

Further on they entered an area where the ice was badly broken up. The way was steep and slippery, and interrupted by deep crevasses, some partly concealed by snow, or even bridged by it, and in places they had to take detours, but they doggedly continued as straight as they could. As they pressed on, one section of ice suddenly began to crack and groan and shudder.

A moment later it almost seemed to become plastic, and a small wave ran through it. Adam shouted a warning, but his words were lost in a sharp splitting noise. As they watched, an abyss opened a few metres from them.

'The glacier edge must be unstable because of the eruption,' said Adam. 'We were lucky.'

At last they cleared the tumbled area, only to find themselves in a fresh landscape, hardly any easier to cross, dominated by great pressure waves, like frozen ocean rollers. Some were at least ten or fifteen metres high, others were barely a metre or two. The area was also crisscrossed by fresh rifts and cracks, most no more than a few centimetres wide, but a few were broad enough for it to be difficult to find crossings, especially for Marianne and Wan Li, who had to be handed across between Adam and Larsen. Luckily there was less snow, so the walking was less tiring.

The sun was now a pale ball above them, and Marianne and Wan Li were nearing the end of their tether. However, the area was so cracked and broken with crevasses, jagged little peaks and ridges, and brooks and pools of open and frozen water, that there was nowhere to sit and rest. Adam drove them ruthlessly on, and at last they emerged on to a wide field of almost fluorescent blue ice, rippled with sharp wind-cut edges, and scattered snow patches. Here they stopped and huddled together for warmth, with Marianne in the middle.

They did not stop long, for the cold of stillness was almost insupportable. The surface soon grew uneven, and became hard walking once more. Adam was carrying Marianne again, while Larsen kept looking worriedly at Wan Li, who seemed on the very point of collapse, yet somehow kept going.

At last, as the glacier dipped down and a jumbled chaos of white blocks and knife-edged seracs, flanked by transverse crevasses, loomed out of the mist, they stopped for another rest in a large hollow, out of the thin cold wind, and covered by a high ice ridge. Again the four of them cuddled as close as they could, gaining a fleeting relief from each other's body warmth.

'I must rest for longer,' said Wan Li, as Adam started to stand up.

'They may be close on our tracks.'

'I do not care any more,' said Wan Li. 'I must rest.'

'Me too,' came Marianne's weak, piping voice.

She was curled up against Adam, with her eyes closed. Adam

hesitated, then relaxed again and pulled her closer to him, to give her more warmth.

Within moments she was asleep.

The old Chinese man looked at the little Inuit child, and from somewhere deep within he dragged out a smile. Then he turned back to Larsen and Adam.

'I am sorry,' he said. 'But my body betrays me.'

'It is incredible you have kept going as long as you have,' said Larsen. 'How do you do it?'

For the hundredth time the old man wiped his spectacles, then put them back on. His dark eyes looked at Larsen, and seemed to see right inside his skull.

'You are trying to take my mind off the cold. But I am old enough to know what is happening, and still be willing to go along with it. Do not forget that less than ten years ago I escaped China by struggling through the high passes of the Tien Shan. That was like this, but steeper. There is only one way I know to endure pain, and that is to think of the future. Every time I was tortured, I knew I could not stand any more so I promised myself, with complete conviction, that I would confess the next time. Now as I cross this wasteland of ice, I know that in a little way I will give up and collapse, but not quite yet.'

There was a silence. The wind whined over the ice, and Marianne breathed as deeply and easily as if she were in her own bed.

'There is not much more of the ice to cross now,' said Adam. Relentlessly practical.

'Let her sleep,' said Wan Li, nodding at the little girl. 'Let her sleep and me rest, and maybe we will achieve it.'

It occurred to Larsen that as they were high up, and further from the volcano, he might be able to use his mobile. But when he felt for it, it was not there. He had lost it somewhere on the chaos of ice.

An hour later Marianne awoke shivering, and began to cry. 'I want my mummy, I want my mummy. I want Aunt Anita.'

'It won't be long now,' soothed Adam. 'I'll carry you to her.'

He picked her up in his arms, like a baby, and strode on.

The way was growing harder as they reached the far edge of the glacier, where the drag of the surrounding rocks twisted and distorted the ice. Eventually Adam had to put Marianne down, and again she followed as best she could.

The mist was reluctantly lifting, though it still hung heavy and dark behind them. In front the sun glittered on the ice, and showed them the bare mountains less than a kilometre away, but that kilometre was of twisted, cracked and rotting ice of the worst kind. After half an hour of tortuously slow going, they came to a huge crevasse, hung with delicate, lace-like frost tracery. It was far bigger than any they had yet seen, plunging into unfathomable cold, cerulean depths, and stretching on either side as far as they could see. But there was a snow bridge across it, a straight ridge of wind-carved old snow, perhaps five metres wide at its narrowest, and twice that long.

'We are going to have to cross the bridge,' said Adam, after a few minutes casting up and down the crevasse.

'Is it safe?' asked Larsen.

Adam shrugged. 'If it is, we will be off the ice in fifteen minutes. If not, we may have to face another three or four hours' walking. I do not think the other two will last that.'

'No,' agreed Larsen. 'But –'

'We have no choice,' interrupted Adam impatiently. 'Otherwise we will be trapped like seals in a savssat – cut off from the open sea by ice, unable to do anything but wait for the final freezing and inevitable death.'

'Look,' came Wan Li's voice.

They turned round. The old man was pointing to the shifting boundary of the mist behind them. Dark figures had appeared on the tumbled white snow slope.

'It seems they were able to track us after all,' said Adam. His voice was dull with hopelessness.

'There's still a chance,' broke in Larsen. 'If we get over that bridge, we can break it behind us.'

Adam's face changed. He nodded and led them on to the snow bridge.

The first few metres were fairly easy but, as the bridge narrowed, Adam went forward with ever more caution. Behind him, within arm's reach, came Wan Li, Marianne, and finally Larsen. Carefully Adam tested each step before he took it, but the bridge seemed firm and solid. They advanced steadily to just beyond the narrowest section, the centre of the bridge, when there was a sudden sliding, grating sound. The snow fell away under Adam's leading foot, and he staggered, and just managed to jerk himself back as a hole opened immediately beneath him.

All four of them shuffled a couple of metres backwards, then Adam started forward again, trying to edge around that gaping pit.

'Could we jump?' asked Larsen.

Adam shook his head, and inched on, spreading his weight as evenly as possible. Larsen looked at the new hole, and saw water dripping off the underside of the bridge. The sun was melting the bridge, and if they waited much longer, the whole structure might collapse. Still Adam advanced at a snail's pace, testing every step.

There was a sudden fresh rustle of falling snow, but it came from the edge of the crevasse, further up, where a great mass of soft snow flopped down into it. Adam was past the hole, and slowly he began to walk faster as the surface grew harder. The others followed. Wan Li, cautious and upright. Marianne, so light she hardly made an impression on the ice. Finally Larsen, the heaviest of them all. As he passed the hole, there was another hissing, and snow cracked and fell from the edge, close on his left. But the bridge held.

At last they were safely across, on to the far side. Larsen swung round, and saw their pursuers were only two or three hundred metres behind.

'We have to break the bridge,' he said.

'No,' said Adam, holding him back. 'It is too dangerous, it could go any moment.'

'If it doesn't, they've caught us.'

'There,' said Marianne, pointing up the hillside, where some round, ice-smoothed, black boulders lay, embedded in snow. 'You could use those.'

'Brilliant!'

Larsen ran up the hill, and began to push desperately at the nearest boulder. After a moment the others joined him, but the boulder shifted only reluctantly in its snow cradle.

Their pursuers were already within easy rifle range, but they did not fire.

Suddenly Larsen realised what they were doing wrong. He darted round to the lower side of the boulder and began to burrow into the snow that held it back. He could feel it beginning to move. On the far side the other three were still pushing as hard as they could, trying to rock it back and forth. Larsen burrowed deeper. The snow creaked, and the great rock moved a little more.

At last there came a shot, followed almost immediately by a deafening cracking sound, and a bullet whined away from the boulder, a few centimetres from Larsen's left shoulder.

'Stop what you are doing this moment,' came a piercing high-pitched voice.

There was another shot, and a second bullet slammed into the boulder, close by his head. Rock fragments tore his face, and Larsen froze.

'Do not move,' came the voice. 'Do not move, any of you.'

Close beside him, Larsen could feel the boulder tremble. A little snow fell away from it, then a little more. There was a creak, then abruptly it lurched downhill.

Larsen flung himself to one side, even as a third shot echoed, and something hit the snow where he had been standing. The other three were already flat on the ground. The boulder gathered pace, and rumbled and crunched its way down the hillside towards the snow bridge.

'If any of you move, we shoot to kill,' screamed a voice from the far side of the crevasse.

Larsen lay unmoving where he had fallen in the snow, looking below him at the snow bridge. The boulder carved irresistibly over the snow, right on to the bridge, which buckled and fell, sending the boulder crashing down into the blue depths, from where came the echoes of breaking ice. For a moment Larsen breathed, then he realised that only one side of the snow bridge had been destroyed, and there was still a soaring arch that spanned the two sides, though ragged-edged and far thinner than it had been.

'Get up,' shouted that high-pitched voice. 'Get up, all of you. Hands high in the air. Do it now, or I shoot to kill.'

Adam, Wan Li and little Marianne were already on their feet. With a sick feeling of defeat, Larsen too got up, put his hands in the air, and looked across at their captors. Then his heart seemed to burn and wither in his chest.

Two men in heavy duty parkas, hoods up, gloves on their hands, stood there with rifles raised. In front of them were Risa and Kim.

'What are you doing here?' he cried out in confusion.

'It's my fault,' replied Kim. Her voice shaking and panicky. 'Christ knows, this is all my fault.'

'Silence,' snapped out one of the armed men.

But Kim could not be stopped. Confession burst out of her.

'It was back in the US, they came to see me. They said they were members of the Chinese opposition, but even then I wasn't sure. They didn't feel right.'

'Be silent,' repeated the man louder, brandishing his rifle.

She took no notice. 'They offered me money to give them information about Mei Tei, and more, much more, if I could find him. And I ignored my feelings and took it. I needed money to finance my own trip, so I told them what I'd found out – and that was how they got here –'

'Silence. Or I shoot.'

'They were too late the first time. But they smashed up the house and killed Inga after questioning her. And then again they came to me –'

There was the harsh crack of a rifle. A scream from Risa tore the air, followed by a series of sobs. Marianne was whimpering, burying her face in Adam's side. No sound came from Kim. She fell sideways on the snow, almost gently, and lay still. Gradually a brilliant crimson stain blossomed in the snow around her.

Risa ran forward, knelt down beside her, and lifted the American woman's head. It hung limp in her hands.

'You will all do exactly and only what I say,' said the man who had fired.

He turned to his partner, and the two spoke with each other rapidly in lowered tones.

'What are they saying?' asked Larsen, out of the corner of his mouth.

'My hearing is not what it was,' replied Wan Li quietly. 'I suppose they are discussing what to do to us, and how . . .'

He stopped.

'You will cross over the bridge, and join us,' said the leading gunman. 'All of you. One at a time, with Wan Li the traitor first.'

'It will not hold us,' objected Larsen. His eyes were darting back and forth around them, looking for cover. But except for the boulders further up the slope, the sloping, gravel-lined snow bank offered no protection. Nowhere to hide.

'Old man, walk down to the bridge,' commanded the gunman.

Wan Li shrugged and began to shuffle down the snow slope, towards the precarious arch that represented the only link between the two sides of the great crevasse.

The taller of the gunmen took a few paces forward, watching Wan Li closely, his rifle ready in his hand. He was a few metres in front of his companion, who looked across at where Kim lay, and Risa crouched beside her, cradling that motionless body.

'They're going to kill us all, aren't they?' called Risa suddenly, in Greenlandic.

'Silence,' rapped out the second gunman. He advanced on her and raised his gun to hit her.

As he smashed his gun handle down against Risa's broad back, she lunged at him with the speed of striking falcon. The broad hunting knife she held in her hand, the one she had strapped to her leg beside the rising floodwaters, shimmered in the sun, then tore full into the man's chest.

He collapsed with a strangled grunt.

'Run!' screamed Larsen, throwing himself to one side, and snatching up a rock which he hurled blindly in the direction of the remaining gunman.

Adam had already seized Marianne and was dragging her towards the shelter of one of the great boulders.

There was a burst of fire from the leading gunman's rifle. Wan Li staggered and fell to the ground. There was a creak and click as the gunman reloaded. He fired another burst, then suddenly he became aware of the danger at his back.

He swung round, rifle in hand, to find Risa almost upon him, the knife upraised in her blood-smeared hand. There were two shots. Risa spun round with a scream of pain, and the knife flew from her hand. A moment later, carried on by the momentum of her rush and the steep slope, she crashed into the gunman.

As Risa sprawled forward on to the snow, the gunman tottered backwards several paces, struggling to keep his balance and firing again as he did so. He managed to stay on his feet for a moment, then the slope caught him, and he stumbled further down, before falling. The ice immediately above the bridge was steep and stripped of snow, worn and slippery, and he slid down it, desperately clawing for a grip, but finding none. His rifle clattered away into the crevasse.

At the bottom, he struck the bridge. A great piece of snow fell from it, and a moment later cracks appeared, lancing out like a hundred clutching tendrils. Another piece fell, but still the bridge survived. Just. The gunman struggled to his knees, and began to crawl with excruciating slowness back up the glassy slope, towards where Risa lay. No emotion went through Larsen as the crawling gunman slipped again, lost his footing, and slid back down.

The bridge did not break, rather it seemed that the snow opened up to receive him. He slid straight through, and plunged into the crevasse without a sound.

Larsen turned round to where Wan Li lay, but it was instantly obvious that the old man was dead. His face was buried in the snow, his thin body lay unmoving, steaming blood carved a pink runnel in the ice around him. Behind him he could hear Marianne crying. Then he remembered Risa, and got to his feet.

She was still lying where she had fallen.

'Risa,' he shouted, desperately. 'Risa!'

Painfully she looked up, then struggled to her knees. Her shoulder had been hit, and her anorak was blackened and burnt by the blast, and reddened with blood. Her right arm hung uselessly by her side.

'Are you OK?' he called stupidly.

'Are you out of your mind?' she retorted, through teeth clenched in pain. 'Of course I'm not. I've just been shot.'

'I mean . . .' He stopped. He didn't know what he had meant.

'Shit!' she exclaimed, gritting her teeth. 'I thought Edvarth was an orphan then.' And she collapsed back on to the snow.

Larsen shouted again, but she didn't move. He took a step down towards the snow bridge, and heard a crunch beneath his boots. He looked down, and saw that he had trodden on Wan Li's spectacles.

'Where are you going?' called Adam, who was emerging from his hiding place behind one of the boulders. He had Marianne in his arms, and she was sobbing into his shoulder as if her heart was broken.

'I have to get across,' said Larsen.

'You can't.'

'The bridge is still there.'

'Not for long,' said Adam. 'The places where it broke are growing all the time, with this sun on them. I doubt it would even take a fox now.'

'But Risa . . .!'

'You will have to find another place to cross. Go that way.' He pointed east.

'That's further up towards the inland ice.'

'Which is where there is the best chance of another bridge. Or of the crevasse closing altogether. I'll stay here with Marianne.'

Even as Larsen set off, floundering and tumbling through the snow as fast as he could, there was a soft hissing and a volley of small cracking sounds, and the bridge collapsed and fell into the crevasse.

It took Larsen just twenty minutes to find another, larger snow bridge further up the crevasse. He crossed it easily, and as he did so it struck him that if the gunmen had searched more thoroughly, they probably could have caught them all with no trouble. Quarter of an hour later he was back beside Risa.

She was still breathing, though her eyes were shut. Hands shaking with cold and fear, he began to tie up her shoulder with the torn and ragged edges of her anorak.

'You took your time,' she gasped suddenly, looking up at him with long eyes.

'I'm sorry.'

'Yes.' She closed her eyes, and a spasm of pain ran over her face. The makeshift bandage he had put over her shoulder was already wet with fresh blood. 'It hurts like fuck,' she muttered.

'Don't worry. We'll get you out of here.'

'What, to that place they call a hospital where I work? No thank you. I want to go to Nuuk for my treatment.'

'Don't waste your strength talking,' he said gently.

She took no notice. 'What did I come back for? There I was, no problem, sitting in the chopper that was going to take me out of Ikerasak for good. Then I jumped out, and came tearing up here – to get half-burnt, half-drowned, half-frozen, and have the rest of me blasted away by a crazy with a rifle.'

'You saved our lives.'

'Whose lives?'

'Adam, Marianne, and me.'

'So the old man's dead.'

'Yes.'

'And that dumb journalist too. I liked her.' There were tears in Risa's eyes. 'She never got her exclusive interview after all. Never even met the old man. She'd have done better to go back to the guy in Cincinnati, settle down and have kids.'

'Don't tire yourself out.'

'Shut up, I want to talk. Poor Kim. She never found out what she really wanted. And those geologists are all dead too. The cloud got them. Did you see the cloud? It was like death. It was death, and I thought it was going to get me too, and everyone. But Sigrid and the rest were burnt alive.' She shivered convulsively. 'Maybe you're right. Maybe I am talking too much.'

He held her tight.

'I'm getting cold, Tomas,' she whispered. 'Don't leave me.'

'I won't,' he said.

'Promise.'

'I promise.'

23

SEEING THE CHIEF

The helicopter, alerted by Jette's call, had been searching for them for over three hours when it finally landed on the flat upper surface of the glacier. After Adam, Marianne, Larsen and Risa were safely inside, and the bodies of Wan Li and one of the gunmen, in their black body bags, were stored in the side of the helicopter, the co-pilot went over to where Kim lay, another body bag in his hand.

He bent over her, frowned, then stripped off his glove and laid his fingers on the artery below her left ear.

'I think this one's still alive,' he called. 'Just!'

Adam jumped down and helped him strap Kim to the emergency stretcher, and carry her back to the helicopter.

As they set off towards Paamiut, Larsen glanced down and saw Ikerasak beneath them, undamaged by the catastrophes that had encircled it. The great floods that had covered the lower ground to the north of the village were draining sluggishly away, though there were many new lakes and pools, and the Isortoq still ran ten or twelve times its previous size. The volcano was clearly visible, a forty metre high cone of ash and rock and black clinker, still smoking and spitting flame, lava and rocks. Beside it a shoulder of the shadowing mass of Mount Iviangeq had vanished, and the glaciers and snowfields that had covered the mountains around were also gone. Even the edge of the inland ice beyond had retreated, exposing a wasteland of bare, dead rock.

The co-pilot saw where Larsen was looking. 'Been big news,' he said. 'Expeditions are coming from all over the place to study it. Apparently new volcanoes aren't supposed to behave like that.'

'What do you mean?'

'New volcanoes don't explode. So they reckon that mountain above it must be an old volcano.'

So Sigrid was wrong after all, thought Larsen. It wasn't a new volcano, and she wasn't the first person ever to predict the birth of a new volcano, and the mistake cost her her life. Because new volcanoes don't expel burning clouds, but old ones do.

Another thought came to him. It had been because of the fear of an old man – a dormant, but once fire-spitting, volcano – that men had been sent to kill Wan Li. And they had succeeded. But Larsen remembered the old man had spoken out against hero worship, and if the young were now going to have to sort things out for themselves, perhaps that was – in a way – what Wan Li had wanted.

Larsen looked behind, to where Kim lay in motionless silence, then across to Risa. She had been given a pain-killer, and had relapsed into uneasy sleep. Marianne, sitting by her, caught Larsen's gaze, and tried to smile. He smiled back at her, found his own eyes wet with tears, and brushed them aside impatiently. He felt suddenly cold.

It was three days later. Risa was sitting up in her bed in a small hospital ward, talking to Edvarth. Her shoulder was heavily bandaged, and her right arm was attached to a drip. As Larsen came in, she gave a hint of a smile.

'You're very wet. Is it raining?'

He nodded. 'How are you feeling?' he asked, handing her a small bunch of yellow flowers.

'Arctic poppies, how kind of you, Tomas. Did you pick them yourself?'

'I'm afraid they won't last long, but –'

'But I'll be out soon,' she said. 'The doctors are very pleased with me. My son here is less pleased. He's been telling me that I was a fool, and that we only survived because it was a small eruption. If it had been a big one, apparently we wouldn't have had a chance. So I shouldn't have left him in the helicopter, and he's not going to forgive me, and other things . . .'

Edvarth looked away, embarrassed.

'I'm interrupting,' said Larsen uncomfortably. 'I'll go and see Kim. She's just up the corridor, isn't she?'

'I haven't been allowed to see her yet. Give her a message from me – tell her that being shot is one hell of a way of making sure you get married – OK? And come back soon.'

'I have to go to debriefing in less than an hour.'

'So come back after then.'

Kim was lying down on her back in a room of her own. She too was hooked up to a drip, an oxygen mask covered her mouth and nose, and there were other monitors and attachments, which

Larsen squeamishly did not look at too closely. A nurse sat beside the bed, with a trolley of equipment at her back.

'Is she awake?' asked Larsen quietly.

The nurse nodded, glanced at one of the monitors, then went over and carefully unstrapped the oxygen mask.

'You can have three minutes,' she said. 'Not a moment more.'

Kim's face was bloodless and drawn. Her cheeks had collapsed in on themselves, and around her eyes were great black shadows. She blinked as if it took all her energy just to keep her eyes open.

'I don't look up to much, do I?' Her husky voice was barely audible, and Larsen had to lean towards her to hear. 'I feel shit, and this catheter hurts like sin . . .'

'But you're going to be OK.'

'So they tell me. I think they're lying. How's Risa?'

'Pretty good. She sent a message for you, but I don't understand it. She said that being shot is a hell of way to make sure you get married.'

Kim tried to laugh, then began coughing. The nurse frowned and came over.

'That's enough,' she said, reaching for the oxygen mask.

'No, wait,' gasped Kim. 'Tell Risa there's no way I'm going back to Cincinnati. I've got a wicked story to file, and my insurance is going to have to pay me not such a small fortune.' She paused, and breathed painfully a few times, then went on. 'Tell her getting shot is the best thing that could have happened to me, it'll make me rich enough to go on with journalism.'

The nurse was leaning over her, the oxygen mask in her hand.

'OK, OK,' said Kim, surrendering, and closing her eyes.

Larsen took the message back to Risa, who laughed loudly.

'I didn't think she was the sort to settle down,' she said. 'I'm glad.'

'I have to go,' said Larsen.

Risa looked at him keenly. 'You look tense. What is it?'

'I'll tell you later.'

Larsen was fighting not to show anything as he entered the station, took off his dripping wet coat and hung it on one of the hooks.

'You've been living it up,' said Jette, as he went by.

'Thanks for passing on that message,' he said. 'Without it, we'd have all frozen to death up there.'

'You're welcome,' she said.

'I'm sorry about Pieter,' he said quietly.

Chief Thorold, pallid and nervous-looking, was sitting at his desk. As usual, he was reading a form, and as usual he let Larsen wait for a minute or two, then performed an elaborate charade of realising that he was there.

'Ah, Tomas. Sorry, I hadn't noticed you come in. Have a seat.' The insincere smile. Or maybe it wasn't insincere – maybe it was just that Chief Thorold was unable to smile a real smile.

Larsen sat down, and waited for the usual, pointless summary of events. It seemed everything was going to be the same as usual.

Except that this time it wasn't.

'You shouldn't have done it, Tomas,' said Thorold, his expression delicately balanced between disapproval, understanding and sympathy.

'Done what, sir?'

'You know perfectly well. Taking advantage of my good nature like that – pretending that you were visiting Paamiut, when really you were on your way off to Ikerasak again. I must admire your sheer determination, but there comes a moment when determination spills over into stubbornness. I think, Tomas, that you find it too difficult to let things go – that you lack a certain sense of proportion. It is something you must cultivate in yourself, especially if you are to advance in our profession. Much of what I do is about weighing up different calls on me, balancing competing priorities, judging degrees of significance – and that is something that, I am sure you agree, you would find very difficult.'

'I did solve the matter, sir,' said Larsen doggedly.

'Most of it, yes. And I must say it was a remarkable piece of work, though fortune certainly favoured you. Not of course that I am belittling what you have achieved. It was ... very well done. Though the end was somewhat unfortunate. And of course there is still some serious question about exactly who the old Chinese man was.'

He settled back in his chair, and steepled his fingers. Rain hammered against the window.

'Ikerasak has been taken over by geological teams,' he remarked conversationally. 'Eight or nine of them, from all over the world. I suspect you would scarcely recognise it now. Anyway, to return to the point, I have decided to ignore certain actions you took, even though they were in contradiction of your instructions.' A sting came into his voice. 'But I would be grateful if, in future, you paid close attention to what you were told, and obeyed orders. I will be watching your progress very closely. You understand, Sergeant Larsen?'

Larsen knew what was expected. A humble, mumbled apology, then withdrawal. But he had other things in mind.

'I wondered what was happening about the murder of Sergeant Norlund, sir,' he asked.

'There is no evidence that Sergeant Norlund was murdered.'

'With respect, sir, there is. While I was in Paamiut, on my way back, I went up the fjord to identify the body found there.'

Thorold glanced at him. 'Well done, Tomas. That was very thorough of you.' Thorold sounded like a schoolteacher dealing with a pupil who was being too clever. 'I gather it was very badly damaged.'

'Yes, sir. But it was Pieter Norlund.'

'Can you be sure, Tomas? I was told –'

'I am certain, sir. Though if you wish to double-check, it would be straightforward to cross-reference with Sergeant Norlund's dental records.'

'Good idea, Tomas. Good idea.' Thorold held up his hand before Larsen had time to say anything. 'No, no. You deserve a rest. I shall take this matter on myself. If a member of the Royal Greenland Police Force has been murdered, then that, of course, is a top priority matter. Such things cannot be permitted.'

He spoke as if he were discussing an unlicensed fishing trip.

'Thank you, sir. But I can already tell you who murdered Sergeant Norlund.'

'Really?'

'Yes. His plan had been for Wan Li and him to hide out for a while in a hut near Paamiut – to throw any pursuers off their track. Of course Wan Li had no intention of doing that – as we know, he went straight back to Ikerasak without telling anyone. However, it's clear that Sergeant Norlund thought Wan Li had gone to the Eqaluit hut. So, shortly after arriving, he hired a boat to take him there, but not to take him back.'

'Why should he have done that?' asked Thorold, frowning.

'Presumably to make it more difficult for anyone tracking him. One boat to take him there, another – which I suppose he would have telephoned for – to get him and Wan Li away. However

Wan Li was not there. Someone else was there, or arrived shortly afterwards, and they murdered Norlund and hid his body.'

'That makes sense, as far as it goes,' agreed Thorold judiciously. 'But . . .'

'But who was the killer? It was clearly someone unused to Greenland – in our country the cold means corpses rot only very slowly, if at all, and with animals and hunters searching everywhere for food, it was virtually certain that Norlund's body, hidden under a few stones near a well-known hunting base, would be found very rapidly.'

'You mean you think that the Chinese assassins killed him?' said Thorold.

Larsen nodded. 'I don't think there can be any doubt about it. Either they thought he was arriving with Wan Li, or they seized him and questioned him about where Wan Li was before killing him. Presumably an accomplice of theirs then travelled to Copenhagen on the ticket booked in Norlund's name.'

Thorold looked at his soft white hands. 'Yes, I am sure you are right about this. I will have the body double-checked, to make sure it is Sergeant Norlund's, then we can let the whole business drop.'

'Except for one thing, sir. One thing that has been worrying me. How did the assassins know of Norlund's plan to hide at the hut?'

'Presumably they followed him.'

'I thought that, so I asked the boatman who took Pieter there if he had seen anyone during the trip. He said no one.'

'Which only goes to prove that he did not notice them.' Thorold sighed. 'And after all, at the bottom, this is not important. What matters is whether or not Norlund is dead. The person I feel most sorry for is his widow – if she is indeed a widow. And of course she has a newly-born baby, too. I believe you know her, don't you?'

Larsen had a sudden sense that some sort of pre-emptive strike was about to be launched at him.

'Well?' said Thorold.

'Yes, I do know her.'

'Quite surprising that. I would not have thought you had much in common with – what's her name – Gerda, isn't it? I remember her at the last Christmas party, a rather dull, vulgar girl I thought. And very young. Though perhaps not unattractive, if you like that sort of woman.'

Larsen said nothing.

Thorold leaned forward. His pale eyes were fixed. 'And now, as the wife of a murdered police officer, she'll be getting a good pension. Another attraction.'

'I don't understand.'

'I think you do,' Thorold said quietly. 'Norlund knew you were seeing his wife, didn't he?'

'What has that to do with anything?'

'Quite a lot, I would say. Because Norlund wasn't happy about what was going on, was he? In fact the last time you saw each other, he gave you a serious beating. And then came that mysterious disappearance, when it now seems he was shot down by an unknown assailant. At a time when you were just up the coast from him. Coincidental. Very coincidental. If I was you, I might be keen to blame some dead Chinese men too.'

'I was in Ikerasak.'

'Which is only a three or four hours' boat trip from where Norlund was murdered. Do you have an alibi, Tomas?'

'I was lying unconscious at Ikerasak, until Risa and Edvarth found me.'

'So you tell us. But the doctor was quite surprised how little serious damage you had suffered.'

'Are you suggesting that I somehow followed Norlund all the way to the hut, killed him there, then returned to Ikerasak and lay down in the hills waiting to be found?'

'It's not impossible.'

'It's ridiculous. Of course I didn't kill him.'

'I am sure you didn't,' purred Thorold, sitting back in his chair. 'But I would not be doing my job if I didn't notice there are pointers the other way. Wouldn't you agree? Plenty of motive. And the complete lack of an alibi for the time of the murder.'

'You're not serious, Chief?'

Thorold said nothing.

For a long, long time, the two men looked at each other. Larsen felt his hands shaking slightly, but stiffened his resolve, and took a deep breath.

'Very well,' he said. 'It's time I put my cards on the table also. Norlund visited here on his way to Paamiut, and had a meeting with you.'

'There is too much gossiping and idle talk in this office, and not enough work,' said Thorold coldly.

'I think during that meeting Pieter told you where he intended to hide Wan Li.'

Their eyes were still locked. Pale blue and dark brown. Larsen drove on.

'So only two people knew where Wan Li was going to hide – Norlund and you, Chief. As we can assume that Norlund was not such a fool as to give away the old man's hiding place, it must have been you who informed the killers where they could find Wan Li. And if you contacted them that time, then you must certainly have spoken with them before. Where did you get enough money to buy a big new car, Chief? Was it by telling the Chinese government men just where to find the old man who they wanted to kill?'

Thorold said nothing.

Larsen's slow-burning anger was hot in his throat.

'Did you think about Pieter Norlund when you told them where to find Wan Li? Didn't it occur to you that as well as murdering the old man, they might kill his police escort as well? I wasn't Pieter Norlund's greatest friend, but he didn't deserve having his boss finger him for the assassins. Maybe there's every reason for you to feel sorry for his wife.'

The silence sank over them afresh. Quivering with tension, yet heavy and somehow unbreakable.

Thorold flicked a pencil round and round in his fingers, but his face showed nothing.

'Is that all?' he said at last.

Larsen sat glumly by the side of the hospital bed. Risa was watching him with compassionate eyes.

'Well?' she said.

'What could I do? I couldn't prove a thing. Not a bloody thing. And he'd as good as told me what he would do if I pursued the matter – have me suspended on suspicion of having been involved in Norlund's death myself.'

'So you've sort of tacitly agreed not to mention the matter again?'

'I suppose so. Neither of us said anything, but I suppose that's how it is. But Risa, he was corrupt – he took money from those killers; and if it hadn't been for him, Norlund would never have been killed. And he knows I know that. He can't continue to let me work for him under those circumstances.'

'You don't say that you can't continue to work for him.'

'I meant that too.'

'Did you?' she asked gently.

'I suppose I'd better find another job,' he said.

'Do you want another job?'

'No. But . . .'

'He can't throw you out, can he?'

'Not without a very good reason.'

'Then make sure he doesn't find that reason.'

'But . . .'

Risa leaned forward, put her hand on his knee, then winced as the drip tugged at her. 'God, this is sore! Look, Tomas. Do you want to be a policeman?'

He hesitated. Then nodded. 'I can't imagine myself doing anything else.'

'That's not what I asked you. I said do you want to be a policeman?'

'Yes. It's the only thing I've ever been able to lose myself in.'

'Then go on doing it. And don't worry about Thorold. Or if you find you can't do that – and maybe you can't – then watch him. Show him you're watching him. Maybe he'll treat you with respect.'

Larsen nodded. 'I suppose you're right. But –'

'But nothing. Now, how's Edvarth making out? Not too much of a nuisance? He tells me that he likes staying with you.'

'I think he likes it in Nuuk.'

'So do I.'

'The weather's the worst in Greenland. It's been raining without stop ever since we got here.'

'Maybe it will have stopped when I get out tomorrow lunchtime.' She paused. 'Edvarth's told me there's a job for a nurse going here.'

He realised that her hand was still on his knee.

'I'll pick you up,' he said.

As he left the hospital, he thought of Thorold – and those cold, remorseless eyes. Not the eyes of a man who would forgive or forget easily. But the depression passed, and he realised that it had stopped raining, as Risa had said it would. As he walked along the street, in the August sunshine, he was smiling to himself.